Sylvia stood in the presence of Sir Robert Sheldon, a fierce giant of a man who stared disdainfully at her and at the beautiful child at her side.

Had she made the right decision? Should she not have bowed to Fate and accepted the grudging generosity of her uncle? What right had she, penniless and without a protector in the world, to embark upon this foolish adventure?

"You wanted to see me?" Sir Robert's voice was sharp, clear, and compelling.

"Yes," she replied, her calm voice belying the confusion stirring now in her fluttering heart, "I have brought you your daughter. . . ."

Pyramid Books

by

BARBARA CARTLAND

THE HIDDEN HEART

Barbara Cartland

PYRAMID BOOKS ▲ NEW YORK

THE HIDDEN HEART

A PYRAMID BOOK

Copyright © 1946 by Barbara Cartland

Pyramid edition published April 1970
Eighth printing, March 1977

Printed in the United States of America

Pyramid Books are published by Pyramid Publications (Harcourt Brace Jovanovich, Inc.). Its trademarks, consisting of the word "Pyramid" and the portrayal of a pyramid, are registered in the United States Patent Office.

PYRAMID PUBLICATIONS
(Harcourt Brace Jovanovich, Inc.)
757 Third Avenue, New York, N.Y. 10017

1

'I've never laid out a more beautiful corpse,' Mrs. Bootle said dramatically, throwing open the door and waddling into the room, her vast bulk seeming to dominate the delicately polished furniture with its innumerable little knick-knacks.

The girl sitting by the fireplace sewing black braid on to a heavy black serge skirt looked up.

'Can I go upstairs?' she asked.

Mrs. Bootle advanced towards her like a tidal wave.

'I should wait a moment or so, dearie. Give yourself time to think. It's always a bit of a shock the first time you sees one. Cold as marble, yet beautiful in their own way. And beautiful your mother is, you can take it from me, and after thirty-five years as the best layer-out in this neighbourhood I should know what I'm talking about.'

'I'm sure you do,' Sylvia said gently.

All the same she rose to her feet, slipping the heavy skirt from her knees on to a stool beside her chair.

Mrs. Bootle settled herself in the armchair.

'Now before you goes upstairs to have a good cry,' she said, 'I could do with just a little something. Mine's a hard job, though, mind you, it's a good one as jobs go and . . . well, when it's over it's usual for me to take a little refreshment.'

'Oh, I'm sorry, Mrs. Bootle,' Sylvia said quickly. 'You must think me most neglectful. I will get you something to eat—and drink—but I'm afraid there is nothing . . . but tea.'

'That will have to do then,' Mrs. Bootle said graciously. 'I could have done with something a little bit stronger, mark you; but there, it's always the same when there's no man in the house! A cup of tea and something to eat'll do me fine, my dear. What did you say was in the larder?'

'I think there are some eggs,' Sylvia replied, 'and the remains of a pie.'

'That'll do me splendidly,' Mrs. Bootle said. 'Very lightly poached, if you please, and I could eat those while you're heating up the pie, couldn't I? And don't forget,' she added as Sylvia moved towards the door, 'that I like my tea strong, really strong. I need something to put a little life into me.'

'I will be as quick as I can,' Sylvia promised and hurried from the sitting-room across the dark hall and down the uncarpeted stone steps which led to the basement kitchen. There was a smell of must and damp which no amount of cleaning could eradicate, but it was warm from the red glowing coals in the big black range. She put the kettle on to boil and went to the larder for the eggs. There were only two, and she realised that when Mrs. Bootle had finished the remains of the pie there would be nothing at all left for her own supper.

'I don't want anything,' she told herself, but was conscious nevertheless of something like a pang of hunger within her. She had eaten nothing since her mother died. Somehow the mere idea of food had seemed nauseating, but now she admitted to herself honestly that she was hungry. She made some toast for Mrs. Bootle's eggs and cutting off the crusts ate them herself with something like relish.

'It is wrong to feel hungry at such a moment,' she thought, then told herself that such a statement was nonsense. If she cried now, if she appeared prostrated with grief, it would, she knew, be for herself rather than for her mother. For six years Mary Wace had been incurably ill and no one knew better than Sylvia what it was to wait on an invalid day in and day out with no respite and no holidays—an invalid who despite every resolution was querulous and miserable because of the particular nature of her illness.

No one could have wanted Mary Wace to go on living. She had suffered agonies. No doctor could help her and the real tragedy was that she took such an unconscionable time in dying. Despite the momentary shock, it was indeed with relief that Sylvia had found her mother dead when she had entered her bedroom that morning. At first she could hardly believe it was true. Then looking at the thin, white face, she had known with a sudden springing of her heart that her mother was at peace. Mary Wace looked immeasurably younger and many of the lines of pain and irritation had vanished under the hand of death. She had died in her sleep with a faint smile on her lips, and Sylvia, looking at her, had known that she could not be hypocritical enough to pretend that she wished her mother back.

Now, while she prepared the eggs for Mrs. Bootle, she faced the fact that if tears were to be shed she should, indeed, shed them for herself. What was to become of her? Her mother's pension died with her—a meagre pittance, but it had kept a roof over their heads, had kept them alive as long as they practised the most frugal economies and considered the spending of every penny.

'I'm twenty-one,' Sylvia reminded herself, 'and what do I know of life?' She knew the answer to that question, for what chance had she had to learn anything except how to please an exacting invalid, how to fetch and carry and act the part of an unskilled nurse; how to clean and scrub and sew so that a dress that was really threadbare would give just another few months' service? And what use were such talents to anyone except, perhaps, a husband?—and she had little chance of meeting a prospective husband in the life she had lived here. Her mother had been too ill to receive visitors, even if there had been people who wished to visit her, and Sylvia had been unable to leave the invalid except for very short intervals when she must do the shopping or get just a breath of air in the tiny, overcrowded, untended garden.

The house was not theirs; already they were overdue with the rent. The furniture belonged to her mother, but as Sylvia well knew there was nothing of value left to sell. Everything that the dealers were prepared to purchase had been sold long ago.

At last the poached eggs were ready and the kettle boiling. Sylvia made the tea, popped the pie into the oven and carried the tray upstairs.

Mrs. Bootle was sitting comfortably in the armchair, her legs stretched out before her, her head sunk forward on to her ample bosom. She woke with a start as Sylvia opened the door.

'I just closed my eyes for a moment, dear,' she said. 'I'm tired, that's what I am. It's this weather—enough to upset anyone if they have to be out in it. As I said to Mr. Bootle this morning, "It's a poor way to bring in the New Year with a bitter wind as goes right into your bones; peace and good will is what we hoped for in 1903, but we'll have half the population down with pneumonia before you can say knife." '

'Oh, I hope not,' Sylvia exclaimed, arranging a small table by Mrs. Bootle's side and setting the tray upon it.

'I've got my hands full as it is,' Mrs. Bootle said. 'We really need someone else in this district with a knowledge of nursing. Not that any of my old clients would have anyone but me. "Mrs Bootle," they say, "I don't know where we'd be without you," and I couldn't argue with them, I couldn't really.'

'It must be interesting in some ways,' Sylvia suggested.

'Oh, it is and it isn't,' Mrs. Bootle replied. 'I'm getting on in years now and I get fed up with my life at times, I can tell you. I never sit down to a meal at home but there isn't a rap-rap on the door. "Can you come along, Mrs. Bootle, my wife's feeling queer?" Or the doctor says, "Mrs. Bootle, I don't think the gentleman in No. 16 will last the night; you'd better sit up with him." He always tries to warn me so that I can readjust my engagements, but then when I think I have got everything straightened out something happens all of a sudden—like your Ma upstairs.'

'I'm sorry,' Sylvia said.

'Oh it can't be helped, dearie. It's the hand of the Lord, and when He's ready to take us there's no gainsaying Him. All the same it's inconvenient and a shock to the relations. You look a bit pale; wouldn't you like a cup of tea? I see you've put an extra cup on the tray.'

'Yes, please, Mrs. Bootle, but not as strong as you are having it. There is some water there, too.'

'I always say there's nothing after a shock like a cup of tea with a good spoonful of sugar in it, too. Better help yourself, dearie, so you gets it to your liking.'

'Thank you,' Sylvia said. She sat down in the chair opposite Mrs. Bootle.

'Well, as I was saying,' the good lady went on, 'what I likes is things well ordered and planned in plenty of time. Three days is to my mind the right time to take for dying. It gives one an opportunity to call in the mourners. A nice deathbed scene is always to my taste. But you don't want to keep it up for too long, people get bored, especially men—you know what they're like.'

Mrs. Bootle spoke with scorn, as one who holds a poor opinion of the opposite sex. Then she added:

'But there, I don't want to make you feel uncomfortable.

Perhaps it was the happiest way for your Ma, and anyway, she's in a better place at this moment.'

'At least she is out of pain,' Sylvia said softly.

Mrs. Bootle nodded. 'That's always something to be thankful for—always. Have you made arrangements about the funeral?'

Sylvia nodded. 'Yes, the doctor sent along the undertaker. But it all seemed dreadfully expensive; I don't quite know how I am going to pay for it.'

'But surely you've notified the relations?' Mrs. Bootle said in tones of shocked horror.

'Yes, yes, of course,' Sylvia replied. 'But I would rather have paid for that myself. We haven't many relatives—only my Uncle Octavius, my father's brother. He's the Vicar of St. Mathias, Hastings. I sent him a telegram, I expect I shall have a reply tomorrow.'

'And he'll be taking you home with him, I suppose,' Mrs. Bootle said.

Sylvia sat very still and then at last the words were forced between her lips:

'I'm . . . afraid . . . so.'

Mrs. Bootle looked up over her second cup of tea.

'You don't like him?'

Sylvia shook her head.

'He is a good man, I'm sure of that. But I used to stay there when I was a child and I hated every moment of it. My aunt and cousins never let me forget that I was the poor relation and . . .' Sylvia hesitated. 'They didn't approve of my father and my . . . and some of my other relations.'

'I know the sort,' Mrs. Bootle said. 'Keep getting in nasty, back-handed remarks. I've met them—and often. They think themselves Christians, but you'd be surprised what I've seen—and in parsons' houses, too.'

'But I suppose he will offer me a home,' Sylvia said, 'and I must accept it gratefully. There is nothing else to do.'

She looked into the fire as she spoke, but instead of the glowing coals and the warm flames leaping upwards she saw the large, pompous vicarage at Hastings, the tight-lipped, sharp-featured face of her aunt and her cousins looking disdainfully at her worn clothes and darned stockings. Then she heard her uncle's voice saying sharply:

'You quite understand, Sylvia—that name must never be mentioned in this respectable household.'

And she heard her own voice saying tearfully:

'No . . . Uncle . . . of course not. . . .'

'You must forget—erase this—er—memory entirely from your mind.'

But she had known by the glint in his cold eyes that he would remember and go on remembering always—whenever he saw her.

Suddenly Sylvia covered her face with her hands at the humiliation of it, at the agony she had suffered. And now she had to go back to them, knowing quite well that her life would be that of an unpaid servant, a servant whom they could treat as they would because she would never have the temerity to give notice. Slaving for her aunt who had never liked her, fetching and carrying for her cousins who despised her, and watched—yes, watched all the time by Uncle Octavius.

On an impulse she turned to Mrs. Bootle.

'Oh, Mrs. Bootle, isn't there anything else I can do? Surely there is some work however hard that I could take up. I would do my best, I would really. Can't you think of anything?'

Mrs. Bootle scratched her head.

'It's hard on you, dearie, being a lady. I've never thought of it quite like that before. I suppose if I had a daughter of your age we would find her work of some sort, or else she'd get married to some nice, steady chap, then she'd be settled right enough. But with you—well, what is there that you could undertake?'

'I suppose I could be a governess,' Sylvia suggested, 'but I know so little. I wasn't very well educated and these past years while I have been looking after my mother I have hardly had any time to read.'

'Besides, you'd need references,' Mrs. Bootle said. 'You know what the gentry are like, always asking for slips of paper. As I said to Mr. Bootle the other day, "It's a poor judge who bases his judgment on a piece of paper; give me human nature every time." '

'I suppose I could be a shop girl.'

Mrs. Bootle laughed. 'You'd never manage that, you're not the type. They're rough, most of those girls in shops, and besides, when you got the work, you'd have to live somewhere. How would you be able to manage on a few shillings a week in the only sort of neighbourhood you'd be able to afford unless you were prepared to accept . . . well, you know what I mean? No, my dear, I'm afraid you'll have to go to your relations and put up with it.'

10

'Oh, Mrs. Bootle!' It was a cry of desperation and slowly the tears gathered in Sylvia's eyes.

Mrs. Bootle picked up the tea-pot hastily.

'Now don't you take on, dearie,' she said. 'Things will come right one way or another. Here, have another cup of tea. There . . . now you'll have to fill up the pot, and while you're about it, what about that meat pie?'

'Oh, my goodness! I hope it isn't burnt!'

Sylvia jumped to her feet and picked up the tea-pot.

Mrs. Bootle looked after her. 'A nice girl,' she said to herself ruminatively, in the tone of one who is used to talking out loud. 'But too pretty, too pretty by half. No, she'd better go to her vicarage, hard though it is.' Then she gave an exclamation and as soon as Sylvia was within earshot again called out:

'I've got an idea, dearie. Just thought of it, it came to me sudden like. I don't want to raise your hopes and I may be wrong, but I've a feeling that it might be just the thing for you.'

'Oh, what is it, Mrs. Bootle? Tell me quickly,' Sylvia exclaimed, putting the tea-pot down on the table.

'Now I don't want to say too much,' Mrs. Bootle said, 'but one of my patients—a lady, and a real lady if ever there was one—said something to me last week which has just come back to my mind. She said, "Bootle, if anything happens to me I want you to find someone reliable like yourself"—she's always very complimentary in the things she says—"who would take Lucy"—that's her little girl—"to a certain address. It's very important, Bootle." Well, seeing that nothing was likely to happen to the lady, I never gives it another thought, but just this morning—in fact just after I got the message to come along here to you—I sees the doctor in the street and I stops to speak to him. After he'd said a few words about your Ma, he says, "Mrs. Cuningham is bad again. It's her lung, of course. I can do nothing for her. I shouldn't be surprised to see her go any day." '

'Well, I was shocked, you can take my word for it, because I wasn't expecting to hear anything like that.

' "As bad as that, Doctor!" I exclaimed, and he nodded.

' "Pop in and see her as soon as you have a moment, Mrs. Bootle," he says. "That maid of hers is a fool and not to be trusted."

' "I'll go at the first moment I have," I promised him.

But there, what with laying out your Ma I never gives it a thought until this moment.'

'And you think she might want me to take her little girl somewhere?' Sylvia said. 'It doesn't sound very permanent.'

'Who knows?' Mrs. Bootle said airily. Sometimes things turn out quite different from what we expect. And let me give you one word of advice, my dear. If you mean to get on in the world, you've got to grasp opportunities as they present themselves. Many's the time I've said to Mr. Bootle, "There you are again, Fred! Another opportunity gone!" He's steady enough, as men go, but he can't see beyond the end of his nose, not a scrap of imagination in him. Now with you, my dear, if Mrs. Cuningham likes you and Lucy takes to you, well, you might find yourself anywhere. She's a lady born and bred, you can take my word for it.'

'Oh, Mrs. Bootle, it sounds too wonderful to be true! Do see what you can do about it!'

'I'll do more than that,' Mrs. Bootle said ponderously. 'I'll take you along with me now.'

'Oh, I couldn't,' Sylvia said. 'I couldn't really. What would she think? And when Mother . . .' She raised her eyes to the ceiling.

'If Mrs. Cuningham's as ill as Doctor Dawson thought she was this morning, the sooner you see her the better,' Mrs. Bootle said. 'And as for your mother, she's in no position at the moment to object—not that she would, poor soul; she'd want the best for you whatever it might be.'

'Nothing could be worse than Uncle Octavius,' Sylvia said reflectively.

'Well, then, grasp the opportunity,' Mrs. Bootle replied. 'You pop upstairs and put on your best clothes. Make yourself look spruce and tidy. It doesn't matter if they're not black,' she added as Sylvia made a little movement towards the black skirt lying by her chair. 'Few people in the town know that your mother's dead, and it's nearly dark anyway; who's going to see you? Mrs. Cuningham's a stranger to these parts and what's more, she's always kept herself to herself. Now hurry up, dear. You do as I tell you and leave me to enjoy this pie.'

Sylvia did as she was told and picking up an oil lamp from the table in the hall turned it up fully and went slowly up the stairs. As she reached the first floor she paused and then with an obvious effort entered the room where her mother lay.

12

She stood at the end of the bed looking down at the still figure. Mrs. Bootle had been right, Mary Wace looked lovely. She must at one time in her life have been beautiful and for the first time Sylvia saw how closely she resembled her mother. They had the same delicate, perfectly moulded features, the same winged eyebrows under a square forehead on which the hair peaked low. But Mary Wace was prematurely grey and her hair was brittle from her illness and lack of care. In the light of the lamp Sylvia's was golden as glowing corn.

Sylvia stood there for a few moments, the living looking at the dead. Then she spoke, her voice only a whisper.

'Help me, Mother. Help me, wherever you are. I don't want to go to Uncle Octavius.'

She turned away from the bed and closing the door quietly behind her went across the landing to her own room. It was only a slip of a room, cold in winter, hot in summer and a place she could hardly call her own because of the voice she must always listen to across the passage. And yet here she had found the only happiness she had ever known, the only place where she could relax and be herself, where she could think or stare at her own reflection in the mirror hanging over the mahogany chest of drawers and wonder whether anything would ever happen to her or whether her life would continue in its unbroken monotony until she was too old to enjoy anything else.

Sometimes she had been haunted and mocked by her own thoughts of what might have been had she been brave enough to kick over the traces as someone else had done; but always she had known that these were just wild imaginings of a starved brain, a brain which had too little to think about. She had tried to pray, but prayer had been no solution because she had always connected religion in her mind with Uncle Octavius.

In this room Sylvia knew that she had known loneliness, a loneliness beyond the expression of human eloquence; a loneliness which at such times had been stronger even than at this moment when she was really alone in the world. For it had been the loneliness of spirit, without hope.

Now she had a hope, faint it was true, and one in which she kept telling herself she must not place too much reliance. But all the same it was with an eagerness that she took her best dress—if one could call it that—from the wardrobe and slipped it on. It was sadly out of date, she knew, the sleeves not full enough and the skirt too skimpy.

13

But it became her. The soft hyacinth blue of the cheap material threw into relief the whiteness of her skin and the glint of her hair, and the white lace ruched at the neck and caught with a blue bow made her appear very young and unsophisticated. She had always liked this dress, she had been happy when she had made it; happy for no other reason than that it was spring and she had felt a stirring within herself which was unaccountable, but which nevertheless made her feel gay.

Over her dress she put on a dark grey braided cloth coat which she had worn for five years. It had originally been good, a present from the vicarage, of course, for which she had been forced to write a fulsomely grateful letter of thanks. But it was an ugly coat and Sylvia fancied that it must have been a mistaken purchase by one of her cousins who had regretted the impulse as soon as it was made. They had parted with it when it was practically new and Sylvia guessed that the extravagance would have been justified in their minds by their action in making it a charitable gift to herself. 'Poor Sylvia, she'll be grateful for it—and she ought to be, too, it cost a pretty penny.'

'Poor Sylvia.' The words stung, but not half as much as would the tones of their voices could she have heard them. Of course they hated her, why shouldn't they? Plain, gawky girls on whom no amount of money, however carefully spent, gave full value. What did it matter whether they wore silks and satins, bombasine or lace, when their little broad pug noses were always red and their spiteful little eyes were lost in the empurpled flesh of their fat cheeks? Overfed and overpampered!

She had hated them since she was quite small, when they had accused her of dyeing her hair. She could remember her aunt's voice so well.

'Does your mother put anything in the water with which she rinses your hair, Sylvia?'

'Sometimes a little lemon, Aunt Emily.'

'Um. Perhaps that accounts for the colour of it. I should advise her to do nothing of the sort in future. It makes you look conspicuous, which is most undesirable.'

She had never forgotten the tones and jeers which greeted her when she next entered the nursery.

'Who dyes her hair? Who wants to be conspicuous? Yah! Yah!'

They had reduced her to tears, of course. It was only later that she had understood the bitterness and envy which

14

lay behind so many of her aunt's remarks about her appearance. It was to her mother's family she owed her looks. The Waces were dull, stocky and unremarkable. It was all the more galling, therefore, that Arthur, the younger son, the black sheep of the family, should have married a beauty. If his children had taken after him they might perhaps have forgiven them some of the shortcomings of their parent. But from her earliest childhood Sylvia had learnt that she was an offence in the sight of her relations.

She picked up her hat, a plain felt with only a tuft of king-fisher blue feathers to relieve its severity. And yet as so often happened when she put on anything however cheap and ordinary, Sylvia felt she looked over-dressed. She couldn't help the colour of her hair, the shining radiance of her eyes or the natural brilliance of her lips. Lately she had been unnaturally pale, but at this moment, excited because she was going out on what was for her an amazing adventure, there was colour in her cheeks.

She pulled her hat a little lower on her head as if to dull her own radiance and then with a shrug of her shoulders turned towards the door. It was only as she reached it that the full realisation of what she was doing flooded over her. In the room opposite her mother lay dead and yet—she was thinking of herself. For a moment she thought it was impossible, she must not go out, she must stay at home and mourn as it was back her head and raising the lamp high in her hand as if she carried a torch, she descended the stairs. Only in her heart, humbly and pleadingly, she was saying over and over again, 'Oh, please understand, please, please understand.'

2

Outside in the street it was snowing and very nearly dark. Mrs. Bootle's huge form, with her black alpaca cape flowing behind her in the wind, revealed intermittently in the flickering light of the street lamps, looked monstrous and sinister.

Poolbrook was a small town with a long street of prosperous shops and porticoed houses behind which lay a labyrinth of small lanes and narrow passages where the poor lived in squalid and airless dwellings. After dark none of the more respectable citizens of Poolbrook ventured to walk about its less frequented thoroughfares, but Mrs. Bootle was well known and no one would have interfered with her progress, let alone have attempted to insult her.

She was the only midwife in the town, and although she had a reputation for enjoying her liquor and for being sharp-tongued and disagreeable if called out in the night, there were few women in Poolbrook who had not had reason to be grateful to her at some time.

There were others, however, notably in the more prosperous part of the town, who inferred that Mrs. Bootle was too good-natured and that at times her kindness overstepped her discretion, especially if such kindness was well paid. But although this gossip gathered weight and momentum in the passing years, there had as yet been no scandal such as might have involved Mrs. Bootle within the arm of the law; and therefore, though people might have their suspicions, nothing could be proved.

Despite her vast bulk, Mrs. Bootle moved quickly and Sylvia had to hurry to keep up with her.

'It's cold enough in all conscience,' Mrs. Bootle grumbled.

They turned out of the High Street into the countryside, coming shortly upon a white gate which stood open and led into a laurel-bordered drive. It was very quiet and still now they had left the town and Sylvia suddenly found herself nervous and a little afraid of what new experience might lie ahead.

'Don't you think,' she asked shyly, speaking a little breathlessly because of the speed at which they had travelled, 'don't you think, Mrs. Bootle, it might be wise if I waited outside until you have seen Mrs. Cuningham? She might not want to interview me after all.'

'Now leave all this to me, dearie,' Mrs. Bootle replied. 'When I sets my hand to the plough, I don't turn back, and I knows what women are. Whether they be born in a high or low degree, you've got to tie them down. Don't be put off with promises or an "I'll see to it later" reply. Make them see to it now and at once or you'll never get anything you want in this world. You remember that.'

Sylvia murmured that she would just as they reached the front door under its gabled archway supported by two white pillars.

Mrs. Bootle pulled the bell and far away in the depths of the house they could hear its imperious clanging. They had not long to wait before they heard footsteps and the door was opened.

The maid who answered their summons was young; she looked scared and her frilled cap was awry.

'Oh, it's Mrs. Bootle!' she exclaimed when she saw who stood outside. 'We've been expecting you for a long time.'

'Expecting me?' Mrs. Bootle echoed, entering the hall with Sylvia behind her.

It was a largish hall with a staircase running up to a balcony landing off which opened several bedroom doors. Even as they entered one of these was opened and a man looked out. When he saw who stood below he gave an exclamation and shutting the door quietly behind him came quickly to the top of the stairs.

'Mrs. Bootle,' he said, 'at last!'

'Evening, Doctor,' Mrs. Bootle replied in her cheery voice. 'You've been wanting me?'

Doctor Dawson descended the stairs.

'Wanting you?' he answered. 'I have been sending people to look for you all the afternoon. Where on earth have you been hiding yourself? There is practically nowhere in the town that hasn't been searched, including the better-known public-houses.'

Mrs. Bootle, drawing off her black gloves, gave him a resigned look with which a fond mother might contemplate a backward child.

'Had you forgotten that I had to lay out Mrs. Wace this afternoon?'

'God bless my soul!' the doctor exclaimed. 'So that is where you were! How extremely remiss of me! I thought of everywhere else, but not Mrs. Wace's.'

'Well, that's where I was,' said Mrs. Bootle. 'And what was the urgency, if I might ask?'

'You may well ask,' Doctor Dawson replied. 'I told you this morning Mrs. Cuningham was bad. Well, she had another relapse about lunchtime. Her maid—that hysterical woman—came running for me in such a state that she hadn't even bothered to put on her hat and coat.

17

But I must say her anxiety was understandable. It was a bad haemorrhage, Mrs. Bootle, a very bad one. I telegraphed this morning for a nurse, but there is little chance of her being here till tomorrow. Between ourselves'—he lowered his voice—'I don't think she will last as long as that. I wanted to notify the relations, of course, but, would you believe it? she will give me no names and asks for only one person—for you, Mrs. Bootle.'

'There, I might have guessed it,' Mrs. Bootle said, obviously much gratified. 'I know what's worrying the poor soul and I think I can set her mind at rest. I'll go up to her at once. You wait here, dearie,' she said, turning to Sylvia.

She started up the stairs and Sylvia and the doctor were left looking at each other a little uncertainly.

'I came in with Mrs. Bootle because she felt . . .' Sylvia began, but the doctor waved her explanation on one side.

'I'm very glad to see you, Miss Wace. Do you good to get out of the house for a breath of air. You have been cooped up for too long. You will be leaving Poolbrook, I suppose, now that your mother . . .' He paused as if lost for words.

'I don't know yet,' Sylvia replied.

Doctor Dawson said nothing and she realised suddenly how little she did know about herself and her future. She quite liked Doctor Dawson, although at times she had felt irritated by him because he was unable to relieve her mother either of pain or of the life she had found so burdensome. Now she saw with an unexpected clarity that he was ageing, a tired man, and guessed that his medical knowledge was not very great.

His coat was stained and frayed at the cuffs; his trousers were badly creased and baggy at the knees. His linen was none too clean and he had not shaved particularly well that morning. She felt suddenly an impulsive pity for him; she had the idea that he was conscious at the moment of his own inadequacy to cope with the vast problem of disease.

'Death is such a shock,' Sylvia said, realising that she was expressing a platitude, but feeling that she must say something.

Doctor Dawson sighed as if with an effort he forced himself to consider her.

'You have relations who will look after you, Miss Wace?' he questioned.

'My uncle should arrive some time tomorrow,' she
18

replied. 'And I feel sure, Doctor, that he will settle the outstanding accounts.'

She spoke shyly. Doctor Dawson smiled at her.

'I wasn't thinking about remuneration, Miss Wace, for the small services I hae been able to render you. I know you and your mother were not in prosperous circumstances and I assure you I shall take that into consideration when presenting you with my very modest account.'

'Thank you,' Sylvia answered, embarrassed by his generosity, but knowing she could not refuse it.

At that moment Mrs. Bootle came out on to the landing.

'Will you come up?' she said, adding, 'and you, too, Doctor.'

They climbed the stairs side by side. As they reached the landing Mrs. Bootle said in a whisper:

'Can't you give her something, Doctor? There's a lot she wants to say before she goes, poor soul.'

The doctor looked doubtful.

Mrs. Bootle asked him another question in a voice too low for Sylvia to hear what she said. He seemed to hesitate, then replied:

'Can't do any harm now, I suppose.'

Mrs. Bootle preceded them into the bedroom. It was a large room and to Sylvia almost overpoweringly luxurious.

There was a fire burning in the grate and the betasselled curtains of rose pink damask were drawn over the windows. Lying in the big lace-covered bed and propped up by pillows was Mrs. Cuningham. Sylvia's first reaction was that she was beautiful; and then as she drew nearer to the bedside she saw how wasted the face was, the skin stretched tight over prominent cheekbones, the neck so thin that it seemed too slender to hold the head with its cloud of waving hair.

Mrs. Bootle went over to the bed and wiped Mrs. Cuningham's lips with a lawn handkerchief.

'This is Miss Wace, Ma'am, who I was telling you about,' she said. 'You asked me for someone reliable. She's a lady and sensible. I couldn't recommend anyone more highly.'

Mrs. Cuningham looked at Sylvia with dark brown eyes which seemed unnaturally large.

'Come nearer, dear,' Mrs. Bootle said to Sylvia. 'She doesn't want to have to raise her voice to speak to you.'

She made Sylvia take her place at the bedside. Sylvia waited nervously, conscious of Mrs. Cuningham's eyes

19

searching her face. There was a heavy heady fragrance of perfume such as she had never smelt before; it was not the scent of the hothouse flowers which were arranged on several tables in the room. it was more exotic, a disturbing, haunting sweetness, which seemed to Sylvia to numb her intelligence and make her head swim dizzily. At last in a voice that was hardly above a whisper Mrs. Cuningham spoke.

'Would you do something for me?' she asked.

Her voice was curiously defenceless and Sylvia's response was genuine.

'I will do anything I can.'

Mrs. Cuningham turned her head a little towards Mrs. Bootle.

'My tin box, Bootle. It is by the writing desk.'

Mrs. Bootle moved across the room to fetch it. As she did so, the doctor came to the bedside with a medicine glass in his hand.

'Drink this, Mrs. Cuningham,' he said. 'It will make you feel stronger for a little while.'

She took it from him and drank with an air of impatience as if she was straining every nerve in her body in the effort to concentrate on what she wished to do and say.

Mrs. Bootle brought her a small black box with a heavy lock.

'The key, the key!' Mrs. Cuningham's voice was stronger and with her hand she indicated where the key lay.

Mrs. Bootle unlocked the box and raised the lid. Inside was a mass of papers and below them many little perforated paper bags such as bankers use for money.

Mrs. Cuningham drew out a paper and held it towards Sylvia.

'This is where I want you take my daughter Lucy when I am dead,' Mrs. Cuningham said slowly. 'I don't want you to communicate with anyone beforehand. I want you to take Lucy there and ask to see Sir Robert Sheldon. Do you understand?'

'Yes, I understand.'

'Do not be put off by anyone else. Ask for Sir Robert Sheldon. And when you see him, tell him you have brought him his . . . daughter.'

Mrs. Cuningham said the last words with a gasp, her head fell back against the pillows and she closed her eyes. For a moment Sylvia wondered if the strain had been too much for her, but she opened her eyes again and taking one of the bags out of the tin box held it out to Sylvia.

'Here is money for the journey and for yourself,' she said. 'But you quite understand that you are to leave Lucy with her father; whatever else is said or suggested, she is to stay with him. There is no other provision for her—no other arrangement is possible. Will you make that clear?'

'Yes, yes, of course,' Sylvia answered.

'That is what I want you to do. And one more thing. Be careful, very careful of Lady Clementina . . . she is bad . . . wicked . . . she drove me to . . .'

She spoke vehemently and then the words were choked in her throat. She began to cough, the effort shaking her frail body to and fro. She choked, coughed again and then a bright crimson flow of blood stained the handkerchief she held against her mouth and spilled over on to the lace bedspread. Mrs. Bootle and the doctor rushed forward. Mrs. Cuningham's breath was coming in frightened gasps.

Sylvia holding the little bag and the paper in her hand was pushed to one side, but there was nothing she could do. She felt as if she intruded and turned towards the door.

Mrs. Cuningham coughed again and Sylvia slipped outside. She stood on the landing, irresolute, her heart beating quickly. It all seemed unreal, as if she took part in some stage drama; she felt too inexperienced and unprepared for what was happening. It was all like a dream moving swiftly towards a preconceived inevitable climax. At last, after what seemed to her an age, Mrs. Bootle came out.

'She is going, poor soul,' she said to Sylvia, but in the calm tones of one who is well conversant with death. 'I wonder where that maid of hers is,' she went on. 'I want some warm milk and some hot water, too. Let's see if we can find her.'

'And the child?' Sylvia asked. 'Ought we not to inquire about her?'

Mrs. Bootle did not answer, but opened a door on the other side of the landing. She entered without knocking and the maid who was kneeling before a chest of drawers looked up in startled surprise. She was an unprepossessing woman with a shifty look in her eyes and it was quite obvious that she felt herself to be discovered at a disadvantage. The room was strewn with clothes: dresses, petticoats, stockings and frilly underwear thrown on the bed and on the chairs. Some were already packed in a shabby black trunk which stood open by the fireplace.

'Getting ready to leave?' Mrs. Bootle asked.

The maid jumped to her feet and smoothed down her apron.

'That's my business,' she replied tartly.

'Who said it wasn't?' Mrs. Bootle asked. 'But as your mistress isn't dead yet, perhaps you wouldn't mind serving her.'

'What's she want?' The question was surly.

'Hot water and hot milk.'

'It's not my job to do the cooking.'

'Maybe not, but it is your job to bring it into your mistress's room so you'd better find someone to get it ready for you and sharp about it,' Mrs. Bootle said.

There was an air of authority about her now which the girl did not dare to disobey. She flounced to the door, tossing her head as she went and muttering to herself.

'That's the sort of servant she'd had to put up with, poor soul,' Mrs. Bootle sighed. 'Well, we often pays for our sins in small ways.'

'What do you mean?' Sylvia asked, but her curiosity as to what Mrs. Bootle meant was overcome by her interest in the clothes.

Never had she seen anything so exquisite as the petticoats trimmed with Valenciennes lace and the nightgowns with long sleeves goffered and frilled, their bodices tucked and embroidered until they were as fine as lace. There were dresses, too, dresses such as Sylvia had believed existed only in fairy tales Ball dresses with velvet ribbon threaded through silk net and backed by shimmering satin; gowns of watered silk, enriched with fold upon fold of gossamer tulle which was but the background for bunches of rosebuds glistening with dewy diamonds; creations of satin, silk, chiffon, velvet and lace, all combined to make femininity a picture of loveliness and enticement. Then there were furs—muffs of sable and of marten with stoles and capes to match each, ornamented with dozens of pointed tails. A chest of drawers was piled high with hats—hats clustered with feathers and flowers, hats trimmed with buckles and jewelled hat-pins, hats cunningly draped with veils and ribbons And everything, big or small, showed such a delicacy and refinement of taste and choice that Sylvia could only stare, her head whirling. Could any woman possess so much, so many beautiful things?

Mrs. Bootle looked at her rapt face, and then drily she spoke:

'A lot of good they've done her, haven't they? She's not more than thirty if she's a day and her life is ended.'

'So young?' Sylvia exclaimed. 'Oh, Mrs. Bootle, why should she be so ill? What caused it?'

'I haven't time to tell you that story now, dear. Later on, perhaps. In the meantime we had better see to the child.'

'Yes, of course,' Sylvia replied neekly.

She turned towards the door, but as she did so Mrs. Bootle bent towards the bed and picked up a dress that was lying on it. It was a black dress trimmed with braid, its sombreness relieved by touches of white chiffon at the neck.

'That's elegant, isn't it?'

'Lovely,' Sylvia agreed.

'Just about your size, my dear, I should think.'

Mrs. Bootle looked at Sylvia and again at the dress as if measuring them with her eye.

Sylvia sighed. 'One day, perhaps, I shall be able to afford one like it.'

It was wrong of her, she knew, to be thinking about clothes with her mother dead and poor Mrs. Cuningham dying. And yet despite herself the faces of her cousins swam before her eyes. The ugly dresses she had had from them all through her life seemed uglier at this moment than ever before. Reproaching herself for the thought she went out on to the landing.

'Where is Lucy?' she asked. 'I must see the little girl.'

It was an effort to force her mind from the temptation to linger, to touch what belonged to another woman.

Without saying any more, Mrs. Bootle threw the dress back on to the bed and preceded Sylvia across the landing. There was a passage and at the first door they came to Mrs. Bootle paused and turned the handle gently.

'The child may be asleep,' she said in a whisper.

The room was not in darkness for a night-light was flickering on the wash-stand. There was a little cry.

'Who is it?'

'It's Mrs. Bootle, Lucy. Aren't you asleep?'

'Oh, Mrs. Bootle, do come in.'

Mrs. Bootle and Sylvia entered the room. Sylvia from just inside the door could only see a small figure sitting up in bed, then Mrs. Bootle struck a match and lit the gas.

'There, that's better,' she exclaimed. 'And now, why are you awake, young lady?'

'I can't sleep,' Lucy answered. 'Mamma is ill and Annie is frightened. I can always tell when she is frightened 'cos she won't talk to me. She just put me into bed and went away.'

'Well, you ought to go to sleep like a good girl,' Mrs. Bootle said.

'Who is that?' Lucy asked, pointing to Sylvia.

Watching her, Sylvia could see that she was an unusual-looking child. Her face had too much character and too much distinction to be pretty by conventional standards. For one thing, instead of the rounded face of the average child her chin was square as was her forehead above clearly marked, almost forceful-looking dark eyebrows. Her eyes were dark, too, as far as one could judge in the artificial light, but the most remarkable thing about her was her hair. Parted in the middle, it framed her cheeks, fell to her shoulders in graceful ringlets and was red, a vivid, tawny red that Sylvia never remembered seeing before. It gave Lucy a strangely unchild-like look, throwing into relief the whiteness of her skin and her unusual square-cut features.

'I am Sylvia Wace.' As she answered the child's question, Sylvia moved towards the bed. 'Your mother has just asked me if I would look after you for a little while. We may even have to go on a journey together. Would you like that?'

'Shall we go in a train?' Lucy asked.

Sylvia nodded.

'Oh, I would like that,' Lucy replied. 'I like trains. Mummy says they make her head ache, but I like them even though they are dreadfully dirty.'

'I like them, too,' Sylvia said. 'How old are you, Lucy?'

'I'm six, nearly seven,' Lucy replied. 'That is getting old, isn't it?'

'Yes, very old,' Sylvia said solemnly.

'Old enough to be good and helpful,' Mrs. Bootle put in. 'Now you go to sleep, young lady, and in the morning Miss Wace and I will see about this train journey of yours.'

The child obediently cuddled down beneath the bed-clothes.

'I'm glad you've come, Mrs. Bootle,' she said. 'Mummy kept asking for you and Annie went to all sorts of places to look for you. She couldn't find you anywhere.'

24

'Well, I'm here now,' Mrs. Bootle replied. 'And I'm going to turn out the light; are you ready?'

'Yes, I am ready,' Lucy answered. 'Good night, Mrs. Bootle. Good night, Miss Wace. Don't forget about the train journey.'

'I won't,' Sylvia promised.

She went from the room with Mrs. Bootle, leaving the child alone with the flickering night-light.

'Well?' Mrs. Bootle asked as they got outside.

'She looks a sweet child,' Sylvia said, and was conscious as she spoke that she still held the money and the paper that Mrs. Cuningham had given her. She looked at the name written on it in a flowing, well-educated hand. 'Sir Robert Sheldon, Sheldon Hall, Picton Fell.' She read the address carefully, then looked up to see Mrs. Bootle watching her.

'Where is it—Picton Fell?' she asked.

'North Country,' Mrs. Bootle replied. 'You'll have a long journey to get there.'

Sylvia was about to ask further questions when suddenly there was a cry from the landing.

'Mrs. Bootle!'

It was the doctor. Mrs. Bootle sped away and the bedroom door closed behind her.

Sylvia went slowly downstairs. She slipped the money she carried into her coat pocket, and after reading once again the address to which she was to take Lucy she put that away, too.

She sat down in a chair and warmed her hands. She looked round the hall, and through an open door into what she guessed was the drawing-room. The chairs covered with shiny chintz, the wall-paper elegantly dadoed with a replica of blue and pink ribbons, intertwined; the water colours in their gilt frames, the Oriental china which graced the mantelpiece were all impressive to someone who had lived in cheap and shabby surroundings for so long. 'Mrs. Cuningham must be rich,' Sylvia thought and wondered again at the strange instructions she had been given. Was Lucy really Sir Robert Sheldon's child? Then her name must be Sheldon and not Cuningham. And yet, if Sir Robert was alive, how could Mrs. Cuningham have married again? A divorce, could there have been a divorce? Sylvia felt startled at the idea. Such an impropriety and disgrace seemed impossible where Mrs. Cuningham was concerned. Sylvia remembered the sweet tones of her voice.

She must have been very beautiful. Even now when she was ravished by disease, abnormally thin and strained as if by a long illness, it was possible to see that she had had both beauty and charm. And her clothes! Sylvia's mind, despite an effort on her part to think of more serious things, turned to the creations she had seen lying in that room upstairs. And yet as Mrs. Bootle said . . . what was it Mrs. Bootle had said? The words came back to Sylvia and for the first time she felt slightly apprehensive of what lay before her. Would Sir Robert Sheldon be pleased to see his daughter? Apparently he was not to expect her if she was to go straight there without warning. Did he know that Mrs. Cuningham was dying? It seemed not. But if he were the father of Lucy would it not have been right to let him know, to demand his presence at such a moment? Sylvia remembered how Doctor Dawson had wanted to notify Mrs. Cuningham's relations, but she would give him no names. It was all so confused in her mind that she felt she couldn't even try to straighten out the story for herself, but must wait with what patience she could command for Mrs. Bootle.

There was a footstep and a tinkle of china, and she saw the lady's-maid going along the landing, carrying a tray in one hand and a polished brass can of hot water in the other. She still looked sulky and ill-tempered, and as she reached her mistress's door she seemed to rattle the tray unnecessarily loudly. She had put down the can preparatory to knocking when the door opened. Doctor Dawson stood there. He looked at the maid for a moment and then Sylvia heard his voice.

'You are too late,' he said sharply. 'Your mistress is dead.'

3

They had been travelling for nearly nine hours and Lucy, who had been bright and gay at the beginning of the journey, darting from side to side of the railway carriage and exclaiming at everything she saw, was now dozing in the shelter of Sylvia's arms, her dark lashes falling over her sleepy eyes and her tousled red head warm against Sylvia's breast.

It was hard to anticipate when they would reach their journey's end. The snow was falling fast and the country through which they were travelling was already shrouded in white. Passengers spoke of missed connections and snow-bound trains further north, and contemplated philosophically the possibility of arriving a day late at their destinations.

Sylvia closed her eyes, but she was not sleepy. She was thinking, wondering with an ever-deepening anxiety what awaited them at their journey's end. She was physically tired, but she knew she would be unable to rest with anything approaching peace of mind until she knew the answer to all the questions which were harassing her.

It had been very late when she returned to her own home last night. She had waited for Mrs. Bootle and when at last they had started their journey back through the snow the streets of Poolbrook had been quiet and still, its inhabitants having long retired for the night. They had walked in silence, saving their breath for the swiftness of their pace, for the effort of keeping their feet from slipping in the snow which, slushy in the centre of the roadway, had drifted deep into the gutters. At last home was reached and Sylvia had turned on the doorsteps to say in a voice which was more pleading than she knew:

'You will come in, Mrs. Bootle, won't you?'

'Yes, I will come in, dearie,' was the answer. 'I don't want to stay long, but there are things that I must say to you and to which you must listen before we are either of us much older.'

27

Sylvia shut the door and hurried to light the oil lamp on the hall table. It took her a few moments to get the sitting-room fire going again, but when at last the flames licked the splintered wood she looked up inquiringly at Mrs. Bootle standing there vast and impressive, her snow-sprinkled black cape enveloping her like a tent.

'That's better,' Mrs. Bootle said. 'And now, dearie, we'll get down to brass tacks.'

She threw back her cape as she spoke and produced a large bundle from under her arm. Sylvia had thought that she was carrying something as they left Mrs. Cuningham's house; now as Mrs. Bootle undid the bundle she opened her eyes wide in astonishment and was speechless. A black dress was revealed first—the black dress that she had seen in the maid's room and which Mrs. Bootle had held up to show her; next came a black coat which obviously matched it, a white petticoat trimmed with lace, and an evening dress of mauve silk ruched round the neck and having sleeves with folds of chiffon caught by big bunches of imitation Parma violets.

'Mrs. Bootle!' Sylvia's exclamation was hardly above a whisper.

'Wait a minute, that's not all,' Mrs. Bootle said.

From the voluminous folds of the mauve dress she produced a hat, black and trimmed with feathers and flowers and edged with a diaphanous black veil. It was a beautiful hat—a hat such as Sylvia had never seen except in the advertisements of the fashion papers.

'Oh, Mrs. Bootle!' she exclaimed again.

'Now unless I'm a bad judge they'll fit you.' Mrs. Bootle said. 'They may need a pinch here and there, but unless I'm very much mistaken you and Mrs. Cuningham were much the same size.'

'Oh, Mrs. Bootle, how could I . . . I mean to say, they are . . .'

'Yes, I know what you're going to say,' Mrs. Bootle interrupted. 'But if you call that stealing, I don't! The poor lady—God rest her wherever she may be—would just as soon that you should have her things, seeing that you are to look after her daughter, as that thieving hussy of a maid. Why, she'd have given them to you herself if she'd had time to think of it, poor soul. And what I didn't like was that woman packing them before she was even dead! There's gratitude for you! But there, one can't expect it these days. The old-fashioned type of servant doesn't exist now—anyway, not for the Mrs. Cuninghams of this world.'

'Oh, Mrs. Bootle, I couldn't . . . I mean, do you really think it is all right?'

Sylvia had jumped to her feet and stood looking at the clothes, reaching out one hand to touch the softness of the mauve dress.

'Now look here, my dear,' Mrs. Bootle said. 'There's degrees of what's right just as there's degrees of what's wrong in the world, and to my mind there's nothing wrong in your making yourself look your best to do the job that's been allotted to you. And besides, where you're going, as far as I can make out, you'll need all your wits about you and there's nothing gives a woman more assurance and confidence than to know she's well dressed. They're lovely clothes, straight from the best shops as you can see from the labels inside them. Now you wear them and think no more about it. I'd have taken more if I'd had the time, but I didn't want that young hussy saying things about me behind my back—not that anyone would listen to her! All the same, one never knows!'

'Will she take all the other things?' Sylvia asked.

'Not if I knows it she won't,' Mrs. Bootle said grimly. 'Mrs. Cuningham's solicitor will be arriving tomorrow. The doctor found his address in that very box from which she gave you the money. Once the lawyers are in the place it's not so easy to make off with any bits and pieces, as that young woman will find or my name's not Bootle.'

'But suppose,' Sylvia said anxiously, 'suppose she said something about these?'

'Now will you stop worrying,' Mrs. Bootle said. 'You leave it to me, dear. And when you goes to see Sir Robert Sheldon you'll go dressed decent and respectable-like, as a lady should be. You'll be leaving tomorrow morning, so you haven't got time for any shopping.'

'Yes, I must be up at the house early, before Lucy wakes up. She might be frightened to find herself alone with . . .' Sylvia hesitated to say the words.

'Poor child,' Mrs. Bootle spoke softly. 'But you'll do your best for her?'

'You know I will,' Sylvia said. 'And, Mrs. Bootle, I want to say thank you, too, but I just haven't got the words.'

'Don't waste your breath thanking me,' Mrs. Bootle replied.

'Even if nothing comes of it,' Sylvia said earnestly, 'even

if I just leave Lucy at Sheldon Hall and come away, I shall at least have had a short respite before I have to go to . . . to Uncle Octavius.'

Unbidden came to her mind the thought of what her uncle would say if he could see her now accepting clothes from a woman who had only been dead an hour or so, planning a journey before her mother was decently buried, and hoping, yes, hoping with all the strength that was within her that she need never see him again. With determination Sylvia fought against the fears rising within herself.

'Mrs. Bootle,' she said pleadingly, 'won't you tell me all that you know about Mrs. Cuningham, and . . . Sir Robert Sheldon?'

Mrs. Bootle took off her cape and hung it over the back of a chair to dry. Then she settled herself slowly and deliberately in the armchair and started to unlace her boots. When she had removed them she held out her stockinged feet to the blaze, with a sigh of relief.

'Now let me start at the beginning,' she said quietly. 'Mrs. Cuningham came here two years ago. She took the house you've seen tonight and settled in with her small daughter. There was, of course, a great deal of local talk and speculation about her at first; people wondering whether they should call on her or not and trying to find out who she was and where she came from. Soon after Mrs. Cuningham arrived I was asked by Doctor Dawson to attend to her. It wasn't anything serious—just a bad cold which made her keep to her bed for some days, and she didn't want to go to the trouble of sending for a trained nurse.

'As soon as I set eyes on her I knew there was something radically wrong with her health. After a day or two she confided in me that she'd been in two sanatoriums and had come to Poolbrook because she had heard the air was good for chest complaints. Well, I told Doctor Dawson this confidentially and he made a point of examining her next time he called. Sure enough, he found that her lung was affected, badly affected. She knew as well as he did that there was no chance of a real cure, she must just take life carefully and hope for the best. Well, it didn't take me long to find out something else as well and that was that Mrs. Cuningham—as she called herself—didn't want to live. "I've had my life, Bootle," she said to me over and over again. "It's been fun while it lasted, but there's nothing left for me now, nothing at all."

'She didn't say much more to me herself at the time, but visiting the houses round about as I do I soon learnt a good deal more. Mrs. Cuningham, it appears, wasn't Mrs. Cuningham at all. She was Lady Sheldon, wife of a nobleman. It appeared she had run away from her husband, run away with a young gentleman by the name of Cuningham. They'd spent several years abroad travelling on the Continent and had a pretty gay time together from all accounts. And then, later on, when I got to know Mrs. Cuningham better, she told me a few things, too. First of all she let them slip out unawares and then at last one day she says: "Bootle, I can talk to you, you're a human being which is more than most women are. I've been frightened of women all my life," she says, "but men have been kind, yes, kind and sweet to me—that is with the exception of my husband—my real husband, I mean." She laughed bitterly and I said to her boldly:

' "What's happened to Mr. Cuningham, Ma'am?"

' "Mr. Cunningham?" she replies. "Oh, he's gone back to a life of respectability in the bosom of his family. The prodigal son in modern clothes! You see, Bootle, he couldn't marry me, though he wanted to at first, poor lamb. My husband wouldn't divorce me. Sir Robert is like that, stern, unforgiving and cruel if it suits him. But it is his mother that I hate. I have no words in which to describe Lady Clementina. She is sinister—inhuman! It was her fault that I ever ran away." '

'Oh,' Sylvia interrupted, 'that is what Mrs. Cuningham was trying to say when . . . when she died.'

'She was always saying it,' Mrs. Bootle remarked. 'It became quite an obsession with her—sick people get like that, you know. She hated her mother-in-law. She even declared it was Lady Clementina who encouraged her to pay attention to young Mr. Cuningham's advances; but still, you can't be certain, ill people get strange fancies into their heads. Anyway, she ran off with him sure enough, and they were happy as long as she had the health to stand the type of life they lived. Then she got ill—she could never have been constitutionally strong—so he gives her enough money to live comfortably and they parts company. If you ask me, he tired after he realised what an ill women she was, poor lady. There's few men who can

31

stomach illness for long, they get bored with it. You can't blame them in some ways. But though she was brave about it, I always had the feeling that Mrs. Cuningham made up her mind to die from the moment he deserted her. There was really nothing else for her to do. She wasn't likely to find another man to look at her when she was in that state of health, and where could she go where she'd be accepted socially, where anyone respectable would wish to be friends with her?'

'And the child?' Sylvia asked.

'There's the mystery,' Mrs. Bootle said. 'From all I can make out, Lucy was born after her mother had run away with Mr. Cuningham; but she was emphatic, always very emphatic that it was not his child.'

'And supposing,' Sylvia said in horror, 'that Sir Robert Sheldon refuses to take Lucy in and insists she is not his daughter either?'

Mrs. Bootle shrugged her shoulders.

'We must just hope for the best, dearie. You heard her instructions; you're to leave Lucy there whatever happens.'

'Yes . . . but . . .' Sylvia expostulated.

'Now it's no use crossing that bridge until you comes to it.'

Bending forward, Mrs. Bootle took up her boots and put them on again.

'Now I must be getting along home,' she said at length. 'There's little more I can tell you, and no good can come of guessing what's ahead. You must just wait and see. You pop off to bed and get as much rest as you can and be up to fetch that child first thing in the morning. You want to be away before your uncle arrives.'

'That is true,' Sylvia said.

She, too, got to her feet, but her eyes were held by the clothes lying on the settee.

'You are quite sure, Mrs. Bootle?' she asked, and there was no need to ask to what she referred.

'Quite sure,' Mrs. Bootle said. 'You're as entitled to them as anyone else. Now take them upstairs with you and mind you travel in that black dress. First impressions are important. Well, good night, dearie, it's been a long day and I shall be glad of a bit of rest myself.'

'Good night, Mrs. Bootle. And thank you once again.'

On an impulse Sylvia bent forward and kissed the elder woman's cheek.

Mrs. Bootle seemed gratified.

'There, there, I've only done what any Christian would do in the circumstances.'

She moved towards the door, then stopped.

'You're not frightened here alone?'

She raised her eyes to the ceiling and Sylvia knew what she meant.

'No,' she said doubtfully; and then more firmly: 'No, why should I be frightened of Mother? It only seems strange that she won't call me—ever again.'

Sylvia tried on both dresses before she went to bed. The mirror in her room was not a large one and she could see only a little of herself, but it was enough to show her she was transformed.

In the few hours left her in which to sleep she had little real rest. Excitement and anxiety do not make good bed-fellows, and after tossing and turning, her brain chaotic with all that had happened, she heard the clock strike six and got up and dressed. It did not take her long to pack her own few meagre belongings into a small trunk on the top of which she placed the mauve evening dress, strangely incongruous beside her own threadbare and out-of-date dresses.

There was nothing in the house for breakfast. Sylvia made herself a cup of tea and cut herself some bread and butter. Then when at last she was ready, she said good-bye to her mother. It was difficult to feel any emotion save an eagerness to be gone, to sever the last ties with the restricted, inhibited past. She bent forward to kiss her mother's cold forehead and kneeling at the foot of the bed she tried to pray, but all the time she was conscious of the need for hurry, of the desire to be on her way. Before it was yet daylight she hurried up the street to wake Lucy, dress her and help Annie pack her clothes.

It had been a relief to board the train, to know that their luggage was in the van and they were really off on their journey. Up to that moment it had all seemed unreal, a dream from which she might so easily be awakened abruptly by the arrival of Uncle Octavius, or by some other authoritative circumstance which they had overlooked.

But when at last the train started, when Mrs. Bootle's waving figure was out of sight and Lucy, slipping her hand confidently into hers, said, 'I do like going in trains; don't you, Miss Wace?' Sylvia knew the die was cast. For better or for worse she had taken this step; she had accepted the

33

responsibility of Lucy; she had performed an action which she knew would both horrify and shock her uncle when he arrived. To consider a situation of any sort without his advice and approval would seem revolutionary; to leave her mother before she was buried, to slip away on what was unquestionably an adventure would be, Sylvia knew, almost too reprehensible for forgiveness.

But she did not care. For once she had thrown aside the dependence which had been hers all her life. While her mother lived she had never failed her. Now that she could no longer be of service, what did it matter what happened? She had put the key of the house into Mrs. Bootle's hand feeling as if she laid aside the yoke of many years.

Only at the last moment on the station platform had her courage failed her.

'Supposing everything goes wrong, just supposing?' she said, trembling.

Mrs. Bootle, calm and serene, replied:

'If it does, you come right back to me here, dearie, and we'll cope with your uncle together. Don't worry, and let me know if you arrive safely and what's happening. I shall be disappointed, though, if I get you back instead of a letter.'

Perilously near to tears, Sylvia had laughed.

'I will do my best to spare you that disappointment,' she said and got into the train.

Now she wondered over and over again whether she had done right, whether it would not have been wiser to wait and interview Mrs. Cuningham's lawyer. And yet she knew she was not so afraid, so scared of what she was doing as she would have been yesterday. Mrs. Bootle was right: the clothes she was wearing gave her confidence. Although she had only been able to see a portion of herself, as it were, in the mirror in her own room, in Mrs. Cuningham's house she had seen herself full length and had been startled into an almost audible exclamation by her reflection. The black dress, beautifully cut and in perfect taste, had given her not only an elegance, but a dignity which she had never before possessed. The clothes had accentuated her looks, but in the right way; well dressed for the first time in her life, she nevertheless did not feel over-dressed. She looked right. She looked a lady. For the first time, Sylvia was sure of her own beauty. There was, indeed, nothing garish about the colour of her hair or the purity of her complexion; it was only because of the ill-fitting, badly chosen garments she had been forced to wear that they had seemed conspicuous, thrown into relief by the ugliness of the clothes which framed them. Now everything was moulded into a harmonious whole and Sylvia knew that dressed like this she need never feel humble or ashamed in whatever society she found herself.

The coat which matched the dress was not really warm enough for a long journey, but Sylvia would have suffered a good deal more than cold rather than have covered it with the grey cloth coat which she had inherited from her cousin.

She had known from the look on the other passengers' faces that she and Lucy made a distinguished couple. The child's clothes were chosen with the same exquisite taste as marked her own. Lucy's blue coat with its wide collar and pouched sleeves was matched by a wide-brimmed beaver hat and a little white fur tippet and muff. She looked both adorable and a little aristocrat. Now she was tired. Her hands were dirty from the smuts in the carriage and sticky from the food which Mrs. Bootle had wisely insisted that they should carry with them.

'I wonder how much longer it will be before we reach Mickledon,' Sylvia thought, and even as she wondered the train stopped with a jolt and she heard the porters shout, 'Mickledon! Mickledon! All change, all change!'

Hastily putting on Lucy's hat and muff, she gathered up their belongings and alighting on the platform informed a porter that their trunks were in the van.

'We want to get to Picton Fell,' she informed him.

'Ye won't do that t'night. Ma'am. Last train for Picton Fell left nearly an hour ago. 'Tis due out at six o'clock and 'tis getting on for seven now.'

'Oh, dear, what can we do?' Sylvia exclaimed.

'Next train is 5.30 t'morrow morning,' the porter said.

'And is there no other way we can get there?'

'Ah don't know whether Mr. Robb at Green Man can fix ye up with a conveyance. If ye likes to walk across and ask him, Ah'll take care of t'luggage. Ye can't miss Green Man, 'tis straight across road opposite t'station.'

He pointed the direction and Sylvia, taking Lucy by the hand, walked across the dark, snow-covered road to where the lights of the Green Man shone invitingly.

The public-house was an old one built on spacious lines, and entering by the front door, Sylvia found herself in a square hall off which on one side lay a big, comfortable

35

sitting-room where logs flared up the chimney, and on the other the taproom from which came the sound of raised and jovial voices. She hesitated, wondering how to attract someone's attention, when a man in shirt-sleeves, wearing a big white apron, came out from the tap-room. He was an elderly man with grey hair and side-whiskers, and somehow Sylvia felt warmed by the smile on his face and the quiet, respectful manner with which he bowed to her.

'Can I be of assistance, Madam?'

'The porter at the station said that Mr. Robb might be able to help me.'

'I am Horatio Robb, at your service.'

'This little girl and I want to get through to Picton Fell. We have missed the connection; is there any kind of conveyance that would take us there?'

'To Picton Fell. It's a tidy step at this time of night. And where might you be going in Picton Fell?'

'To Sheldon Hall.'

'To Sheldon Hall!'

It seemed to Sylvia that Mr. Robb looked astonished. He bowed politely once more.

'I'll see if it can be done, Madam. If you and the young lady will sit by the fire . . . and if there's anything you'd like to eat or drink . . .'

'We would welcome both,' Sylvia said. 'We have been travelling since early morning.'

She drew Lucy into the sitting-room and took off the child's coat. Lucy was wide awake now and full of questions as to where they were and how soon it would be before they got home.

Sylvia had broken it to her early in the morning that her mother was dead; but now she realised that Lucy did not understand, for after darting about the room looking at first this and then that she came to Sylvia's side and asked:

'How long will my Mummy be dead? Shall we be going back to her soon?'

Sylvia shook her head.

'No, dear, your mother has gone to God.'

'To stay with Him for ever?' Lucy asked.

'Yes, dear.'

Lucy thought this over for some time and then she said:

'But you will stay with me, won't you, Miss Wace? I shall be awfully lonely otherwise. I don't like Annie very much. Mummy and I thought her terribly stupid. But if

36

Mummy's gone away, there would only be Annie, wouldn't there?'

'Annie is not going to look after you,' Sylvia said. 'I hope to do that. But if I can't, there will be somebody very nice who shall do so.'

'Who?' Lucy asked.

As Sylvia could not answer this, she tried to turn the conversation, thinking to herself that she had just as many questions to ask as Lucy, questions to which at present there were no answers.

They had not long to wait before a waiter told them food was served for them in the dining-room. They went to it quickly and while they were eating, Mr. Robb appeared again to inform them that he had persuaded a friend with a four-wheeler to take them to Sheldon Hall.

'I'm afraid he'll charge you a guinea for it, Madam, but the roads are bad and he's not over keen on taking out his horse.'

'I shall be glad to give him a guinea,' Sylvia replied. 'And thank you for all the trouble you have taken.'

'It'll be a little time before he's ready,' Mr. Robb said. 'If you and the young lady will stop by the fire and make yourselves comfortable, I'll let you know as soon as he's round and he can fetch your luggage from the station first.'

'Thank you,' Sylvia said again.

She and Lucy finished their meal and went back to the warmth of the fire. They had been alone in the sitting-room before, but now they were joined by a young man ostentatiously and extravagantly dressed, with a long waxed moustache and a flashing diamond ring on his little finger. He opened a conversation almost immediately.

'Are you waiting for the London train?'

Sylvia shook her head.

'No,' she said quietly, not wishing to snub him, but at the same time as discouragingly as she could.

'That's surprising,' the stranger said; then he added: 'You'll forgive me if I make a personal remark, but you look as if you ought to be going to London.'

'Indeed.'

Sylvia's voice was distant. At the same time she felt shy and awkward. Nothing in her life had ever taught her how to behave to strangers who attached themselves without introduction in a hotel sitting-room.

'Shall I tell you why?' the stranger asked and without

37

waiting for Sylvia's answer went on: 'All the smartest and prettiest women are to be found in London; that's why you look like a Londoner to me. Is that your little girl?'

'I am looking after her,' Sylvia said, and noticed that the man took a quick glance at her ungloved left hand.

'A pretty child. Not that I've ever cared for red hair myself, but there are men who are crazy about it. Golden hair is my preference, the longer the better.'

Sylvia bent her head and spoke in a low voice to Lucy, hoping that the man would understand that his conversation was not desirable. But he was quite unabashed. She realised now from the side glances and the almost unbearable way in which he was looking at her that he was trying to flirt with her and she felt not outraged, but awkward and at a loss.

'Let me tell you something,' he said, edging a little nearer and dropping his voice to a whisper. 'With your looks and figure you'd be the rage in London. Now supposing, just supposing that you were earning your living by looking after that little girl, what future is there in it, I ask you? But in London you'd find yourself really appreciated, and I'd not be the only one to do the appreciating.'

Sylvia turned to face him and looked him straight between the eyes.

'Thank you, but I am not interested,' she said firmly.

Quite unrepressed he winked at her. 'But you might be one day. Who knows?'

It was at that moment that Mr. Robb came into the room again. Sylvia got up quickly.

'Oh, Mr. Robb, is the carriage ready?'

'Not quite, Madam,' he replied.

And then as if he sensed what had been happening he gave the man by the fire a quelling look.

'Mr. Cuthbertson,' he said, 'you'll find your drink waiting for you in the tap-room.'

'Now, Robb, don't start getting up-stage,' Mr. Cuthbertson begged. 'I want my drink in here by the fire and I think this young lady would join me in one. What about a small port, Miss?'

'The lady can order what she wants for herself,' Mr. Robb said sternly, adding in a low voice but loud enough for Sylvia to hear, 'Don't be a fool, man. She's going to Sheldon Hall.'

Mr. Cuthbertson gasped. Sylvia was aware of his expression even while she pretended she was not looking at him.

'Good Lord! Why didn't you say so?'

He got up without another word and left the sitting-room. Mr. Robb followed him to the door, but turned back and bowed.

'I'm sorry, Madam.'

He would have left her but Sylvia stopped him with a question:

'How far is Sheldon Hall?'

'About ten miles, Madam.'

'Do you know the place?'

'Very well indeed. I think everyone does in this part of the world.'

'And you know Sir Robert?'

'Yes, Madam.'

'He is at home.'

'I think so, Madam; I saw him driving this way two days ago.'

That was all she wanted to know—or was it? She felt that Horatio Robb was keeping something back and yet she liked him and felt that he was an honest man who could be trusted, and she sensed that there was more than kindness in his eyes as he looked at her: sympathy, perhaps, or could it be—pity?

'Mr. Robb?' Sylvia made up her mind with an effort.

'Madam?'

'If . . . if . . . if for any reason I was not able to stay at Sheldon Hall, could you offer me a bed here?'

'My premises, such as they are, are at your service.'

'Thank you.'

Sylvia felt that she had made a friend and was curiously relieved.

Mr. Robb said no more. He bowed and left the room.

Here at least was some haven, some refuge if the worst came to the worst. And yet of what was she afraid? What could the worst be?

'The carriage is at the door, Madam.'

Now there was the last part of their journey to be faced. Lucy was growing sleepy again. Mr. Robb produced a rug and Sylvia wrapped it round her.

Outside the door the four-wheeler was waiting, smelling of must and hay, the horse shaking its bit as if irritated at being taken out at this hour of night.

'You'll have to take it slow, Joe, the roads are none too clear,' Mr. Robb called to the man on the box.

'Ah'll get 'em there, don't ye worry!'

Mr. Robb helped Sylvia and Lucy in.

'I've put a foot-warmer for you, Madam, and there's an extra rug if you need it.'

'Thank you, Mr. Robb.' Sylvia held out her hand. 'I'm grateful, very grateful for all you've done.'

There was strength and reassurance in his handclasp. As they drove off he brought his fingers up to his forehead in a countryman's salute.

'A good journey to you!'

Then they were off, travelling the road which led to Sheldon Hall.

4

The carriage drew up with a sudden jerk and Sylvia, who had been dozing, opened her eyes with a startled exclamation. She leant forward and rubbed the carriage window with her gloved hand. Then she saw that they had not arrived at the house, but at the lodge. Outside the moon had risen and she could perceive two high wrought-iron gates flanked by stone lions holding heraldic shields. Joe, the coachman, gave a shout, his voice echoing clearly in the silence which surrounded them. For a moment nothing happened and then a door of the lodge opened and a shaft of yellow light illumined the figure of a man coming quickly to the gates.

Sylvia roused Lucy who, nestled against her, was sleeping soundly.

'You must wake up, darling. We shall arrive in a few minutes.'

Lucy opened her eyes and was instantly wide awake.

'Where are we?' she asked. 'It isn't morning?'

'No, it isn't morning yet,' Sylvia replied. 'You haven't been to bed, you know.'

Lucy laughed the spontaneous, care-free laugh of a child. 'I thought I had,' she said. 'Aren't I silly?'

Sylvia bent down to kiss her. she felt just then the need for human contact, for some reassurance to still her own fear, a fear amounting almost to panic now that the moment was upon her, a moment in which it seemed to her that not only Lucy's future, but her own was at stake.

The carriage started forward again. Sylvia smoothed her hair beneath her smart black hat. Mrs. Bootle had said that first impressions were important and she wished that she could see how she looked. To forget herself she turned again to Lucy, arranging her hair, tying the ribbons attached to her hat tidily beneath her chin. The child was jumping about in her seat, trying to look out of the window.

'Where is the house, Miss Wace? I can see only trees. We can't sleep in trees, can we?'

'This is the drive,' Sylvia said, glancing at the oaks silhouetted in the moonlight, their branches heavily laden with snow.

She was searching for a handkerchief in her handbag when suddenly Lucy gave an exclamation.

'Oo, there it is . . . there's the house!'

Sylvia looked up and was suddenly still, unable to find words for what she saw. A bend in the drive had revealed Sheldon Hall and Sylvia was never to forget her first sight of it. From where they were they looked across an unbroken expanse of white snow, and a little above them, standing majestically alone, stood the Hall full in the light of the moon, the grey stone a sombre background for the shining iridescence of a hundred windows. The façade was supported by six great fluted columns and below them were steps balustraded in stone and curving down to the courtyard from which the winged sides of the house spread away. Perfectly proportioned, designed by a master mind, the house was a poem in stone.

What Sylvia had expected to see she could never afterwards remember, but never in her life had she imagined anything so imposing and yet so beautiful as this house as it was revealed to her now. In the moonlight, too, it seemed to possess a fairy quality as if it were unreal, a figment of the imagination, and it was only as they drew near that its immensity became apparent and her first wonder was lost in a feeling of being overpowered.

The carriage drew up at the foot of the stone steps. Sylvia, hurriedly putting still more finishing touches to Lucy's toilet and her own, heard Joe, the coachman, climb heavily down from the box and walk up the steps. He must have

41

rung the bell and come straight down to the carriage door, for even before he reached it a golden light came streaming forth from the door above them. Joe opened the door of the carriage.

'Here ye are, Miss. Delivered safe an' sound. Ah'll tak t'luggage round t'back.'

'Thank you.'

Sylvia got out and after paying him took Lucy by the hand and walked up the steps. Standing in the doorway was a white-haired man whom she guessed must be the butler.

'Good evening. I wish to see Sir Robert Sheldon.'

Her eyes were a little dazzled by the light, but even so she was aware of the surprise on the butler's face and his momentary hesitation before he asked:

'Sir Robert is expecting you, Madam?'

'No, but I wish to see him.'

As she spoke Sylvia stepped forward and drew Lucy in through the doorway to what she now perceived was a big high hall panelled in dark oak and lit by innumerable candles set in silver sconces. The butler shut the door behind them.

'If you will wait here a moment, Madam, I will inquire if Sir Robert will see you.'

A log fire was burning in an open fireplace and Sylvia drew Lucy towards it.

The butler walked across the hall to a door that was almost directly opposite the fireplace. He waited a moment as if he listened and then gently opened the door. There was a burst of laughter and the sound of men's voices. Through the partially open door Sylvia could see a side-table covered with a white cloth and laden with silver dishes. Sir Robert was here then and at dinner! She sighed with relief. Here at least was one anxiety allayed, for all the time she had been haunted by the fear that after they had travelled so far and for so long the man they sought might be away from home.

There was another burst of laughter and then quite suddenly silence. She heard a voice exclaim, 'A woman and a child to see me? What the devil do you mean, Bateson?'

There was a little buzz of conversation and then a man's tones rather slurred as if with heavy drinking:

'Perhaps a bit of your past has caught up with you, Robert.'

'Tell them to come in here.'

The words came commandingly from the man who had

spoken first and then once again there was laughter—mocking, derisive laughter. Sylvia felt herself pale. For a moment she was afraid and then as she saw the butler cross the hall she felt a sudden anger aroused by a pride she had not known she possessed.

"Will you and the young lady be good enough to come this way, Madam?"

The butler's manner was quiet, correct and impassive and yet Sylvia, sensitive and quivering, suspected impertinence.

'Kindly ask Sir Robert to come here to us.'

She spoke slowly. There was an authority in her voice which surprised even herself.

Bateson inclined his head.

'Very good, Madam. I will take Sir Robert your message.'

Sylvia did not move. Lucy was fidgeting a little, staring round her wide-eyed, pulling off her gloves and stuffing them into her minute muff. But Sylvia did not look at her; her eyes were fixed on the butler's retreating figure. There was the rising chatter of voices as he opened the dining-room door, and then once again came silence, a silence in which Sylvia was not really conscious of her own feelings; and yet something instinctive within her told her that this moment was important.

The dining-room door was thrown open wide. She had a momentary glimpse of a long table around which half a dozen men were seated. There was a gleam of candles, a shimmering of glass and silver, but she had eyes only for the man striding across the hall towards her. For one startled moment she thought his face seemed familiar, that she knew him. And then the explanation was obvious. She waited until he reached her side. He was frowning, the black brows almost meeting across his forehead. A tall man, she was aware of an arrogance about him, a forceful pride which was somehow in keeping with the magnificence of the house.

'You want to see me?'

His voice was clear, sharp and compelling.

Sylvia looked up at him.

'Yes,' she said quietly. 'I have brought you your daughter.'

As she spoke she put out her hand and drew Lucy's hat from her head; it hung down her back by its blue ribbons and the light from the leaping flames shone on the burnished red of her hair, a colour echoed unmistakably on Sir Robert's head.

He said nothing, made no movement, gave no exclamation, and yet Sylvia knew she could not have surprised him more had she fired a pistol straight in his face. Father and daughter looked at each other. They were absurdly alike not only in the colour of their hair, but in the darkness of their eyes, their clean-cut features, square jaws and the smooth dark brows etched sharply against white foreheads.

It was a moment of tension, a moment so poignant that it seemed to Sylvia as if the silence would never be broken, until Lucy, looking around her, asked in her clear, childish treble:

'Are we going to stay in this big house?'

Sir Robert turned to Sylvia.

'Who is she? Where have you come from?'

Sylvia felt some of her composure leave her.

'Her mother asked me to bring Lucy to you,' she said. 'I knew her as Mrs. Cuningham, but I understand she was in fact Lady Sheldon.'

The expression on Sir Robert's face did not alter. It was as if he held himself in an iron grip through which it was impossible for any emotion to penetrate. The tone of his voice was cold and impersonal as he asked:

'Where is she now?'

'She died yesterday.'

He looked again at Lucy and arrested the child's wandering eyes, holding them with his own.

'How old are you?'

'I'm six, nearly seven.'

'When is your birthday?'

Lucy hesitated a moment, her forehead contracting with the effort of remembering and making her even more ridiculously llike the man interrogating her.

'The ninth of April,' she said at last slowly, 'I shall be seven.'

Sir Robert looked round.

'Bateson.'

From some dark corner of the hall where he must have been waiting, Bateson appeared as if by magic.

'Is her ladyship awake?'

'Yes, Sir Robert.'

'Then show these ladies upstairs.'

'Very good, Sir Robert.'

Sir Robert looked at Sylvia. She felt his eyes flick over

her from her faced down to her boots. She had no idea what the glance meant and yet she felt he drew some conclusion from it.

'You will excuse me?'

He spoke stiffly as if his politeness was an effort, and then before she had time to reply he walked across the hall and re-entered the dining-room.

'I want something to drink, Miss Wace.'

Lucy tugging at her hand aroused Sylvia to her responsibilities.

'We'll see about it in a moment, darling.'

Bateson was at Sylvia's elbow.

'Will you come this way, Miss?'

She felt he had successfully catalogued her——he was subtly more familiar in his intonation. She realised, too, that he had seen her ringless hand from which she had withdrawn her glove quite unconsciously while talking to Sir Robert.

Bateson led them up a broad oak staircase. Now for the first time Sylvia had eyes for what lay around them: the great gilt-framed pictures hanging on the panelled walls, the thick carpets into which their feet seemed to sink, the tapestries, polished furniture, heraldic newels and high-backed chairs covered with ancient needlework. It was all so lavish, so luxurious that she felt as if her eyes were incapable of taking in anything individually, it was only a kaleidoscope of beauty such as she had never imagined.

They reached the landing from which they could look back into the depths of the hall below, and suddenly Sylvia had the impressioon that they were being watched, not by a human being, but by something vast and mighty and overpowering.

'This way, Miss.'

Bateson's voice drew her on. It was as if he added, 'It's not for the likes of you to linger.' He stopped at a door, knocked and then opened it.

'This way, Miss, if you please.'

He ushered them in, Sylvia a little apprehensive of what they would find, Lucy clinging to her hand, though whether from fear or tiredness Sylvia had no time to consider.

The room though large was dominated by a four-poster bed with hangings of blue brocade surmounted by great fronds of ostrich feathers. In the centre of the bed, propped up by pillows and seeming at that moment in-

45

significant because of the height and breadth of her surroundings, was a little old woman.

'Who is it? What do you want?'

The voice was sharp and somewhat shrill.

'Sir Robert's instructions, my lady. These ladies have
just arrived.'

'Ladies, at this hour of night!'

The voice was now querulous. As Sylvia and Lucy came
forward, the old lady bent and peered at them.

'Come here. Who are you and where have you come
from?'

The words were shot at them staccato fashion.

Sylvia obeyed the command by moving towards the bed
holding Lucy by her hand. The child's hat was still hanging
down her back and Sylvia was aware that after the first
searching glance the old lady's eyes were fixed on Lucy.
They drew nearer and nearer to the side of the great bed.
There were two great silver candelabra on either side of it
and at least a dozen candles burning in each. They revealed
a raddled, withered face, a sharply arched nose, dark,
piercing eyes and a wealth of white hair piled high in innumerable curls. Round her shoulders Lady Clementina
wore a cape of Russian sable and her fingers, thin and
pointed, were ornamented with many sparkling rings.
There was a flash of diamonds, too, on her wrist, and
round her scraggy yellow neck were three rows of magnificent pearls.

On a closer scrutiny it was difficult to believe that one
had thought her small. She had a presence. There was
something vital, almost dynamic about the small figure sitting up in bed and speaking in her quick, commanding
manner. As Sylvia looked at her, she felt afraid. This was a
woman, she thought to herself, who would be utterly
ruthless, who would have her own way at whatever cost,
who would have mercy on none and ask none for herself.

Because of the feelings Lady Clementina aroused within
her, Sylvia was unprepared for the command:

'Explain your presence here!'

Now Lady Clementina was looking at her. Sylvia could
see those dark eyes peering at her, taking in every detail of
her appearance.

'This is Lucy,' Sylvia began and was aware that her own
voice faltered and sounded curiously weak. 'Her mother,
whom I knew as Mrs. Cuningham, died yesterday. Her last

46

request was that I would bring the child here—to her father.'

'As a little surprise, eh?'

Sylvia fancied that a faint smile twisted the withered lips, and then without waiting for an answer Lady Clementina cried:

'Bateson, stop trying to listen and go and fetch Nannie.'

'Yes, my lady.'

Lady Clementina dropped her voice, speaking as if to herself.

'So Alice is dead, is she? I never expected she would last long, but I am surprised at the child. I didn't believe she was capable of producing one. But it is Robert's all right.'

'You are sure of that, I suppose?'

The cool voice from the doorway made Sylvia start. She turned to see Sir Robert advancing from the shadows into the light of the candles, tall, handsome and, it seemed to her, incredibly arrogant.

Lady Clementina laughed, an unpleasant laugh which was almost a cackle.

'Have you looked at her, Robert? You can't deny that hair! Alice has had her revenge. We can only be thankful it isn't a boy.'

'I should have thought that would have solved your problems without more ado,' Sir Robert replied.

He moved across to the fireplace and stood with his back to the fire.

'The type of son which Alice could produce would be of no use to Sheldon Hall,' Lady Clementina replied; and Sylvia had the impression that this was the reiteration of an old argument.

'I always understood you to say, dear Mamma, that Alice was incapable of producing any child, male or female,' Sir Robert said suavely. 'And yet it apppears you have been proved wrong.'

Mother and son looked at each other—a strange look. Was it hatred? Sylvia wondered and then thought she must be tired, that the effects of the journey and the strange surroundings in which she found herself were bewildering her, giving her queer ideas.

It was at that moment that Lucy began to whimper. 'I'm tired. I want a drink. Oh, Miss Wace, let us go home.'

Sylvia went down on her knees and put her arms round the child.

47

'It is all right, darling,' she said.

She looked across the child's bowed head to Lady Clementina.

'We have been travelling since very early this morning. Could I please put Lucy to bed?'

'It is too late for the child. Any fool can see that. Where is Nannie? I sent for her.'

There was a knock at the door.

'Come in, come in,' Lady Clementina said testily; and then as a woman entered, 'Oh, there you are, Nannie. I expect Bateson has told you what has happened so you need no explanation from me. See that the child is put to bed, and Miss . . .' She stopped.

'Wace,' Sylvia interposed. 'Sylvia Wace.'

'. . . will go with you. Afterwards bring her back here. There are several questions I wish to ask her.'

'Yes, my lady.'

Nannie came forward, Sylvia saw with relief that she was a woman of about sixty with a smiling, good-natured expression on a plump, unwrinkled face. Her ample bosom and rounded arms seemed made to cuddle babies, and there was a homeliness about her white cap and sensible apron. 'The only human being I have seen so far in this house,' she thought to herself, as getting to her feet she picked up Lucy and, following Nannie, carried her from the room. The child cried a little as they went along the passages, but almost before she was undressed she was asleep.

'I will stay with her,' Nannie said. 'Her ladyship will want to see you.'

They had undressed Lucy together and were now unpacking her luggage. Sylvia already felt that she liked and could trust this older woman.

'I was Sir Robert's Nannie,' she said, 'and I would have known this child anywhere. Why, if you cut her hair short she would be Sir Robert himself just as he was as a little boy, and a sweeter child you never saw.'

Sylvia longed to say, 'It is a pity then that he has altered so much since he grew up,' because now she knew that Sir Robert frightened her. There was something inhuman about him, as there was about his mother. 'Perhaps it is because I am not used to people of this class of life,' Sylvia thought humbly; and yet she knew that was not the truth. There was something strange, something almost sinister about them, and although in the warmth and cosiness of

48

Lucy's bedroom with Nannie chatting away to her she felt that she exaggerated her feelings, she was well aware that she shrank with an almost physical emotion from seeing Lady Clementina and Sir Robert again. This, however, did not prevent her when she had washed her hands and tidied her hair from telling Nannie with a quiet bravery she was far from feeling that she was ready. Her own reflection in the mirror reassured her a little; at least, she told herself, she need not be ashamed of her appearance. Nevertheless she felt overwhelmingly insignificant as she walked beside Nannie through the long corridors which led to Lady Clementina's bedroom. Nannie left her at the door.

'Just knock,' she said. 'You'll be all right.'

Her smile was reassuring and yet Sylvia felt far from confident. She knocked and there was no reply, and then as she listened intently against the thickness of the big oak door she heard voices: Lady Clementina's and the other voice, deeper, quieter, and yet almost as perturbing.

'So Sir Robert is still there,' she thought, and wondered what had happened to his guests downstairs. She would have gone away, afraid to interrupt them now that her first knock had gained no answer, but the door was flung open.

'I thought I heard someone outside,' Sir Robert said. 'Mother, Miss Wace is here.'

'Tell her to come in,' Lady Clementina replied; and then as Sylvia advanced. 'You have been a long time. You could have left Nannie to put the child to bed.'

'I wanted to look after her myself,' Sylvia replied gently. 'Lucy might have needed me.'

'Um.' Lady Clementina made a noise which might have expressed anything and indicated a chair beside her bed. 'Sit down.'

Sylvia did as she was told, feeling rather like a delinquent housemaid.

Sir Robert took up his position in front of the fireplace.

'Now,' Lady Clementina said, 'will you tell us why you are here?'

Sylvia explained, making her story as coherent, but as short as possible. She told of Mrs. Cuningham's death, the sudden unexpected haemorrhages, and her last request that Sylvia should bring Lucy to Sheldon Hall.

'So he abandoned her!'

Lady Clementina looked across at her son with an expression very like satisfaction on her face.

'I knew that,' Sir Robert said.

49

'You knew it?' Lady Clementina ejaculated. 'You did not tell me.'

'There was no reason for you to know,' Sir Robert replied.

'Fiddlesticks! Why should I not know?'

'Because I rather expected to hear from Alice herself,' Sir Robert answered. 'As it was, my informant was merely a friend of the family who told me that Bertram had returned to the fold.'

'And if Alice had writtten to you?'

'I might have been tempted to ask her to return.'

'Pah!' Lady Clementina spoke with disgust. 'You always were ridiculously sentimental. The woman left you when she had no further use for any of us.'

'At least she has had the courtesy to send me—my daughter.'

Lady Clementina looked at him angrily. 'I suppose it does not strike you that it was the only thing she could do with the child! I don't suppose young Cuningham would go on paying for her!'

'That is beside the point,' Sir Robert replied. 'Let us give Alice her due. She has sent me Lucy and I am delighted to have her.'

'Why? What good can it do you?'

Lady Clementina's tone was harshly suspicious.

'Well, she might even bring a little happiness within these dark walls.' There was something subtly mocking in Sir Robert's words.

Lady Clementina watched him as he moved across the floor to stand beside Sylvia.

'Allow me to thank you, Miss Wace, for your part in bringing my daughter here. I am most grateful. You will, I hope, be able to stay with Lucy, at least for the time being.'

'Thank you.'

Sylvia was half afraid that he would see what a relief his words were to her. Even as she had helped unpack Lucy's trunks the question presented itself whether she would be needed with Nannie in the house—an old and trusted servant. Why should they want a stranger? Why, indeed, should more than one attendant be necessary for Lucy?

'Miss Wace may have other plans,' Lady Clementina said sharply and Sylvia realised that her positioon was by no means secure. She replied quickly, but speaking to Sir Robert.

50

'I have no other plans and I would very much like to stay with Lucy if it is possible.'

'I hope you will make yourself at home here,' Sir Robert said, and again Sylvia had the idea that he was mocking—not her, but Lady Clementina. He walked towards the door. 'My mother will tell you what a very happy family we are—at Sheldon Hall.'

There was bitterness as well as mockery now in his voice. Then the door shut behind him.

5

Sylvia woke with a sense of foreboding, but when she had opened her eyes and realised where she was a feeling of excitement stole over her. This was a new life and an adventure.

She sat up in bed, pushing her long fair hair from off her shoulders, then as the last mists of sleep left her she jumped out of bed and, drawing wide her curtains, looked out. Her window faced the front of the house and from it she could see the drive along which they had come the night before. The park-land was covered in snow and the great expanse of lake which lay a little to the left of the house was a sheet of ice, the ducks and swans sitting disconsolately upon it as if they were unable to understand why the water with which they were so familiar should have become solid beneath their feet.

At the far end of the lake was a little Grecian temple, beautiful in its simplicity, and it drew Sylvia's eyes, filling her with a kind of awed wonder that so much beauty and loveliness could be hers for just this moment.

It was an effort to turn from the window and look at the room; but when she did, the memory of what had happened in the night came flooding into her mind. At the time she had thought she must be dreaming, but now as she looked at the communicating door which led to Lucy's room she knew that it was no dream.

Lucy was sleeping in the larger room of the two and she

had been allotted a smaller one, which was generally in use as a dressing-room. Both rooms were large by Sylvia's standards, and the heavy damask hangings and great suites of mahogany furniture seemed to her very impressive. She had looked round the rooms before she had gone to bed feeling a little awed, even a little afraid of such luxurious surroundings, and it had seemed to her then that Lucy, fast asleep in the big bed, was her only link—and a very small one—with the world she had left behind. She had bent over the sleeping child, seeing with satisfaction the expression of quiet contentment on her face. The tears she had shed had been only the result of over-tiredness, and yet it occurred to Sylvia that Lucy might wake in the night and be frightened. Accordingly she left the communicating door ajar and moved her bed a little so that she could see Lucy from where she lay.

Sylvia had thought she would find it difficult to sleep, there was so much to think about, so many new impressions to sort out and consider, and yet almost as soon as her head touched the pillow she had fallen into a deep, dreamless sleep. How long she slept she had no idea, but she had woken suddenly and for a moment experienced the strange, bewildering sensation of wondering where she was, expecting to recognise the familiar outlines of her own small slip of a room at home. The fire was sinking low in the grate, but it still gave enough light to glitter on the picture frames and mirrors and throw a monstrous shadow behind the heavy wardrobe.

Then she heard with a sudden sense of shock the opening of a door. Her heart beat quickly; but it was not her door that had opened, but the one in Lucy's room which opened on to the passage Someone was entering the room. She would have sat up in bed, but sheer fear held her motionless; she could not force her limbs to obey her instinct which was to move and cry out There was a light moving slowly into the room until it reached her line of vision, and then at last, as the thumping of her heart almost suffocated her in its intensity, she saw a candle held level with a head vivid as the flame itself.

Now she was thankful that her first instinct had not been obeyed, for unseen she could watch Sir Robert advance across the bedroom toward his daughter's bed. He moved slowly and when at last he reached the bed he stood at the foot and looked long and intently at the sleeping child. Sylvia could see him in profile, the clear-cut

52

features, the burnished hair brushed back from his square forehead. 'He is handsome,' she thought, 'extremely handsome.' Then as she watched she realised that he was swaying slightly. For one startled moment she thought he was ill and wondered what she could do, but with a sense of horror the true explanation came to her. The candle flickered in his unsteady hand, spilling its grease on the satin-covered eiderdown and the polished bedstead. Wild thoughts crept into Sylvia's mind. Then as slowly as he had come in, Sir Robert turned and went from the room, the door closing beind him, and she heard his footsteps die away down the passage.

Sylvia had lain shivering in the darkness. She had been inexplicably afraid of what she had seen; and then because of her utter exhaustion, both mental and physical, she had fallen asleep, too tired even to speculate further on the strangeness of this very strange place.

Now what had happened came back to her so vividly, so sharply etched that its verity could not be questioned, but before she had time to consider it fully, Lucy called her from the next room.

'Are you awake, Miss Wace? Please, can I get up?'

Sylvia hurried in to the child and while they were dressing Nannie knocked on the door. She was surprised to see that they were nearly ready, saying that she had not had them called as she hoped they would have their sleep out.

'I've ordered breakfast for you in my room,' she added.

Sylvia was relieved. She had been half afraid that breakfast with Lucy might be in the dining-room and that she would be forced to meet Sir Robert so early. She felt that she wanted time to prepare herself before she saw him again.

And yet when she did see him her fears and apprehensions seemed ridiculous. As she and Lucy were exploring the garden later in the morning he came riding towards them through the snow, two large dogs bounding by the side of his horse. Lucy waved to him happily. She was a friendly child untroubled by any form of shyness.

'What a lovely horse,' she exclaimed as soon as he was within earshot. 'Please can I have a pony soon? Mummy always promised me one.'

'We will see what can be done.' Sir Robert said, and then he raised his hat to Sylvia.

'Good morning, Miss Wace. I trust you and Lucy have slept well.'

'Very well, thank you,' Sylvia replied, feeling the blood rising in her cheeks and ashamed of herself for displaying any emotion. But Sir Robert was not looking at her; he was looking at Lucy.

'Would you like to come round to the stables and see my horses?' he asked.

Lucy clapped her hands in delight.

'Oh, please take me—now at once.'

'What about riding in front of me?' he suggested. 'Would you be afraid?'

Lucy shook her head.

Sir Robert spoke to Sylvia. 'Will you lift her up?'

Sylvia did as she was asked and he bent down to grip Lucy under her arms and swing her into the saddle in front of him.

'I will bring her back to the house when we have finished, Miss Wace,' he said as they rode off, and Sylvia felt herself dismissed.

She walked slowly back along the freshly swept paths towards the front of the house. In daylight Sheldon Hall had lost some of the fairy-like beauty with which it had captured her imagination the night before. Now close to it, she felt overpowered by its largeness, by the formal grandeur of the building with its big stone cupolas and terraces which stretched on each side of it down to formally laid-out gardens. There were no trees near the house for behind it, stretching away to the horizon, were the moors, rising higher and higher until the tops of them were silhouetted white and shining against the pale winter sky. There was not another house or habitation in sight and suddenly Sylvia felt the utter loneliness of it. Sheldon Hall was beautiful, but a place, she thought, that one could admire, but never love. Even as she decided this, she wondered how much this impression was due to the atmosphere she had found inside the house. It was only a ridiculous fancy, she knew, and yet the silence of the long corridors, the vastness of the great hall and the magnificence of every room she entered struck her with a kind of chill, as though she walked in a place of death rather than in the home of the living. 'It is because it is all so strange,' she told herself; the contrast with her previous surroundings was too sharp, too poignant.

She entered the house by the front door. The sunshine was left outside; despite the leaping flames from the huge logs burning in the open fireplace the hall seemed chill and

54

formal. The curtains were drawn back from the high windows, but the coats-of-arms embodied in the glass diffused the light in colourful patches which made strange shadows and patterns. Now that she was alone, Sylvia had time to look at the pictures ornamenting the walls. Nearly all were family portraits and in practically every one she saw an echo of Sir Robert's and Lucy's red heads. The Sheldons were a handsome lot, the men especially.

Sylvia was looking at a portrait labelled 'Sir Hugh Sheldon, 5th Baronet,' when a quiet voice beside her made her jump.

'Sir Robert's father, Miss.'

It was Bateson.

'Oh, you startled me,' Sylvia exclaimed, and meeting the man's eyes felt somehow as if interrogated her without words.

'I was just going upstairs,' she said weakly, and was annoyed with herself for explaining her actions to him.

'There is no hurry, Miss,' Bateson said suavely. 'Seeing your connection with her ladyship it's understandable that you should be interested in the family.'

She felt somehow that there was an impertinence beneath his words, and turning away with what dignity she could command she walked across the hall and up the stairs. Only when she had crossed the landing and was out of sight did she hurry, almost running down the passages until she reached the homely comfort of Nannie's room.

Nannie was sitting sewing in front of the fire as she entered.

'Have you enjoyed your walk?' she asked looking up. And then added before Sylvia could reply, 'Where's Miss Lucy?'

'We met Sir Robert,' Sylvia explained, 'and he took her to the stables to see the horses.'

Nannie put down her sewing. 'Well, I never did!' she exclaimed. 'But I'm glad, very glad.'

Her tones were heartfelt.

'She went with him quite happily,' Sylvia said. 'She has been brought up not to be shy.'

'Her ladyship had pretty manners,' Nannie said. 'One would expect them from her child, but I was afraid that Sir Robert . . .'

She bit off her words quickly as if she thought she was saying too much. Sylvia wondered if it would be indiscreet to confide to Nannie what had happened the night before,

55

and then a sense of loyalty to Sir Robert himself prevented her betraying him. If he wished to come and see his daughter, whose business was it but his own?

Nannie broke in on her thoughts.

'You're fond of Miss Lucy?'

Sylvia sat down in the chair opposite her.

'To tell the honest truth,' she replied, 'I have only known the child such a short time. I had never even seen her till the night before last. I didn't tell Sir Robert and Lady Clementina that, it seemed unnecessary.'

'But you'd like to stay with her?' Nannie asked.

'Very much,' Sylvia replied. 'I have nowhere else to go and I need a position badly.'

Nannie nodded.

'I thought that might be the case. Well, you've been frank with me, Miss Wace, and I'll be frank with you. I think it would be to Miss Lucy's advantage to have you here. I'm too old for a young child, who should have someone young and active like yourself. But it isn't my views that count, you must remember that, and there's other people in this house who might not see eye to eye with me.'

'You mean Lady Clementina?' Sylvia ventured.

'I'm mentioning no names,' Nannie replied. 'You must draw your own conclusions. But if you wish to stay here, you must "go canny," as the Scotch say. It's not going to be too easy.'

Sylvia was thankful for the warning when just before luncheon she was sent for by Lady Clementina. Lucy had been brought to her a few moments earlier by Bateson, the child pink-cheeked and glowing with excitement over what she had seen in the stables and the fun she had had with the horses.

'I rode one, I did really, Miss Wace,' she cried. 'And I'm to have a pony of my own, my very own, as soon as the snow has gone. Then I can go out every day.'

'That will be lovely,' Sylvia smiled.

She changed Lucy's shoes and stockings and dressed her in one of her pretty frilled muslin dresses ready for luncheon.

It was then that the message came from Lady Clementina and they went together to her bedroom. The room still seemed shadowed and sinister even with the curtains drawn back from the three high windows which looked on to an inner courtyard of the house, and despite the huge vases of hothouse flowers it had a faint smell of must and age as if it had been lived in too long.

In the daylight Lady Clementina looked even more extraordinary. Her skin was like parchment and the massive, glittering jewellery she wore only showed up the lines and wrinkles of old age.

'Come here! Come here!' she called imperiously as soon as Sylvia and Lucy came to the door. 'Why haven't you been to see me this morning?'

'I'm sorry,' Sylvia said in a quiet voice. 'I didn't know you expected Lucy.'

'Lucy must learn that her grandmother always expects her. You must always come and say good morning to me, child. Do you understand?

Lucy, round-eyed, but unafraid, stared at her.

'Are you my grandmother? I've never had a grand-mother before.'

'You haven't? Well, that's a good thing,' Lady Clemen-tina commented. 'Yes, I'm your grandmother. What do you think of this house?'

'I think it is lovely,' Lucy replied. 'And I'm going to have a pony, a pony of my very own.'

'Who said so?' Lady Clementina asked sharply.

'That . . .' Lucy turned to Sylvia at a loss for words.

Sylvia looked at the child and then realising this was the first time it had been said took the plunge.

'It was your father who promised you one, Lucy.'

'My father?'

Lucy looked puzzled for the moment and then accepted it as if it was nothing unusual to be presented with a whole flock of new relations in one day.

'Do I call him Daddy?' she asked.

'I think that would be very nice,' Sylvia said; and looked up to meet the keen eyes of Lady Clementina.

'So it is all settled?' the old lady remarked dryly, her words more of a question than a statement of fact.

'I believe so,' Sylvia replied, pretending not to under-stand that Lady Clementina spoke of wider issues than the gift of a pony.

'And now what about yourself, Miss Wace?'

Sylvia had a feeling that Lady Clementina had been waiting for this moment.

'About myself?' she queried.

'You have plans, I imagine, for the future.'

Sylvia took a deep breath.

'I hoped after what was said last night that I might stay here and look after Lucy.'

'That depends, of course,' Lady Clementina said. 'You have relations?'

'My mother is dead,' Sylvia replied, 'and it is essential that I should find employment.'

'So you think the rôle of governess at Sheldon Hall would suit you?'

The words were simple enough and yet Sylvia had the idea that Lady Clementina baited her.

'I should very much like to offer myself for the situation,' she answered gently.

'We must discuss various aspects of it,' Lady Clementina said. 'The salary would be one of them; but I am afraid, Miss Wace, that you will be too expensive for us. Judging by your clothes, you must be a young woman of means.'

Sylvia felt herself flush crimson. Somehow she knew instinctively but surely that Lady Clementina had been leading up to this. The black dress she wore, expensive and cut by a master hand, had not escaped the elder woman's eye. She had known its value and—Sylvia knew this now—had suspected a governess who was too well dressed.

'Perhaps I had better explain,' Sylvia said; and then turning to Lucy she said, 'Run back to Nannie, dear. You know the way, don't you?'

'Yes, I know the way,' Lucy said. 'Good-bye, Grandmother; I expect I shall see you later.'

'I expect you will,' Lady Clementina replied, and then as the door closed sharply behind Lucy she asked, 'Well, Miss Wace?'

Sylvia drew in her breath. 'She is enjoying this,' she thought. 'She is getting a sadistic satisfaction out of humiliating me and making me feel a fool.'

Unconsciously she raised her chin higher and her blue eyes were defiant as she faced Lady Clementina.

'You asked me about my dress,' she began. 'Perhaps I should explain. My mother died the same day as Lucy's mother. I had no time to get mourning before starting off on the journey I had promised to undertake to bring Lucy here to Sheldon Hall. I was given this dress at the last moment.'

'By my daughter-in-law?' Lady Clementina asked. 'It is very much in her taste.'

Sylvia longed to reply that it was no business of hers,

but instead, because she was inexperienced in dealing with older people, she told the truth.

'No, her nurse gave it to me. As you rightly suspected it belonged to your daughter-in-law.'

'I thought so.'

Lady Clementina lay back on her pillows.

'Well, Miss Wace, I am glad you have been honest with me. I was curious, you know, for young women anxious to take the post of governess do not usually wear clothes made by Worth.'

Sylvia said nothing. She felt as if she had fought a hard battle and been defeated.

'That will be all, Miss Wace, for the moment. We will discuss the other matters I mentioned—principally that of your remaining here—another time.'

'Thank you.'

Sylvia moved towards the door, conscious that she was being watched, that her every movement was criticised. When she was outside in the passage she was aware that her heart was beating and that her forehead was damp. She would have given anything at that moment to have left the house.

She went to her own room to fetch a handkerchief. The coat belonging to the dress was lying over the chair where she had left it when she got ready for lunch. Now she picked it up to put it in the wardrobe and as she opened the door was at once aware that her things had been moved. It was difficult to know why she was so certain of this except that she felt sure that the order in which she had hung them when she unpaacked was not quite the same. 'I'm imagining things,' Sylvia thought, but as she caught sight of the mauve evening dress she knew she had not been mistaken. The inner petticoat with its label of the Court dressmaker sewn to it was hanging inside out. Someone had handled it, had perhaps even taken the dress along the passage to show Lady Clementina.

It was all so obvious, Lady Clementina's questions and the way she had been forced into admitting that the clothes were not her own. Yet why should anyone spy on her? And why should Lady Clementina be interested? Sylvia suddenly had the idea that Lady Clementina was like a spider and that everything and everybody who came into this house was caught in her web. Mrs. Cuningham had warned her—and Nannie.

Sylvia shut the wardrobe door. She was angry and yet
59

her anger was tempered by fear. This was something she did not understand, something too subtle, too unexpected and queer for her comprehension. What did it all mean? And if she was dismissed, what was the alternative?

With a sinking in her heart, Sylvia thought of Uncle Octavius and the vicarage at Hastings. What did anything matter beside her fear of that? Was she not more afraid of her life there than of Lady Clementina and Sir Robert or anything that this house might hold?

She knew the answer. With a little sound that was half a sob and half a laugh she opened the door and ran in search of Lucy.

6

'Nannie, I am afraid"

Nannie put down her sewing and looked at Sylvia who was sitting on the other side of the fireplace.

'Of Lady Clementina?' she questioned.

Sylvia nodded. 'She is not going to keep me here. She means me to go, I know that, although so far she has said nothing definite.'

Nannie sighed. 'I expected it.'

'Has she said anything to you?' Sylvia asked.

'Well, not in so many words, but that's often her ladyship's way. Sometimes long after she's made up her own mind she'll play cat and mouse, as it were, with anyone she has decided to dismiss.'

'But why, Nannie? Why does she dislike me? What have I done?'

Nannie pursed her lips and Sylvia knew she was wondering just how much to say or how little, for she had learnt that above all things Nannie was loyal to the house she served and to those who employed her. There was so much information that she might have imparted to a newcomer these last few days, but she had remained silent, trying, Sylvia knew, always to put the best complexion on everything, to make things seem pleasant and agreeable

60

for Lucy's sake, if not for her own. And yet there was so much that could not be hidden.

'It's like this,' Nannie said at length, choosing her words with care. 'Her ladyship has ruled this house for nearly half a century. She isn't fond of women. I have often heard her say that she would like to be waited on only by men. Besides which, you're young and you're pretty.'

Nannie smiled at the end of her sentence and Sylvia tried to be pleased by the compliment.

'Thank you, Nannie. At the same time that is not much consolation if it drives me from where I want to stay, if it prevents me from earning my living.'

'It's hard and unfair,' Nannie agreed; 'but I've known many a good girl suffer because of her looks. Unless she's rich, looks in a woman are more of a curse than a blessing, and that's the truth.'

Sylvia bowed her head in despair, fighting against the tears which gathered in her eyes. It all seemed cruel and unreasonable. If it had not been for Lady Clementina, she told herself, she could have been happy here. It was true that she was frightened of Sir Robert. To take Lucy down to luncheon in the dining-room when he was present was almost agonising for her. She was afraid of him, afraid of his cool, impersonal arrogance; of the way he seemed hardly to be aware of her presence while having the strange effect upon her that she was tinglingly conscious of him the moment he entered a room. She told herself that she would get used to this, that it was just the unusualness of meeting a man casually and regularly after years of being shut up alone with her mother. It was shyness, nothing more, and she believed that in time she could force herself into making conversation with Sir Robert, into behaving naturally when he was present.

But Lady Clementina was her enemy, she was sure of that, sure of it from the moment when with subtle cruelty she had been forced to confess that the clothes she wore were not her own. And since then, as Nannie had put it very graphically, Lady Clementina had played with her as a cat might play with a mouse. She said nothing definite, either about her staying or going, and yet she loosed little barbed shafts at Sylvia every now and then which kept her in a state of quivering anxiety and fear.

Only this morning, for instance, when Lucy was visiting her grandmother, Lady Clementina had said to the child:

'When the snow goes, Lucy, you must ask Bateson to

take you up on the roof and show you the view. You can see for miles and miles over the countryside.'

'I would like that,' Lucy exclaimed. 'And can Miss Wace come, too?'

Lady Clementina had looked at Sylvia with an enigmatical expression in her eyes.

'Perhaps Miss Wace would not be interested—even provided that she were here.'

That was all, but for Sylvia it was enough. She knew only too well what Lady Clementina was trying to convey to her.

'I don't want to go, Nannie,' she said now agonisingly.

'I'm sure you don't,' Nannie said. 'But when her ladyship's made up her mind there's no gainsaying her. She's always been the same. I remember when I first came here. She was young, then, young and very beautiful though you wouldn't think it; but that headstrong and with a will of her own that no one dared to cross.'

'Not even her husband?' Sylvia inquired, thinking of the handsome face of the portrait at which she had looked in the hall.

'Sir Hugh idolised her in those days,' Nannie said. 'It was only afterwards . . .' She paused and picked up her sewing quickly as if she had said too much.

'After what?' Sylvia inquired curiously.

'I'm talking too much,' Nannie said. 'What's past should remain past and is best forgotten.'

'I always have a feeling that there is something mysterious about Lady Clem . . .' Sylvia started but ceased to speak as the door opened and Bateson came into the room.

'Sir Robert wishes to see you in the study, Miss.'

Sylvia gave an exclamation and got to her feet.

'I wonder what he wants,' she said half to herself, and noted a kind of triumphant look on Bateson's face.

'It is something unpleasant,' she thought, 'and Bateson is pleased.'

She had known in the last few days that as surely as Lady Clementina disliked her, Bateson did, too. It was nothing that he said, nothing in his manner, which was outwardly and conventionally correct; but she felt as if he watched her; why, she could not fathom. Always if she were in any other part of the house except the rooms allotted to Lucy, she would find Bateson lurking somewhere, speaking to her in that soft insinuating way, trying for some reason she could not understand to make her feel a stranger, unwanted and alien.

She smoothed the front of her dress and walked past Bateson without looking at him. She preceded him along the corridors and down the big oak staircase, conscious all the time of the man behind her, of his quiet, almost shuffling footsteps.

They reached the library door and Sylvia waited for Bateson to open it. He paused for a moment, before with a faint smile on his lips he announced her.

'Miss Wace, Sir Robert.'

Sylvia walked in. She saw Sir Robert start to rise from the big, high-backed chair in which he was sitting, and then she saw who was with him and her heart stood still. She had been right in suspecting something unpleasant, and nothing at that moment could have been more unpleasant than the sight of Uncle Octavius in his dark, clerical garments, waiting for her with a forbidding frown on his forehead, his fat, white fingers interlaced across his portly stomach.

'Uncle Octavius!'

Sylvia faltered the words which were hardly above a whisper.

'You seem surprised to see me, my dear niece.'

'Yes, I am. I didn't expect you to come as far as this.'

'Nowhere is too far in the course of duty. When our conscience dictates an action, we must obey. I must admit that my journey has been long and arduous, but I am prepared to make such a sacrifice of self in your interssts.'

'In my interests?' Sylvia echoed.

'Certainly. I was surprised, nay horrified, when I arrived to conduct the burial of your dear mother to find that without a thought of filial affection, without any respect for my feelings, you had left the neighbourhood that very morning.'

Sylvia took a deep breath.

'Uncle Octavius,' she protested, 'I thought you would understand.'

'Understand what? That you put the needs of a stranger before that of your own family? That you considered your own inclinations rather than obey even the commonest rules of decency and respect? However, we need not argue the point just now. I have explained the circumstances to

Sir Robert. I have a carriage waiting at the door and if you will pack your things there is no reason to waste further time.'

'Pack my things?' Sylvia ejaculated. 'Then you want . . .'

'Need I explain myself further?' her uncle asked testily. 'I am taking you home with me to Hastings. Your aunt out of the kindness of her heart has agreed to let you live with us, to be, as it were, one of our own family. There are, of course, certain duties that you will perform, but otherwise you will be treated as if you were our own child. Need I say more?'

He glanced towards Sir Robert as if for approval.

'But, Uncle Octavius, I would rather earn my own living. It is kind of you, I know, but I would like to be independent.'

'Independent!' The word was ejaculated in tones of horror as if such an expression were indecent. 'I don't think you know what you are saying. Go at once, Miss, and pack your boxes. I have no time to waste bantering words of this sort.'

It seemed to Sylvia as if he passed sentence of death upon her. She gave him one last despairing look and turned towards the door, but at that moment there was an interruption from an unexpected source.

'One minute, Miss Wace.'

It was Sir Robert speaking from the fire-place where he had stood during the whole interview.

Sylvia stopped and raised her eyes to him. 'How good-looking he is,' she thought. He was indeed very different in his well-bred elegance from the stocky, stout figure of her uncle who despite his grey hair could never have managed to look distinguished. The contrast between the two men as they stood side by side was almost cruel.

'Am I to understand, Miss Wace,' Sir Robert asked slowly, 'that you do not wish to accompany your uncle to his home?'

'I would so much rather stay here with Lucy,' Sylvia answered, and even as she spoke the words they sounded feeble and ineffective in her own ears.

'And Lucy, I think, would like you to stay,' Sir Robert said. 'In that case, sir, surely there can be no possible objection to your niece remaining here?'

'Bu I have already explained to you,' Uncle Octavius replied, 'that I consider my niece's behaviour most reprehensible, most reprehensible indeed. Her attitude

64

towards her mother can only be described as callous in the extreme. To leave my sister's body alone in an empty house while she came gallivanting north on a journey . . .'

'. . . of mercy,' Sir Robert interrupted. 'As I see it, sir, your niece had to make the choice between serving the living or the dead. She chose the living—a not unreasonable selection if one thinks of it in that light. Nevertheless the fact remains that she came here in charge of my daughter and she offered to remain on as companion and governess to the child. Believing her to be a free agent, I took Miss Wace into my employment. Unless there is any particular deterrent that concerns her moral character or she herself wishes to terminate the agreement, I see no reason why my plans should be disarranged.'

Sir Robert spoke with an authority which could not be gainsaid. Seeing the dismay and the surprise in her uncle's face, Sylvia felt excitement leap within her. Here was a reprieve at the last moment and from a source from which she had least expected it. It was strange to see her uncle, who was always so authoritative, looking nonplussed and at a loss for words.

Uncle Octavius paused before he spoke.

'Of course, I see your point of view, Sir Robert,' he said at length. 'At the same time, as her legal guardian I consider my niece is too young to earn her own living.'

'How old are you, Miss Wace?'

Sir Robert addressed her abruptly.

'I was twenty-one last October,' Sylvia replied.

It was as if the ground had been cut from beneath Uncle Octavius's feet. Without elaborating the point, Sir Robert had proved that she was her own mistress, free to take a position should she wish without the permission of her guardian. The expression in Sylvia's eyes was eloquent as she looked at Sir Robert, and then she faced her uncle again. He was angry, she could see that, so angry that now he was gripping his fingers together, the knuckles showing white; and yet he could find nothing to say.

Sylvia guessed that he had followed her hot-foot to Sheldon Hall not only because he had discovered a position in his household in which she could be useful, but also because he had suspected from the first the tale Mrs. Bootle had told him. It would be like Uncle Octavius to be suspicious of any story that was straightforward or honest. He had always suspected her, and had watched, Sylvia knew, for some lapse in her behaviour, for some evidence of heredity peeping out, for some laxity which would prove only too clearly that her morality was only surface deep.

'How disappointed he must have been,' she thought to herself, 'when he saw Sheldon Hall, when he saw Sir Robert.' And she could have laughed aloud at the discomfiture that he was now experiencing.

At last Uncle Octavius spoke.

'If you are satisfied with my niece, Sir Robert,' he said, 'and she wishes to remain in your employment, there is, of course, nothing I can say.'

He spoke stiffly, the expression in his eyes when he looked at Sylvia one of bitter anger. They were like an animal's baulked of its prey, she thought suddenly and shuddered.

'As for you, Sylvia, I can only hope that you will conduct yourself in a fitting manner. I cannot say that your present attitude or your behaviour gives me reason for confidence. I shall pray for you. Good-bye, Sir Robert.'

He bowed and Sir Robert, bending forward touched the bell beside the fire-place. Almost immediately as if, Sylvia suspected, he had been listening, Bateson opened the door. Without another word or a glance, Uncle Octavius went out into the hall. Bateson shut the door behind him and Sylvia was alone with Sir Robert.

'Thank you. Oh, how can I thank you for saving me?' Sylvia asked.

There was a faint smile on Sir Robert's lips. For the first time since she had known him he looked human, and Sylvia had the idea that he saw her as if for the first time.

'I assure you, Miss Wace, it was a pleasure to rescue you from such a dragon. I am not surprised that you shrank from a life at the vicarage.'

'It would have been horrible beyond words,' Sylvia said. 'My uncle is always frightening.'

'Perhaps you are easily frightened?' Sir Robert suggested.

Sylvia knew there was a meaning in his words.

'I am afraid I am very inexperienced,' she said. 'You see, I have not met many people.'

He looked at her for a moment as if he would say more and then abruptly he walked towards his desk.

'While you are here, Miss Wace, shall we discuss the matter of your salary? Would a hundred a year be sufficient?'

Sylvia gasped a little. 'I don't think I am worth that, Sir

Robert. You see, I have had no experience. I can teach Lucy all I know, but that is not very much.'

'Well, we might put the rest on account for keeping her happy,' Sir Robert suggested.

He sat down at the desk and took a piece of crested paper from the drawer.

'That is settled then,' he said. 'and if you will tell me your Christian names the whole matter will be dealt with by my agent.'

'Sylvia Mary.'

'Both pretty names,' Sir Robert remarked as he wrote them down. He put down his pen and rose to his feet. 'Now, Miss Wace, may I give you one word of advice?'

'But of course.'

'My mother is getting old. Sometimes she is a little difficult. Will you try and make allowances for her? We all have to do that. She has one great absorbing love in her life—a love of this house. It means everything to her. If you can understand that you can understand a great deal about her.'

Sir Robert had spoken seriously, yet it seemed to Sylvia that there was a strange expression in his eyes—almost one of pain. She had little time to be sure of anything except the sudden joy in knowing that he was confiding in her, that he was trusting her; and now that he had chosen to champion her, she knew that nothing, not even Lady Clementina should force her to leave Sheldon Hall.

'I will do anything for you, Sir Robert,' she said, and added quickly—'and Lucy.'

'Thank you, Miss Wace. That will be all for now.'

She felt as if he had suddenly withdrawn into himself, had ceased to be human and had donned again that cold, reticent mask which he had raised a little for the first time.

She was dismissed, she knew that, and yet she paused a moment, watching him walk across the book-lined room towards the windows and stand with his back to her looking out over the snow-covered garden. She hesitated, why she was not sure, and then softly she opened the door and went out.

She had one idea and that was to tell Nannie at once what had happened, but even as she hurried across the hall towards the stairs, Bateson appeared beside her.

'Her ladyship wants you, Miss.'

'Now, this moment?' There was something like dismay in Sylvia's voice.

'Immediately, Miss.'

She looked at him and knew without words or further confirmation that Bateson had been to Lady Clementina and told her about Uncle Octavius. 'So he is the spy,' she thought. 'That is how Lady Clementina knows everything that goes on in the house. It is Bateson who tells her!'

She mounted the stairs quickly, pausing only for a moment before she knocked, conscious that Sir Robert's last words had the power to alleviate just a little of her fear of his mother.

'Come in.'

She entered the room. Lady Clementina had a pile of papers on the bed in front of her. She pushed them aside as Sylvia came in, then watched her as she walked across the room. It was an ordeal, Sylvia realised some time ago, for anybody to walk the whole distance from the door to Lady Clementina's bed with the old lady's eyes watching and criticising silently, though obviously, every moment.

'Why haven't you gone with your uncle?' Lady Clementina asked, as soon as Sylvia stopped at a respectful distance from her.

'Sir Robert was kind enough to say that he wished me to stay to look after Lucy,' Sylvia replied.

'Um.' Lady Clementina made one of her strongly expressive sounds. Sylvia was well aware that this was not news, she knew it already.

'And you wish to stay? Why do you wish to stay here?'

The words were intimidating, but for the first time Sylvia was not intimidated.

'Wouldn't anyone in my position want to stay in such a place?' she queried.

'You are no fool,' Lady Clementina sniffed. 'You have seen the place by this time. It is miles from a town and there are no amusements. There are not even any young men about—unless you count my son.'

The last words were spoken with intention. Sylvia raised her chin a little higher.

'I am used to doing without amusements and without men,' she said. 'I am content to be here for as long as I can be of use to Lucy.'

Lady Clementina lay back against her pillows.

'You have got a certain amount of spirit,' she said, 'and in a way I suppose that is a good thing. If only you were not so . . .' She stopped speaking.

Sylvia knew what she was going to say. Hadn't she heard

the same words only a short while ago from Nannie? She made an effort to capture the elder woman's confidence.

'I assure you, Lady Clementina, that I am interested not in myself but in Lucy. She is a sweet child and I will do all I can to make her happy. I want nothing else, nothing.'

'Then you are very different from other women of your age,' Lady Clementina said. 'I am an old woman, Miss Wace, and I have seen a good deal of life, and I have learnt that if you put a young man and a young woman together the result is always very much the same.' She made a sudden gesture of impotence and then she bent forward. 'Very well, then. You can stay here. But remember what I am telling you now. My son is not for you.'

Instinctively Sylvia stepped backwards.

'Lady Clementina, I never thought . . .'

'If you have not thought of it already—and I am not sure I believe it—you will. But remember, I have warned you. My son has married one fool and as long as I am alive he will not marry another. This house is more important than personalities, greater than individuals. It holds the history of our family, and the woman who bears an heir to the Sheldon name has to be worthy of it.'

Lady Clementina almost snarled the last words at Sylvia. There was a frightening, fanatical look upon her face and her eyes gleamed from the shadows of the bed. Sylvia had the feeling that at that moment she was not quite sane. She was certainly overpowering. One could feel that every sinew of her body, every ounce of dynamic power within her was concentrated on this thing for which she lived. She stared at Sylvia for a long moment and then slowly, as if the energy she had conjured up died within her, she relaxed.

'You can go.'

She spoke harshly and Sylvia, feeling curiously weak, went gratefully from the room. Outside in the passage she took a deep breath. She felt as if her strength had been drained away from her, but she was less afraid than she had been. Now she understood why Lady Clementina had wanted to get rid of her.

She turned not towards Nannie's room, but towards Lucy's. The child was lying down, in her arms a doll to which she was singing softly. Sylvia walked across the intervening space and knelt beside the bed. She put her arms around Lucy and hugged her close.

'Everything is all right, darling,' she said. 'I am going to stay with you.'

'But of course, you are.' Lucy said, not understanding, 'And now can I get up? I have rested for hours and hours, haven't I?'

'Not quite as long as that,' Sylvia said smiling, 'but you can get up.'

'Are we going down to luncheon with Daddy today?' Lucy asked.

Sylvia nodded. 'I expect so.'

She went across the room to get Lucy's dress from the wardrobe and as she did so she caught sight of herself in the mirror. There was a smile on her lips, her eyes were shining. She stared at her reflection and knew the truth. She was pretty, extremely pretty. 'And I am glad, so very, very glad,' she thought.

7

Lady Clementina, exhausted by her interview with Miss Wace, lay back and shut her eyes. After a moment or two she put up her hand and pulled the embroidered bell-pull hanging within the folds of her bedside curtains. Had she said too much, she wondered, or perhaps too little? If she had asserted herself earlier this might never have occurred.

'You rang, my lady?'

Her maid answered the bell. Purvis was a thin, sharp-nosed woman of middle age. She had a refined, mincing manner which at times infuriated Lady Clementina. But she retained her, partly because Purvis for all her affected ways was a good maid, and partly because she believed that at heart Purvis was as fond of her as she was capable of being fond of anyone except herself.

'Tell Bateson to bring me up half a bottle of champagne,' she said. 'I am tired.'

Purvis drew near and straightened an imaginary wrinkle in the bedspread.

'Very good, my lady,' she said primly. 'But you'd be better without it.'

70

Lady Clementina looked at her with impatience. It always irritated her when Purvis took upon herself to consider her health and make suggestions which curiously enough were always in opposition to her own wishes.

'Tell Bateson I want the champagne at once,' Lady Clementina said sharply.

'Very good, my lady.'

Purvis moved away with the martyred expression of one who has done her best and can do no more.

As the door closed behind her, Lady Clementina's thoughts went back to Sylvia Wace. 'I ought to have sent the girl packing the first night she came here,' she thought. She was too pretty, and pretty people, as Lady Clementina well knew, usually meant trouble. It was like Alice to make mischief in the house, to send someone who would be, if nothing more, at least at variance with her own rule at Sheldon Hall. But Lady Clementina guessed it was unlikely to have been intentional on Alice's part—she had not the brains or the subtlety to think out anything of that sort; it must have been just chance. Alice was too simple, too wrapped up in herself to conceive such an ingenious way of annoying her mother-in-law.

All the same, Alice had proved a surprise in that she had produced Lucy. Lady Clementina remembered her rage when Robert had brought home his bride. She had taken one look at the elegant figure and empty face of her new daughter-in-law and had known that Robert had made a mistake.

She blamed herself for letting him stay in London for so long. With his looks and money he was bound to be run after by every ambitious mother. But who could have foreseen that what she imagined was a safe enough love affair with a married woman should have ended so abruptly and launched him straight into the arms of Alice? Yes, she had caught him on the rebound; caught him with her stupid, frivolous little airs and graces, her kittenish playfulness and her foolish conversation. And who could have foreseen that or have expected Alice and her mother would be clever enough to insist on a secret speedy marriage because of family mourning.

Lady Clementina could remember her own horror all too vividly as she opened the letter which told her the news of the marriage and that they would be returning to Sheldon Hall that same evening. At first she had been almost numbed by the shock and then she had hoped against hope that Robert would have chosen wisely and have selected a wife worthy of the position that awaited her and of all his mother hoped for on his behalf.

How much she loved Robert! How much she had done for him, always! Too much, maybe, by some standards, but never, never by her own.

And yet, much as she loved this handsome son of hers, she loved Sheldon Hall more. There was the real love of her life.

There was a knock on her door. It was Bateson bringing her champagne. She watched him, precise and pompous, fill a delicate high-stemmed glass with a little of the golden liquid. Lady Clementina took the glass from the salver.

'Thank you, Bateson.'

He put the bottle within reach of her hand. 'Anything else, my lady?'

'No, thank you, Bateson. Where is Sir Robert?'

'He has gone round to the stable, my lady. He left a note for Mr. Jameson. I think it informed him of the amount to be paid to Miss Wace in salary.'

'Um. He is taking a great deal of trouble over this.'

'An unusual amount, my lady.'

The eyes of mistress and servant met in a look of perfect understanding. Bateson bowed respectfully and went towards the door.

Lady Clementina sipped her champagne. A good man, Bateson! What she would do without him she did not know. He kept her informed of everything that went on in the house. She had few secrets from him and was sure that he had none from her. It was a pity he had not been with Robert when he went to London. If he had been, there would have been no marriage—at any rate not without her being aware of it first. But Bateson had been here with her at Sheldon Hall. She had needed him at that particular time. Indeed it was difficult to imagine now what she would have done without him; but of that she did not want to think; that was something best hidden, a secret between herself and Bateson, one which she thrust deep down in her conscience and which must for ever and ever be unspoken, if not forgotten.

No, it was of Robert that she must think, Robert first and always. Robert linked with Sheldon Hall, Robert and the heir that he had not yet produced. On her first sight of Alice, Lady Clementina had felt certain that she would not produce the grandson she wanted for the house—the boy

72

who must carry on the line which had been unbroken since the twelfth century. She could see Alice now standing there in the hall, elegant and good-looking in her own insipid way, laughing happily at something Robert had just said to her. She had looked picturesque enough, but where was the stamina, the strength that she required—nay, demanded in her daughter-in-law? It was not there; she had known it, been certain of it. Alice looked delicate; her gaiety was the feverish energy of someone who could drive herself as long as she was amused and interested, but who would flop weakly when faced with anything difficult or boring. How well Lady Clementina knew the type! She who had so much wiry strength in her small body that she could do more than the average man and be less exhausted. Alice was not the daughter-in-law she had prayed for and she felt both dismay and despair at what Robert had done without her approval or advice.

Then had come those long four years when Alice produced no son and she either giggled or sulked her way through the days spent at Sheldon Hall, longing only for London and the gaieties she had once known and enjoyed and which she now missed bitterly and regretfully. The country bored her; she admitted as much as soon as the first ecstasy of the honeymoon was over. She hated the rough, bracing air which blew over the moors and which to Lady Clementina was more stimulating than any champagne. She found the details of the great house with its horde of servants and its feudal traditions troublesome and a nuisance. Perhaps Lady Clementina in time might have forgiven her much else, but that she should not love Sheldon Hall was the final and unforgivable crime. She despised Alice at first because she knew her for the weakling she was; but when she realised that she had no feeling for Sheldon Hall she began actively to hate her.

She remembered her own feelings when first she saw the house which had afterwards become the absorbing love of her life. She was a child of twelve and she had driven over with her father and mother for a visit. Her mother had been a Sheldon before she married the Earl of Glendale and Clementina had looked forward to meeting her young cousin, Hugh Sheldon. She was too young to put into words what Sheldon Hall meant to her at that first glance—the great pile of stones with its lovely lines, its terraces encircling it like a necklace, and the barren, treeless beauty of the moors in the background.

73

Hugh had been a schoolboy at the time, four years older than herself. She had looked at him with awe instead of the friendly affection she had anticipated, because she realised that he was the future master of the house. He was a handsome boy with good manners, and if he was bored with a girl cousin he did not show it too obviously. But from the first moment of meeting he was not an individual to Clementina, he was a part of Sheldon Hall and, something already hard and calculating within her whispered, a very important part.

She had been a strange child, spoilt and self-willed, but already showing promise of the great beauty that was to be hers in later life. She had gone home that night and dreamt not of her cousin Hugh, smiling at her as they patted the horses or sailed their boats on the lake, but of the house itself with its long galleries and elaborate plaster ceilings, its stained-glass heraldic windows, polished floors and wealth of tapestry, its great rooms, some panelled or lined from floor to ceiling with books, some delicately coloured in primrose and wedgwood blue, some hung with brocade or delicate, laborious needlework. Sheldon Park became for her a fairyland into which she could escape in her dreams; and when she was worried or unhappy, angry or depressed, she would close her eyes and imagine herself under the glittering lustre of the chandeliers in the ball-room, standing at the head of the grand staircase looking down into the hall below, or hidden in some big curtained bed shut in with the ghosts of the past—ghosts which lingered because of the black secrecy of love of or violence and death. Sheldon Hall! She grew up with it hidden in her heart.

She had been an amazing success when she made her debut at the Court of St. James. She had been courted and fêted and had attracted more attention than any other débutante of her season. It had been a year of gaiety and achievement. Members of the noblest families in the land had asked her hand in marriage and she had flirted coquettishly with them while waiting for something, she knew not what.

And then one day as she stood beside her mother in the crowded ball-room of Devonshire House she had seen a red head forging its way steadily towards her.

Hugh Sheldon! She had recognised him at once. He had altered very little from the schoolboy she remembered, only he had grown taller and better looking.

It was then she had known what she wanted. She had

74

known it clearly and unmistakably and had applied herself with her usual strength of will to getting it. It had not been hard, for Hugh had fallen in love with her and he fought as hard as she did against relations who frowned forbiddingly on a marriage between cousins.

Clementina had always had her own way. Her parents had spoilt her and it was unlikely that they would make a stand now to deny her the one thing on which she had set her heart. They talked vaguely of waiting, of giving herself time to consider, but she side-stepped such suggestions.

It was only as she went up the aisle of St. George's, Hanover Square, on her father's arm and saw Hugh waiting for her at the chancel steps that she admitted honestly to herself that she was marrying not Sir Hugh Sheldon, but Sheldon Hall.

From the moment when she took her place there as mistress she felt a savage, fierce emotion rise within her which resembled nothing so much as a primitive animal's love for its young. It was hers, she told herself, hers! This house of which she had dreamed for so long and which in realisation was even more wonderful and more splendid than her dreams. She almost loved Hugh in those first few years of marriage because he had given her what she wanted; at least she submitted to the ardency and the insatiable hunger of his lovemaking with a good grace because within her heart she was grateful to him.

Then she set herself the task of making the house perfect. Hugh was a rich man, very rich. And there were experts who were only too willing to advise her on what she should do to clear away the rubbish amassed by each succeeding generation and use to its best advantage that which was most valuable. Luckily she was well advised and under her guidance Sheldon Hall was polished and improved until it shone like a jewel, flawlessly perfect.

It was then that Nature reasserted itself. After several years of what to the world appeared complete and absolute domesticity, Clementina Sheldon knew that her task was finished. And because she had kept away from life for so long, she went back to it with renewed ardour. It was amusing now to remember how startled everyone had been. Beautiful Lady Clementina Sheldon had been the talk of the season. As her father's daughter she had, of course, the entrée into the best society, a society which clustered round the Court and kept strictly to the standards expected and imposed by its Royal mistress.

It took the newly awakened Lady Clementina only a few months to find how dull this society was, how limited in its interests. She looked about her and with an apparently complaisant husband to protect her she began to enjoy herself.

What wagging of tongues, what chatter of shrill voices arose! It was not long before tales of her doings echoed round the Court and reached the ears of the Queen. Lady Clementina was warned, at first gently and then more severely. Three times she was saved from final disgrace by the intervention of her relations and her father's friends at Court.

And then at last because she was too wilful, too rebellious to heed such warnings the blow had fallen. 'That wicked Lady Clementina' was banned from all Court functions.

At first Lady Clementina had laughed. What did it matter to her, she who had half the men in London at her feet, whose beauty drew them to her side and whose wit kept them spellbound? But she was to learn that a woman, however fabulous, cannot live with the friendship of men alone. The great hostesses followed the Court lead; the few women friends who remained to her visited her only secretly and with abject fear of being seen. The men began to change, too. They remained friends and lovers, but there was a subtle alteration in their attentions—they became at once too familiar and too demanding.

A weaker character might have capitulated, have sought to reinstate herself or even have clung to the faded glory as it hung in tatters around her. Clementina, whatever her faults, had never been weak. With one swift blow she severed her connection with the life she had known and retired to the country. She informed the world that she was going to devote herself to her husband and to her home.

Hugh was not certain whether he was glad or sorry. He was a stupid man for all his good looks, and while he had chafed and raged at times at Clementina's behaviour he half admired her because she had more grit and determination than he had ever had. At first he was sulky at having to live nearly the whole of the year at Sheldon Hall and having the decision made for him as if he were too immature to make it for himself.

There was, however, no question of their being lonely or idle. Clementina filled the house with friends. It was one thing to be seen openly consorting with the notorious Lady

Clementina in London, where people were only too willing to report such an action to the Queen, and quite another to travel north to stay at Sheldon Hall; to be amused and captivated by one's hostess and know that what occurred was within an intimate circle and that the knowledge was unlikely to spread further.

In the countryside, too, there were people who were not so squeamish and who cared little or nothing for the Royal approval they had never sought. The shooting was good at Sheldon Hall and in the summer there were other sports to be enjoyed, besides the knowledge that the food was superlatively excellent and that the hospitality one was accorded within its walls was quite without its equal anywhere in the land.

From being an undutiful subject in London, Lady Clementina became a queen at Sheldon Hall. While her parties, her extravagances and her behaviour kept the countryside agog and gave everyone something to talk about, she personally became more and more obsessed with her home, with the house which had become a background for herself and her activities. She had always been possessed by a kind of superstrength. While other women of her generation swooned at the thought of walking a mile or so, she could ride or walk all day over the moors, could dance all night and at the same time manage with the shrewdness and perspicacity of a man the great household and its finances.

Hugh gave up attempting to run his own estate or to interfere with her arrangements. He became querulous and indeed jealous of a wife who relegated him too much to the background. But he could do nothing, she was too strong for him, as she had been too strong all her life for those who crossed her path. When he died, the Fifth Baronet was an embittered, querulous man who had raged at his own impotence and been powerless to enforce any authority over his wife or his household.

It was almost a relief to Clementina to be alone. She had married Sheldon Hall and so was content to have it to herself. All her life she had intrigued for what she wanted, sometimes openly, sometimes subtly; but always she had known she was to succeed because of the will that was within her.

Sheldon Hall would be inherited by her son; she had made that inheritance a splendid one. She had not reckoned on Robert's taking the bit between his teeth and

77

marrying where he would. She had known when she had seen Alice that she was no good. She set out to get rid of her and had succeeded so cleverly that only Robert knew that she was at the bottom of it.

Robert was not a jealous husband and soon after his marriage he was worried and perturbed, and Lady Clementina was well aware that a man with something on his mind is not a good husband. She watched Alice getting more bored, saw her love for Robert dwindle and fade because it was unfed by flattery and unceasing protestations of affection. She was a shallow girl; yet if she had been left to live an ordinary and uneventful life she would doubtless have settled down and been a good wife.

But she had no hope against the machinations and schemes of her mother-in-law. When Alice was bored to the point of distraction, Lady Clementina produced a series of young men. Many of them lived locally, among them young Bertram Cuningham who had been brought up to believe that anything which belonged to Sheldon Hall was attractive, glamorous and inevitably exciting. It was not long before he was in love with Alice.

Lady Clementina saw it happening and knew that here was the weapon she most needed ready within her hand. She overwhelmed young Cuningham with invitations. 'Such a nice boy,' she told her son, 'and we must be kind to him for his parents' sake.' Robert was made to ask him to shoot and dine, to go on picnics in the summer, to play tennis as a partner for Alice, who looked ravishingly pretty in her full white skirts and neat belted waist.

Lady Clementina knew the first time that Bertram Cuningham kissed Alice. What she did not see with her own eyes was usually reported to her through Bateson who seemed to be everywhere, ready to overhear everything. Casually and as if apropos of nothing at all she talked to her daughter-in-law.

'You are young,' she said. 'You must enjoy your life while you can.'

'Is that a wise philosophy?' Alice asked.

Lady Clementina shrugged her shoulders. 'The only things I regret in my long life,' she said, 'are the times I said "no". There are very few compensations in old age. Make the most of your beauty, my child.'

She watched Alice glance at herself in the long mirrors and knew the thoughts that were passing through her empty head: Was she getting old? Was youth passing her by? And Robert! What did he feel about it? It was months since he had made love to her. He seemed taciturn and difficult, he had been like this ever since they were married.

Alone with her son, Lady Clementina had another story to tell.

'Give Alice time and I suppose she will settle down,' she said. 'It is an heir that we need, an heir for Sheldon Hall. The line has been unbroken for so long. The girl does not seem strong and perhaps we are wise to give her her head and let her enjoy herself unhampered by the cares of married life. But it must not be left too long or too late, your sons are waiting to be born.'

Robert was by no means as stupid as his father. He knew his mother, and even while he had an unwilling admiration for her because of her capabilities and her strength of character, he understood her better than anyone else. When Alice had run away and her piteous childish note was found conventionally pinned to the pillow on an unslept-in bed, he had confronted Lady Clementina.

'This is your doing! Are you satisfied?'

She had not prevaricated. She faced him without fear, her eyes glinting.

'You had better start divorce proceedings immediately.'

'What then?'

'Then you can set about finding yourself a wife worthy to bear your name.'

'And if I don't?'

Lady Clementina had laughed at him. 'You will. You are a young man and an extremely handsome one. There will be plenty of women who will want you to marry them; you will find them.'

But he had not. Instead of divorcing Alice as she had wished, Robert had remained single, obstinately and despite every argument and the unceasing plea of his mother. He was young, there was still time, she knew; and yet always the fear persisted at the back of her mind that the line would die out and the house pass into alien hands. She believed that sooner or later she would wear her son down and force him into obeying her; but the word 'marriage' loomed like a barrier between them. They would seldom be alone together without her referring to it, and now she believed it gave him pleasure to laugh at her, to mock her ambitions for him.

She was groiwng old, her body had not the fabled power of her youth and middle-age, yet her will was indomitable. The doctors had told her that her heart was weak. The strenuous life she had always led had begun to take its toll. It was then that Lady Clementina made another of her amazing decisions. She had ever intention of living and seeing Robert settled, of knowing that the succession was secure; therefore she would take no risks. Sheldon Hall, the house she had always loved, needed her still, and until that need no longer existed she must concern herself with serving the great love that had always possessed her.

She retired to her bed. She lay there conserving her strength, making her room the pivot round which everything in the house revolved. She was just as much a power, just as dominating as she had been when she could move about. She was feared and respected by the whole household. Bateson was not the only one who spied for her; she had many and various ways of knowing things. The cooks could not leave a saucepan dirty, the footmen smash a glass, or the housemaids forget to darn a torn sheet without being afraid of being summoned to her ladyship's presence. Someone would report it, someone would inform against them, and they would be called upon to face their just retribution. Sheldon Hall was Lady Clementina's kingdom, a kingdom ruled over by a despot. And its only rebel was her son.

Lady Clementina poured herself out the rest of the champagne and sipped it slowly. Over and over in her mind she turned the problem of Sylvia Wace. She could quite understand how it had happened that Robert had begun to champion her. He ignored women as a rule in these days, driving her to a frenzy when she invited suitable and eligible girls to the house only to have him aloof and indifferent, treating them with an impersonal politeness which was even ruder than if he had ignored them. She should have got rid of Miss Wace within a day of her arrival. It was too dangerous to keep a girl as pretty as that and with decent antecedents alone in the house with Robert, even though it had seemed unlikely that he would look at her. Then he had done so, had taken her part against her uncle was due, Lady Clementina calculated, entirely to the bad luck that Uncle Octavius had called in person. She knew her son well enough to realise that he would person. She knew her son well enough to realise that he have enjoyed outwitting the pompous clergyman. His concern would have been not with Miss Wace's unhappiness, but with her uncle's overbearing authority. Robert was lazy in some ways—at least by his mother's standards—but when he wished he could override those who presumed and crush an impertinence with a word or a look as competently as she could herself.

Bateson had given Lady Clementina a pretty graphic description of what had occurred inside the library. It made her chuckle to think how astounded the clergyman must have been; she imagined his anger and frustration at the thought that his long journey had been abortive, that he had accomplished nothing, not even the humiliation of his recalcitrant niece.

That was all very well in its way, but now the girl was becoming a danger. She had often accused Robert of being sentimental. At heart he as. He liked his women soft and feminine; and now that he had played St. George and had rescued the fair maiden from the Dragon, what could be more natural than that he should take an almost proprietary interest in her? 'And she is the type,' Lady Clementina thought, 'who will demand marriage.' Should it be just a love affair, she would welcome it. She believed that a mistress might make Robert more human, more understanding, more ready for the marriage she had planned for him. But she knew, because she was no mean judge of character, that for Sylvia it would be marriage or nothing.

Lady Clementina finished the champagne and put the empty glass down beside her. At the moment her wishes had been challenged, but it was only a minor set-back and she was by no means defeated.

8

A week after their arrival, Sylvia was informed that Lucy and she were to use the old nurseries at Sheldon Hall. These were situated on a higher floor than the rooms they were using at the moment. When Lucy first saw the day nursery she exclaimed with excitement and glee. It was a large, sunny room looking south with a traditional screen made of scraps, coloured pictures of children and animals, and containing an assortment of toys which the child fell upon in a perfect ecstasy of delight. There was a rocking horse, a big golliwog and a great teddy bear; there were forts with tin soldiers and a cannon which shot big lead pellets, and a Noah's ark with all its animals covered with real fur. Sylvia found herself infected by Lucy's joy and together they explored the cupboards and chests, discovering all sorts of strange things which children of another generation had played with and loved.

It was difficult for Sylvia to visualise Sir Robert as a child. Was he ever a natural, spontaneous, affectionate little boy? she often wondered and after over a month's acquaintance she still felt him to be the most complete stranger she had ever met in her life. He never seemed to relax, never dropped for a moment that air of aloof detachment, as if he were only an onlooker at life.

And yet strangely enough he inspired love. Lady Clementina adored him, that was obvious, although at times mother and son seemed bitter antagonists fencing with each other fiercely with their tongues as if they would be glad to inflict mortal wounds. But Lady Clementina's wrinkled face softened when she spoke of her son and her eyes followed him when he was in the room. Sometimes it seemed to Sylvia that Sir Robert was deliberately callous towards his mother, that he knew she craved his love, but was determined to withhold from her even a glimpse of any feelings that he might have for her in return. It was as if there was a barrier erected between them which Lady Clementina wished at times to ignore or forget while Sir Robert was conscious of it always and at every moment.

Sometimes when she was alone, Sylvia speculated as to what could be the cause of this barrier. She felt it was not Sir Robert's marriage; all trace of the dead Alice seemed to be effaced from Sheldon Hall. If in her lifetime she had any influence here it was long forgotten. Even Nannie, devoted and loyal to every member of the family, spoke of her as if she were little more than a name. And if her pale ghost wished to haunt them, she did it very ineffectually. 'No,' Sylvia thought, 'it must be something deeper and more weighty than Alice, something which held mother and son apart and at the same time linked them together.'

When Sylvia had such thoughts she chided herself for being over-imaginative, perhaps over-sensitive. Why could she not accept things as they were, at their surface value, and be grateful and content with the comfort she enjoyed at Sheldon Hall and the knowledge that in some degree at least she was her own mistress and not under the jurisdiction of Uncle Octavius and Aunt Miranda?

'I am happy,' she told herself fiercely, only to find her thoughts returning persistently to the point from where they had started. Sir Robert was loved, that was what she had been thinking, loved by his mother in her own strange, dominating way: by Nannie whole-heartedly and warmly—the love of a woman for the child she has nursed which having once clung to her and sought her protection can never seem entirely grown-up and independent. What could be finer than such a love, which is often more maternal than that of a mother because it is utterly selfless and demands nothing in return?

Then there was Lucy. It was obvious that Lucy had grown to love her father and if in front of other people he was often coolly abrupt, Sylvia had the idea that when father and daughter were alone together things were very different. They would walk round the estate hand in hand, and when they returned Lucy's cheeks would be glowing and her eyes sparkling and she would have an enormous amount to say about what they had seen and done. Already she was clever with Sir Robert and at her tender age something of a coquette, flattering him with her enthusiasm for his company, greeting with an eager cry his entrance into the room where she was. Sometimes, too, with an enchantingly natural gesture she would rub her cheek against his hand.

Sylvia had grown wise to the fact that Sir Robert liked to have Lucy entirely to himself, and when he came up to the nurseries she would withdraw quietly and unobtrusively. After this had happened several times she guessed that Sir Robert was aware of her tactics, and once when she returned to say that Lucy must get ready for tea, he had on leaving said simply, 'Thank you, Miss Wace.' She understood for what he thanked her and she had almost been tempted to repeat the spontaneous words which had come to her lips when he had saved her from Uncle Octavius—'I will do anything for you, Sir Robert.' But she had grown wiser. Sheldon Hall had taught her one thing—that one did not express one's feelings without thought and consideration. It was in her nature to be keenly observant and she had come to the conclusion that everyone within that great house was hiding what they felt behind some kind of mask. Even Nannie thought before she spoke—an attitude entirely alien to one whose character originally had been open-hearted and spontaneous.

One day Sylvia, going alone to the maids' room to borrow some cleaning material for one of Lucy's dresses, had found Purvis, the lady's maid sitting before her fire, her head in her hands.

'Is anything wrong?' she asked quickly.

Purvis raised her head and Sylvia saw that she had been crying. Her thin nose which was always red at the tip was redder than usual, and her eyes which always appeared slightly shifty because of their pale lashes were swollen.

'It's all right, Miss Wace,' she said in a low voice. 'I'm just a bit upset, that's all.'

'Have you had bad news?' Sylvia asked sympathetically.

Purvis shook her head. 'I'm just making a fool of myself,' she said. 'There's times when it's more than I can bear, this continual nagging and fault-finding. I do my best, and nobody can do more, but there's no pleasing some people. If the Angel Gabriel himself came down to wait on them, he'd do it wrong.'

Sylvia was well aware of whom Purvis spoke. She had heard the harsh, irritable way in which Lady Clementina often spoke to her and she was not surprised that Purvis found it unbearable. The really surprising thing was that she had stood it for so long and put up with so much.

'I am sorry,' she murmured, feeling there was nothing else she could say.

'I shouldn't be so foolish as to take any notice,' Purvis continued, 'but I haven't been feeling myself lately. I suppose between ourselves it's my time of life, but I get such buzzings in the head that sometimes I feel I'm going mad, I hardly know what I'm doing or saying. And then when she goes at me like she does, well, it's really a wonder I don't say or do something terrible.'

'I have got some medicine in my room,' Sylvia suggested, 'that the doctor prescribed for my mother's headaches. Do you think it would do you any good?'

'Oh, no, I shall be all right,' Purvis said, getting to her feet and wiping her eyes determinedly. 'But sometimes I just hate this place, the house and everybody in it. As I wrote to my sister only last week, they aren't human—that's the real answer, they're just not human.'

Sylvia thought how she had echoed this sentiment over

and over again, but she felt it unwise to express her own feelings to Lady Clementina's maid. She did not like Purvis; there was something unpleasant about the woman; and although at the moment she was ready to accept sympathy, Sylvia knew that the next day she might be waspish and disagreeable when they met and ready to vent her ill-humour on everyone with whom she came in contact. What was more, she did not like children. Even Lucy, who had captivated most of the household, could make no headway with Purvis.

Having obtained the cleaning material that she had come for, Sylvia went back to the nurseries. Lucy was still finding new things to excite her in a big chest which contained bricks and puzzles and lots of the small miscellaneous objects which children love to collect.

'Look, Wacey,' Lucy said, running up to the table where Sylvia was working. 'I have found two wooden swords. Do you think Daddy played with them when he was a little boy and pretended to be a soldier?'

'I am sure he did, dear,' Sylvia answered 'You must ask him about them when you see him.'

'I wonder why he wanted two?' Lucy questioned. 'They have both got something written on them. What is it, Wacey?'

Sylvia put down her sewing and took the swords from Lucy. 'Your Daddy's name is written on this one,' she said. 'See, you can spell it out for yourself. R-O-B-E-R-T. That stands for Robert, your Daddy's name.'

'And what is on this one?' Lucy asked, giving Sylvia the other sword.

'This has got "Edward" written on it,' Sylvia replied. 'I expect he was a little boy who came and played with your father.'

'Did they have battles like real soldiers?'

'I expect so; but you had better ask Nannie. She will remember what they did.'

About ten minutes later Nannie came up to the nursery bringing a cup of hot milk for Lucy and some fruit.

'I met one of the girls on the stairs bringing this up,' she said, 'and a cup of tea for you, Miss Wace. Stone cold it was already! I sent her back to get another one. Don't you put up with anything of that sort. If your tea isn't served right, send it down again.'

Sylvia smiled. She was grateful for Nannie's championship, but she had learnt that a governess was considered a person of little importance by the other servants and that she must often put up with bad attention and scarcely veiled impertinence from those who were confident that she was too nervous and inexperienced to report them.

'Thank you, Nannie,' she said. 'Come along, Lucy. Drink your milk while it is hot, darling. And then we had better go out for a walk before luncheon.'

Lucy came reluctantly across the floor, carrying her precious swords.

'Lucy has discovered even more treasures this morning,' Sylvia told Nannie. 'Two swords are the latest find. One is marked "Robert" and the other "Edward." We are both wondering who Edward was.'

There was a pause before Nannie answered. Then with a strange expression on her face she replied in a low voice ,'It belonged to Sir Robert's elder brother.'

'An elder brother?' Sylvia exclaimed in surprise. 'I don't know why, but I always imagined that Sir Robert was an only child. Is he dead?'

Nannie nodded. 'Yes, he's dead. It's hard to come up to this nursery without seeing their little red heads bent together in the corner as they played with the fort or with those very swords.'

Lucy had been listening. 'Was my Daddy sorry when Edward died and couldn't play with him any more?'

'Yes, dear,' Nannie replied. And then she added quickly, 'But you don't want to go talking to your Daddy about your Uncle Edward. It's best not to mention him in this house.'

'Why not?' Lucy asked; and Sylvia, who longed to ask the same question, waited for the answer.

'Them that asks no questions isn't told any lies,' Nannie said. 'Now remember what I've told you—don't go talking about your Uncle Edward to anyone. Do you understand?'

'Yes, Nannie,' Lucy answered; and added as if she needed some reasonable explanation for the command, 'Does it make Daddy and people sad if we talk about him?'

'Yes, dear, it makes them sad,' Nannie replied, 'and you wouldn't want to do that, would you?'

Lucy shook her head. She finished her milk and went back to her toys.

Sylvia was silent. There were so many questions she wanted to ask, but she felt a little shy in the face of Nannie's reluctance to be communicative.

'When did he die?' she asked at last, unable to resist this one question.

'Nearly eleven years ago,' Nannie replied.

'As little as that?' Sylvia said. 'Why, you were saying the other day that Sir Hugh had been dead for fifteen years. That means that his son Edward must have been the Sixth Baronet.'

'That's right; Sir Robert is the Seventh.'

There was something in Nannie's voice which told Sylvia she did not wish to continue the conversation, but in spite of herself Sylvia could not help asking questions. She was so curious about Sir Robert's brother that her interest overcame her better judgment.

'Did he die through an accident?' she asked.

Nannie got to her feet. Sylvia had never seen her look so grave.

'Listen, Miss Wace,' she said. 'It is much better for us not to speak of it. I loved Master Edward. I looked after him from the moment he was born. But as he grew older he was not like other people. He was not quite normal. It upset her ladyship, she couldn't bear to think of it or even to see him.'

'He was deformed?' Sylvia said in horror.

The tears came suddenly to Nannie's eyes. 'He . . . he never grew up. He was always gentle, always child-like. That was what he was—only a child. He went on playing with toys while his younger brother grew to manhood. He was always a baby—my baby.'

The last words came with an effort and Nannie pressed her handkerchief to her eyes and went from the room.

For a little while Sylvia sat watching Lucy brandishing a sword in the sunlight. So here was yet another mystery of the house! The eldest son who had never grown up, who had been mothered and nursed by Nannie long after he should have grown to man's estate! What a tragedy! For once she could sympathise with Lady Clementina and be sorry for her. Could there be any anguish more bitter than that of a mother who knows she has produced an abnormity? No wonder there was no portrait of the Sixth Baronet to hang beside his father in the great hall.

'Come along, Lucy,' Sylvia said, suddenly getting to her feet. 'Let us go out in the fresh air.'

She wanted to take the child out of the nursery, away from the toys which seemed all at once contaminated, from something slightly horrible. She had a vision of a young man bending over them, fingering them with soft, white useless hands.

When Lucy was dressed it was time to go down to Lady Clementina's bedroom to say good morning.

'Don't let us be long,' Lucy whispered as Sylvia knocked on the door.

Sylvia smiled at her comfortingly.

Lady Clementina, however, greeted Lucy perfunctorily and absent-mindedly. Sir Robert was with her and Lucy ran across the room to slip her hand into her father's.

'Well, what are we to do about tonight?' Lady Clementina asked irritably, ignoring Sylvia. 'With Mary Erskine falling out you will be an odd number at dinner. It really is too annoying and I can't think whom we can ask at this eleventh hour.'

Sir Robert looked bored, appearing to care little about the arrangements. There had been talk in the household for several days about the dinner party which was taking place that evening and which was to be followed by a small dance. Sylvia had gathered that it was to be nothing on a grand scale, but merely a pleasant method of entertaining some neighbours.

'You must think of someone,' Lady Clementina insisted. 'One of the grooms can ride over with a note if you will decide whom you would like to ask.'

Sir Robert was not listening. Lucy was standing on tiptoe to whisper something in his ear and he was bending down towards the child. As if the sight was suddenly intolerable to her, Lady Clementina broke in sharply.

'Robert!' she said. 'Will you answer me? This party is given in your interests.'

Sir Robert straightened himself. 'On the contrary, my dear mother, my interests are never consulted. I don't care for the country dowagers who ogle me in the hope that I will present their plain daughters with a free tenancy of Sheldon Hall. And I care less for their husbands. I gather that my own cronies are not to be invited tonight?'

'Most certainly not!' Lady Clementina snapped. 'A lot of drunken wasters whose only interest is in gambling!'

'Drink and gambling are the best means to make the time pass when one's real interest is in its passing.'

There was such a weariness in Sir Robert's voice, as if he carried a burden too heavy to be borne, that Sylvia felt a pang of sympathy for him.

'You should add women to your vices,' Lady Clementina retorted. 'It is noted as the best cure for ennui.'

Sir Robert sighed. 'Must we go over all this again?' he asked impatiently. 'I have agreed to your wishes on this occasion. We will have these bumpkins to dinner. I will listen to their giggling platitudes, and I will, when dinner is over, propel them around the parquet while they swoon at the beauty of the ballroom and assure me that I am their ideal partner. I have agreed to all this; don't trouble me with any more in case you drive me too far and I refuse to attend your party.'

'You are being ridiculous,' Lady Clementina said with some asperity. 'As Master of Sheldon Hall you have certain obligations to the neighbourhood. This is one of them. The only difficulty now is to find one other woman to complete the table. Shall I ask one of the Shipton girls or poor Freddie Fielding's widow?'

Sir Robert was about to declare that he had no preference and that she could do what she liked when his eyes suddenly fell on Sylvia waiting patiently by the doorway for Lucy. A pale shaft of wintry sun striking through the window illuminated her for a moment, turning her hair to living gold, lighting the pale transparency of her face, and making her eyes unexpectedly and vividly blue. A faint smile touched the corners of Sir Robert's lips. There was on his face at that moment a reflection of what he must have looked like as a small boy when about to do something particularly mischievous and naughty.

'Why go so far afield, Mother,' he asked, 'when a substitute for Lady Erskine is here at hand?

'What do you mean?' Lady Clementina inquired; and then in a flash she understood. For a moment she met her son's eyes across the room. Wordlessly they wrestled with each other.

'I shall be delighted to see Miss Wace at dinner,' Sir Robert said after a moment. 'And now I think it is time for Lucy and me to feed the horses. They will be waiting for us.'

He turned towards the door, Lucy dancing beside him. And then they were gone, leaving the two women speechless behind them.

Lady Clementina looked at Sylvia.

'You have not forgotten, I hope, the warning I gave you when you first came here, Miss Wace.'

'No, Lady Clementina.'

'It would be a pity if you got ideas above your station.'

'I hope I shall not do that.'

Sylvia spoke calmly, but her heart was beating fast. Would Lady Clementina allow her to go? Despite her shyness she had a sudden longing to be present at this party. She had never been to a party or a dance since she had been grown-up. She knew instinctively that Lady Clementina was considering whether it would be wiser to allow her to go to the party or to risk Sir Robert's further championship by refusing her permission. There was always the chance that if she were to refuse it would make Sylvia even more important in his eyes. It was Lady Clementina's fervent hope that she should remain a nonentity, one of the vast company of employees who moved about the house, often unseen and forgotten by those they served.

Lady Clementina's fingers were tapping on the book which lay beside her, her brows were knitted. She was thinking deeply, 'Robert is a fighter—after all he is my son.' Finally she made up her mind.

'Very well, Miss Wace,' she said, 'you may take your place at dinner. You will, of course, make your position in this household clear to the gentlemen who sit on either side of you. There must be no understanding, no pushing of yourself forward to be on equal terms with my son's guests. After the dance has started, you will retire to your own room.'

'I quite understand,' Sylvia replied.

'You have, I believe, an evening dress in your wardrobe?' Lady Clementina continued.

'Yes,' Sylvia stammered.

'I have heard of it. It came, I believe, from the same source as the black dress you wore on arrival?'

'Yes, that is so.'

'When you are dressed I would like to see you. If I do not consider the gown suitable for someone who is entrusted with the care of a young child, you will not be able to attend the party.'

'I understand.'

'That will be all, Miss Wace.'

Lady Clementina was angry. Sylvia was well aware of that as she crept from the room; but she was not so intimidated as she might have been for she was excited at the prospect of what lay before her.

Going downstairs to her room she looked at the mauve

dress. It was certainly a lovely gown, and yet she was almost sure that, however suitable and attractive it might be, Lady Clementina would disapprove of it. Was it, she wondered, another of her cat and mouse schemes to allow her to get dressed and then at the very last moment to cancel the arrangements? There was nothing else, however, which she could wear and she turned from the contemplation of the dress to the window.

How utterly helpless one was! How dependent on the whims and will of someone else! She felt very young and inexperienced and very much alone. If only she had a friend with whom she could talk, just one person to whom she could confide her feelings, from whom she could ask advice! 'I am being ungrateful,' she thought. 'I am asking more of life when it has given me so much already.' Nevertheless she felt as if she were caught and imprisoned by something which held her back from living fully, from grasping the wonder of all that life held just out of her reach.

The thaw had set in. Already there were patches of green in the park. Only where the snow had drifted did it still lie as white and unsoiled as the snowdrops raising their heads below the terraces. Soon it would be spring and already it seemed to Sylvia that the air was milder and that there was a promise in it of warmer days to come. Was it an omen, she wondered, that she, too, had passed through the winter of sterile unhappiness? If so, what did her future hold?

She laid her cheek against the coolness of the windowpane. She had an idea, just an idea of what she wished it to hold for her; but she was afraid to put her thoughts into words.

9

'Oh, Miss, you look lovely!'

It was Ethel who spoke, the little maid who had been allotted the task of waiting on the nurseries.

'It certainly fits me,' Sylvia said critically, seeing in the long mirror a vision of mauve from which her shoulders and arms emerged dazzlingly white.

'I have never seen anything so lovely!' Ethel exclaimed, clasping her hands together. 'You look a dream, you do really, Miss!'

'Thank you, Ethel.'

It was pleasant to have someone so genuinely sincere in her flattery. She turned this way and that—something more was needed.

'I wish I had a necklace,' Sylvia sighed at last.

'It looks beautiful just as it is, Miss,' Ethel replied.

But Sylvia, having uncovered her neck and shoulders for the first time in her life, felt shy and half naked. And yet she would have been blind or dishonest if she had not admitted to herself that the dress did suit her. She was transformed. The 'ugly duckling' had become a swan.

Then in the midst of her delight she thought of Lady Clementina and her elation faded. She looked pretty, even beautiful; but she certainly did not look like a governess. After what Lady Clementina had said about her being suitably dressed it was impossible for her not to realise the improbability that she would be allowed to attend the dinner party.

Glancing at the clock on the mantelpiece she saw that it was a quarter past eight. At any moment the guests would be arriving, for dinner was at half-past. But she would not see them. She was certain of that, as certain as if someone had already told her what Lady Clementina's judgment would be. Suddenly she felt angry. She knew that Lady Clementina having seen the mauve dress had decided that it was unsuitable and far too smart. Yet to raise her hopes only to dash them to the ground at the last minute was, Sylvia felt, such a refinement of cruelty that it incited her to rebellion. She was young, she wanted to enjoy herself, she wanted to go to her first grown-up party. Why should anyone, even Lady Clementina, deny her that pleasure?

For the first time in her life Sylvia was mutinous. For years she had been subservient, had looked after her mother, accepted the arduous task of ceaseless attendance on a querulous, difficult invalid. She had accepted meekly the sacrifice it entailed of all the interests that might have been hers. Loyal to a fault, however, she had never rebelled against her lot, not even in her heart. Now she felt passionately that some joy, some excitement must be hers before she grew any older. After all, Sir Robert had invited her; why should his mother cancel that invitation? She lifted her head higher. Lady Clementina was an old woman who had lived her life. It was unfair that she should deny a younger woman just a few of the crumbs which might fall from the rich man's table!

At that moment there came a knock on the door. Sylvia made up her mind in a flash. As Ethel started to cross the floor she seized her by the arm.

'If it is someone for me,' she whispered, 'say I have gone downstairs. You understand?'

Ethel nodded. Then with her finger to her lips Sylvia ran across the room and opening the door of the big mahogany wardrobe slipped inside. Her heart was beating as she waited in the scented darkness. Ethel opened the door.

'Oh, Miss Purvis!' Sylvia heard her say. 'Were you wanting anything?'

'Tell Miss Wace her ladyship wants her.'

'Miss Wace has gone downstairs.'

'Gone? Already? But I thought she knew that her ladyship wanted to see her first.'

'I expect she forgot,' Ethel said. 'She was excited at being dressed up and frightened, too, of being late. You'd be the same, Miss Purvis, if it was the first party you'd ever been to.'

'Is that what Miss Wace told you?'

Purvis was interested and Sylvia guessed that this information would be carried back to Lady Clementina.

'Yes, that's what she told me,' Ethel replied. 'She's been looking after her sick mother for years. Couldn't leave her for more than an hour at a time. It's hard what some people have to put up with, Miss Purvis.'

'When you're as old as I am, Ethel, you can begin to talk about putting up with things,' Purvis replied with some asperity. 'You get on with your work like a good girl and don't go wasting time. There's no call for you to wait on Miss Wace personally, if you know what I mean.'

It was an upper servant asserting herself. Ethel from long training became meek and monosyllabic.

'Yes, Miss Pruvis.'

'Well, I don't know what her ladyship will say, I'm sure, but I'll go and break the news to her that the bird has flown.'

Purvis left the room. Ethel closed the door behind her and then came running towards the wardrobe.

'She's gone, Miss Wace.'

'Thank you, Ethel. I am grateful.'

Sylvia stepped out of the wardrobe, gave her hair a last touch, and catching up her gloves and a handkerchief went towards the door.

'If only I don't meet anyone,' she said, 'I shall be all right.'

Without waiting for Ethel's reply she threaded her way along the passages, the silk of her petticoats rustling as she went. She ran down the great staircase, only to stand hesitating and uncertain as she heard the sound of voices coming from the drawing-room.

Bateson was waiting at the hall door for other arrivals; there were several footmen beside him. He walked across the hall giving the impression of a pompous, patronising bishop with his white hair and slightly portly figure. Sylvia was well aware that he saw her uncertainly and was amused by it.

'Won't you go in, Miss?' he asked. 'Or would you like me to announce you.'

Sylvia shrank with horror from her own name being cried aloud in Bateson's stentorian tones.

'No, no, I will go in,' she said. And because she was anxious to escape from him she entered the drawing-room precipitately.

There were about a dozen people grouped round the fire-place and in the centre of them, wearing his usual look of aloof boredom, stood Sir Robert. He glanced up and saw her in the doorway. For a moment it seemed to Sylvia as if he did not recognise her and then with a faint smile on his lips he went towards her.

'Come in, Miss Wace.'

He drew her forward until they reached the oldest and most distinguished-looking woman in the gathering.

'Duchess,' Sir Robert said, 'may I present Miss Wace? She is staying here with us to look after my daughter Lucy whom I do not think you have met. Miss Wace—the Duchess of Melchester.'

A sudden silence fell on the group of people in the room. Sylvia saw the surprise on the face of the Duchess and guessed that the same expression was echoed on the faces of those around her. She felt utterly at a loss, feeling that Sir Robert had used her merely as an instrument through which he could startle and perhaps shock his guests.

'I had no idea you had a daughter, Robert,' the Duchess said, raising her eyebrows.

Sir Robert laughed. 'Indeed I have,' he said. 'A most attractive young creature and exactly like me. Isn't she, Miss Wace?'

Her voice scarcely above a whisper, Sylvia agreed with him. This might be amusing for him, but for her it was mortifying in the extreme. She was not so insensitive as not to know the questions that were seething through every mind. Who was this daughter? Why had they not heard of her before? Was she legitimate or was Robert merely brazening out a difficult situation? Surely Miss Wace was too young and too well-dressed to be a governess? Desperately Sylvia tried to appear at her ease. Now the Duchess was asking her a question.

'How old is your charge, Miss Wace?'

'Nearly seven, your Grace.'

Sylvia was aware of the calculations that were going on. Yes, that was all right. They all knew when Alice had run away. It was just possible that Lucy might be Robert's child.

'And where has she been living all this time?' the Duchess asked.

Sir Robert was not going to allow the game he was playing with his guests and neighbours to end so quickly.

'Forgive me, Duchess,' he said before Sylvia could answer, 'but I want to introduce Miss Wace to my other guests.'

He touched her arm as if to draw her across the room to another somewhat austere-looking dowager. Sylvia went obediently. The names he murmured meant nothing to her, her mind was in a whirl; and yet some part of her relished the surprise on the well-bred faces, the glint of curiosity in every eye she encountered.

More people arrived, and still more. She found a gentleman standing by her side. He was fair and not unattractive-looking.

I say, Miss Wace, I hope you are going to enjoy this part of the world.'

'I am sure I am,' Sylvia replied. 'But why?'

'Well, you'll be a definite asset in the neighbourhood. We're very short of pretty girls.'

Sylvia felt herself flush and then was angry at her own inexperience. It was the first compliment she had ever received from a man and she wished she knew how to parry it adroitly.

She was thankful when dinner was announced by Bateson and Sir Robert offered his arm to the Duchess and led the procession to the dining-room. Sylvia found herself being escorted by the fair man and discovered that his name was Captain Davidson.

'My estate adjoins Sir Robert's,' he said as soon as they were seated. 'You must come over one day to Hartley Towers. It is only an hour's drive.'

'Have you any children of your own, Captain Davidson?' Sylvia asked.

Her companion laughed heartily at the idea.

'I am what is called an incorrigible bachelor, Miss Wace. But I assure you that merely means that I am an idealist. I am still looking for the one woman, and until I find her I merely enjoy myself. Won't you help me?'

Sylvia wondered what she should say next. In this sort of conversation she felt out of her depth. She wished that she could remain silent, merely taking in impressions of what she saw around her. She glanced at Sir Robert at the head of the table, leaning back in his chair and listening with an air of attention to some long story the Duchess was pouring into his ears. She looked at the other women, at their bare shoulders and twinkling diamonds, the aigrettes nodding in their high-piled hair, their fingers shining with costly gems. They looked unreal, puppets come to life from some picture book. The men talking to them, with their shining white shirt-fronts, high collars and long moustaches, were elegant beyond anything she had imagined. They were so very different from the few men she had known in her sheltered life—from Uncle Octavius, Doctor Dawson and the business men she had seen passing down the street at Poolbrook. She liked the elegant tones in which they spoke, the slight drawl in their voices and she felt shy and excited when they looked at her with that speculative, yet admiring glance which said so much without words.

The table, too, was worth seeing. The spotless white damask of the cloth and the napkins; the heavy silver candelabra, their candles shaded with rose silk; the great dishes of hot-house fruit and the picturesque arrangement of flowers and smilax twined among the dishes and silver ornaments—all made a perfect pattern, a connoisseur's piece in the way of decoration. The food was new to Sylvia,

96

too. There were delicacies such as she had not only never tasted before, but of which she had never even heard: ortolans and quails, *pâté de foie gras*, truffles and *marron. glacés.*

There was so much she wanted to savour and to watch, but all the time she must remember to listen to her neighbours, to keep them talking and to answer their questions as intelligently as she could. On her right she had an elderly man whom she soon learnt was a hunting bore. Whenever she turned to him he started some long and interminable story of his hunting experiences, which, being unconversant with hunting in any shape or form, she found quite incomprehensible.

'You must get Sir Robert to mount you,' the enthusiast said at last. 'This is not a first-class huntin' county, mind you, but we will give you as good a run as you will get anywhere, I'll promise you that. You will enjoy it, and don't forget I said so!'

Sylvia, thinking it was the last thing she would enjoy, thanked him for his kindness and then while he drew breath to begin his next question she found her attention caught once again by Captain Davidson.

'I say, do you ever get a day off?' he asked.

'What do you mean?' Sylvia inquired ingenuously.

'Well, you can't have the child with you all the time,' Captain Davidson replied, lowering his voice. 'What about meeting me some time? I know all the country round about here; I can bring along the trap and take you for a drive. What's more, in a week or so I shall have something better to offer you. I'm buying a car.'

'Oh, how exciting! But aren't you frightened of the things? I have never been in one.'

'Well, I don't mind betting you you won't say that in a month's time,' Captain Davidson replied. 'Leave it to me, little woman; I will think out a plan. But mum's the word, fo course.'

'I don't know . . . I mean . . . I don't promise anything,' Sylvia said rather desperately.

At that moment the Duchess rose to lead the ladies from the dining-room.

'It's a cert—but don't you say a word to a soul,' Captain Davidson muttered, as he stood aside to let her pass.

The Duchess announced that she was going upstairs to see Lady Clementina.

'Tell her that I would like to see her, too,' another Dowager remarked.

'I will give Clementina your message,' the Duchess replied graciously. 'How many people she can see will, of course, depend on how she is.'

The other ladies were led upstairs to one of the big bedrooms, which had been put at their disposal, and Sylvia took the opportunity to slip up to her own room. She looked at herself in the glass and saw that her eyes were sparkling and there was an excited patch of colour in each cheek. She wanted to rearrange her hair, but she did not dare to linger as she was afraid that the long arm of Lady Clementina would be reaching out for her.

She slipped into Lucy's room. The child was fast asleep, clutching a somewhat tattered doll she had found the day before. Sylvia tucked in the bed-clothes and went through the room into the nursery where Nannie was sitting by the fire, keepng watch in case Lucy awoke.

'Well, are you enjoying yourself?' Nannie asked; and then stopped with an exclamation. 'Why, for a moment you looked just like her late ladyship. It is the dress, I suppose. Is that the one you were telling me belonged to her?'

'Yes, this is the one,' Sylvia said. 'Do you like it?'

'It's lovely,' Nannie said. 'But then her ladyship always had perfect taste. You were lucky to get it.'

'Yes, I was, wasn't I?' Sylvia replied, thankful that Nannie did not know exactly how she had obtained it.

'Well, what is the party like?' Nannie asked.

'Rather frightening,' Sylvia confessed. 'You see, I have never been to one before.'

'Are you going down again?'

'Lady Clementina said I was to stay until they started dancing and then come upstairs. Oh, Nannie, don't you think I could stay for one dance? That is, if anybody asks me.'

'I should think they'll ask you all right,' Nannie said dryly. 'You must please yourself, but remember Lady Clementina can be hard if she is crossed.'

'I feel exactly like Cinderella,' Sylvia sighed wistfully. 'But at least she was allowed to stay until twelve o'clock.'

'It will be nearly that before it's time for you to come away,' Nannie said uncompromisingly. 'But I'll stay here until you do. I don't like to leave Lucy alone on this floor.'

'No, of course, not,' Sylvia agreed quickly. She felt that

kindly, but firmly, Nannie was recalling her to a sense of duty.

'I shall not be long then,' she said, turning towards the door. 'And thank you, Nannie.'

When she reached the first floor she found the ladies had already left the bedroom and gone downstairs. Sylvia had inspected the ball-room with Lucy, but they saw it unlit and its chairs and sofas covered in dust-sheets. Now with its glass chandeliers sparkling with hundreds of candles, with the massed decorations of ferns and flowers and with the brocade and gold chairs uncovered, it was a very lovely sight. As Sylvia entered the room and looked at the dancing couples, seeing the whole scene like a picture set before her, she thought, as she had thought so often before, that half the beauty of Sheldon Hall lay in the fact that in the big reception rooms and in the hall Lady Clementina insisted on the use of candles, keeping the modern gas lighting to the bedrooms and passages upstairs. Now in the candle light every woman seemed to be looking her best and she knew that she, too, had nothing to fear. Intent on her thoughts, she suddenly found herself clasped in Captain Davidson's arms and whirled away into the centre of the room.

'I didn't stop to ask permission,' Captain Davidson was saying. 'I saw you wanted a partner and I wanted to dance with you, lovely little lady in mauve.'

'But I must not dance,' Sylvia said quickly. 'Please stop. You see, Lady Clementina said . . .'

'Forget her. From all I hear, Lady Clementina is always saying things but why should you worry? She is old and ugly and you are the prettiest little filly I've seen for a long time.'

'But, please, Captain Davidson, please . . .' Sylvia pleaded, when to her relief at that moment the music came to an end.

Captain Davidson put his hand under Sylvia's elbow and led her from the ball-room into the conservatory.

'Come in here,' he said, 'and tell me what all this is about. Why aren't you allowed to dance? Is there anything wrong with so delightful a recreation?'

The sweet fragrance of hot-house flowers was almost overpowering. Captain Davidson led the way to a seat arranged in an alcove and shadowed by palms. Sylvia sat down; then recovering her breath she looked at him with a smile and said:

99

'I am a governess. You seem to forget that.'

'I couldn't forget anything about you,' he replied fervently. 'But may not governesses dance? Is there some law against it?'

'There is in this house,' Sylvia said, laughing as she said it so that there was no hint of bitterness in her words. 'And now having broken the rules,' she added, 'I am going to slip away. Thank you, you have been very kind.'

'But I say, this is ridiculous,' Captain Davidson expostulated; but Sylvia had risen to her feet.

'Good night, Captain Davidson.'

'I refuse to let you go,' Captain Davidson cried. 'I insist on having another dance with you.'

Sylvia laughed. 'I am afraid you have got more chance of getting your own way than I have,' and she held out her hand.

As Captain Davidson took it they heard voices and looked up to see Sir Robert enter the conservatory, a lady with whom he had been dancing on his arm.

'I say, Robert,' Captain Davidson called, still retaining Sylvia's hand much to her embarrassment. 'I want you a moment.'

'What is it, Tim?' Sir Robert asked, walking towards them.

Sylvia noticed that the woman with him was not particularly attractive. She was inclined to be stout and was fanning herself with the sequin-sprinkled fan she held in her gloved hand.

'I am making a formal complaint to you as my host,' Captain Davidson said. 'Miss Wace, the one person I wish to dance with, insists on going to bed. Is this the lavish Sheldon Hall hospitality of which I have heard so much?'

He spoke with a jocular, debonair air which was slightly forced. As he finished his sentence, Sylvia managed to slip her hand from his. She felt extremely foolish, especially as Sir Robert loooked at her gravely, while the woman who held his arm giggled openly.

'But if Miss Wace wishes to retire . . .' Sir Robert said after a moment's pause. He looked at Sylvia.

She knew she had only to say that these were Lady Clementina's orders to drive him into revolt. She had learnt already that it was quite easy in small matters to incite Sir Robert to defy his mother and suddenly she felt ashamed to do such a thing, ashamed, too, of herself, of the position in which she had been caught. There was something in Sir

Robert's eyes which seemed to tell her that he was disappointed in her. All sense of excitement immediately died within her. She wanted only to escape and be alone in her own room.

In the meantime, Sir Robert was waiting. Sylvia tilted back her head to look up at him—an unconscious gesture of pride, and then quietly she said:

'Lucy is alone, sir Robert. I think I should be with her in case she wakes.'

She felt rather than saw the expression change in his eyes. She had touched the right cord, done the right thing.

'Your complaints are overruled, Tim,' Sir Robert said, while the woman giggled again and remarked, 'It is good for Captain Davidson not to get what he wants for once. We poor women give in to him so often that he's getting quite spoilt.'

Captain Davidson looked nonplussed, and while there was still the opportunity, Sylvia said good night quickly and respectfully and slipped away. She did not have to pass through the ball-room, there was a passage which led from the conservatory back to the great hall. She hurried along it and as she reached the hall she saw Bateson standing there supervising the footmen who were clearing the dinner-table. At the sight of her, Bateson came forward and before she could escape up the stairs had reached her side.

'You have enjoyed the evening, Miss?'

'Very much, thank you.'

'Her ladyship asked me to inform you when it was half-past eleven as she felt that was the right time for you to retire. It still lacks a few minutes to the half-past; you are early, Miss.'

Sylvia raised her chin. 'I am quite capable of carrying out her ladyship's instructions without being reminded of them,' she said coldly. 'Perhaps you will remember that in future.'

She sped up the stairs, leaving Bateson looking after her in surprise. She felt glad at her own courage.

Nannie was waiting in the nursery. She thanked the older woman for sitting up and told her to go to bed.

When she had gone, Sylvia sat down on the hearth-rug in front of the fire. How strange life was! She had looked forward so much to this evening, longed for it with what amounted almost to greediness. Yet now she felt not elated, but slightly sad, as if nothing she had anticipated

101

had come up to her expectations and all that she had experienced had only left a sour taste in her mouth.

What had she wanted? She was not sure. Was it to be as carefree as the women who danced downstairs, carefree because they were born into a different social status? A few weeks ago she had felt she would be utterly content if only she could stay at Sheldon Hall. This morning she had felt that she would be utterly content if she could be present at tonight's party. What was wrong with her that she should be discontented, that she should want more and still more? She had looked lovely; the mauve dress had changed her from a quiet, drab little person into a creature of splendour who drew men's eyes and made other women jealous. She had Mrs. Bootle to thank for that and she made a mental note to write to Mrs. Bootle tomorrow and tell her what a success her dress had been. Yes, the dress had been a success, but not she herself. What was it she had missed?

Sylvia leant her head against the side of the armchair. How complicated life was, giving with one hand and taking away with the other! She stared into the glowing coals. Some people could tell fortunes in the fire. How she wished that she could tell her own fortune, could know what lay ahead of her! And yet, would it make her happy to know? Was it to be a life of looking after children and going from post to post as a governess, a position in which she was suspended, as it were, in mid-air, the equal neither of her employers who ignored her nor of the servants who despised her. Sylvia closed her eyes.

She thought of Captain Davidson's arm round her waist, the look in his eyes and his suggestion that they should meet. She did not want to meet him again or for him or anyone else to make advances to her of that sort. She knew that because she was only a governess he would make no attempt to see her openly, to court her except clandestinely. Was that what the future held? Romance which had to be snatched and hidden, becoming more sordid, more degrading with the passing years? And what was the alternative? A life of sterile emptiness, becoming withered and bitter and unwanted—an old maid?

Sylvia moved her arm on to the side of the chair and dropped her head on it. Must every girl who earned her own living find her path beset by such obstacles and suffer such humiliations? She had asked for independence, was this the inevitable result? If so, had she been wrong to choose it?

Questions kept presenting themselves to her and she h
no answer to them. She only knew that she was young, that
there was something crying out within her for satisfaction
. . . that what she wanted was out of reach . . . she was
wishing for the moon. Gradually the tumult within her died
away and like a child tired out Sylvia slept. . . .

She woke with a start. She raised her head from her arm
and her eyes, heavy with sleep, blinked uncertainly in the
light of the dying fire. Standing on the hearthrug looking
down at her was Sir Robert.

'Oh, it is you!'

There was no surprise in her voice. For a moment he
seemed to be part of her dream. She had been dreaming of
him. . . .

'You have been asleep.'

'Have I? Yes, suppose I have . . .'

'It is three o'clock,' Sir Robert said. 'I was just going to
bed and I thought I would come up and see if Lucy was all
right.'

Sylvia tried to collect herself and made an effort to rise
to her feet. She was cramped and stiff with sleeping in such
an unnatural position. Sir Robert put out his hand and
drew her up. It seemed to her that his hand, strong and
supporting, was like a rock to which she could cling.

'Thank you,' she said. 'I am sorry that you found me
like this.'

'Why? It doesn't matter.'

'But . . . I should have gone to bed . . . I sat down to
think . . .'

'Of the evening?'

'Yes.'

'You enjoyed it?'

'Of course, and thank you ever so much. It was so kind
of you to ask me.'

'Kind?' He gave a short laugh. 'To inflict upon you what
I found incredibly boring! I envy Lucy who is too young to
suffer the demands and machinations of the social world. I
suppose that is why I came up to see her tonight—to com-
pare my evening with hers—to her advantage.'

'You are very fond of children?' she asked, wondering
how often he paid these visits to Lucy when she was not
aware of them.

He looked across the room and it seemed to her that in
his eyes there was an expression of sadness.

'Very.'

103

She was surprised at the quiet humanity of his voice.

'This house could do with a dozen children in it,' Sylvia said, not stopping to think, but speaking the first words that came into her mind. 'How true that is,' she thought, even as she spoke. The gloom would be dispelled, the silence of the corridors, and the feeling that the house sheltered the dead rather than the living.

'I know that,' Sir Robert said. 'But I shall never marry again, never.'

He spoke almost fiercely, as if he answered some urging within himself.

'But why?' Sylvia asked, and even as she spoke the words faltered because she was speaking to Sir Robert, inquiring perhaps too personally into his private life. He stared at her as if he hardly saw her, as if he looked inwards for something which was secret to him alone. Suddenly, abruptly and in a voice curiously harsh, he said:

'Do you know how lovely you looked tonight when you came into the drawing-room?'

Sylvia looked up at him in amazement. It was the last thing she had ever expected him to say. His face had changed, his eyes as they looked into hers were deep pools of flame. She felt something vibrate between them, something strong, dynamic and forceful, something which seemed to join them both and which in itself was so powerful that she could not draw her eyes from his nor his from hers. She felt her mouth tremble and a flame leap through her. He reached out his arms and drew her to him.

'Why do you tempt me?' he asked in a voice of pain.

He pressed his lips to hers and she felt her senses reeling as he held her closely, kissing her passionately, fiercely, possessively.

Then with a sound that seemed to her almost one of horror, he flung her from him. She fell against the armchair, and without another word or glance Sir Robert strode from the room. She heard the door close behind him. She was alone; alone with her own tumultuous thoughts and the dying fire.

10

Ethel drew back the curtains and put a tray containing an early morning cup of tea beside Sylvia's bed. Then she stood hesitating, and Sylvia knew from past experience that she had something on her mind and wanted to talk.

She forced herself to open her eyes and smile at the girl. Although she had hardly slept at all in the night she did not feel tired, but rather as if she was drawing on some secret source of energy which made her feel more invigorated and stimulated than ever before.

'Good morning, Ethel,' she said.

This was the cue for which Ethel was waiting.

'Oh, Miss, such excitement!' she exclaimed. 'The whole household has been up since five o'clock.'

'Why, what has happened?' Sylvia asked, sitting up in bed half alarmed.

'At five o'clock exactly,' Ethel said dramatically, 'Sir Robert rang his bell. Mr. Bateson hurried along to his room thinking the Master must be ill, but to his surprise he finds Sir Robert up and dressed, and what do you think? He gave orders there and then that he was leaving for London and wanted to catch the eight o'clock train from Mickledon. He made us scurry, I can tell you. Everything had to be packed and the carriage got round; but we managed it, although Mr. Bateson kept saying he couldn't do impossibilities.'

Ethel paused for lack of breath.

'The eight o'clock train,' Sylvia repeated slowly. 'So he has gone then.'

'Oh, yes, he's gone,' Ethel said. 'The carriage was round at a quarter to seven. Sir Robert was waiting for it on the doorstep, his watch in his hand.'

Sylvia said nothing. She felt as if a heavy hand had blotted out the light, leaving her quivering and lost. Why, why, had he run away?

Annd yet despite a disconsolate sense of loss, she was aware that deep inside her there was a springing happiness which nothing could quench. He had kissed her; she had been in his arms, and she knew now that she loved him, had in fact loved him for a long time. It was pointless to deny that he had attracted her from the first moment she had seen him; and though to start with she had felt repulsion and indeed anger at that imperious air, at his arrogance and obvious indifference to herself, she had been aware all the time that there was another side to him for which she yearned and which, despite herself, had commanded her love. That side, she knew, revealed the real Robert Sheldon, the man whom Lucy knew, whose eyes softened at the sight of his child and who had within him the humanity to love and to command the love of a little girl. Something had made Sir Robert don a mask and hide a nature capable of deep emotion and generous impulses behind a screen of cold reserve. The bitterness in his voice and his harshness seemed to tell of some secret pain which he could never altogether shake off and seldom, if ever, forget. What was it? What had caused him to adopt this attitude to life, this deliberate restraint and subjugation of all traces of a capacity for warm feeling? That, Sylvia told herself, was what she had to find out, for until she knew what it was she could not help the man she loved.

The thought of loving Sir Robert brought the colour to her cheeks and yet she was not ashamed. She knew now that he was a man who suffered and because of that she was no longer afraid, she only wanted to help him, to offer any sacrifice in an effort to assuage his suffering.

It was difficult, she found, not to let her thoughts wander away from the present while she was giving Lucy her breakfast and later when they were occupied by the simple lessons which immediately succeeded breakfast every morning.

'No, Lucy, twice three are not ten. Think again,' Sylvia said and found herself thinking of that moment when Sir Robert had caught her in his arms, of the queer note of agony in his voice . . . of the touch of his lips. . . .

'Isn't that right?'

She was startled into awareness by Lucy touching her arm.

'I'm sorry, darling. What was it you said?'

'I have said nine three times,' Lucy said in an aggrieved voice. 'Are you cross with me this morning?'

'No, of course I am not, my pet.'

Sylvia bent down to put her arm around the small figure

beside her and give it a squeeze. 'I am never cross with you really, you know that. I am just feeling rather stupid and I think some fresh air would do us both good.'

'Oh, that would be lovely,' said Lucy, throwing aside her lesson books and jumping to her feet. 'Look, Wacey, the sun is shining. Let's go down to the park and try to feed the deer. I nearly got one to eat out of my hand yesterday. Oh, hurry, Wacey, hurry!'

Lucy danced about the room. The sun glinting through the window made her hair into a halo of burnished light around her red head. Sylvia felt her heart contract, thinking of someone else whose hair was so very red and whose eyes were so dark—those eyes which had looked into hers last night, overpoweringly, possessively.

'I am coming, Lucy,' she said quickly, as if by talking she could try to keep her thoughts at bay. 'Let me put on your coat and hat and then we must go in and say good morning to your grandmother.'

'Oh, must we?' Lucy pouted.

'Yes, darling. Don't forget she cannot go out in the sunshine as you can. You must try and remember that and be sorry for her.'

'It is very difficult, somehow, to be sorry for grandmother,' Lucy said refelctively, her head a little on one side. Though Sylvia agreed with her, she felt that this was not the moment to encourage such ideas in Lucy. Instead she fastened up her coat, helped her to do up her gloves and get all the fingers into the right places. When she was ready, Sylvia found her own coat and hat and buttoned on her thickest pair of boots.

'You won't stay long, will you?' Lucy said in a whisper as they went down the stairs leading from the nursery floor.

'Not if I can help it,' Sylvia replied, feeling that the last thing she wanted at that moment was a prolonged interview with Lady Clementina.

They knocked on the door and a second or two later were standing beside Lady Clementina's bed.

'You are early this morning, Lucy.'

'Yes, Grandmother. Miss Wace thought some fresh air would do us good,' Lucy replied in her clear voice. 'We both felt rather muddle-headed.'

'Indeed.'

Lady Clementina shot a sharp glance at Sylvia. 'Perhaps last night's dissipation has overtired you, Miss Wace?'

'Not really,' Sylvia said quietly.

'And did you enjoy the evening?' Lady Clementina asked.

'Very much, thank you,' Sylvia answered.

She had the impression that Lady Clementina was probing, trying to find out something by her usual method of aasking questions. In the clear morning light she looked unusually old and frail and quite suddenly Sylvia was genuinely sorry for her. She had the impression that Lady Clementina was worried and perturbed, and she guessed that the reason was Sir Robert's sudden departure. 'After all,' Sylvia thought to herself, 'she is an old woman, and she is afraid, afraid of losing the only thing left to her—power.' Because of an unexpected feeling of sympathy with her, she spoke without waiting to be questioned.

'I would like to thank you for letting me go down to dinner last night. It was an unforgettable experience.'

'Um.'

Lady Clementina seemed slightly nonplussed. She had not anticipated gratitude. But she said sharply:

'You did not come in to see me as I asked you to do.'

'I am sorry,' Sylvia replied. 'I forgot.'

'I wonder.' Lady Clementina looked at her reflectively. 'The Duchess informed me that you caused quite a sensation in your mauve dress.'

'It was kind of her Grace to say so,' Sylvia said quietly, 'but I do not think it is quite true.'

Lady Clementina said nothing for a moment, and Lucy, tugging impatiently at Sylvia's hand, cried out:

'May we go now, please, Grandmother? We want to feed the deer and if we don't hurry, by the time we find them it will be time to come back for luncheon.'

'Yes, you can go,' Lady Clementina said wearily. But as Sylvia and Lucy reached the door her voice stopped them. 'Did my son dance with you, Miss Wace?'

It was quite obvious why she made the inquiry. Instinctively Sylvia thought, 'Although she knows nothing, somehow she connects me with Sir Robert's departure.' She was thankful she could answer the question honestly.

'Oh, no,' she replied, 'I came upstairs as you told me very shortly after the dancing had begun.'

Lady Clementina said nothing more and thankfully Sylvia and Lucy sped away, hurrying down the staircase into the hall and through the open door on to the sunlit terrace.

Lucy had already forgotten her grandmother. On her arm she had a little basket filled with bread for the deer and her thoughts were concerned only with them.

'If we could catch a tiny baby deer, Wacey,' she asked, 'don't you think we could keep it in the nursery? We could make it a tiny bed and bring it up all by ourselves.'

'I am afraid it would be unhappy without its mother,' Sylvia replied.

Lucy considered this for a moment. 'I don't think it would,' she said at length. 'I am not unhappy without my mother any longer. But perhaps that is because I have got you.'

Sylvia felt warmed. It was good to be wanted, and it made her very glad to know that this small replica of Sir Robert loved and needed her. Despite everything she could not help feeling happy this morning. Some instinct, prompting in spite of her own inexperience, told her that if Sir Robert had not cared for her, if she had meant absolutely nothing to him, he would not have run away.

They found the deer feeding under the great oak trees.

'You must keep quite still, darling,' Sylvia admonished Lucy. 'If you jump about or talk you will frighten them. Keep still and they will come to you.'

Patience was at last rewarded and one of the does took a piece of bread from Lucy's fingers. She was like a little bit of quicksilver with excitement as they turned their steps towards home. At the end of the park, not far from the drive gates, there was a small grey stone church. As they passed it, Lucy gave an exclamation.

'Look, Wacey, there is Nannie; I can see her black bonnet! Can I run to her?'

Without waiting for Sylvia's permission she sped away, her fat little legs carrying her swiftly through the lychgate and into the churchyard. Sylvia followed and saw Nannie kneeling before a grave. Lucy, running soundlessly across the grass, reached her and flung her arms round her neck. Nannie looked up in surprise; then as she saw who it was her mouth smiled, but she could not hide the tears in her eyes and on her cheeks.

'A deer eated a little piece of bread out of my hand. It did really!'

'I'm so glad, darling.'

Nannie got slowly to her feet as Sylvia reached them.

'Perhaps Nannie doesn't want to be disturbed at this moment, Lucy,' Sylvia said, trying somewhat inadequately to apologise to Nannie for allowing the child to catch her unawares.

Nannie took out her handkerchief and wiped the tears unashamedly from her eyes.

'It is all right, Miss Wace,' she said in the tone of one who understands. 'That the deer ate from her hand is the most important thing in Lucy's life at the moment, and who should grudge her happiness where she may find it?'

'Are you crying, Nannie?' Lucy asked. 'Has someone made you unhappy?'

Nannie shook her head. 'No, dear. I was only remembering another child when he was about your age, that was all.'

'Is he dead now?' Lucy inquired.

Nannie did not answer. She turned to look at the grave by which they were standing.

Sylvia followed her eyes to the tombstone and read:

'In Memory of Sir Edward Sheldon, Sixth Baronet, of Sheldon Hall, who died on February 20th, 1892.'

'Eleven years ago today,' Sylvia said softly.

Nannie nodded.

Sylvia looked at the small bunch of white flowers Nannie had laid at the head of the grave. Almost involuntarily the next words came to her lips.

'Doesn't anyone else remember him?'

Nannie gave her a strange glance.

'I have told you her ladyship can't bear him spoken of,' she said, adding in a lower voice, 'Be careful in front of the child.'

Sylvia took Lucy's hand in hers.

'Who is buried there?' Lucy asked curiously, pointing to the grave, conscious of where the thoughts of the grown-ups were focused, and sensing instinctively that they were trying to distract her attention.

'A little boy Nannie once looked after,' Sylvia replied. 'Now come along, dear, we must get back to the house.'

Nannie went with them and Lucy walked between them, chattering away and telling Nannie over and over again about the deer. As they reached the terrace Lucy dropped a little way behind and Sylvia took the opportunity to ask Nannie the question that had been in her mind for some time.

'Was Sir Robert fond of his brother?'

'He adored him.'

Nannie said the words as if they were dragged from between her lips; and then sharply for her, because Sylvia had never seen her cross or irritable with Lucy, she said, 'Come along, Lucy, and don't dawdle or you'll be late for luncheon.'

In her own bedroom, Sylvia found herself thinking over the events of the morning. How strange everyone was about Sir Edward. But surely it only made matters worse that no one would speak of him? Why not treat the whole matter nromally? It only intensified sorrow to have everyone so repressed about it.

But her thoughts did not linger long with the dead, they were so vitally concerned with the living. Before she went down to luncheon she opened her wardrobe and looked again at the dress she had worn the night before. 'It brought me happiness,' she thought to herself.

Then as she closed the door upon it, she thought of that other woman who had worn it, the woman who had been Sir Robert's wife, and for the first time she knew jealousy. She had half forgotten Mrs. Cuningham, no one ever referred to her at Sheldon Hall, and somehow it was difficult to imagine Sir Robert anything but aloof, a man walking alone, unattached. Yet he had loved his wife. Why else should he have married her? And even though she had deserted him and run away with another man, he had not divorced her. Did not that show love?

Sylvia felt as if a viper had thrust its fangs into her flesh. Another woman had lain against Sir Robert's heart, and he had loved her. With a little cry she covered her eyes with her hands. This, then, was love. A love which tortured and betrayed one. A love which gave one a sudden springing happiness only to supplant it with a depth of misery and depression.

She moved across the room and stood against the window, looking out on to the moorland. Somehow its vast expanse had for the moment the power to bring her comfort; it seemed so much bigger than the bitterness of human jealousy and the trivial pin-pricks of daily existence. It seemed to tell her that it was no use fighting against the inevitable; that one had to be big enough to accept the universe as it is, to raise one's eyes from the ground to the skies.

'Oh, Robert, Robert . . .' Sylvia whispered.

She was startled by a knock at the door and Ethel entered, carrying a silver salver on which lay a letter.

'Mr. Bateson asked me to give you this note, Miss. It was delivered by the carrier about noon today.'

'A note for me,' Sylvia said in some surprise as she took it from the tray.

'Mr. Bateson said he did not know if there was an answer, Miss,' Ethel said, 'but if there was, the carrier will be calling in about three o'clock on his way home.'

'Thank you, Ethel.'

Sylvia was well aware of the curiosity on Ethel's face, but she waited until the door had shut and she was alone again before she studied the envelope. Her name and address were written in a bold hand and it struck her that in all likelihood it was from Captain Davidson. And yet, why should he send such a communication by carrier? she wondered. Surely he would have posted a letter if he was too discreet to send it over by one of his own grooms?

She slit open the envelope and then as she drew out the letter and opened it to read the signature she went pale and sat down suddenly on the chair beside the dressing-table. Looking at the violet-tinted paper she saw it was ridiculous of her to have imagined even for a moment that it might have come from a man; the handwriting was too feminine with its elaborately curling capitals. The paper was also impregnated with perfume, fragrant, but exotic and disturbing. Aware that her hands were trembling, Sylvia turned to the beginning:

My dear Sylvia,

You will doubtless be surprised to hear from me after this long time; but you will, I feel sure, be delighted to know that at the moment I am quite near you. I am in fact staying at the Green Man at Mickledon and am anxious to see you as soon as possible. Will you therefore on receipt of this note let me know when you can come and see me, or, if prefer it, I will come to you. That will be of no inconvenience to me as there is little to do here and I am impatient to see you again.

Your affectionate sister,
Romola,

Sylvia read the letter through twice and then set it down on her dressing-table and sat staring at it. Romola at Mickledon! Romola anxious to see her! It seemed unbelievable.

Sylvia got to her feet and walked up and down the room.

112

How long was it since she had seen her sister? Over six years! She could remember all too vividly the horror of her departure; Romola defying her mother, her voice a little strident in the hushed dimness of the sickroom.

'I am going, Mother, and nothing and nobody shall stop me! I am sick of this place, sick of all this pinching and saving, of being poor and humble and beholden to our relations for charity! I can earn money on the stage; Mr. Groseman has promised me a part at once.'

Sylvia could hear her mother's tones, pleading, begging, beseeching Romola not to shame them, not to throw away her good name for a dubious future.

Romola had laughed.

'What can you offer me here but drudgery and slavery? What is there to do except make the beds and cook the meals? Is that a life you think worth while? Have you forgotten that I am twenty-four? Yes, twenty-four years old and so far not one single man has proposed marriage to me. Shall I tell you why? Because I never meet one, because the only men I ever see are those who happen to serve me in shops. Do you think I want to be an old maid? Don't you realise that I want to be loved and admired, to have a chance of marriage like other girls of my age?'

'You will not marry on the stage.'

Momentarily Mary Wace conquered her weakness to fight desperately with her daughter.

'How do you know?' Romola had retorted. 'And if I don't marry, well, at least I shall have known masculine society, perhaps even a man's love and adoration.'

'Romola!'

Mary Wace had given a cry of horror and collapsed on her pillows.

'Good-bye, Mother. I am sorry you should take it this way, but when I am a success perhaps you won't feel so badly.'

'You have broken my heart, Romola,' Mrs. Wace sobbed.

But Romola had not listened. She had gone from her mother's room on to the passage where Sylvia was waiting, white-faced and stricken.

'Oh, Romola, don't leave us,' Sylvia begged. 'Don't do this terrible thing.'

Romola looked at her younger sister. 'I am putting the whole burden on you, aren't I, my poor darling?' she said. 'You will have to do all the work now and I am sorry about that. But you are young and I am getting old; I can't afford to waste this last chance. Perhaps you, too, will escape one day. Good-bye, baby.'

She bent down and kissed Sylvia; then as if ashamed of the softness in her eyes and the sudden quivering of her mouth she ran down the stairs.

Sylvia controlled her tears to run after her, crying:

'But, Romola, your luggage, your clothes! You've forgotten them!'

Romola turned at the front door.

'Those old rags?' There had been unutterable scorn in her voice, as if she had suffered in this particular respect for too long. 'I've been promised a complete trousseau when I get to London.'

The door slammed behind her and Sylvia realised that she had gone—for ever.

What had happened after that was stamped unforgettably on Sylvia's memory, Mary Wace had sent for Uncle Octavius. He came hurrying with what had seemed an almost lustful eagerness to know every detail of what Romola had said or intended to do. Sylvia had been cross-examined again and again and Uncle Octavius had hinted at dark, sinister, unspeakable things, at horrors which seemed unutterably evil, as his eyes glinted and he licked his dry lips.

'Did Romola tell you where she was meeting this man? Had you any idea of what they did together? Did she mention when you two were alone if he had . . . ? If he touched . . . ? If he . . . ?' Over and over again Uncle Octavius asked the same questions.

While she continued to proclaim her ignorance of Romola's movements, Sylvia was well aware that Uncle Octavius did not believe her. And finally the verdict:

'Your sister is to be thought of as one who is dead, and dead she is to all common decency. Your mother agrees that it is best that her name should never be mentioned. She has brought shame upon us all and particularly upon you, my dear child. You must forget her very existence. Never let the thought of her enter your mind nor her name pass your lips. Your sister Romola is dead. You must forget—erase this—er—memory entirely from your mind.'

But how had it been possible to forget Romola, especially when Sylvia knew that Uncle Octavius was watching her and waiting for her also to show evidence of the same bad blood that apparently had been responsible for her

114

sister's misdeeds? Her bed, standing there empty, the things she had used in her girlhood lying scattered about the house were perpetual reminders; and the years they had spent together, years in which she had looked up to Romola and thought her wonderful, when she had believed her the most beautiful girl in the world were printed indelibly on her heart.

However long she lived, Sylvia would remember Romola with her shining hair and velvet brown eyes, her full red lips and mischievous, dancing smile—Romola, greedy for excitement, hungry for life, who had wanted so much and had chafed at and loathed the cramped, poverty-stricken existence they had to live at Poolbrook; who had always seemed like a wild bird in a cage, imprisoned . . . cramped!

It had not been surprising that Romola had flown away, but Sylvia had been bitterly hurt and wounded when the weeks and months had passed without a word from her, without any indication that she was even alive.

Hope died hard. Sylvia had lain awake at night making excuses for Romola—she was afraid—she was ill—she was too busy. The last excuse presented itself over and over again, and when the years brought only silence she knew it for the truth. Romola was too busy for her family, for the little sister who had almost worshipped her.

Sylvia turned the letter over and over in her hands. What did she feel for Romola now? Had her love died from neglect or would the sight of that lovely laughing face bring it pulsating back to life?

Romola wanted to see her. Why and for what reason after six years of utter indifference? Quite suddenly Sylvia was afraid. Afraid of a sister from whom she had grown apart, afraid of how this visitation from the past might affect her life here at Sheldon Hall.

The letter she held in her hands fell to the floor. The room was warm, but she was shivering. . . .

11

Romola Roma, as she was known on the stage, stood looking out of the window of the Green Man and drummed with her fingers on the window-pane. The road stretching away towards the moors was empty.

She turned with a gesture of impatience and moved across the room to the fire, holding out her thin fingers to the blaze. Then sinking down with a rustle of her silk skirts into a cushioned chair, she lay back as if to relax. Nevertheless every nerve in her body was tense.

'This waiting is intolerable,' she told herself, though she knew quite well that she must have patience if she was to achieve anything. But what exactly did she wish to achieve? That remained to be discovered. Some instinct told her that she was on the right track.

Romola sighed and moved restlessly, bending forward now to cup her face in her hands and stare into the leaping flames. She wondered what Sylvia would be like. Would she have altered much in the passing years? Charlie Cuthbertson's words came back to her with a little stab.

'A smasher, that's what she is! A real smasher! And a figure which would knock a blind man sideways!'

Was it jealousy, Romola wondered, that made her ache a little to think of Sylvia—her little, insignificant sister—being beautiful? She supposed it was. But perhaps it was just envy of someone so much younger than herself. 'I'm thirty,' Romola thought, and felt with her fingers the sharp line of her cheekbones beneath her tired skin. Yes, thirty! It was six years since she had run away from home—run away to grasp what was, she had believed, a golden opportunity and the chance of a lifetime. Did she regret it? Romola considered the question and answered it honestly: Not really. She had suffered; in a way she was suffering now. She had paid fully for her opportunity, paid in heart-break and disappointment, in speedy disillusionment. And yet underneath all this had been the feeling that at least she had escaped the monotony of the dull, soul-killing existence which would have been hers at Poolbrook. She had known love, gaiety, excitement—and pain. And if she had paid for them with tears, with the sapping of her health and the destruction of the standards and ideals in which she had been brought up, was that too high a price to pay?

Romola got to her feet and again crossed to the window. The road was still empty; a flight of birds whirled against the pale sky; there was no other movement. With another gesture of impatience she moved back again towards the fire. Would Sylvia never come? She wanted to see this beauty who had so infatuated Charlie Cuthbertson that he must lean drunkenly at the bar talking of little else. At first Romola had paid no attention to him. She had no time for Charlie except when he could offer her the chance of a job on the stage. At the moment there were more important people to notice, observe and attract. Then a name caught her ears.

'So I toddled across to the station,' Charlie was saying, 'and had a look at the lugggage labels, and there was her name written for all to see. "Miss Sylvia Wace." A pretty name, but, by jingo! not half as pretty as its owner.'

Now Romola was interested.

'What is that you're saying? Who are you talking about, Charlie?'

'Evenin', Romola.' He bowed to her unsteadily, not troubling to remove his top-hat which was set at a jaunty angle on the side of his head.

'Who are you talking about?' Romola repeated.

'I was just telling my friends,' Charlie replied, 'that Cicely Holme, our most beloved and talented star, will have to look to her laurels.'

'Why?' Romola asked the question sharply.

'Well, it was like this,' Charlie answered, obviously only too delighted to tell the story once again to an appreciative audience. 'I was travelling up north on a little business of my own—or rather, shall we say, old Joe's? He sent me up to Newcastle to see a turn that he heard was worth engaging. My God! it was terrible! One of the worst exhibitions I've ever seen! I said to the manager, "Old boy," I said . . .'

'Never mind what you said,' Romola interrupted irritably. 'Where did you see this girl—the one you mentioned just now?'

117

'I'm coming to it, I'm coming to it,' Charlie answered. 'All in good time. I left Newcastle—kicked the dust from off my feet, so to speak—and started home in a snowstorm. The real stuff, I can tell you! Trains were held up, and I found myself stranded for the night at a place called Mickledon. Ghastly little hole, but thank goodness the pub itself wasn't too bad—at least their cellar was tolerable.'

'Yes, yes, get on!' Romola said, tapping her foot.

'What's the hurry?' Charlie asked. 'The night's still young. Well, I was waiting for the London train but who should come into the hotel but a young woman. I took one look at her and I said to myself, "Charlie, my boy, this is where you open your eyes pretty wide." '

'What did she look like?' Romola asked.

'What did she look like?' Charlie put his fingers together, kissed them and threw them out in a wide, demonstrative gesture. 'She had golden hair,' he continued.

'Was it hanging down her back?' one of the men asked.

'Not at that moment,' Charlie replied. 'But I would have given something to see it that way.'

'Go on,' Romola urged.

'She had golden hair, blue eyes—the bluest I've ever seen, and her figure . . .'

'You mentioned that before,' Romola interrupted. 'Was she well-dressed?'

'Exquisite! You can trust your old friend Charlie when it comes to judging clothes. Her dress had cost some poor bloke a pretty penny. I might have guessed, when I looked at it, there was nothing doing as far as I was concerned; yet I reminded myself "nothing venture, nothing have," and up I toddled. She had a child with her and . . .'

'A child?' Romola shouted the words.

'That's what I thought myself at first,' Charlie said. 'And then what do you think I noticed? No wedding ring. I said to myself, "Charlie, old boy, that girl's looking after that little child; it isn't hers. She's too beautiful to have had so much experience." '

'I've always been told it improves a woman,' someone said, and there was a roar of laughter.

Romola kept her eyes on Charlie. 'Go on, tell me more.'

'Well, with characteristic tact I told her that I knew of better employment than looking after a child. I suggested I had just the place waiting for her here in the heart of the great metropolis. And then what do you think?'

'What?' Romola could not help asking the question.

'I was informed—not by her ladyship, of course, but by the proprietor of the pub—that this lovely creature, this Juno on whom I had set my heart, was not for me but for another! And who do you think that was? Our Cicely's backer, the big noise, the unapproachable, the man to whom we all owe a tidy bit one way or another—Sir Robert Sheldon!'

There were exclamations and screams of surprise from those who had been listening.

'My word, you nearly put your foot in it that time, my boy!'

'It will be the sack for you all right if Sir Robert hears of it.'

'You'd better keep mum and not let Cicely know either.'

'What do you take me for?' Charlie asked of no one in particular. 'A fool? I assure you I haven't told another soul.'

'What did you say her name was?' Romola asked in a low voice. 'And how did you learn it?'

'I was just coming to that. I said to myself, "If our Robert's got something like this up at Sheldon Hall, then maybe it's good-bye to Cicely and the whole lot of us. Why should he spend money in London when he's got something like this in the home?" So I nipped across to the station and looked at the label on her luggage.'

'And the name was . . .' Romola asked again.

'Sylvia Wace. A name to conjure with, a name to dream of. "Who is Sylvia, who is she?" That's what I've asked myself continually ever since.'

Romola had turned away. She had found out what she wanted to know. So it was Sylvia—Sylvia, her own sister, who had been going to Sheldon Hall! But why? Why should she be going? How had she got to know anyone like Sir Robert?

Romola thought of the times when she had passed him at the stage door, waiting to escort Cicely, the leading lady, out to supper; seen him in the stage box on the opening night, a strange, inscrutable smile on his face during the whole performance, never clapping, never applauding anything that happened on the stage. And yet they all imagined the show must please him, for it was mainly his money that backed it.

After a six months' run of *The Girl in a Balloon*, Romola had been ill and her place in the second row of the chorus had been filled, so that when she recovered she had found herself forced, as had happened in the past, to join the party of gaudily dressed women who haunted the promenade and bar, hoping and waiting . . . evening after evening. She had been promised that should a vacancy occur in the chorus she should have it; but such promises were not worth much and she was well aware that this last illness had taken even a more devastating toll of her looks than those she had experienced before. She was tired, nervous and run down, and had been forced to part with her last remaining jewels and furs to pay the doctor's bills and keep herself while unable to work. She was honest enough to herself to own how far she was slipping downhill. And yet she somehow believed that her luck would turn and that this weakness which seemed to sap her energy and vitality would pass. Who could be interested for long in a sick woman? The smoky atmosphere of bars and restaurants made her cough. Often everything swam round her so that she found it difficult to laugh and be gay and keep the eyes of some attentive cavalier gazing tenderly into hers. Besides, the competition around her was not to be under-estimated. Every other woman seemed to have something which she had not—youth and freshness which invariably commanded attention or a strong, robust vitality which enabled her to drink as much as the man who accompanied her and to keep him laughing by a coarse, yet hearty humour which had an appeal of its own. Some inbred refinement in Romola kept her from attempting to emulate this type and Nature itself prevented her from competing with the younger women. She looked faded, she knew that. The fashion called for curves, for rounded breasts, well-covered white shoulders, a jaunty posterior, and she found it hard to conceal the thinness of her neck, the boniness of her arms and legs or the sallowness of her skin due to being undernourished.

But Sylvia was a beauty. Charlie's story festered in Romola's mind until at last she could bear it no longer. She must know the truth, must find out where Sylvia was and force her—yes, that was the word Romola used to herself—force her to offer what assistance lay in her power.

Sir Robert Sheldon had not been seen in London for over six weeks. That fact was added to the knowledge which Romola started to accumulate about her sister. He was a strange, moody person at the best of times, but while Cicely Holme had received flowers from him—delivered no doubt by a standing order at the florist's—he had never stayed away so long or been, so Cicely averred—so uncommunicative. Romola was given a lot of information by Cicely's dresser in confidence.

'You take my word for it, dearie,' the woman told her, 'she's just a bit in love with him—really in love, I mean. Of course, he's handsome; and money—he's made of it! All the same, he's not my idea of a nice cup of tea. Too stiff and standoffish-like. Now young Lord Marlow, he's as different from Sir Robert as chalk is from cheese. Comes in here, cheery as you please, makes us all laugh, and whisks Miss Holme off to the Savoy before you can say knife. But there, we all knows that he's nearly bankrupt, so what's the point? And when this show comes off there's got to be someone else to back our young madam. That's as certain as August follows July.'

'Has Sir Robert given her any idea why he hasn't come to London all these weeks?' Romola asked.

The dresser shook her head. 'Not that I've heard of. I don't believe he even says much. She writes to him pages on her violet-scented paper and hardly gets an answer. Can't think why she troubles except, as I said she's half in love with him. But there, she'll get nothing permanent out of it; he's not the marrying sort, you mark my words.'

'Not the marrying sort.' Romola pondered on this. Did that mean that her quiet, pure, innocent sister, whose sense of duty had kept her at Poolbrook to nurse her dying mother, had gone to Sir Robert on any other terms than marriage? The idea seemed impossible to Romola. And yet, supposing Sylvia really was a governess and had taken the post to look after the child, as Charlie had suggested, where had she got her expensive clothes? Romola knew that Charlie would not have been deceived over the price of a dress. He had been too long in the stage business not to be infallible in his judgment of clothes. He was a travelling contracts man and went all over the country in search of talent. When he thought a turn awas good, he brought it to London for an audition. He knew down to the last sixpence, regardless of the value that they put on themselves. He saved his boss a good deal of money in one way and another by his knowledge and earned in consequence a good, fat salary. If Charlie said a woman's dress was expensive, Romola knew it was expensive; and she knew also that a woman's figure would not call forth such a paean of praise unless it was shown to its best advantage.

121

She speculated on every aspect of what she had heard until at last she came to a decision. She had caught a very bad cold by driving home from the theatre in an open carriage with a young man who was too drunk to know whether it was summer or winter. She was in bed for a week and when she got up felt so curiously weak about the legs and head that she could do no more than sit miserably in her small flat, too feeble even to cook herself any food. It was then she made up her mind. She collected together her last remaining treasures, sent them out to the pawnbrokers, and packed her box. When she arrived at Mickledon, she put up at the Green Man and sent a note to Sylvia. She had been half afraid that by some evil mischance the whole story had been untrue—that Sylvia was not at Sheldon Hall and that her whole journey had been taken in vain.

When the carrier who had taken her letter to Sheldon Hall brought back a reply, Romola felt her heart leap with excitement. She tore open the envelope. Sylvia had written only a few lines:

My dear sister,
If it is possible, I will come to see you tomorrow afternoon. If I cannot manage this, then I will come the following day.

Yours,
Sylvia.

That was all and Romola had to wait, still beset by the many questions which had remained unanswered while she was in London. She was turning them over again in her mind when there came a knock at the door.

'Come in.'

The pot-boy opened the door of the sitting-room which Mr. Robb had promised for her exclusive use that afternoon.

'A lady to see you, Ma'am.'

He stood back and Sylvia entered. She wore the black dress and hat which had so aroused Charlie Cuthbertson's admiration. She was excited, too, at the thought of seeing Romola and there was a bright patch of colour in either cheek and her eyes were shining. She stepped forward, smiling, and as she did so Romola knew that Charlie had been right. She felt herself gasp. Yes, Sylvia was a beauty! Then before she could speak, she saw the expression in

122

Sylvia's eyes, the dismay on her face, the sudden fading on her smile.

'Romola! You have been ill! What have you done to yourself?'

Her dismay broke through her shyness, dispersing it immediately. She held out her hands and impulsively the sisters kissed each other.

'Oh, Romola, it is lovely to see you again!'

That, indeed, was genuine enough. Romola knew in that moment that Sylvia had not really changed; she was still the little sister who loved her and admired her beyond all else.

And with Sylvia, all her resentment, all the hurt of the years passed in silence slipped away when she saw Romola's thin, ravaged face, the deep hollows in her cheeks, the dark lines under her eyes. The sparkling, gay Romola had gone. This was a much older woman—a woman who had suffered and looked frail and ill. Sylvia was instantly ashamed of herself for ever having harboured any feeling of unkindness towards her sister.

'Sit down,' she suggested. 'Tell me about yourself. Why are you here, and what has happened to you all these years? And oh, Romola, why do you look so ill?'

'I have been ill,' Romola replied; and then quickly, as if she took her cue, she added, 'That is why I have come north. The doctors thought the air would do me good. It was only when I got here that I heard you were a near neighbour. At first I could hardly believe it was true, and then I sat down and wrote to you, hoping and praying I should at last see the little sister I had loved so much.'

'Romola, why didn't you write before? Why didn't you let me know where you were?'

Romola made a gesture. 'My dear,' she said softly, 'I felt I hadn't the right. You were so young, so innocent. The least I could do was to leave you in peace, safe in the security of our home.'

Sylvia looked at her quickly. Somehow the words did not ring quite true.

'But, Romola, I nearly went mad, wondering what had happened to you, believing always believing that you would write to me if not to Mother.' Sylvia sighed. 'She never mentioned it, but I think she hoped to hear. She is dead, Romola. I couldn't let you know because I did not know your address. She died at the beginning of the year.'

'Good heavens! I thought she must have died ages ago,'

Romola exclaimed; then realised that she had spoken unfeelingly and her voice softened. 'I mean, of course, that I hoped she would for her own sake—she was incurable, I knew that, and in constant pain. It must have been a happy release. I'm sorry, I would have liked to see her again.'

'We were not so very far away from London if that is where you were,' Sylvia suggested.

Romola turned away her face. 'If you only knew how often I considered coming home,' she said, 'and then I remembered that I had burnt my boats and I felt the door would be closed against me.'

'It would not have been as long as I was there, you must have known that.'

'I tried to protect you, darling. You see, I still thought of you as a little girl.'

'I'm twenty-one, a grown-up and responsible person.'

'That is obvious.' Romola tried to smile. 'And how tell me about yourself. What are you doing at Sheldon Hall?'

'I'm governess to Sir Robert Sheldon's daughter.'

'I had no idea he had any children.'

'Nor had most people,' Sylvia replied; and proceeded to tell the story of all that had happened after her mother's death.

Romola sat listening, interspersing a question here and there, watching Sylvia's face, her thin fingers tightly locked together in her lap.

'And I'm happy; yes, very happy,' Sylvia ended. 'Lady Clementina is rather frightening, and she is insatiably curious. I told her the truth, of course—that I was coming to meet you this afternoon. The only thing I did not tell her was that you had been on the stage. I thought she might be shocked.'

'I'm glad you didn't tell her that,' Romola said. 'I was hoping very much that somehow you could persuade her and Sir Robert to let me come and stay at Sheldon Hall . . .' She saw the surprise on Sylvia's face and noticed that her expression of surprise deepened to one of dismay. 'You don't think it is possible?' Her voice was harsh.

'I don't know . . . I have never thought of it,' Sylvia stammered. 'I don't know what Lady Clementina would say. Where I am concerned she expects me to be very circumspect, very much a governess. After all, I am in charge of the forming of Lucy's character.'

Romola's lips tightened. 'I am sure you do that admirably,' she said. 'You always were rather a little prig,

124

even as a child. Do you remember how you wouldn't steal the plums out of the next-door garden because you thought God wouldn't like it?'

'Now you are cross with me,' Sylvia said unhappily. 'Romola, dear, of course I want you to come and stay at Sheldon Hall. I want it more than anything, but I just don't see how it can be managed.'

Romola got to her feet. 'I understand. I will just stay here alone. I'm ill and the doctors don't think I have got long to live anyway. I just wanted to be with you—with the only person I ever loved and who I believed loved me. I have been through a very difficult, sad time. But I understand that now you have no place for me in your life.'

Romola walked towards the window, her head was turned from Sylvia and her thin shoulders shook a little. Sylvia jumped impulsively to her feet.

'Don't, Romola! Don't say things like that! They are not true! Darling, I will do anything, anything you want. I will ask Lady Clementina. If she says no, I can't help it; but I will ask her. I will ask her right away, as soon as I get back.'

'You will?' Romola turned round eagerly and she was smiling. 'Now listen, Sylvia, you must be very sensible about this. You mustn't say one word about the stage; in fact, we must think of a story, one that is completely convincing. And what is more, we will make it so damned respectable that even Lady Clementina will swallow it.'

'Oh, Romola!' Sylvia ejaculated, half shocked and at the same time laughing.

This was the Romola she knew—dashing, impetuous, daring, and so fascinating that she held her spellbound.

12

Romola ran into Sylvia's bedroom and slammed the door behind her. She placed the tips of her fingers together with a mock gesture of piety.

'Behold,' she cried, 'the widow of the late lamented

Reverend Theosophilus Brent, missionary in Darkest Africa! Do I look the part?'

Sylvia jumped up nervously from the chair in which she had been sitting. 'Hush, Romola,' she said, 'don't talk too loud. Someone might hear you.'

'Don't tell me that anyone is as interested in me as all that,' Romola answered mockingly. All the same, she lowered her voice.

'What happened? What did Lady Clementina say?' Sylvia asked.

'My dear, she was charming,' Romola replied. 'She would like me to stay here with my young sister while I get over the tragic sorrow which has shattered my life. I wish you had heard me recount my life story! It was the best performance I have ever given in my life.'

'Oh, Romola, I am so pleased you are to stay here. But you must be careful. Suppose you forget to keep it up! I was terrified when I was telling Lady Clementina about you because I am certain she thought I was lying.'

'She thought I was telling the truth all right,' Romola said with a laugh. Then looking round the room she exclaimed, 'Well, I must say you make yourself very comfortable. This is a nice room.'

'Yes, isn't it?' Sylvia agreed. 'Lucy's is next door and beyond hers the nursery where we sit.'

'Nursery?' Romola said, raising her eyebrows a little. 'And what about when the redoubtable Sir Robert is at home?'

'Sometimes we go down to the dining-room for luncheon,' Sylvia answered, 'if he is alone; but we always sit upstairs.'

Romola looked at her sister quizzically. 'Don't tell me, darling, that you have been missing your opportunities all these weeks.'

'What do you mean?' Sylvia asked.

'Now, don't be so innocent,' Romola admonished. 'You and Sir Robert alone in this big, lonely house, his mother very conveniently safe upstairs in her bedroom. Now come on, tell me the truth.'

'There is nothing to tell,' Sylvia said quietly, but the colour flamed in her cheeks.

Romola looked at her. 'Then you are either a fool or a liar.'

Sylvia gave an exclamation. 'Really, Romola!'

'I'm only teasing you,' Romola said quickly. 'I might

126

have guessed that you would behave well under any circumstances. Now if I had been here alone in this dismal place all this time, I imagine the story would have already ended very differently.'

'Oh, Romola, you will be careful, won't you?' Sylvia pleaded. 'If you did anything, however slight, which offended Lady Clementina, she would turn us both out. She is very strange about her son—in fact, she made it quite clear to me that if anyone employed by her so much as looked at him it would mean instant dismissal.'

'So you have been warned off the grass, have you?' Romola said. She laughed unpleasantly and threw herself down into the armchair in front of the fire. 'Sylvia, I believe I am going to enjoy myself here. I like the setting. Lady Clementina—obviously the bad fairy; yourself—the shrinking heroine; and Sir Robert, needless to say, the hero. And I—what part do you think I play?'

Sylvia made no reply, so Romola went on, 'I think it is "a *femme fatale*," don't you?—the woman with a past who lures the manly hero from the path of virtue.'

'Romola!' Sylvia's voice held a note of distress which for a moment seemed to soften her sister.

'Darling, am I being a pig to you?' she asked. 'I promise you that I will behave well and not disgrace you. It is just the relief of knowing where I shall lay my head tonight and where the next meal will come from.'

Impulsively Sylvia crossed the room and knelt down beside her sister's chair. 'Has it really been as bad as that?' she asked. 'Why didn't you come home? Why didn't you write to me?—I would have helped you somehow, you know I would.'

Romola smiled. 'I believe you would, but I would rather have starved than admit I was defeated. I very nearly did at times, but at others—well, to put it frankly, I had a good time! Not that good is a well chosen word—perhaps gay or hectic is better.'

'Poor Romola.' Sylvia spoke softly.

'Don't pity me.' Romola said the words almost harshly. 'I have at least learnt one thing and that is, that people pay for being stupid, not for being wicked. Oh no, my dear, the wicked flourish like a green bay tree; it is the stupid who suffer, bitterly and with broken hearts.'

There was so much unhappiness in Romola's voice that Sylvia reached out her arms and put them round her sister as if she would protect her. Romola pushed her away. 'I told you not to be sorry for me. Besides, you forget, as the widow of the late lamented Theosophilus I have no past, only the memories of a life devoted to saving heathen souls and covering their nakedness with cotton shifts made by well-meaning virgins.' She jumped up from the chair to walk across the room and peer into the mirror over the dressing-table, 'Heavens! I look a sight. I am not surprised Lady Clementina believed my story. My best friend wouldn't recognise me at the moment.' She pulled off her grey hat which, shorn of the brilliant crimson feathers which had decorated it only a few hours ago, looked sadly out of date. 'Am I likely to see her ladyship again tonight?'

Sylvia shook her head. 'She might send for you, but I don't think it is at all probable.'

'In which case,' Romola said, 'I can put some rouge on my cheeks. I had no idea how sallow I was until I saw you.'

'You used to have such a lovely natural colour.'

Romola laughed without humour. 'Evil living corrupts good complexions,' she misquoted. 'And now show me the way to my room.'

'I shall have to ask the housekeeper. If you will wait here, I will slip down to her room to inquire.'

Left alone, Romola moved restlessly round Sylvia's bedroom. Then opening the wardrobe she examined the clothes hanging there, finally pursing her lips into a suppressed whistle as she saw the mauve evening dress. She took it down from its hanger and holding it up to her shoulders looked at herself in the mirror; then with a little laugh she hung it up again and closed the wardrobe door. She had no sooner done this than the communicating door with Lucy's room opened and Lucy and Nannie stood in the doorway, both wearing their outdoor clothes.

'Oh, Wacey . . .' Lucy began. Romola turned round and for a moment they all stood looking at each other. Nannie spoke first.

'I beg your pardon,' she said politely. 'I thought Miss Wace was here.'

'I am Miss Wace's sister,' Romola explained, moving forward and holding out her hand. 'You must be Nannie, she told me about you. And you must be Lucy, of course. She has told me a lot about you.'

'I didn't know Wacey had a sister,' Lucy exclaimed, staring at Romola with large serious eyes.

'Well, she has, and I am she,' Romola said. 'But I hadn't

seen her for a very long time. Do you know, I can remember your Wacey when she was just the same age as you.'

She spoke ingratiatingly, eager to make friends with the child, but Lucy having regarded her steadily for a few moments moved backwards and slipped her hand in Nannie's.

'Shall we go and take my clothes off, Nannie,' she asked, 'so that I shall be ready when Wacey comes back?'

'That is a good idea,' Nannie replied. 'Perhaps you will tell Miss Wace when she comes up, Madam, that we are in the next room.'

'I will tell her,' Romola replied shortly.

She had the curious feeling when she was alone again that Nannie and Lucy had both refused her advances. She could not quite explain it even to herself, but she turned to the mirror again scowling and noted with an added sense of irritation the lines which etched themselves sharply from nose to mouth as her lips tightened.

The door was opened. 'You are having the room near mine,' Sylvia said excitedly. 'It is a lovely room, which gets all the morning sun. Come and look at it.'

Romola picked up her hat. As she followed Sylvia from the room she caught sight of her own reflection in the long mirror in the wardrobe door and what she saw filled her with dismay.

The room had been aptly described by Sylvia. It was lovely. The watered silk paper with a flowering dado which matched the shiny chintz curtains gave an impression of spring-like freshness which was not dispelled by the big chintz-hung four-poster bed or by the polished walnut furniture.

'You will soon get well here,' Sylvia said. 'Oh, Romola, I am glad to have you, you know that.'

She spoke seriously and so sincerely that Romola was touched. She looked out of the window on to the green lawns below them. 'Don't be too glad, Sylvia.'

'Why not?'

'I don't know,' Romola replied. 'I don't know why I said that. I want you to be glad, of course. I was just thinking that you have taken me so confidently on trust. How do you know after all these years that I haven't changed, that I am the same Romola that you used to know?'

'But, of course, you are,' Sylvia said looking bewildered. 'Why, you have hardly changed at all except that you have got so thin and ill-looking. When you feel well enough to laugh again and your eyes begin to sparkle as they used to do, I shall forget that we have ever been separated. Then you will be just as you were when you used to come running in from school to tell me of something exciting that had happened to you. You don't know how quiet the house was when you weren't in it.'

'And when I went away?' Romola asked.

'Then the house was very, very quiet,' Sylvia replied.

For a moment the two sisters looked at each other. Romola's face was suddenly haggard and it seemed as if she would speak, that some tension within herself would break. Her eyes dropped; she looked away from Sylvia and her glance wandered round the room with its luxurious furnishings; she stared at the soft comfortable bed, at the delicate china on the wash-stand, at the deep, soft pile of rose-tinted carpet which covered the floor.

'Why are we harrowing ourselves by these sentimental memories?' she asked, and her voice was sharp. 'Let us forget the years between and enjoy ourselves.' She stretched her arms above her head. 'Heavens! If you only knew how tired I am!'

Sylvia was silent for a moment. She knew that some barrier which she sensed but did not understand still stood between them, unsurmounted and unconquered. She reminded herself that Romola was racked with nerves, an ill woman, and that whatever happened she must be kind to her.

'Why don't you go to bed, darling?' she suggested. 'I will order you some supper and you can get a really good night's rest and feel better tomorrow.'

'It is a wonderful idea,' Romola approved.

'I can hear your boxes coming up now,' Sylvia said as she moved toward the door. 'I will unpack for you and you can slip into bed. If you would like a bath, there is one opposite—you and I will be sharing the same bathroom.'

Romola sat down on the chair by the dressing-table and watched her luggage being carried in by two footmen. When the trunks with their black, rounded tops had been set down and unstrapped, Ethel knocked on the door.

'Shall I unpack for Madam?'

Sylvia shook her head. 'No, thank you, Ethel. I would rather do it for her, and it gives us a chance of talking to each other. Tell them downstairs that Mrs. Brent will have her supper in bed, and let me know when Miss Lucy comes back.'

'Very good, Miss,' Ethel said conventionally.

Romola gave an exclamation. 'Oh dear, I quite forgot. Lucy came in with Nannie while you were downstairs.'

'Oh, Romola, and you didn't tell me!' Sylvia got to her feet quickly. 'I won't be a moment, darling. I must run along and see to Lucy at once.' She reached the door and then looked back with her hand on the handle. 'Don't let anyone unpack for you but me,' she said in a low voice. 'If you have anything which might seem to be out of keeping with your part as a clergyman's wife, it must be locked up, otherwise Lady Clementina will hear about it.' She spoke with an air of desperate earnestness.

Romola gave a shout of laughter. 'Good Lord, what a house!'

Sylvia slipped through the door and closed it behind her. As she hurried down the passage, she half resented the scorn and mockery in Romola's voice. She almost found herself making excuses for Lady Clementina's curiosity. If she wished to know more about those who lived under her roof, why shouldn't she? Then hastily she reproached herself for disloyalty to her sister. 'She is very ill,' she thought; 'none of us is quite normal when we are ill.'

She found Lucy in the nursery undressed, ready for bed and having her supper of milk and biscuits.

'Oh, Wacey, I thought you were never coming,' Lucy said reproachfully.

'I'm sorry, darling,' Sylvia said. 'Nobody told me that you were here.'

'I asked your sister to inform you that we had returned,' Nannie said stiffly, 'but she must have forgotten.'

'I am afraid she did,' Sylvia explained. 'You see, she has been very ill and it is easy for us not to remember things then.'

'Has she gone now?' Lucy asked hopefully.

'No, darling, she is going to stay with us for a little while. Your grandmother has invited her.'

Lucy did not say anything for a moment, and then as Sylvia started to ask how she had enjoyed the afternoon, Lucy said firmly and distinctly, 'I don't like her.'

'Don't like whom?' Sylvia asked, thinking Lucy referred to someone she had met that afternoon.

'That lady who says she is your sister,' Lucy said.

'Now, Lucy, that is very unkind,' Nannie interposed. 'It is very nice for Miss Wace to have her sister here. You

131

shouldn't say things like that about people you have only just met.'

'But I don't like her,' Lucy said obstinately.

She had never been a shy child and Sylvia thought, a little apprehensively, she was growing somewhat spoiled lately and had started to have very decided opinions of her own. Sometimes when she was particularly obstinate in her convictions there was a distinct resemblance both to her father and to her grandmother. Sylvia had long ago decided that it was best to ignore her on these occasions, and now she smiled at Nannie over Lucy's head.

'You will change your mind in the morning,' she said. 'I think it is time for bed, don't you, Nannie?'

'I will just clean Lucy's teeth,' Nannie said, fetching a toothbrush and glass. 'She has said her prayers already.'

Lucy having collected the golliwog let Sylvia lead her into the bedroom. As she snuggled down into her small bed she stretched out her arms to hug Sylvia.

'I missed you today, Wacey dear. I wish you had come with us. There was the darlingest little kitten. I wanted it for my very own, but Nannie said it was too young to leave its mummy.'

'Perhaps you will be able to have it when it is older,' Sylvia said.

'I thought you would say that,' Lucy smiled. 'Oh, Wacey, I do love you, but I don't like that woman. I hope she won't stay long.'

Sylvia kissed the child and then went through to her own room. The thought flashed unbidden to her mind that something within herself echoed Lucy's wish. Then sternly she dismissed the idea, angry with herself for thinking it even for a moment. Of course, she was glad to have Romola here, very, very glad. She would look after her and make her welcome. Romola had been unhappy and she would make up to her for that. Good food, plenty of fresh air and she would be better within a few weeks. And then, when she was bored, she could go back to her old life well and strong—that was the main thing, that she should be well and strong.

A little later she went along the passage and knocked on Romola's door. To her surprise when she turned the handle she found the door was locked.

'Who is it?'

Romola's voice coming to her from within sounded harsh and unnecessarily sharp.

'It is I—Sylvia.'

'That is all right then.'

The key was turned and the door opened. Sylvia entered and stood open-mouthed. The room was strewn with clothes. It looked as if Romola had pulled out all her dresses quickly one after another and strewn them down higgledy-piggledy on the chairs and on the floor. They lay everywhere, great splashes of colour—peacock blue, pigeon's blood crimson, apple green—and with them waves of white frilled petticoats and underwear. Sylvia stood speechless and Romola laughed.

'Don't look so astonished,' she said. 'I am trying to find something to wear and there is nothing at all suitable for the widowed Mrs. Brent.'

'Romola,' Sylvia exclaimed, 'I have never seen so many things! How could you afford them all?'

'Oh, I picked them up from time to time,' Romola said airily. 'Many of them are from the shows in which I appeared; the . . . the chorus often have to provide their own clothes.'

'Oh, I see,' Sylvia said, but at the same time she wondered. She had always heard that chorus girls were very badly paid. 'Romola, this is lovely!' She picked up a red flimsy silk dress from off the bed. It seemed to her to be cut daringly low, but the skirt billowed out in great frothy frills.

'Yes, I had that for a very special party,' Romola said. 'It was given by Lord Carstairs, a delightful young man. He was—well, very kind to me at one time.'

'And you bought this dress for a party given by him?' Sylvia asked. 'It must have cost you a lot of money.'

'You don't know what a clever shopper I am!' Romola smiled.

Sylvia put down the dress and picked up another. This was of apple-green chiffon; the skirt was embroidered with tiny silver roses and there were clusters of them on the top of each puff sleeve.

'This is lovely, too,' she said; then picked up another and yet another. 'But, Romola, they are all evening dresses. What have you done with all your day clothes?'

'I haven't got many,' Romola said. 'You will find them in that box over there. You see, I used to go out mostly in the evening; I was always sleeping in the day-time.'

'Yes, of course,' Sylvia replied, and then added quickly, 'We must put these away again and lock them up. Lady

Clementina would hardly expect you to be wearing such dresses in Africa.'

Romola laughed. 'I would like to see her face if I came down in them,' she said.

'I told you how she found out about my dresses,' Sylvia said. 'You must be careful. She gets to know everything sooner or later.'

'Well, pack them away then,' Romola commanded; 'and you had better put the petticoats with them.'

'They are pretty, too,' Sylvia said, holding up one which was trimmed with frilly lace and slotted through with black velvet ribbons. 'What a lot of work there is in this,' she added. 'It seems almost a pity to wear it under one's dress where it isn't seen.'

'Yes, it does, doesn't it?' Romola said drily.

Sylvia folded it neatly and put it away in the trunk, and gradually she put back the other things; the shoes which matched the gowns; the evening wraps, all in brilliant colours and trimmed with shining sequins or brightly coloured feathers.

'Where did you live in London?' she asked suddenly.

'Oh, all sorts of places,' Romola replied. She started to undress and, draped now in a filmy dressing-gown of lace and satin, stood looking down at Sylvia's bent head as she placed the garments neatly folded into the boxes. 'I think,' she said at length, 'that it would be wiser if we made a pact, you and I.'

'What sort of a pact?' Sylvia asked, looking up.

'Not to talk about my past.'

'Oh, Romola, you don't think I was prying or being inquisitive, do you?'

'No, of course not. At the same time I would rather not talk about it. Let us forget all about it. Let us pretend that I really have been abroad, that I really have had a husband and lost him and that I have lived a good life for six years.'

Sylvia said nothing. There was something in Romola's face which revealed to her all too clearly what her heart shrank from knowing.

'Yes, let us forget the past,' she said quickly. 'That is an excellent pact, a sensible one.'

'And give me your word, too,' Romola said, 'that whatever happens you will never tell anyone the truth about me—not unless I give you permission. Do you promise?'

'But, of course, I promise,' Sylvia said quickly. 'Why should I want to tell anyone things about you.'

'One never knows,' Romola said lightly. She walked across the room and opened a drawer of her dressing-table; then with a faint mocking smile she looked over her soulder at her sister. 'And now,' she said, 'I am really going to shock you, so be prepared. I am going to smoke a cigarette.'

Sylvia got to her feet. 'You smoke? she said.

'Yes,' Romola answered, 'I smoke. Are you shocked?'

'No, of course I am not,' Sylvia answered. 'But don't smoke here, Romola, it isn't safe. Somebody will smell the smoke and Lady Clementina will be told.'

'It soothes my nerves,' Romola argued.

'Jump into bed and I will get you something from Nannie,' Sylvia suggested. 'She has got a medicine cupboard full of all sorts of things. She will give you a little bromide or some soothing syrup. That is better than cigarettes, it is really.'

'This place is exactly like a girls' school,' Romola said half irritably, but she put the box of cigarettes back in her drawer and let Sylvia go in search of some sedative from Nannie.

Later in the evening, when Sylvia had finished her dinner, she came along to find Romola tucked up in bed having eaten her supper. She put some more coal on the fire and sat down beside her.

'I am not going to stay long,' she said. 'You must go to sleep early and then you will feel better tomorrow.' She looked across the bed and thought that already Romola was looking better. Her brown hair, loosened against the pillow, framed her face and made it seem less sharp and haggard then it had earlier in the day.

'I am so comfortable,' Romola said, 'I almost wish I could die.'

'What nonsense you talk,' Sylvia said. 'And it is very unlike you, Romola; you used to be ready to challenge anything. I always felt half alive and listless beside your vitality.'

'You should try the life I have led,' Romola said, and then added quickly, 'In darkest Africa, of course.'

Sylvia looked across the room to see if the door was shut. 'Do you know anything about Africa?' she asked.

'Precious little.'

135

'We must look tomorrow to see if there is a book in the library about it. We had better learn all we can. It would be awful if someone came here who really knew and we were caught out.' She looked away from her sister into the fire. 'I wish we didn't have to lie,' she continued. 'As you know, I am afraid of Lady Clementina. But although in some ways she seems rather a tyrant, I hate lying to her. Afterall, I am in this house to set a good example to Lucy.'

'Which I am sure you do admirably,' Romola said, 'Well, what about Sir Robert? Does he set a good example up here at his country estate?'

'I am sure he does,' Sylvia answered.

'He keeps his wild oats for London, I suppose,' Romola suggested dryly.

'What do you mean?'

'Well, he is known as rather a gay lad in Town.'

'In what way?'

Romola looked across at her sister's raised face.

'You are very interested.'

'But naturally,' Sylvia said quietly. 'He is my employer. You are hinting that he has a side to his character that I haven't seen. Have you any reason to believe that what you are saying is true?'

'Every reason,' Romola retorted coolly. 'But I certainly won't besmirch your pure little ears with it. I will keep what I know to myself.'

Sylvia looked away, struggling with her pride and her curiosity. Then at last she said quietly, 'Perhaps you are right.'

'I am sure I am.' Romola said. 'And now I think I will go to sleep. Some day perhaps I will tell you how I came to hear you were staying in this place.'

'Tell me now,' Sylvia pleaded, unable to resist the prompting of her own heart.

Romola shook her head. 'It is too long a story. Besides, we have agreed to forget my past.' She shut her eyes. For a moment or two Sylvia stood irresolutely by the bed, but as she started to tip-toe out of the room believing her sister to be asleep, Romola opened her eyes again. 'There is an old maxim which says, "Always keep something up your sleeve." I am keeping a bit up mine, just in case. One never knows!'

She shut her eyes once more and Sylvia left her.

13

'Such excitement, Miss!'

This morning, Ethel did not wait to see if Sylvia was awake. She pulled back the curtains and talked at the same time.

'Why, what is happening?' Sylvia asked.

She was not asleep when Ethel came to call her. After a restless night, sleep left her early in the morning and she had been thinking of Sir Robert, thinking of him with an intensity which somehow made her believe that he was thinking of her. She had dreamt of him in the night and in her dreams her lips had felt once again that strange, compelling, passionate kiss.

'Sir Robert's coming home,' Ethel announced dramatically.

Sylvia felt the news was no surprise, it seemed the natural sequel to her dream.

'When?' she asked, sitting up in bed.

'Today, Miss. And he's bringing a big party back with him, too.'

'A big party?'

'Yes, Miss. Her ladyship got the letter this morning. She sent for Mr. Bateson and after that things started to hum, I can tell you. Mr. Bateson says it's years since the house will have been so full. They're even opening the guest rooms on the second floor.'

'Who are these people Sir Robert is bringing?' Sylvia asked, aware that she should not encourage gossip from Ethel, yet unable to check her own curiosity.

'I don't know, Miss. I don't expect her ladyship knows either, or else she didn't tell Mr. Bateson. It will be exciting, though, won't it, Miss, having so many people here? Grand ladies, I shouldn't wonder.'

Sylvia said nothing. The glamour and happiness of her dream faded away from her and she came back to reality. Sir Robert had his own friends, his own life; she had no real part in it. Suddenly she felt very alone and very defenceless. What was she to him, and what could he be to her? Her heart had ached for the sight of him, yet now that he was coming back he was returning not to her but to the splendour of his home, and he was bringing his own friends to fill it.

She realised that Ethel was waiting, looking at her with an almost god-like devotion, hoping for her comments. Sylvia made an effort.

'I am sure it will all be very exciting, Ethel. Perhaps we shall be able to catch a glimpse of Sir Robert's guests in the distance, and that will be very interesting.'

To her own ears her voice sounded false, but Ethel seemed satisfied.

'I've told Mrs Brent, Miss, and she's worrying that she won't have enough things to wear. But you've got your lovely mauve dress, so you'll be all right.'

The door shut behind Ethel. Sylvia sighed. So Romola was expecting to participate in the entertainment, to take her place in the house party! She would soon be disillusioned; she would soon learn that she would be privileged if she was allowed to be a spectator, let alone to mix with Sir Robert's guests. Sylvia could recall all too vividly the humiliations of the one evening when she had been invited to the dinner party downstairs. At the time every other thought had been swept away by the emotions she had experienced at Sir Robert's kiss and the wonder and happiness of being in his arms; but now other memories returned and she could recall such separate and subtle humiliation. The Duchess's raised eyebrows; the curious and then disdainful glances of the other women when they realised that she was only Lucy's governess; the way they conveyed without comment that they considered her strangely and unexpectedly overdressed for such a part. She thought of Captain Davidson and his suggestion that she should meet him clandestinely; of being told to retire when the dancing started; Bateson's words to her in the hall; her own sense of being set apart and treated as an inferior. Was it likely she could forget all this or for one moment believe it enjoyable? Romola would learn the same lesson if she had social aspirations at Sheldon Hall.

Getting out of bed Sylvia walked towards the window. As always the beauty of the landscape stretching away to a blue horizon had its power to touch her with healing hands. 'I could be really happy here if . . .' She could not complete the sentence even to herself and was afraid of the magnitude of her own desire. She wanted Sir Robert, that was the truth; wanted him to be hers—hers alone; wanted to know herself beloved, even as she loved him.

Slipping on her dressing-gown, Sylvia went along the passage to Romola's room. To her surprise, Romola was already out of bed and sitting at the dressing-table, peering at her face in the big gilded mirror.

'You've heard the news?' she asked gaily as Sylvia entered the room.

'Yes, Ethel told me, and she told me, too, that you were worried about what to wear.'

'Who wouldn't be? Romola asked. 'I wonder who Sir Robert is bringing. Have you any idea?'

'None at all,' Sylvia answered. 'But, Romola, surely you don't think that you and I will have anything to do with the house party? Lady Clementina would not think of allowing such a thing.'

Romola laughed. 'Dear Sylvia, how easily you are always defeated. Leave things to me.'

'What do you mean?' Sylvia asked. 'What are you going to do?'

'I have my plans,' Romola answered, 'and I shall not tell them to you in advance. You never were a good strategist. I was always the convincing liar of the family.'

Sylvia looked at her in dismay. 'Romola, do be careful,' she begged. 'If you do anything at all rash, we shall both have to leave.'

'And you would hate that, my dear little sister, wouldn't you?' Romola teased. 'And not only because you like looking after Lucy.'

Sylvia felt her colour rising at the implication in Romola's words. 'What do do you mean?' she asked.

'You know quite well what I mean,' Romola retorted. 'I have just told you that you never were good at lying. My dear, I have known for a long time—in fact ever since I came here, that you were in love with Sir Robert. Your face gives you away every time his name is mentioned—apart from the fact that you can't control your voice when you talk about him.'

Sylvia put her hands up to her cheeks. This was unexpected.

'Oh, Romola,' she said desperately.

Romola threw back her head and laughed. 'Let us hope that Lady Clementina is getting a bit blind in her old age, otherwise you will have given yourself away to her long ago.'

'I don't know what to say,' Sylvia confessed.

'Well, I should tell the truth and admit—at least to me—that you are madly in love with him,' Romola suggested.

Sylvia got to her feet and moved agitatedly across the room. 'I don't know that I am . . . it is so difficult . . . he is strange, aloof . . . and yet . . .'

'And yet?' Romola prompted.

Sylvia could not be drawn any further. That moment in the nursery was, she thought, her own secret, her very own. She could not speak of it to anyone, not even to Romola.

'Wait until you see him,' she finished lamely.

'You always were a fool, Sylvia,' Romola said softly. 'I was the one who made the most of my opportunities.' She returned to the contemplation of her own face in the mirror. 'I am looking better,' she said.

Sylvia forced herself to concentrate on her sister. 'But, of course, you are, darling. You look a different person since you came here.'

That was indeed the truth. The rest and good food at Sheldon Hall had transformed Romola in three weeks from a tired, faded, emaciated woman into a girl, young, pretty and sparkling. Her eyes were brighter, her hair had recovered much of its sheen, and her figure was beginning to fill out a little; the deep hollows in the base of her neck and the lines which had been etched sharply from nose to mouth had vanished. She laughed more easily and some of the bitterness had gone from her voice. It seemed to Sylvia that at times there was even an echo of the Romola who with eagerness and excitement had once found life a thrilling, absorbing and lovely adventure.

'Yes, I look better,' Romola repeated; 'but there is plenty of room for improvement. At the moment you still remain the beauty of the family.'

She made the compliment sound reproachful, and Sylvia said softly:

'Of course I am not. You were always lovely, Romola, and it is only ill-health that has made you believe anything else.'

Romola smiled. 'You were always generous in your affections, Sylvia,' she said. 'I believe you would really like me to be happy.'

'You know I would,' Sylvia said solemnly. 'I want your happpiness more than anything in the world.'

Romola looked at her and again it seemed to Sylvia that a mocking expression crossed her face.

'Even if it affected your own?' she asked. 'Remember I left you once to bear the brunt of our family misfortunes while I escaped.'

'I never reproached you for that,' Sylvia said quickly 'not even in my heart. You had the opportunity. If the position had been reversed, I am quite certain that I should have gone and left you.'

'I wonder,' Romola said. 'I have a feeling that you would have been self-sacrificing. But don't let us argue about that now; let us hope that the future will hold something better for both of us.'

'I hope so, too,' Sylvia said.

'"God helps those who help themselves,"' Romola said with a sharp change of tone: 'you will have to buck up and be a bit more alive to your opportunities, Sylvia. It is no use lying down weakly and expecting life to hand you things on a plate. It doesn't, you know. You have to fight and grasp and kick for what you want; even then you don't always get it.'

Sylvia smiled. 'I doubt my being able to do that,' she said.

'No, that isn't your type,' Romola stretched her arms above her head. 'Mostly money . . . power, position, security . . . again money. Money can guy those things. Nothing else matters.'

'Not even love?' Sylvia asked softly.

'Love!' Romola put a wealth of scorn into her voice. 'I've seen too much of what is called "love" to consider it at all. You can buy love with money—the sort of love that most people understand anyway. Love without money is only slavery or worse.'

'Don't, Romola.' Sylvia walked across to her sister and put her arm round her shoulders. 'I know you have suffered, darling, but don't let it make you bitter. One day you will find someone whom you will love and who will love you, and then you will think differently.'

Almost roughly, Romola pushed Sylvia's arm aside. 'I know too much about love to listen to such nonsense. It is money I want, and money I mean to have.'

There was something ugly in her expression and Sylvia looked away from her and turned towards the door. 'It is time for Lucy to be getting up,' she said. 'I will see you at breakfast.'

Romola did not answer and Sylvia closed the door quietly behind her, feeling as if she had escaped from something ominous and rather beastly. 'I must be kind to Romola,' she thought, and she went along the passage. 'She must have suffered so terribly. I suppose that the man she loved let her down.' And yet although she tried to think kindly of Romola, she was afraid of that brooding look; Romola was planning something and the vague hints that she had thrown out made Sylvia uneasy and troubled.

As the day advanced there was no doubt that the news of Sir Robert's return had thrown the whole place into a turmoil. Housemaids scurried to and fro, footmen were busy opening up the big dining-room and polishing silver ornaments that were used only on special occasions. Gardeners came into the house with great armfuls of hothouse flowers, arranging them in the big reception rooms downstairs and sending vases of them to the bedrooms. Together the fragrance of carnations and lilies permeating the house and the bustle of servants to and fro created an atmosphere of expectant unrest which communicated itself to the whole house, even to Lucy.

'My Daddy is coming home, my Daddy is coming home,' she sang, running up and down the passages and bursting into Lady Clementina's room unannounced. 'My Daddy is coming home, Granny. Are you pleased?'

'Very pleased. But who said you could come down here?'

'I came all on my own,' Lucy answered, and at that moment Sylvia appeared behind her in the doorway.

'Oh, there you are, Lucy. I wondered where you had gone to,' she said. 'I am sorry if she has been disturbing you,' she added to Lady Clementina, 'but she is so excited at the prospect of seeing Sir Robert again that it is difficult to keep her occupied in the nursery.'

'Come here, child,' Lady Clementina said to Lucy.

Lucy obeyed her grandmother, running across the room to stand beside the bed and looking up at her with wide eyes.

Lady Clementina looked down into the child's face and then she reached out her hand and touched her cheek. She said nothing for a moment and it seemed to Sylvia, watching her, as if there was suddenly an expression of great sadness in her eyes. 'You love your father, don't you, Lucy?' she said at length.

'I love him better than anyone in the world. Don't you love him, Granny?'

'Yes, I love him,' Lady Clementina answered, and her voice was low and unsteady.

'I wish we could have some flags to wave when Daddy comes home,' Lucy said suddenly. 'We could hang them out of the windows, couldn't we, Granny? It would make the house look very gay and bright for him.'

'I think your father will realise you are pleased to see him without the addition of flags,' Lady Clementina said dryly; and then sharply, as if she had been caught off her guard, 'Now run along, Lucy, and do not be a nuisance. Do as Miss Wace tells you. And do not come here another time unless you have been told that you may.'

'All right, Grandmother,' Lucy said, but she was quite unabashed. By the time Sylvia had followed her out of the room she had reached the stairs and was doing her best to slide down the banisters. Sylvia took her up to the nursery, but Lucy escaped once again and slipped up to the top storey where Sylvia found her chattering to Purvis.

'I am sorry, Miss Purvis,' Sylvia said. 'Lucy is rather naughty today. I know it is only excitement, but she is upsetting everybody, rushing hither and thither. I think I had better take her or a walk, although it is beginning to rain.'

'Oh, I don't mind her, Miss Wace,' Purvis said. 'She likes sorting through my button boxes. There's never been a child as didn't enjoy doing that. Here you are, Miss Lucy.' She handed her the big tin box which contained every sort and size of button.

Lucy sat down on the floor and pouring out the buttons started to arrange them in patterns. Purvis looked at her with a smile. She did not like children, but Sylvia guessed that she liked the satisfaction of being able to amuse Lucy when other people failed.

'She is excited about seeing her father again,' Sylvia explained.

Purvis sniffed. 'All this fuss! And isn't it just like him, giving her ladyship so little notice? The letter comes this morning and he's here this afternoon. Every room in the house to be got ready and no time to do it. I said to her ladyship when she told me, "It isn't fair, that it isn't, and least of all on you, my lady." But, of course, you know what she is—dotty about him, thinks he's perfect. Why, I can't imagine.'

'I expect all mothers are the same about their sons,' Sylvia said.

'Not by a long chalk,' Purvis said sharply. 'No, her ladyship just dotes on Sir Robert; almost an abnormal affection I should call it, especially when he treats her the way he does.'

'What do you mean?' Sylvia asked.

She knew that really she should go away and take Lucy with her. It was wrong staying here to gossip with Purvis who, she always felt, was a bitter, frustrated woman. But there were so few people in the house from whom she could learn anything about Sir Robert. Now she felt she must listen to what Purvis had to say.

'You ask me what I mean?' Purvis inquired. 'Well, look at his goings-on! And there's her ladyship just giving up her life to him! She thinks of him, and she thinks of this house, because it is his, all the time. I don't believe she would care if everyone else in the world died as long as her Robert was all right. And what does she get for it? More kicks than thanks, I can tell you. I've heard him be downright cruel to his mother, talking to her in that nasty, sarcastic way of his which cuts one like a knife. It would break some women. But her ladyship stands up to him. She may be old, but she's got a lot of fight left in her. And when he's away—that's the time; I've seen her lie there for hours with a brooding look on her face, staring out through the windows and not saying a word.

'But once she did say to me, "Purvis," she said, "never love anything with all your heart and soul. If you do you are lost." And when I asked her what she meant, of course she wouldn't say. Contrary as always. But I knew what she meant. She meant Sir Robert. Men—they're all the same! Take what you offer them and not give you so much as a thank you for it.'

'But I feel sure Sir Robert is fond of his mother,' Sylvia said, feeling that she must defend him.

Purvis sniffed; then she glanced over her shoulder at Lucy playing absorbedly on the floor and lowered her voice. 'Sometimes, Miss Wace, I think he hates her.'

'Hates her?' Sylvia was startled.

Purvis nodded. 'That's what I think, and if you ask me, there's something behind it all. There's something he doesn't want her to know, something that he's afraid of her finding out. But I'll find out what it is before he's finished and that will teach him to sneer at her ladyship—and at me, for that matter.'

'Oh, Miss Purvis, I am sure you are exaggerating,' Sylvia said.

She felt suddenly nauseated by the sinister, hissing note in Purvis's voice, the gleam in her eyes and the compression of her thin lips. It was all nonsense, of course, yet she felt at that moment as if this woman might harm Robert, do him an injury.

'Well, wait and see, Miss,' Purvis said. 'You remember the saying about them who laughs last . . .' She picked up her sewing.

Sylvia felt she must ask one question. 'Don't you like Sir Robert, Miss Purvis?'

Purvis looked up at her. It seemed to Sylvia as if she was going to refuse to answer the question, then she said:

'If you want the truth, I hate him, and that's that! I never could abide his stuck-up, sarcastic ways.'

Sylvia felt there was nothing more to say. She was sorry now that she had stayed so long. Purvis seemed somehow to have poisoned the air around them, making her feel perturbed and unhappy. With a note of unusual authority in her voice she told Lucy to put the buttons back into the box and took the child downstairs.

In the nursery, Romola was sitting on the sofa with her feet up, reading a novel.

'Where have you been?' she asked. 'I couldn't find you anywhere.'

'I am sorry,' Sylvia replied. 'Lucy ran up to the top floor to Miss Pruvis's room. 'Did you want me for anything?'

'Nothing in particular,' Romola answered; then added casually, 'Lady Clementina asked me to go down to see her at four o'clock.'

'Lady Clementina?' Sylvia said. 'What does she want?'

'I have no idea,' Romola answered. 'I merely got the message that she would like me to have tea with her at four o'clock.'

Sylvia looked horror-struck. 'I wonder what it means,' she said. 'Do you think it means she has found out something?'

'What a coward you are, Sylvia,' Romola said scornfully. 'I expect she just wants the pleasure of my company.'

'But it is so unusual!—and today of all days!'

'Well, don't get agitated,' Romola said annoyingly. 'We shall know everything in due course, and, personally, I am not afraid of her.'

'Nor am I,' Sylvia said untruthfully, and Romola laughed.

Sylvia and Lucy had tea together in the nursery, Sylvia trying to talk intelligently and naturally to the child while all the time her thoughts were with Romola, wondering what Lady Clementina had to say to her and why she had suddenly been singled out for such attention.

It seemed to Sylvia that in the last few weeks the dangers surrounding her position in the household had increased rather than diminished. Romola's presence there made her nervous and anxious; she could never be quite certain how her sister would behave, what she would say or what she would do. Even her joy at the idea of seeing Sir Robert again was overshadowed by this anxiety and what amounted to a fear of Romola.

The time passed slowly; and then as Ethel came up to clear the tea, they heard the sound of carriages outside on the drive.

'It is Daddy, I'm sure it is Daddy,' Lucy said, running to the window and peeping out.

Sure enough there was a stream of carriages rounding the drive in front of the house. Without waiting for Sylvia's permission the child gave a scream of joy, rushed across the room and was down the stairs before Sylvia could do anything but follow her. By the time Sylvia reached the front hall there was already a group of people there. Several of the women were exclaiming in loud voices at the house or saying how tired they were after the journey, and in the background Bateson was hovering with a number of footmen. The centre of the picture was entirely occupied by Sir Robert. He had lifted Lucy up in his arms and was kissing her, and Sylvia watching them felt her heart contract.

'Oh, Daddy, I am so glad you are back.' Lucy's voice was high and excited.

'Have you missed me?' Sir Robert asked.

'Of course we have, all of us.'

'I am glad to hear it, but I expect you are just flattering me,' Sir Robert said.

He looked across the room and saw Sylvia. He gave no sign of recognition, but their eyes met and held each other. In that moment for both of them time stopped still.

Sir Robert set Lucy down on her feet. 'Come and meet my friends.' He drew her towards the women who had moved eagerly towards the warmth of the big log fire.

At that moment the door opened and another carriage load of guests came streaming in.

'What a wonderful house, Robert!'

'I had no idea anything could look so magnificent.'

'I thought at first it must be the Town Hall.'

There was a shriek of laughter and another voice said, 'What she really means, Robert, is that she didn't know you were so rich.'

Again there came laughter. There was something in the quality of it and the shrillness which made Sylvia look for the first time closely and critically at Robert's guests. She was standing in the shadows at the foot of the staircase. Unobserved by them, she studied the fashionably dressed, high-voiced young women, several of whom were being helped from their travelling coats.

Then her heart began to beat almost agonisingly, for she knew without being told and without fear of contradiction what type of people had come to Sheldon Hall as Sir Robert's guests.

14

Robert Sheldon walked into his bedroom. There was still an hour before dinner, but his valet was waiting for him, his evening clothes laid out ready for him to put on.

'I will ring when I want you, Turner.'

'Very good, Sir Robert.'

Turner withdrew quietly and Robert walked across to the side-table which held a decanter and a siphon of soda. He poured himsellf out a strong drink and sat down in a chair facing the fire. There was a knock at the door.

'Come in.'

It was Bateson.

'About the wine for dinner, Sir Robert . . .'

'I thought I told you to bring up the best we had.'

'We've only five dozen of the Perrier Jouet '90 left.'

'We will drink it then.'

'And the brandy, sir?'

'The best, Bateson.'

'Not the Napoleon brandy, Sir Robert?'

Robert Sheldon twisted round in his chair to look at the older man.

'These guests who have arrived tonight, Bateson, are my intimate friends. I wish to accord them my best hospitality. Is that understood?'

Bateson's face was impassive, but his voice was not so perfectly under control.

'Very good, Sir Robert.'

He walked across the room with dignity and the door closed behind him.

Robert smiled wryly and looked into the fire. He was perfectly aware of Bateson's feelings and he knew he had just committed, or rather was making Bateson commit, what almost amounted to an act of sacrilege. Good wine, the best wine, fit only for connoisseurs, was to be poured down the throats of people who would not appreciate it and would drink it as lightly as and with no more enjoyment than they would quaff a sparkling German Moselle or the cheapest and most fiery cognac. Never mind. He had made the gesture as much to convince himself as anyone else that these people were his friends, entitled to his utmost consideration and the very best he could offer them.

Robert finished his drink and then as he rose to pour himself another he swore queitly and forcibly under his breath. What a fool he had been to ask them here! How stupid to imagine for one moment that it would be a success! He was honest enough with himself to admit that he would have given a great deal at that moment to have come home alone, to have left the raffish, exotic crowd whom he called his friends behind in the place to which which they belonged—London. He had given the invitation on an impulse after a supper party at which they had all dined and wined well and when for once he had felt some exhilaration in his blood, some lightening of his habitual sombre gloom, so that for the moment he believed that he was cured and to prove it must defy all common sense and all good taste.

Cured! Was it likely that he could or ever would be? Even as they had driven up the drive and had seen the great house there waiting for them, he had known how ridiculous such an idea had been. He had entered the hall and Lucy had run forward, holding out her arms, her childish welcome so spontaneous that he had felt the warmth of his own response, the sudden leaping of his heart dispelling caution and restraint.

Then he had looked across the hall and seen Sylvia's face. He had forgotten how beautiful she was. It was the expression in her eyes; she was so unsophisticated, so unspoilt, that she had not yet learnt to control her feelings and they showed there in the transparency of her smile. He missed nothing, neither the joy which told him he was welcome, nor the sudden change to surprise and dismay as his guests intruded themselves between them. That is what they had done—intruded on a moment which, timeless to them both, had held them spellbound; a moment when they had looked into each other's eyes and known beyond all doubt, beyond all questioning, beyond all pretence that their hearts beat in unison.

Wearily Robert dropped his head into his hand. There was no escape, either from the torture within his heart or from the agony within his mind. He closed his eyes. Would he ever be able to forget her eyes raised to his when he had held her in his arms and kissed her, unable to control the hunger that had tortured him for so long? He supposed that he must have wanted her from the moment he first saw her, but the consciousness of it had crept upon him almost insidiously. Gradually he had found himself listening for the sound of her voice on the stairs, for the tread of her footsteps and then waiting for the sight of her. He had never believed that a woman could look so breathtakingly beautiful, yet so innocent and untouched—perhaps inviolate was the word.

Robert groaned. What was the point of going all over this again? He had got to forget her; he had got to cure himself somehow. God knows he had tried! He had drunk until other men had fallen under the table, drunk until his legs were unsteady though his brain still remained cool, calculating and observant. He had drunk until he had believed no human being could remain sober, but still some detached part of himself had survived to remember . . . to remember . . . and to go on remembering. . . .

For a second antidote he had tried women. But with a bitter cynicism he had known that they would fail as they had failed in the past to make him forget other things. How

149

they had bored him with their flutterings and flattery, their ridiculous laughter and equally inane jokes! He thought of the money he had poured out and knew that the waste of it mattered not one iota compared with the waste of time, of energy and vitality.

But what did any of that matter when he was a man alone, a man who must go through life unaccompanied because of the past, a past from which he could never escape? 'If only I could hate her,' he thought, and knew that it was only himself that he must hate because, when he had found the one thing that he had wanted all his life, he was not worthy of it but must let it pass him by. It was the only course he could take, and yet the Devil tempted him. . . .

'She is only a woman like the rest. Take her, make her yours. What does it matter if one day her love should turn to hatred and loathing, that she should shrink from you, knowing the truth. Perhaps she will never know the truth, perhaps it will always remain hidden from her. Anyway, whatever happens, you will have had her, she will have been yours—yours to have and to hold, to touch and to caress . . .'

Robert got to his feet and paced up and down the room. He had listened to it all before, had gone over and over it in his mind. But it always presented itself to him afresh, a problem to which there was no solution, and yet a problem which he must perpetually consider. And when finally, as he always did, he told himself, 'Enough of this! You know the answer: I will not murder the thing I love!' the devil had another suggestion, more subtle, more hard to credit, yet whispered in the silence of Robert Sheldon's soul.

'How do you know that she is so pure, so innocent as she appears? Remember Alice; she took you in; remember the other women you have known, those you have sought, those you have chased and captured. When they surrendered, what did you find? That they loved money and possessions; that they were not innocent or saintly but of the earth—and none the worse for that. Why should not this woman be greedy even as they were? Why should you imagine that she is any different from the rest? Take her; take her on any terms you like and you will find that all this high-flown stuff is only part of your imagination, that all you are crediting her with is probably false.'

Damn it! Damn it! What was he to believe? Impulsively

Robert threw his glass into the fireplace and heard it shatter into a thousand shining crystal pieces. He stood looking down at the broken glass glistening in the light of the flames. The fragments were like tear-drops.

There was a tap on the door. He did not answer and after a moment the door was opened.

'Excuse me, Sir Robert, but it is after seven-thirty.'

'Very good, Turner, I will change.'

They would be waiting for him, these guests of his. He could imagine them in their bedrooms, twittering away in awe-struck voices.

'My dear, the footmen, and the size of the hall!'

'Did you notice the flowers?'

'And the pictures! I bet they're all masterpieces.'

'He must be richer than we thought!'

'I always said he was a millionaire.'

'Do you think the Cicely episode is finished? She must have made a packet out of it.'

Yes, the women would be talking!

And the men? Robert could well imagine their thoughts even if they were wise enough not to put them into words. They would be wondering how they could 'stick' old Robert for a 'monkey,' or pondering what was his weak spot, planning a campaign of assault upon his pocket like the veterans they were in that particular art. He would give them the opportunity. There would be cards after dinner. If he was the loser, his debts would be paid; if he was the winner, their's to him would be forgotten.

He knew his guests only too well, and there was not one of them who before leaving after the visit, would not touch him for some petty cash.

'I'm sorry, old boy, I didn't get the chance to cash a cheque before I left London. You understand, I know, it's only a loan.' Only a loan . . . only a loan. . . .

Yes, he despised them, and not only them. He despised his own class, the people who came here because he was rich and it was convenient for them to forget the scandal that Lady Clementina had caused in her youth. People who brought their daughters, as ready for the marriage market as any fat duck being taken to the fair. The people who 'kept in' because Sheldon Hall was a landmark, a name which mattered in the county. He despised all these even more, despised and loathed them, because indirectly they were responsible, they and their kind, for all that had ever happened to him in his life—the glorification of a name until it became a religion, the adoration of a house until it had become idolatry.

Robert looked back into the past. Faces, faces, and more faces, awe-struck, fawning, vacuous and flattering. Faces which expressed every emotion, except honesty and truth and purity. And then one day he had found a face which expressed all those things, a face such as he had sometimes imagined in his dreams—soft, tender and unawakened. If things had been different, he might have been the one to awaken her, to watch the cool perfection of those frank, sweet eyes become first shy, then radiant as the knowledge of love came to her in the full blossoming of its magic beauty. He would have taught her tenderly and with patience; he would have worshipped her, then taken her when she surrendered as a conqueror might, knowing that as a woman she would love him the more in her very subjection to his manhood. . . .

Fool! fool! to think such things; it was too late.

'Your gardenia, Sir Robert.'

Turner's voice recalled him to himself.

'Yes, yes, of course.'

He took the flower with its insidious, exotic scent and set it in his button-hole. For the first time since he had dressed he glanced at himself in the mirror. He saw his face, dark and scowling, the brows knit together, the mouth a hard line; and then he turned away. Why should women look at him except because they wanted his money? He had shown them often enough and all too clearly what he thought of them. Playthings of the moment, that was all they were.

He went downstairs. There was the sound of laughter coming from the drawing-room and voices raised a little too shrilly. He entered the room. For a moment there was silence, then they all started talking at once.

'Oh, Robert, it's too, too deevy!'

'It's the most marvellous place we've ever seen.'

'Darling, why didn't you tell us that you were a kind of king? Not that we would have believed it.'

They fluttered round him, their hands reaching out to touch his arm, to stroke the lapel of his coat; their perfume, heavy and overpowering, was in his nostrils.

He glanced across the room to meet the eyes of the menfolk, envious, greedy and calculating. Poor devils! he would give them their chance later.

When dinner, at which everyone over-ate and over-drank, was finished, the card-tables were got out; but the women wanted to dance. Robert knew their reason only too well. They were out to exercise all their feminine wiles on him, and proximity was a necessary part of this.

'Oh, do let us dance first!'

'If you men once settle down to cards, we shan't get a word out of you!'

'Oh, Robert, it's the perfect setting for a waltz.'

He had not expected this. Bateson told him in an aside that the ball-room had not been opened and was not warm enough.

'We will have a proper dance tomorrow night,' Robert promised them; and then as their faces fell, 'We can take a turn in the hall now if you like. The footmen can move the piano there from the drawing-room.'

The idea was hailed with enthusiasm and soon they were dancing, while the family portraits stared down at them. As they became warm through the exercise, more and more champagne was brought by Bateson to sit cooling in the great crested silver ice-pails and then poured sparkling into the long-stemmed crystal glasses.

It was as he raised a glass to his lips that Robert first became aware of a shadow on the balcony. For a moment he thought he was mistaken, then it moved and he was sure. Someone was watching them from above. He had a glimpse of a face, but it disappeared too quickly for him to be sure and yet he knew instinctively that it was not one of the servants. They would not dare, for one thing; they were far too well supervised. Now the shadow had gone.

He danced round again, in his arms a pretty little un-natural blonde who did her best to nestle against him. She had lisped her way through nearly ten years of stage life and she could still manage *ingénue* parts and get away with them.

'I don't believe you weally like us poor women.'

'What makes you think that?'

Robert was talking conventionally; he glanced upwards as he spoke—yes, the shadow had returned.

'Well, we know what you think of Cicely, but most of her friends are vewy kind to us, too.'

'But aren't I kind to you?' Robert asked.

His partner shook her blonde head.

'Not weally. You give us fings, but you don't weally fink about us.'

Heavens! but she was right in her own shrewd little way. She knew the truth; he could not bother to think about them, not when his mind kept straying, even as his eyes were straying now, towards something else, something which drew him, magnetised him. Did she care enough then to come down from the nurseries and stand there in the shadows? Had she, too, got to the stage when the mere sight of a person so beloved was enough in itself and one dare not ask for more?

She had moved! Robert took the blonde back to the buffet table and plied her with champagne. He did not know what he said, but it must have been something complimentary for she was laughing excitedly and her voice cut across his thoughts.

'Wobert! I never knew you felt like that! Will you weally put a teeny weeny bit of money into a new play if the governor will offer me the part?'

'Yes, of course.'

He had no idea what he promised, but he would have promised anything at that moment. Now she had gone again. Was he too late, or should he go upstairs and confront her? He had sworn to himself that there should be no repetition of that night in the nursery. He had lost his head then, he admitted it, but the temptation had been too great as she lay there asleep, the dark lashes lying on her cheeks, her mouth drooping a little like a child who has been frightened before going to sleep and who is still wistful and sad in its dreams; one hand lay in her lap and her head was resting on her other arm on the seat of the chair. She had given him the impression of being completely defenceless, and he had wanted to raise the fingers of her open hand to his lips, to touch the soft palm; but sternly he had prevented himself and had stood looking down at her. He had known in that moment just how great a hold she had over him. Everything which was chivalrous and fine in his nature and which he had tried to thrust from him had come forth shining and splendid, denying the degradation he had sought with which to deaden his unhappiness. He would have tip-toed away, but she had wakened and looked up at him sleepily and then happily, with a confidence he knew came only from some inner trust. And still he had held himself in check. Then he touched her, drew her to her feet, and like the bursting of a dam within himself he could withstand it no longer. He had taken her into his arms because he must, because the compelling magic in the air around them was unbearable; he had to feel her lips against his. Even as he kissed her he had known himself for the cad he was and had thrown the cup of ecstasy away.

He had been on fire with a desire that was deeper and more consuming than passion, and he had run away. But what good had it done him? He had to come back.

'I will make her hate me!' How often had he repeated such words to himself, but without conviction. All he had achieved was a hatred for himself. He hated his life, he hated his thoughts, he hated his feelings; he hated the sham and emptiness of all that he knew and all that he had ever known. Once before he had believed that he had touched the depths, that nothing worse could happen to him, that the humiliation of an utter degradation was unalterably and completely his. Now he knew that he had not known the half of it. Then he had nothing with which to make a comparison. Now he had Sylvia.

He took up a glass of champagne and held it towards the blonde, clinking it against her glass.

'To the future,' he said.

She gave a little cry of excitement. 'Oh, Wobert, how marvellous you are to me!' Then she lifted up her face to his invitingly.

After a moment's hesitation, Robert, with bitterness in his heart, bent to kiss the reddened lips raised to his. 'This should teach her the truth,' he thought, but he was not referring to the blonde.

The pianist broke into an inspirited polka. 'Come on, all of you,' he shouted. 'You are getting too sentimental.'

Robert was well aware of the reason for this sudden command. The man who was playing had seen the kiss and the enrichment of an uninspired *ingénue* was not part of his plans. There were so many axes to grind, so many irons in the fire; everyone had something to pull off, everyone was resentful, afraid and suspicious of someone else's good luck, driven always by the hidden fear that there might not be enough to go round. Good fortune for A might mean less for B and nothing at all for C. What a world, and what petty fools inhabited it! And yet who was he, Robert Sheldon, to speak harshly of foolishness or of fools?

He saw the man next to him was not smoking. 'What you want, old boy, is a good cigar,' he exclaimed. 'I will get you one.'

Bateson, who was hovering in attendance, stepped forward. Robert silenced him with a gesture. He crossed the hall and made his way quickly along the passage which led to another staircase. His heart was beating faster. Would she still be there, he wondered, or when he left the floor would she have hurried away?

The staircase was nearly in darkness and as he reached the top he felt elation flooding over him with a warmth and a rising crescendo of desire. She liked him enough to leave the child alone on the top floor so that she could come down and watch him. She must have been there nearly an hour by now. It was reprehensible, certainly; yet did it not show that she cared sufficiently to dare everything? Robert felt a sudden stirring of his pulses. Why must he go on refusing what was being offered him? Why must his own fastidiousness hold him in check? Were the barriers he himself had erected really necessary?

He moved quietly forward down the long passage leading to the balcony. Now he could see her at last, the soft folds of her dress billowing over the floor. She was bending forward, peeping over the oak balustrade. He stood still a moment, then reaching up his arm he turned out the gas. It died with a soft plop, but it was not loud enough to startle her. Now the passage was in darkness; there was only the light rising from the hall below, hardly enough to reflect the gilt frames of the portraits or the colour of her hair as she stood with her back to him.

He moved towards her, but before he reached her she turned. He knew without being told that something had alarmed her; perhaps she had heard someone move or had only just realised that he himself was missing. Whatever it was, she was coming towards him. He heard the rustle of her dress and suddenly, almost before he knew it, she had reached him and he held her in his arms. . . .

He held her tightly, heard her give a little gasp before his mouth sought hers. He kissed her and felt his kiss returned. There was something in her kiss that inflamed him, something that was different. He felt her slim body nestle even closer to him, and then he knew. Drawing back he held her at arms' length and turned her round so that the light from the hall fell upon her.

He saw what his senses had told him some seconds earlier—that he held a strange woman in his arms, a woman he had never seen before, and she was smiling at him!

'Who the devil are you?'

He did not release her and his hands tightened on her shoulders, but the pain of it did not seem to affect her.

'One of your guests, Sir Robert.'

'One of my guests? Indeed, that is news to me.'

'I thought it might be. Nevertheless I have had the privilege of enjoying your hospitality for some weeks.'

'You have! Well, suppose I have a look at you.'

He moved, still not releasing her, till he had his back to the balustrade and she was standing before him, the soft upthrown light falling directly on to her face. He wondered then how he could have mistaken her for Sylvia. Her hair was dark for one thing and she was much older. But she had a certain charm of her own, a charm which seemed to him vaguely familiar.

'Well, what have you got to say for yourself?'

'Where do you wish me to begin?'

Her eyes were mocking but her smile inviting. He thought instinctively of those swift responsive kisses, and for a moment he was prepared to play her game. His arms dropped to his sides.

'Won't you introduce yourself? You have the advantage of me.'

She swept him a little curtsy. 'Romola Brent. At your service. Mrs. Brent, if you wish to be formal.'

"Really. And who is Mr. Brent—if there is one?'

'There is not. The Reverend Theosophilus is merely the late lamented.'

Her voice was flippant and it jarred on Robert.

'So you are a widow. Undoubtedly a merry one.'

'I have been ill.' Romola's voice rebuked him. 'And before that I was for many years in Africa. My existence there could be described by many adjectives, but "merry" is not one of them.'

'And who invited you here?'

'Your mother, Lady Clementina. It was kind of her, wasn't it?'

'Very kind. I wonder she didn't mention the fact to me when I saw her before dinner.'

'Perhaps you were in a hurry to . . .' She hesitated, '. . . to return to your friends. Especially the charming little lady with blonde curls.'

Robert smiled a trifle grimly.

'The lady to whom you refer is a very old friend of

mine. And now that at last we have become acquainted, perhaps you will join my guests downstairs and meet the lady in question.'

'I shall be delighted.'

For the first time he noticed that this strange woman was elaborately dressed, so elaborately as to be out of keeping with her rôle of spectator. Her dress was red and cut very low. Her arms were bare and in her hand she held a red feather fan.

Robert gave a short laugh; the situation appealed to his sense of humour. Whoever this woman was, she was obviously hoping to be invited to the party, dressed ready in case she should be. He bowed to her with ceremony and held out his arm to her. She laid her finger-tips on it, laughing up at him. Yes, there was definitely something familiar about her.

'Have I seen you before?' he asked.

'You may have.' She lowered her eyes for a moment. 'But surely it is uncomplimentary for me to have to do all the remembering, Sir Robert?'

She was clever enough to make her evasiveness provocative rather than merely annoying.

Robert laughed. 'Come along then, perhaps my memory will come back to me later.'

They went downstairs together. In the hall the dancing had stopped for a moment and the dancers were crowded round the buffet consuming still more champagne. The laughter was less restrained now, voices were higher and louder. The party spirit was obviously rising.

Robert drew Romola across the floor. Someone turned at their approach and then there was that sudden, quick, instinctive silence which so often occurred when Robert appeared. He took advantage of it.

'My friends, I have not yet had the opportunity of introducing you to another guest under my roof—Mrs. Brent.'

He ran through the names of the assembled company and they each bowed or protested their pleasure at making the acquaintance.

'And now,' Robert finished, 'that you know everybody, what about a glass of champagne?'

'There is nothing I should like better,' Romola declared.

He turned to take it from the attentive Bateson and as he did so caught a sharp whisper between two chorus girls.

'Surely it's her!' one said.

'I'd no idea she was married,' the other replied.

Robert handed Romola champagne and took a glass himself. Before he could speak she had raised her glass.

'To our very charming host.'

There was something almost mechanical in the way she spoke and Robert had the idea that she had raised many glasses in her time and made many such toasts. There was something about her he did not understand, something which was completely at variance with his notion of a woman whom his mother would invite to Sheldon Hall. In the brighter light her dress looked gaudy; it was smart and in its own way attractive; but it had been fashioned with one aim and one aim only—to display to the utmost and only just within the bounds of decency the charms of the wearer.

Everyone was taking now and he moved across to the two chorus girls who smiled up at him coquettishly. Speaking in a low voice so that only they could hear, he asked:

'Have either of you met Mrs. Brent before?'

'We think we have,' came the reply. 'In fact, Dolly and I are certain that it's Romola Roma. She was in *The Scarlet Butterfly* with us. That was, oh, two years ago now, and when we last heard of her she was in your show. But surely you know who she is?'

Robert did not reply; he was staring at Romola. It was an unusual name and, besides, there was something about this stranger's movements and her way of speaking which made it seem more than probable that she had been on the stage, even if she was here under another name. But how in heaven's name had she managed to find her way to Sheldon Hall? Why should his mother have invited her?

He moved back to her side. One of the footmen was handing her another glass of champagne and when she looked up at him he realised that the previous one had already had its effect; her eyes were sparkling, she was making those around her laugh at some witticism, and it was obvious that she was thoroughly at home with these people who seemed so out of place, so alien to their surroundings. She was definitely one of them, and Robert felt that he must solve the problem.

'Come and tell me about yourself,' he suggested.

Romola's eyes met his over the glass she had raised to her lips. 'Don't you like mysteries?' she asked flirtatiously.

'Not particularly.'

159

Romola sighed. 'Very well then. If you insist, I must tell you the banal facts. But I am disappointed in you.'

Her eyes told him that she was nothing of the sort. She bent towards him a little, her face lifted, her lips curling as if she invited his kiss.

'You're a very surprising young woman to find unexpectedly in this house,' Robert said dryly.

'Doesn't that make it all the more exciting?'

'For whom?'

'Surely for both of us?'

The words were soft and cleverly spoken, with just the right intonation. Despite himself, Robert felt he had to admire her technique; she was completely mistress of the situation.

'Set my mind at rest,' he begged. 'Tell me why you are here.'

Romola sighed. 'I have never met such a man for keeping to the point. Very well, then. Be prepared for a very obvious explanation. I am Sylvia's sister.'

For a moment there was no response; then in a voice strangely unlike his own, Robert asked:

'Sylvia's sister? Do you mean Miss Wace?'

'Yes, that's right. Now are you happy?'

She raised her eyes. She was looking into the face of a man whose expression frightened her. The words she was about to say died on her lips. Without a word, Sir Robert turned and left her.

15

Sylvia sat in the nursery, her sewing in her lap; she was worried and could not concentrate on her work. Thoughts and emotions chased one another through her mind in quick succession until the pattern of them became chaotic.

She was experiencing with a deep intensity new sensations which she had not previously known existed. The sight of Sir Robert had stirred her even more than she had anticipated. She had seen him again and known him to be as handsome, imperious and arrogant in his good looks as she remembered; but in her dreams she had imagined him as someone softer, kinder, at times even tender. Now she knew that this was but a figment of her imagination and that the reality was ruthless.

As she watched him in the hall downstairs, standing like a king among those shoddy, gaudy people who clustered round him, she had understood how impossible and how utterly impracticable all her ideas and desires had been during these past weeks. She had yearned for him, and now that he was here she knew they were completely alien, further apart perhaps than ever before. Once in her ignorance she had believed that it was possible to be satisfied with just the sight of him, with knowing that he breathed the same air as she breathed, that they were housed under the same roof. Now she realised that such ideas were merely the romancings of a schoolgirl. She was a woman, and it was a man for whom her whole body ached.

But even so, the man she envisaged was not the Sir Robert she had seen only a few hours before fawned upon by people without breeding, without—as far as Sylvia could judge—anything to recommend them except the looseness and the unconventionality of their lives.

Why had he chosen such people? Somehow instinctively she knew the answer. He was trying to escape. But from what? From his own upbringing? From the class into which he had been born? From his mother? Perhaps even from herself? She didn't know. She only knew that Sir Robert was trying to escape; she could almost feel him stretching out his hands, crying for a freedom which he could not find. He was suffering, suffering in some obscure way which she could not understand. And she had no power to help him nor was she in the position to comfort him.

As the evening progressed she had been certain that sooner or later he would either send for Lucy or come up to kiss her good night. The child had been so excited at his home-coming and she, too, had waited for a summons. Long after it was past her usual bedtime Lucy refused to be undressed.

'I want to go down to Daddy,' she kept saying; but Sylvia dared not give her permission. At last she persuaded the child to have her bath, eat her supper and be tucked up in her own little white bed.

'Wacey, tell Daddy I want to see him,' she commanded

with an imperiousness which somehow echoed her father's.

'He will come when he is ready, darling.'

'Doesn't he want to see me?' Lucy's lower lip quivered and big tears welled into her eyes. 'I thought he would want to see me after all this long time,' she repeated dolefully.

At that moment Sylvia almost found it in her heart to hate Sir Robert. Why should he have this power over women and children to make them love him, and then give so little in return?

'He will come later, I am sure he will, darling,' she comforted Lucy, hoping her words carried greater conviction than she felt in her heart.

'We are all the same,' she thought fiercely. 'We attribute to him greater virtues than he possesses and are disappointed when he fails us.'

She turned out the lights and went into the nursery. Lucy kept calling out, 'Wacey, go to the top of the stairs and see if Daddy is coming.' 'Wacey, what's the time? I'm so tired of waiting.'

At last there was silence for a long time. Sylvia tip-toed in, a shaded candle in her hand, and found Lucy fast asleep. There were tears on each cheek and even in her sleep her breathing was broken by little sobs. Angrily Sylvia smoothed the bedclothes and went back to the nursery. What idiots they were—Lucy, Lady Celmentina and herself! All three loving this man, who understood so little about love that he could leave his child pining for him while he found amusement with painted women with shrill, high voices and common accents.

Angry though she was, Sylvia could not help pitying him. He was missing so much; missing the charm and the sweetness in Lucy which before long he could never have again. How quickly human beings grew from babyhood into adolescence and from adolescence into grown-up men and women, controlling their emotions, hiding their feelings! Only at Lucy's age could one state openly and proudly that one loved a man, and cry because of him. 'I could cry now but I dare not,' Sylvia thought, staring with dry eyes into the fire, conscious of the tempest of tears that lay hidden within her breast.

She was afraid, yes, that was the truth; afraid not only of her feelings but of so much else besides. Lucy's unhappiness had almost driven from her mind another worry which had presented itself when they arrived upstairs in the nursery after Sir Robert's arrival. Romola was waiting for them. Sylvia knew almost as soon as she entered the room that Romola was upset. She was standing very straight and tense before the fire, her head held high and her mouth set in a hard line. Before she had time to speak, Sylvia asked the question:

'What is the matter?'

'You may well ask,' Romola said disagreeably. 'I have been given my *congé*.'

'What do you mean?'

'Exactly what I say,' Romola answered in a bitter, sarcastic voice. 'Her ladyship is delighted that I am better and she regrets there is no longer any room for me at Sheldon Hall. She is sure, now that I ave regained my health, that I have other relations whom I would wish to visit or an tion of some sort which would necessitate my leaving here. Anyway, I am to go, and at once.'

'At once?' Sylvia echoed bewildered.

'Well, tomorrow,' Romola conceded.

'Oh, Romola, I am sorry,' Sylvia said; but her words belied some contradictory little voice within herself which told her that she was in reality glad that Romola was going.

'She is a devil, yes, a devil, that woman!' Romola exclaimed vehemently.

Sylvia made a hasty gesture. 'Hush! in front of the child!'

'I don't care,' Romola retorted hotly. 'I loathe her! A hundred years ago she would have been burnt as a witch, and quite rightly, too. She sat there talking to me, trying to drag out reminiscences, and all the time she was waiting— waiting to tell me that she wished me to leave.'

'Did she give any reason?'

'Not in so many words, but I know the reason right enough.'

'Which is?'

'That her son has come home,' Romola replied. 'Oh, yes, that is the truth and I know it. She is afraid to have me in the house because I am not looking so ill as I was. Heaven knows how she has allowed you to stay all this time. She would like to keep him a monk, a hermit, away from every woman if she could. It's wrong, it's abnormal, and yet she doesn't care! She has the power and she uses it!'

'I don't think that is quite true,' Sylvia said, feeling that she must speak in defence of Lady Clementina. 'She wants

163

Sir Robert to marry—but she wants him to marry someone of his own world.'

'Oh, I realise that all right,' Romola answered. 'We're not good enough for her precious son. Good enough! Somehow, Sylvia, I will have my revenge for this! I will get even with them, you see if I don't!'

'Don't talk like that,' Sylvia pleaded. 'It frightens me. Besides, why should we expect anything else? We should be grateful really. You have been here three weeks; you are better, much better for the change; and after all, it is Lady Clementina's house, or rather, Sir Robert's, and we did invite ourselves, both of us.'

She tried to smile, but Romola would not be so easily cajoled.

'Why should I go now?' she asked. 'I have put up with the boredom of it, of living up the back stairs, and now that there is a bit of life and laughter in the house I am turned out like an unwanted housemaid. Oh, yes, that is the truth,' she added, as she saw Sylvia's shocked face. 'It suited me to be here and I agree that my health is better, but I have been bored, of course I have. No one who wasn't made of milk and water could stand trailing round after somebody else's child and call it enjoyable. The place is comfortable, I grant you that, but I should go crazy if I stayed here long without someone to talk to, without a man to find me . . . at least attractive.'

'We are made differently,' Sylvia said quietly. 'And as you feel that way, perhaps, Romola, it is all for the best. You will go back to London, to your own friends, to your own life.'

'Without any money?' Romola asked, her voice rising.

'I will give you all I can,' Sylvia answered. 'My wages for last month are intact, I haven't spent any of them; you shall have them.'

She fetched the money from the bureau where she had placed it a few mornings previously.

'What is the use of a few pounds to me?' Romola asked, but her fingers closed over the shining golden sovereigns.

'But, darling, what else can I give you?'

'I have got to think; I am going to my own room.'

'Yes, perhaps you had better,' Sylvia said thoughtfully, conscious all the time that Lucy, while outwardly intent on her dolls in the corner, might easily be listening to this strange conversation.

Romola turned towards the door.

'I will come along shortly,' Sylvia said.

She did not, however, get the opportunity until much later. Lucy wanted her and it was not until their dinner had been brought up to them by Ethel that Sylvia had the chance of slipping along the passage to Romola's room. She knocked on the door.

'Who is there?'

'It is I, Sylvia. Dinner is ready, dear.'

'Ask somebody to bring it along here,' Romola said, 'and leave it outside the door.'

'Are you ill?' Sylvia asked. 'Let me in.'

'No, I am busy. Just do as I ask.' Romola's tone was sharp.

Sylvia listened a moment. She heard the sound of rustling paper and Romola moving about the room. 'She is packing, I suppose,' she thought to herself, and went back to tell Ethel to put Romola's dinner on a tray and take it to her room.

Ethel did as she was told and came back with an anxious face.

'Mrs. Brent wouldn't let me in, Miss, but I left the tray outside the door as she told me. And then she said I was to ask Mr. Bateson for half a bottle of champagne. She said to tell him it was her last night and she wanted to celebrate. Shall I do as she says, Miss?'

Sylvia was startled. 'I don't know what to say, Ethel,' she said hesitatingly.

'Shall I ask him, Miss?' Ethel inquired again. 'I don't mind.'

'Yes, perhaps you had better,' Sylvia said, adding weakly, 'I don't know what he will say.'

'It's what Lady Clementina will say that matters,' Ethel retorted, the impertinence somehow forgivable because of the impish smile which accompanied it.

Before Sylvia could reply, she was gone.

Although the meal before her was tempting enough, Sylvia felt that she could not eat it. What was Romola up to? Why was she acting like this?—demanding champagne, shutting herself in her room, bitter with hatred against those who had at least given her shelter and taken her in when she was ill.

Sylvia tried to find excuses for her, but somehow they all merged into that unmistakable feeling of gladness within herself that Romola was going. She was heartily ashamed of it and yet she could not prevent it. She wanted to be alone again; alone with Lucy and with her thoughts. Soon it would be spring; the buds would be coming out in the gardens, the trees would be blooming in the park. She had the curious feeling that spring would mean something in her own life; that for her the winter and the bleakness were nearly over, there was light ahead. She could not explain it, could not put it into words; yet it was there, almost a presentiment that a springtime was approaching her, coming nearer and nearer, soon to be upon her; and something within her wanted to welcome it, to hold out her arms, to surrender herself to whatever was demanded of her.

When she had finished her meal, Ethel came up to clear away.

'Mr. Bateson sent up the champagne, Miss, but he didn't half say some things. If he hadn't been so busy, I think he'd have gone and asked Lady Clementina first. But they're rushed off their feet downstairs. You've never seen such a dinner! And the wine they're having! I'd just like to have a taste of it myself.'

'It wouldn't do you any good, Ethel.'

'I daresay not, but I'd just like to be able to say as how I'd had a drink. But there, it's no use pining after what you aren't likely to get.'

'There is sense in that,' Sylvia smiled.

Ethel went away and Nannie came in to say good night.

'I've got one of my headaches tonight, Miss Wace,' she said. 'I'm going to bed early with a glass of hot milk. Do you want anything?'

'No, thank you, Nannie.'

'You look tired, Miss Wace.'

'I am a little,' Sylvia confessed, although she knew it was worry she was suffering from and not fatigue.

'Well, you take my advice and go to bed. I hope the music won't keep you awake.'

'Music?'

'Yes, I hear that they're going to dance in the big hall. The sound will come up the open staircase; but they're not having a band, so I daresay it won't disturb you. Good night, Miss Wace.'

'Good night, Nannie.'

Sylvia listened at Lucy's door. The child's breathing was even now. Then she went along the passage to Romola's room. Once again she knocked. 'It is Sylvia,' she said. 'Let me in.'

166

There was a sudden rustle, then silence.

'I've gone to bed, I don't want to see anyone tonight. I know you will understand. Good night, dear.'

Romola's voice did not sound sleepy, it sounded light and excited. It occurred to Sylvia at that moment that Romola's voice was always like that when she was up to something.

'Let me in,' she pleaded. 'I do want to see you on your last night.'

'I've locked the door and I'm too tired to get out of bed,' Romola answered.

Sylvia knew it was a lie, but what could she do? 'You are sure there is nothing I can get you?' she asked.

'Nothing, thank you.'

'Good night, then.'

'Good night.'

Sylvia waited a moment and again there was a rustle; but she would not eavesdrop. She walked away from the door conscious of an acute apprehension. What on earth was Romola doing? What was she planning? At least her bitterness was gone, that was apparent from the tones of her voice.

Sylvia hated Romola when she was in a bitter mood. The day before she had found her upstairs gossiping with Purvis in her room, and somehow she had suddenly felt nauseated by the two of them. They were sitting rather unnecessarily close and their heads were stretched out at an identical angle; although they were utterly dissimilar in looks there was something in the expression in their eyes and the twist of their mouths which gave them almost the appearance of being related. And Sylvia realised why. They were being bitter together. They were discussing the people of the house, and Sylvia sensed that Purvis had been telling Romola of her hatred of Sir Robert and the way he treated his mother, exuding poison in her own feline, sharp-tongued way which always left a distasteful impression behind and made one feel unclean and in need of fresh, untainted air.

Romola had been interested in what Purvis had been saying. Later in the afternoon she had said to Sylvia:

'There's been some strange goings-on in this house. Purvis was telling me about Sir Robert's brother. There's something queer about that; don't you think so?'

'Queer? Why queer?' Sylvia asked coldly.

'Well, it was very convenient his dying off at such an

167

early age so that his younger brother could have the title, the house and the estates.'

'We all have to die sometime.'

'I quite agree,' Romola said. 'At the same time, Edward Sheldon was not only a very young man, but he was practically a lunatic. Didn't you know that lunatics always live to a ripe old age—that is, if they are—allowed to live.'

Romola said the last few words slowly and distinctly.

Sylvia moved her chair back from the fire with a sudden gesture of repugnance. 'How can you say such things?' she asked angrily. 'You have been listening to idle gossip. If Lady Clementina knew that Purvis dared to voice such opinions she would dismiss her and quite rightly, too. We are employees here, both she and I, and as long as we take Sheldon money they have a right to ask for our loyalty as well as our services.'

Romola threw back her head and laughed.

'Hoity-toity,' she taunted. 'What temper! Well, well, I will say no more. But I have thoughts about the whole affair and I shall go on thinking them whatever you say. One day you will find out that I am right.'

Sylvia did not answer. She felt at that moment such a blind passion of rage and anger that it was difficult for her to restrain herself from saying things that she knew she would regret. Who was Romola even to think such things about the Sheldon family, let alone speak them aloud? Romola, whose life, Sylvia was quite sure, had been by no means blameless.

Then gradually Sylvia's anger died away; the quivering fury of it diminished and sank to quietness. After all, had not she herself, too, wondered and speculated a little? She went back to the fireplace.

'I'm sorry, Romola, for being cross,' she said, forcing herself to bend down and kiss her sister. 'Let us talk about something else.'

Now, as she went back to the nursery, Romola's words returned to her. Pray Heaven that what she was planning at this moment had nothing to do with the secrets of the house or the secrets of the people to whom it belonged. Sylvia felt as if in some way she had betrayed Sir Robert by bringing Romola here. She had hated at the time to lie, to deceive Lady Clementina, to pretend that Romola was a married woman. And now she knew that she was paying for that deceit by anxiety and apprehension.

The nursery looked quiet and homely. There was a big

bunch of flowers on the table, the fire was glowing in the grate, some of Lucy's clothes were airing on the guard. It was all simple and unpretentious. Why should she be afraid and what was there to fear?

Sylvia sat down in her chair and took up her sewing with resolution. Tomorrow Romola would go. In a few days Sir Robert's guests would go, too. Things would return to normal. But her thoughts kept closing in on her, she could not dispel them. Presently her hands fell idle in her lap; she stared ahead of her, seeing nothing but pictures from the past and Sir Robert's face. He was looking tired, or was it merely dissipated? And yet, there had been something in his smile as he had swung Lucy up in his arms which had made Sylvia catch her breath. That was a side of him which only Lucy knew and that side was, Sylvia was sure, worth loving. Then he had looked across the hall and their eyes had met. She had forgotten for one moment everything except her joy that he was home . . . yes, home . . . .

The little clock on the mantelpiece ticked away the minutes. It was getting late, but Sylvia could not bring herself to go to bed. Far, far in the distance she could hear, as Nannie had predicted, the strains of music. She was not tired, but she was honest enough to admit to herself that even if she had been she would have waited. Waited in the hope that Sir Robert would come up to say good night to Lucy.

Quite suddenly, when she was least expecting it, the door was flung open and he stood there. She looked up and there was an up-flung ecstasy of joy within her. Then she saw his face and started to her feet. He shut the door behind him and came across the room to stand before her. He said nothing but stood looking at her. Nervously she broke the silence.

'Lucy was so hoping that you would come up before she went to sleep, Sir Robert. She asked for you again and again, and when at last she fell asleep she was crying.'

He did not answer her. It seemed to her as if her voice died away on a harsh and unnatural silence. She met his eyes and there was something strange in them, too. Suddenly afraid, she felt herself tremble and her lips went dry. At last Sir Robert spoke.

'I have just met a young woman in the house who calls herself your sister. Is that correct?'

Sylvia took a deep breath.

'Yes, Sir Robert. She has been staying here. Lady Clementina asked her.'

'And her name?'

'Romola.'

'Is she married?'

He shot the question at her sharply. Sylvia paused for only a fraction of a second.

'Yes.'

'What is her name?'

'Brent. Mrs. Brent.'

'And what was her husband?'

'He . . . he was a missionary. He is dead.'

'When did he die?'

'Er . . . er . . . a short time ago.'

'Where?'

'In Africa.'

'Your sister was with him?'

'Yes . . . yes, I think she was.'

'And then what did she do?'

The room seemed to be swimming dizzily around her. She felt that she must hold on to her control at all costs.

'She . . . she came back to England.'

'Recently?'

'Yes . . . yes, of course. Just the other day.'

'You lie!'

Sir Robert spoke the words loudly and then suddenly he raised his hand and hit Sylvia hard across the cheek.

She staggered under the impact of it, and then she stood staring at him, one hand raised slowly to touch her throbbing, burning skin.

'You lie!'

He spoke the words again and abruptly he turned from her and walked across to the window and back again. Then from some distance away he stood looking at her.

'Your sister is an actress,' he said. 'Is that the truth?'

Sylvia did not answer. She felt as if the whole world had fallen in ruins at her feet. She was conscious of feeling terribly cold, except for one burning patch where his hand had struck her, nay, branded her.

'There is no need for you to answer,' Sir Robert went on. 'I know the truth.' He looked at her and his mouth twisted at the corners. 'And I thought you were different from other women. My God! what fools men can be when there is a pretty face about! Yes, I thought you were different. I have known deception so often that for once I

170

imagined I had found someone guileless and innocent. And then what do I find? That you are just like the rest, scheming, pretending, lying and acting for your own ends. Well, have you anything to say for yourself?'

Still Sylvia did not reply. She felt as if her voice had left her for ever.

Sir Robert smiled, an unpleasant, cruel smile with no humour in it. 'So I have hurt you, have I? Well, you deserve it. Never mind, we will soon make it better. What a lot of time we have wasted, dear Sylvia, you and I. Time when we might have enjoyed ourselves. But I, poor, easily deceived fool that I was, imagined that I was not good enough for you. That is funny, isn't it? Robert Sheldon, of Sheldon Hall, imagined he was not good enough for the little, lying governess who had wormed her way into his household. Well, well, it is not too late to make amends. But you must have thought me very slow, my dear. I must apologise for that.'

The cruel sarcasm in his words and voice cut Sylvia like a whip. She threw out her hands in a gesture of protest and helplessness. In a voice hardly above a whisper, she said:

'Don't, please don't.'

Sir Robert dropped his bantering tone.

'Come here.'

Sylvia did not move, and he repeated his words.

'Come here to me!'

Against her own will, despite some protest within herself that she would not obey, she found her feet carrying her across the room until she stood before him, looking up at him. She moved slowly, almost as if she were in a trance, and yet she could not prevent herself from doing what he asked. He waited a moment and then suddenly, so that she was taken unawares, he put his arms round her.

'You are lovely enough for me to forgive you a great deal,' he said, and now there was pain in his voice, pain and something else which she feared.

She raised her hands, and at last she felt as if she could speak.

'Let . . . me explain,' she pleaded.

Through her thoughts went the promise she had given Romola. How could she explain? What was there for her to say? And yet she must clear herself, must tell Sir Robert that she had not meant to deceive him.

'Let me explain. . . .'

She spoke the words again, and then she knew that it

171

was too late. She saw the fire in his eyes, saw the expression of his face alter, and knew that she was in the hold of a man utterly possessed by his own passion and his own desire; and in that fraction of a second she knew, too, that she had released the beast within the man. She struggled to free herself.

'Please, please,' she whispered in panic-stricken tones.

But it was no use. Sir Robert crushed her to him and with his free hand forced back her head. Then he kissed her; kissed her passionately, brutally and cruelly until her lips were bruised, until she could do nothing but lie quivering within his arms, while a tempest swept over her, sapping her strength and leaving her dazed, shaken and humiliated almost beyond fear. There was a roar in her ears as if of running water and she heard his voice saying triumphantly:

'You are mine! I have wanted you and now you are mine! Mine to do with as I will!'

She was lost, bitterly and completely lost. Too weak to move, there was nothing she could do. Her lips were held, stilled beneath the fierceness of his. The waters were closing over her head, she was being drowned in a passion which she knew would carry her to the gates of hell and beyond. Deep in her heart there welled up a sudden prayer. 'Oh, God, save me!'

But it seemed that there was no help for her.

He was carrying her now; he had swept her off her feet up into his arms, her head had fallen back, and her hair fell loose in a cascade of living gold.

'You are mine—beautiful, wonderful, desirable—mine!'

She heard his voce vibrant, pulsating with desire, and triumphant in victory.

'Oh, God, help me!' She was only just conscious. Was there no help from anywhere? And then suddenly it came, the answer.

'Wacey, Wacey. I want you.'

It was Lucy calling. Sylvia felt Sir Robert pause. She tried to speak but she could not; her lips, bruised and burning, could only quiver.

'Wacey, I am frightened. Where are you, Wacey?'

There was a sudden movement and Sylvia found herself released and her feet touching the floor; but the room whirled round her and it seemed hard to focus her eyes. She put out her hand and clutched the back of a chair.

'Oh, Wacey, do come to me!'

172

It was a cry now, the cry of a frightened child.

As from a great distance, Sylvia replied:

'I am coming, darling.'

She made an almost superhuman effort, forcing herself to move across the room, and as she went she heard a door close behind her.

She entered Lucy's room.

'Oh, Wacey, I thought you were never coming.'

Sylvia groped her way in the darkness to the bed and knelt beside it. 'I am here, darling; it is all right.' And putting out her own trembling arms she took Lucy into them.

'Oh, Wacey, I had such a horrible dream . . . I thought you were lost . . . in a horrible place . . . and that you were calling for me.'

Yes, God had heard her prayer.

16

Lucy was asleep. At last Sylvia could move her cramped limbs and very gently extricate her arm from underneath the child's warm and heavy head. She tucked Lucy up, pulling the linen sheet close over her shoulders. Then she tried to rise from her knees and an agony of pain shot through her legs; yet the physical pain was as nothing compared with the agony within her heart.

As she turned away from the bed she saw that the nursery door was ajar; indeed the only light in Lucy's room came from a golden shaft flooding through the crack. Common sense told her to enter the nursery and turn out the lights but the nervous tension within herself made it impossible for her to do so. She was afraid—yes, afraid, even though she knew the room was empty. Never again, she thought, would the nursery mean for her peace and door, she groped her way across the now darkened bedroom and found the door which led to her own room.

Here she lit the gas and stood staring at herself for a moment in the mirror over the dressing-table. It was as if she looked at a stranger; the glass reflected a face white

173

and drawn—the face of someone who had suffered shock and a horror beyond words. And as she stood there the full realisation of what had occurred came to her overwhelmingly. She turned away to stagger blindly to the bed and throw herself down upon the satin eiderdown, her face buried in the pillows. She did not cry, she could not; she was past even the relief of tears. She only suffered silently with a violence and a misery in which it seemed that she had reached the heart of all suffering, so that she lost her own individuality and became nothing but one vast, agonising pain; a pain in which she knew she was lost—lost and alone, a helpless piece of flotsam without direction or purpose.

She had no idea how long she lay tense and still on her bed, but when at last she raised her head she was very cold. The fire in the grate had long since died out. She listened and heard only the soft, almost resilient silence of a house asleep.

And then at last Sylvia knew what she must do. Getting to her feet she started to change her clothes. She went to the wardrobe and saw hanging there the black dress and coat which Mrs. Bootle had given her, it seemed now centuries ago; but she turned away from it. Never, never again did she wish in any way to be connected with or reminded of anything which had to do with Sheldon Hall or the people in it. She chose instead her own worn blue dress which had served her for so many years and put it on with stiff, mechanical fingers, rearranging her hair and placing on top of the piled up curls the old felt hat trimmed with a jay's feather which reminded her only of Poolbrook and of the long winters then when it had served at least to cover her head, though hardly to decorate it.

Then she took a small bag from the top of the wardrobe and started to pack. It was impossible to take anything but the barest necessities—a brush and comb, tooth brush, nightgown and a change of underclothing. When she was packed and ready, she slipped into the grey coat, ugly and old-fashioned, which had once belonged to her cousin.

And then, and only then, did she hesitate. The thought of Lucy arrested her, Lucy sleeping peacefully in the next room in ignorance of what was going on. What would Lucy feel when she awoke in the morning? Suddenly Sylvia covered her eyes with her hand. Could she do it, could she bear to sever all connection with Lucy? She recollected the child's hands holding her, the quick, affectionate, trust-

174

ing smile, her voice calling, 'Wacey, Wacey.' She loved Lucy, but how could she stay? She remembered the look in Sir Robert's eyes, the words he had spoken, first in contempt and scorn and then with a mounting passion which was even more terrifying, more brutal to encounter. Sylvia made a gesture of helplessness. No, there was nothing else she could do.

She opened the door to Lucy's bedrooom and leaving it wide moved across to the bed. In the borrowed light she could see the outline of the child's features—the little oval face, the tip-tilted nose, the dark lashes against her cheeks; and flowing over the pillow and over her shoulders the vivid red of her hair. Sylvia took a deep breath. She wanted to creep forward and take the child once more into her arms; she wanted to know the comfort of that flaming head against her breast, the feeling of Lucy's arms round her neck, of being reassured by her love and affection, so generously and spontaneously given. But no! it was impossible—impossible to do what she was about to do and to say good-bye!

'God bless you, my darling,' she whispered; and because of the tears which suddenly blinded her eyes she had to grope her way back to her own room.

There she picked up the bag lying ready for her on the floor and opened the door into the passage. The lights were turned low as they always were at night, but it was not too dark to see and Sylvia walked to the top of the stairs. Here once again she hesitated; there was some battle going on within her. At last she made up her mind, and as if she refused to take the coward's way she turned briskly and retraced her steps down the passage to Nannie's bedrooom. She knocked on the door and very gently turned the handle. Before the door was fully opened, Nannie was awake with the quick, alert wakefulness which comes from having listened all one's life for the call of a child.

'What is it? Is anything the matter?'

'It is I, Nannie—Miss Wace.'

'Is Lucy ill?'

'No, no, Lucy is quite all right. I wanted to tell you something.'

'Of course, dear, of course. Come in. Wait a minute while I light a candle.' Nannie groped for the matches by her bed.

'No, please, I would rather be in the dark.'

'As you wish.'

Nannie sat up in bed and Sylvia held on to the brass rail at the foot.

'Listen, Nannie. Something has happened, something which makes it impossible for me to stay here. I have got to go away. I am going now. I have only told you because of Lucy.'

'Going away? At this hour of night, Miss Wace? But how? And where are you going to?'

'Don't worry about that, I shall manage. I have only come to you because of Lucy. She woke up a little while ago; she had a bad dream and was frightened .She is asleep now, but she might wake again and I wouldn't like her to find herself alone.'

'No, of course not. I will go along to her. But, Miss Wace, have you thought what you are doing?'

'Yes, Nannie.'

'You are sure? Quite sure? If you leave the house like this, it means you go without a reference.'

'I know that.'

Nannie sighed. 'I'm sorry, Miss Wace. I like you, and Lucy loves you.'

'Don't. She will forget me.'

'Possibly. Let us hope so . . . for her sake.'

There was silence for a moment. Then Sylvia said:

'Thank you for being so kind to me, Nannie, ever since I came here.'

'It has not been difficult. You are certain, quite certain, that you must go?'

'There is nothing else I can do.'

Nannie sighed again. Somehow Sylvia felt that she not only understood but knew a great deal more than the little she had told her.

'Good-bye, Nannie.'

'Good-bye, Miss Wace. And I hope that one day you will find happiness.'

Sylvia had nothing to say to this. She found her way to the door.

'Look after Lucy. Even if she forgets me I shall always love her.'

Her voice broke on the last words; and then quickly, because she feared for her self-control, Sylvia slipped into the passage and shut the door behind her. She picked up her bag and went down the front stairs; then as she reached the hall and went towards the back entrance door she heard someone approaching. Her heart gave a sudden leap of fear.

She hesitated whether to run back the way she had come; but knowing there was not time to retreat without being seen, she pressed herself instead into the deep shadows of the door leading into the drawing-room. The footsteps drew nearer. Her heart beat so suffocatingly loud that she felt that whoever it was who was approaching must hear it. Then she saw a moving light and knew it was only the night watchman making his rounds as he did every night to guard the premises against fire and theft. She kept very still while he walked into the hall, his lamp swinging beside him, opened the door of the library and went inside. This was Sylvia's opportunity. She slipped from her hiding place and crept on tip-toe down the passage from which the night watchman had just come. At the far end was a second flight of stairs and beyond that a door leading into the garden. It was a door which Lucy and she often used and although it was locked and bolted it only took her a moment to turn the key and shoot back the bolts; they were well oiled and made very little noise—not enough, at any rate, to attract the attention of the watchman still investigating the big reception rooms opening off the hall.

She stepped out into the garden, shutting the door quietly behind her. The sharpness of the night air on her face was icy cold, and the wind, too, threatened to lift her hat from off her head. For a moment she shrank back, every nerve in her body crying out for the warmth and shelter of the house she had left behind her. Then with her chin up and holding the bag in her right hand, she started to walk quickly down the paths which would lead her to the drive. Once she had got going she was almost glad of the wind and the chill in the air; she could keep her thoughts on the inclement elements, think of her physical discomforts rather than her mental ones.

It was not a dark night, the moon was nearly full and the sky clear and starry. Except under the shadows of the great oak trees it was not hard to find her way. She reached the lodge, opened the small gate beside the great wrought iron ones and slipped through.

She had walked for nearly two hours before the first signs of dawn appeared in the sky. The wind grew sharper and the hand holding her bag became numb with cold, so that every few minutes she must change hands, slipping the free one into the pocket of her coat to warm the stiffened fingers. The stars were fading in the sky and in the east the faint glow of dawn appeared creeping high over the moors.

Sylvia walked on, scarcely glancing to the right or left but keeping her eyes on the road ahead and moving with a determination of will which defied tiredness. On, on, on. The road seemed endless. Now the pale light of dawn had turned to gold, the last star flickered and disappeared and the first voices of the birds could be heart. It was very beautiful and very still, the sun touching the great expanse of moor, their heights glowing as they lay silhouetted against the tender iridescence of the sky.

But Sylvia could see only the road ahead. Six miles . . . seven miles . . . eight miles. . . . At last in the distance there appeared the roofs of Mickledon. The bag she carried seemed now to be made of lead and weighted with stones. She had been walking for nearly four hours and yet she would not let herself rest, would not relax even for a moment. She must go on, there was no stopping now she had started. Soon, she thought, it would be discovered that she had left the house. What would Nannie say? What could she say except that she had gone? Ethel would know first when she came to call her and found either the room empty or Nannie there. And Ethel would chatter with the household. This indeed would be a bit of news to gossip about! Soon her absence would be reported to Lady Clementina. But Lady Clementina was not called until nine o'clock, she had that much grace at any rate. Nine o'clock; it must be getting on for seven now, she had two hours in hand. But would they, dare they, come after her? She was certain that Lady Clementina would not trouble to search for her; but in thinking in the plural Sylvia was including another name, a name which she had sworn to herself should never pass her lips. She would not think of him either!

Such a resolution was easier to make than to keep. How could she not think of him? How could the memory of what he had said and what he had done ever be erased from her mind and her thoughts? It was branded there upon her, even as he had branded her cheek the night before so that it still felt bruised and tender. She would not think of it; she must not. She must force herself to forget the bitter twist of his mouth, the biting words which had fallen from his lips, and . . . and . . . the fire in his eyes.

Mickledon at last! Only a quarter of a mile more, and yet these last yards were harder to cover than any of the preceding miles. Now that she had reached the outskirts of her objective, Sylvia felt as if she could not extract the last

178

ounce of strength which it required to go further. Her whole body ached almost intolerably; there was a blister on one of her heels and she felt as if her bag would drag her to the ground so that she would never rise again.

On, on, she forced herself on, until at last she stood before the door of the Green Man and raised her hand to the knocker. She rapped sharply and then a sudden weakness overcame her so that she had to put down the bag she had carried so valiantly and so far and lean against the portal with her eyes closed, the world swimming dizzily around her. She felt a sudden cloud of darkness encompass her and a weakness creep insidiously over her so that she longed to sink into an easy oblivion, to let herself drift, to escape both from herself and from the world.

'What's ailing tha', Miss?'

A voice beside her recalled her to her senses. She opened her eyes and saw the pot-boy staring at her in wide-eyed concern. She opened her lips to answer him but no sound came.

'Eh, but tha' do look bad!'

He turned and was gone, his feet clanking down the flagged passageway.

'Mister Robb! Mister Robb!' she heard him call.

She could have gone in, but she felt as if it was impossible to move. She heard Mr. Robb approach, felt a firm hand on her arm and his voice say soothingly:

'It's all right, Madam. You come in here and sit down. It's early for a lady to be out, that's what made you feel queer. You'll be all right.'

Her feet stumbled as she walked with his hand on her arm assisting her, and then she felt herself being gently lowered into a comfortable chair.

'There you are, Madam. Boy, get that fire going and sharp about it!'

The relief of sitting down and taking her weight off her tired feet seemed to Sylvia to give her new strength. At last the darkness was gone and she could look up at Mr. Robb and hear her own voice say:

'Thank you so much. I felt faint for a moment; I am all right now.'

'What you want is a cup of coffee,' Mr. Robb said. 'Or shall it be something stronger?'

'Coffee would be very nice.'

'Hear that, my boy? Find cook and tell her to hurry. My instructions, mind you.'

'Ay, Ah'll tell her.'

The boy was gone.

The fire was already ablaze and in a few moments Sylvia felt the frozen numbness of her body begin to disappear.

'I hope you hadn't been waiting long at the door,' Mr. Robb said. 'It's strange none of us heard the carriage arrive.'

Sylvia smiled faintly. 'There was no carriage, Mr. Robb.'

'No carriage, Madam?' He stared in bewilderment. 'Then how did you get here?'

'I walked.'

'From Sheldon Hall?' Now he looked incredulous.

'Yes, Mr. Robb.'

She saw the questions in his eyes and respected him for the restraint which left htem unuttered. Then she pulled herself together, forcing herself to make the speech which had been turning over and over in her mind for innumberable miles.

'Mr. Robb, will you help me?'

There was no hesitation before he replied, 'I will do anything that is within my power, Madam.'

'I want to catch the first train which will get me back to Poolbrook. It is in Oxfordshire, it is where I came from.'

'That shouldn't be difficult, Madam.'

Clasping her hands till the knuckles showed white, Sylvia spoke in a low voice. 'Mr. Robb, I have no money with me, none at all. I want to ask you to trust me, to lend me enough for my travelling expenses. I will repay you, I promise you that, but I have nothing to offer you except my promise.'

Mr. Robb looked her straight and squarely in the eyes. 'I may be only a working man, Madam, but I know a lady when I meet one. I shall consider myself privileged to help you in any way I can.'

'Oh, Mr. Robb!' His name was just an ejaculation of relief.

'Now don't worry any more about it, Madam. Your coffee will be along in a moment. In the meantime if you would like to wash there is an empty bedroom at the top of the stairs. I'll call the chambermaid and she shall take you up.'

Mr. Robb turned away, but Sylvia stretched out her hand and touched his arm.

'Won't you let me thank you?' she asked, and she held

out her hand. He took it and gripped it hard before without another word he left her.

Why were people so kind? Sylvia wondered. She sank back in the chair and felt a sensation of sheer and utter relief steal over her. It was only after she had left Sheldon Hall and had walked nearly two miles that she remembered that she had no money. She had picked up her handbag automatically when she had packed, and as she always carried what money she had about with her, she had not given the question of finance a thought until suddenly, moving along the open, isolated road, she had remembered that Romola had taken all the money that she possessed in the world. She had spent the previous month's wages on some material to make a dress and on a doll for Lucy. It had been an expensive present, but Lucy had seen it advertised in Hamley's catalogue and had wanted it so much and with such ardency that Sylvia could not bear to disappoint her. She had half hesitated, wondering whether she should go to Lady Clementina, and then the desire to give pleasure herself had over-ridden the prudence which told her to keep her own money by her for a rainy day. She had written for the doll and paid for it, secure in the knowledge that she could save most of the next month's wages. Instead she had handed them intact to Romola.

When she realised her plight, she had also realised that it was impossible for her to go back. How could she? If she had thought of it before she could have borrowed a few pounds from Nannie; but now, having once started on her way, there was no looking back. She had walked on wutomatically, wondering desperately what to do, till suddenly she had remembered Mr. Robb at the Green Man. She recalled his kindness to her when the young man had proved impertinent and the way he had looked after her and Lucy; somehow she was sure that she could trust him, that he would prove a friend, that he would not turn her away. She was right. She need not have worried and she was grateful to him with all her heart.

A moment or two later the chambermaid came along to take her upstairs. There was hot water in the basin, a clean towel and a sweet-smelling cake of soap. Sylvia washed her hands and face and felt fresher. Downstairs she found some coffee awaiting her and with it a plate of eggs and bacon. She had not known that she was hungry until that moment. She remembered now that she had eaten very little dinner the night before; and although the thought of food in the abstract nauseated her, when it came to the point her body, young and hungry, was ready for the nourishment which her brain wished to deny it. She ate and drank and felt immeasurably better; the weakness which had kept a dark shadow hovering at the back of her mind disappeared and she felt more courageous. She wanted above all else to get away, to leave far behind her Mickledon, its moors and the road winding over them . . . the road to Sheldon Hall.

'I have made inquiries,' Mr. Robb told her after a little while. 'The 8.53 will take you as far as Crewe, Madam. You will have to change there.'

'Thank you, ' Sylvia said. 'And thank you for breakfast. I will go on go the platform and wait for the train.'

'There is no hurry,' Mr. Robb said in surprise. 'You have nearly half an hour yet.'

'All the same,' Sylvia replied, 'I think I had better move across to the station.'

Mr. Robb looked at her and understood her anxiety. 'You are safe here, Madam. If anyone asks for you, I will tell them that you haven't been seen.' He saw the relief in Sylvia's eyes and knew now of what she was afraid. 'You can trust me,' he said gravely.

'I know that,' Sylvia answered. 'And, please, Mr. Robb, if anyone does ask, you don't know where I have gone. Can I rely on you to keep my secret?'

'You can, Madam. Many people honour my poor house day after day, but there's no reason for me to remember one lady more than another.'

There was a faint smile on his lips, but he was completely respectful; and he was thanked by the eloquence in Sylvia's eyes, an eloquence she found hard to express in words.

It was with the utmost delicacy that he brought her some minutes later her ticket and some money in an envelope.

'Here is everything you require for the journey, Madam.'

He handed them to her on a tray and for a moment Sylvia did not understand what the envelope contained until she looked inside. When she saw several sovereigns she gave an exclamation.

'But it is too much! Please, Mr. Robb, I cannot take all this.'

'You may need it, Madam. I advise you to take it to be

on the safe side. One never knows when one is travelling, or indeed what one may find at the end of the journey. You can pay it back at your convenience, but I would feel happier if I knew that you were provided for in any emergency.'

'Oh, thank you.'

There was nothing else Sylvia could say, but his kindness brought the tears to her eyes and it was a moment or two before she could speak.

'You've got someone to go to, Madam?' Mr. Robb asked. 'A relation perhaps?'

'A friend,' Sylvia replied. 'I think she will be glad to see me.'

She need not have been afraid of her welcome. It was late that evening when she reached Poolbrook; but when she got out at the station it was to find there was no conveyance of any sort, so she walked down the hill and across the river into the town. It was misty, but the street lamps were lit and Sylvia could not help remembering another night when she had walked through the snow beside Mrs. Bootle. That had been the turning point in her life. It was no use thinking of it now, no use wondering if it would have been better not to have taken the initiative into her own hands but to have waited for the arrival of Uncle Octavius. If she had, she might at this moment have been sitting in the vicarage at Hastings. She would never have known Lucy or Lady Clementina, Sheldon Hall or the magnificent luxury of such an existence. And she would never have known pain or suffering and heartbreak and the utter, humiliating misery of seeing someone she had idolised scorn and despise her.

Sylvia hurried along the road. Soon she would pass the turning which led to her old home. How shadowy that life had become! It seemed so long, long ago since she had looked after her mother, had managed the house, done the shopping and waited for the querulous, unceasing call of an invalid. So much had happened since then. She knew, too, that she had become alive. For good or for evil, Sheldon Hall had brought her to life; oh! why not admit it?—not Sheldon Hall, but Robert Sheldon. Yes, he had brought her to life and then he had killed that life or tried to kill it. Loving him she had begun to blossom—as a flower will bloom as it turns its face to the sun—only to be withered and stricken down by a storm, violent and brutal in its intensity.

She had come back to Poolbrook, but Sylvia knew now that there was no real return. The girl she had been no longer existed; now she was a woman, a woman who had loved and suffered; who still loved and would go on loving.

She turned off the main street and went down a long, ill-lit passage. There were men lolling in the doorways; one of them spoke to her and laughed obscenely. She hurried on even faster, the blood mounting to her cheeks at the encounter. At last she came on a little row of houses standing back from the roadway. Sylvia found the one she sought—No. 7—and with an impatience that was born of fear hammered on the door.

'See who it is, Father,' she heard a well-known voice say, and the door was opened.

A man peered into the darkness. 'Who is it?'

'It is Miss Wace—Sylvia Wace. Please can I come in?'

There was a cry of welcome from the fireplace.

'As I live and die!' Mrs. Bootle rose to her feet, her great bulk seeming to dominate the room. 'What a surprise! But come in, dearie. And if I wasn't just talking about you this very morning to Father. Come in and tell me how you got here.'

Sylvia entered and put down her bag. Then as she saw Mrs. Bootle standing there so huge, so monstrous and yet with smiling good humour and friendliness oozing from every wrinkle of her face and twinkling in her bright eyes, she felt the horror and misery of her plight and the long journey slip away from her, leaving her weak and vulnerable, her over-strained resolution no longer needed now that she had achieved what she had set out to do. In that moment Sylvia forgot that she was a woman, that she was grown-up, and she became a little girl again, a little girl who had come home, who had run away from troubles and and dangers and unhappiness to the one friend she had ever known, the one person who had always shown her tenderness and kindness. And because she was so utterly glad to see Mrs. Bootle, she put her arms round her neck and burst into tears on her shoulder.

'Now you drink this up, dearie, and then you can tell me all about it,' Mrs. Bootle said, coming into the tiny bedroom like a ship in full sail, a glass of hot milk in her hand.

Sylvia looked up gratefully from the bed and struggled into a sitting position against the pillows.

'I never believed a bed could be so comfortable,' she confessed.

Mrs. Bootle laughed. 'When the body's weary enough, any place of rest is a feather bed! There's many a one that has complained about that mattress, including that young varmint of mine to whom it rightly belongs.'

'I feel dreadful, turning your son out of his room,' Sylvia said.

'You needn't,' Mrs. Bootle chuckled. 'He's used to it. He'd sleep on anything, that boy! He curls up on the couch and has a real good night. There's always people coming and going in this house. Father often laughs at me and calls it a home for waifs and strays.'

'That is exactly what I am at the moment,' Sylvia sighed.

Mrs. Bootle drew up a chair.

'Now drink your milk while it's hot,' she commanded, 'and then I'm ready to listen.'

'You are kind to me,' Sylvia said. 'You always have been. My one idea was to get back to you . . . I had nowhere else to go.'

'I've told you before there's always a welcome for you wherever I am,' Mrs. Bootle answered. 'But I'm disappointed, dear, very disappointed. I had such hopes of that job.'

Sylvia dropped her eyes for a moment and there was silence; then having drunk a little of the milk, she said:

'Perhaps it is wrong and disloyal of me to talk to anyone about . . . well . . . Sheldon Hall . . . but I have got to tell someone. I have got to ask advice, and I know I can trust you.'

'You can that dearie. Now come on, out with it and don't be shy. I'm as safe as the grave, if not a good deal safer.'

Sylvia smiled wanly and then she forced herself to start her story. She began at the very beginning, from the moment when the train had steamed out of Poolbrook Station leaving Mrs. Bootle waving on the platform. She told of the long journey, of her fear that the man they sought would not be at home—and then she spoke of her first encounter with Robert Sheldon. She had no idea how her voice altered or the expression on her face when she talked of him. Mrs. Bootle would have been blind and deaf if she had not realised that he meant something special in Sylvia's life.

Mrs. Bootle had been startled at her appearance when she had first arrived. The girl was looking worn out and utterly fatigued. But now as she spoke of Sir Robert the colour came back into her cheeks and her eyes shone. She spoke his name softly and Mrs. Bootle knew beyond all doubt, long before Sylvia revealed it in so many words, that she loved him.

The story went on, told at times hesitatingly, at times quickly as if Sylvia in a rush of words could skip over the dangerous emotions that had been aroused, the fears and the wonderings which in reality had taken so long in their passing. At last she came to the end, to that moment when Sir Robert had come up to the nursery, had catechised her, and then accused her of lying. . . .

It was then that the tears which had been gathering in her eyes ran unchecked down her cheeks. She tried to continue, tried to control her voice, to speak steadily, but it was no use; she broke down, put her head between her hands and sobbed.

Mrs. Bootle understood. She could without any tremendous effort of imagination fill in the gaps. She let Sylvia cry for a few moments before she said briskly:

'Now, dearie, tears aren't going to do you any good. They'll only make you feel worse and there's nothing to be gained by that.'

'I can't help it,' Sylvia faltered. 'If you only knew what happened; but I can't tell you, I can't tell anyone.'

'I can have a shrewd guess,' Mrs. Bootle remarked dryly; and then, lying back in her chair, she said casually, 'So you ran away and left that young minx Romola in possession, so to speak.'

Sylvia stopped crying and dropped her hands. If Mrs. Bootle had wished to shock her, she had succeeded.

'What do you mean?'

'What I said, ' Mrs. Bootle replied. 'Romola's out to get Sir Robert by fair means or foul, and you've gone and left her a fair field.'

'Romola . . . I never thought of it . . . I mean, why should you think . . . ?'

Mrs. Bootle gave a short laugh. "If I could tell you all I think about that sister of yours it would fill a volume and leave some over. Oh, I know you're fond of her, or you used to be, and more's the pity. I must say I never wept any tears when she ran away from home. It was the best thing that could have happened as far as you and your mother were concerned.'

'Oh, Mrs. Bootle! How can you say such things!'

'I can say them and a good deal more,' Mrs. Bootle retorted. 'I've watched that young miss ever since I first used to come and treat your mother, and a more selfish little hussy I never saw. Never a hand's turn did she give in the house. It was "Sylvia will do this," or "Sylvia will do that," or "Sylvia will fetch it for you," and all she was thinking about was dolling herself up and making eyes at half the young men in Poolbrook.'

'Oh, I'm sure that isn't true. You are just making it up!'

'God strike me dead if I'm speaking anything but the truth,' Mrs. Bootle said solemnly. 'You were only a child at the time; I don't suppose such an idea ever entered your head, but I saw her goings-on. How do you think she ever met that theatrical man that she went off with? Not by going to church or doing any of the other things that she told you and your mother she was doing. If anyone was born in original sin it was her. Never have I seen a girl who I was more sure would sooner or later go to the bad, and the night she ran away I said to Father—you ask him if this isn't the truth—I said to him, "That Romola Wace has gone off just as I said she would. It doesn't surprise me, but I'm sorry for her mother and sister. They knew nothing of the world and less about the people who live in it. That girl will be a sorrow and a grief to them all the days of their lives." Now you ask Father if I didn't say those very words to him. That's what I said at the time, and I knew that sooner or later she would turn up in your life and make trouble.'

'I can't believe it even now,' Sylvia protested. 'I loved Romola so much, I love her still.'

'Do you?' Mrs. Bootle asked shrewdly, 'or are you just telling yourself you do? I can't really believe that you've got much in common.'

'No, perhaps we haven't,' Sylvia admitted; 'and yet she is the only relation—a close one—that I have left now that Mother has gone.'

'When I hear people talking about their relations,' Mrs. Bootle said, 'I always remember that God gives us our relations, but we choose our friends. You can't help Romola being your sister, but you can help making a friend of her, letting her rule your life by her selfish goings-on and interfering with your happiness.'

'Perhaps she didn't mean any harm,' Sylvia said. 'I think she only wanted a good time.'

'Didn't mean any harm?' Mrs. Bootle echoed. 'I bet £1,000 to a postage stamp that your sister knew exactly what she was doing. Pretending to you that she was packing in her bedroom and then going downstairs all dressed up to kill, I shouldn't wonder.'

Sylvia thought of all those evening dresses packed away in the trunk. Was that why Romola had locked the door and refused to let her in? Yes, she must have dressed up deliberately and forced herself upon the man whose hospitality—unconscious of it though he might have been—she had enjoyed for over three weeks. Something fastidious in Sylvia revolted at the whole idea, even as she had been disgusted and ashamed of the lies she had to tell at Romola's insistence. And yet she couldn't be disloyal; not even to Mrs. Bootle could she confess her horror and dislike of much that Romola had said and done.

'Romola has suffered,' she said; 'she has suffered so much that we have got to make allowances for her.'

'Well, you've made them already,' Mrs. Bootle snorted. 'As I said, she's got her own way and what more could she want? You're out of the running and it's up to her to win the prize.'

'You mean Sir Robert?' Sylvia asked. 'But I am quite, quite certain he would never marry her; Lady Clementina would never allow it.'

'There's other things than marriage for that sort,' Mrs. Bootle said enigmatically. And then looking at Sylvia's pale cheeks and tired eyes, she added, 'Now you get to sleep; it's no use worrying, and it's no use lying awake trying to decide whether you've done the right thing or the wrong. It's done now and I'm not saying that I blame you. At least you've shown that you know how a lady should behave, and that's something.'

Sylvia suddenly reached out her hand to clasp the other woman's. 'I did do the right thing, didn't I?' she asked. 'I didn't mean to go, I didn't want to leave Lucy; but I can never, never see him again. I could never bear to look in his eyes and know what he felt.'

There was so much pathos in her voice and so much pleading in the expression on her face that Mrs. Bootle, whatever her inner convictions, knew that she must agree.

'You did the right thing, my dear,' she said soothingly. 'But let's talk about it tomorrow. There will be plenty of time, and when you're feeling stronger we will consider the future and forget the past. What is the point of looking back? As I always say to Father, "It's today and tomorrow that counts. We can't have yesterday again, not for all the wishing in the world!"'

'Yes, that is true,' Sylvia said, and added softly, 'Thank you, dear, dear Mrs. Bootle, and good night.'

'Good night, my dear.'

Mrs. Bootle rose and taking the candle with her turned towards the door.

In the darkness Sylvia closed her eyes. Clearly as if he stood there she could see Sir Robert's face, see his lips curl as they spoke those words of bitterness, see the pain and anger in his eyes as he denounced her for the liar that she was. Sylvia gave a little cry and buried her face in the pillows. At this moment he would still be thinking such things of her, still believe that she had deceived him, deliberately and with intention. She thought of all that Mrs. Bootle had implied. Could Sir Robert really be interested in Romola? 'Robert, Robert.' The name burst from her lips to be smothered in the softness of the pillow. 'Oh, Robert, I love you.' She had said it, admitted it at last—aloud and in the darkness . . . 'I love you, I love you . . .' The words taunted her and yet she must go on saying them, must know that they were true and that every nerve and feeling in her whole body vibrated to the harmony of them. She loved him, and once it might have been possible that he would love her.

She understood now why he had gone away that night after the dinner party when he had come up and found her asleep. It was because he was protecting her from himself;

189

it was because he respected her. And now that respect had gone; she had killed it by her own stupidity, by agreeing to Romola's suggestions and plans. Fool that she had been! And yet, what else could she have done? How could she have left her sister alone and ill, without friends and without money?

At the thought of money, Sylvia remembered Mr. Robb's kindness. He had trusted her even as she had trusted and believed in other people. Surely there was no harm in that? Surely it was better to be robbed than to suspect everyone, to miss the chance of doing a good turn to someone in trouble? That was all she had tried to do—to do Romola a good turn, to nurse her back to health. And if they had gone to Lady Clementina with the truth, what hope was there that Romola would have been allowed to stay at Sheldon Hall? From one lie all this had come—this misery, this humiliation, this exile!

'I have been punished—yes, punished,' Sylvia sobbed.

Once again she felt her cheek burn where Sir Robert had struck her. How angry he had been! But physical violence had mattered little beside the knowledge that she had failed him. He had spoken like a man who had been betrayed by treachery. He had cared, yes, he had cared; cared enough to be brutal, to be cruel, and yet at the same time inflamed by his desire. And now she would never see him again.

It seemed to her then that her life was completely over. There was nothing to look forward to, nothing the future could hold except misery and a vast, utter loneliness beyond words. All hope had gone, and without hope there could be no happiness. None!

She must have fallen asleep from sheer exhaustion. When she opened her eyes again, the light was coming from between the curtained window and for a moment she wondered where she was, expecting to see the familiar outlines of her room at Sheldon Hall. Then the smallness of the room struck her and she remembered yesterday and all that had happened. She turned over and saw the clock beside the bed. It was nearly noon.

Sylvia sat up with an exclamation. In the room below she could hear voices and she called out:

'Mrs. Bootle, I've just woken up. Is it really nearly 12 o'clock?'

'Coming, dearie,' Mrs. Bootle called, and a few moments later she entered the room.

190

'Well, you've slept the clock round,' she said, 'and a good thing, too.' She pulled back the curtains, letting in the sunlight. 'There, let's have a look at you. Yes, you look better already. I peeped in at you when I went down to breakfast. You were asleep, as quiet and comfortable as a baby. "The girl's fair worn out," I said to Father. "Don't you make a noise now." And I kept him creeping about in his stockinged feet until it was time for him to go out.'

'Oh, Mrs. Bootle, you shouldn't have done that. I am ashamed of myself. I will get up at once.'

'That you won't, not until you've had some breakfast,' Mrs. Bootle said. 'I've got the kettle on now, and it won't take me a moment to fry you some bacon. Now lie back and don't worry about anything until you've had something to eat. If there's one time when it's wrong to think, it's on an empty stomach.'

Mrs. Bootle sailed away and Sylvia did as she was told, or at least tried to. But despite every resolution her thoughts turned immediately to Sheldon Hall. By now everyone would know that she had run away. She wondered what Lady Clementina would think. Lucy would be upset. And Sir Robert, what would he say? There was Romola, too. She would have to leave today if Lady Clementina's instructions were to be carried out. Or would she be clever enough to get Sir Robert on her side so that Lady Clementina would be forced to allow her to stay on? Sylvia had some idea of how Romola would react to the news of her disappearance. It would be a grand opportunity for her to appear distressed. She would have the right to be consulted on what should be done, and now for the first time Sylvia began to worry in case Romola should guess where she had gone. She had been quite sure that neither Sir Robert nor Lady Clementina had ever heard of Mrs. Bootle. They might write to Uncle Octavius; but even he was unlikely to guess that Sylvia would find sanctuary in such lowly surroundings. Romola was different; Romola knew Mrs. Bootle, and Sylvia had told her how kind the woman had been during their mother's illness and how she had been instrumental in getting her the job as Lucy's governess.

Then, unconsciously admitting Mrs. Bootle's estimate of her sister, Sylvia realised that, even if Romola guessed, she would be in no hurry to voice her suspicion if she wished to remain at Sheldon Hall; and if she wished the attention to be focused on herself it was all the more important that

Sylvia should not be found too soon or too easily. No, Romola was not likely to solve the mystery; she was far more likely to add to it—that was, if anyone was sufficiently interested to find out what had become of her. 'Perhaps they won't care,' Sylvia thought, and felt the idea wound her out of all proportion.

By the time Mrs. Bootle came up with her breakfast tray she was feeling dejected and even a little sorry for herself. The sadness of her expression did not escape Mrs. Bootle's sharp eyes.

'There now, you've been thinking,' she said, 'and you know I told you not to. What's the point of me talking, I'd like to know? Now eat every bit of this and you'll feel a different person.'

'I wish I was sure of that,' Sylvia said.

Nevertheless she did as she was told, eating up the crisply fried bacon and pouring herself out a cup of tea.

'Now it's no use moping,' Mrs. Bootle said briskly. 'Moping never helped anybody, neither man nor woman. What you want is something to occupy your mind.'

'I know that. What do you suggest? You found me one job and I haven't been very successful in that. Can you be bothered to help me again?'

'See here, dearie, it's no trouble. I've always been fond of you. I saw the way you looked after your mother and I admired you for it. It was not an easy job, no one knows that better than I do, but you did it and you kept smiling in spite of all the difficulties and a good deal of ingratitude. Your mother didn't mean it, poor soul; it was part of her illness; but I've heard her speak many a sharp word to you and you took it like the little Trojan you were. Well now, it's time for somebody to do something for you and if I'm the one to do it I'll be glad of the opportunity.'

'Oh, Mrs. Bootle, you are much too kind and I don't deserve it. I have been a fool in lots of ways, I realise that now.'

'We all are at times. If we didn't make mistakes, the world would come to an end and then what would happen? Never you mind about what's happened in the past. Let's get on with worrying about the future. First of all, have you got any money?'

Sylvia flushed. 'I was going to tell you about that. I am afraid I haven't, and what is more, I owe quite a lot.'

She told Mrs. Bootle about Mr. Robb's kindness.

'How did you come to run away with nothing in your purse?' Mrs. Bootle asked. 'It's well after the first of the month; what have you done with your wages?'

Feeling almost ashamed of her own generosity, Sylvia told her.

'So Miss Romola's got that, too, has she? Well, I don't know, but it seems to me that you've been had for a mug all along the line. But there, what's the use of talking? It's done now.'

'I must get a job of some sort, and quickly. I must pay back Mr. Robb and you, dear Mrs. Bootle.'

'Now don't you start talking like that,' Mrs. Bootle said sharply. 'It isn't money as I want, and you know it. But a woman's got to have some money in her purse. Well, we shall have to put on our thinking caps. There must be something to be found hereabouts. Perhaps there's a lady wanting a companion, or even a governess.'

'Not children,' Sylvia said quickly. Then seeing the expression on Mrs. Bootle's face, she added quickly, 'That sounds ungrateful, but I am not really. Somehow I don't want to look after a child, not after Lucy. She is so sweet, so affectionate, I should feel disloyal if I looked after any other child but her.'

'Well, you take things easy for the moment,' Mrs. Bootle replied, 'and I'll be keeping my ears open for what I can hear.' And with that she left Sylvia to get up.

When Sylvia came downstairs, it was to find Mrs. Bootle cooking the lunch, while a delicious smell of stew pervaded the small kitchen.

'I've been thinking,' Mrs. Bootle said. 'I believe you might get a bit of employment with Doctor Harris. He was saying the other day that he had got in a muddle with his accounts. His wife used to do them for him, but she died nearly twelve months ago and he's got nobody there except a young son of his reading for the Church.'

'Do you think he would have me?' Sylvia asked. 'But I know nothing about medicine or medical terms.'

'I don't expect you have to,' Mrs. Bootle said. 'What he wants to know is who has paid him and who hasn't. These doctors are all alike, never give themselves a chance to get straight. I don't suppose he'll pay you much, but you could stay here with us for the time being and that won't be expensive.'

'Mrs. Bootle, are you sure?' Sylvia asked. 'I can't take your son's bedroom, not permanently.'

'Oh, Bill! He's all right,' Mrs. Bootle answered. 'He can stay with his friend Harry up at the Cross. They're always asking him and the two boys are such friends that they'd rather be together.'

'I had no idea until now that you had a son,' Sylvia said.

Mrs. Bootle smiled. 'Well, he isn't really my son, if it comes to that; but I always call him son and think of him as such. He's my sister's child—my youngest sister's. She died nearly ten years ago and we've had the lad with us ever since. He's a nice boy and Father and me, we look on him as if he was our own, the Lord never having blessed us with children.'

'So you had a sister,' Sylvia said softly.

Mrs. Bootle nodded. 'Yes, I had a sister. She was a sweet girl and there was no harm in her. The man she married was a brute; he knocked her about and then deserted her. I sould never be surprised to learn that they weren't really married; he looked the type that might have a wife in every port, one of those rolling stones which bring no good to man or woman. Anyway, we've got young Bill and it's a joy to have him.'

'That is what I mean,' Sylvia said. 'You are complete in your little household and I can't possibly intrude on it. If you will just find me a job to bring me in enough money, I will find a room somewhere; there must be lodgings to let.'

'There's lodgings to let all right,' Mrs. Bootle said with scorn, 'but I'd rather see a child of mine dead than living in most of them. Dirty, verminous places with old harpies charging a top price for accommodation that most people wouldn't offer to an animal. No, my dear, you're going to stay with me—at any rate for the present.'

Sylvia expressed her relief and grateful thanks. She had no desire to leave Mrs. Bootle and yet she felt somewhat ashamed of imposing on her. But the more she talked of leaving, the less Mrs. Bootle would listen to her; so finally she gave in, thankful beyond words that she need not trouble about where to lay her head for the time being.

True to her word, Mrs. Bootle went up to see Doctor Harris, but the news she brought back with her was not particularly good.

'He says he could do with someone, but if you are untrained he doesn't see why he should pay you much. He offers you fifteen shillings a week and you are to be there from nine to six. Slavery I call it.'

'At least it is something,' Sylvia said quickly. 'And he is right; I am certainly untrained. But fifteen shillings is better than nothing and I can start to pay off my debt to Mr. Robb. Do you think you could feed me on seven-and-sixpence a week?'

'Now don't you worry about that,' Mrs. Bootle said in a brusque voice, and then added as if in explanation, 'Sometimes you remind me of my sister. She was a pretty girl, though you wouldn't think it to look at me, and as she was much the youngest I used to look after her rather as I am looking after you. If she had taken my advice she would never have married that man and might even be alive today. But there, however fond a woman is of you, when a man comes along you go to the wall. Always remember that. It's men first every time.'

Sylvia wondered if it was true, and then to test herself asked the question: If she had known what was to be the result of her action, would she still have helped Romola when she found her sick, lonely and ill at the Green Man? Could she there and then have made up her mind to offend Sir Robert? She knew the answer and in all humbleness admitted that Mrs. Bootle was right.

The following day she went up to Dr. Harris's house. It was a dark, gloomy, Victorian villa standing a little way back from the road and enclosed around with dark shrubs and laurel bushes.

She rang the front-door bell, but no one came to answer it. Then she knocked with the same result. Finally she started to tour round the house, trying to find the back door. She walked through an untidy, ill-kept garden and came to a yard where a youth was mending a puncture in a bicycle tyre. He did not notice her until Sylvia, shy and hesitant, said:

'Excuse me, but is there anyone at home?'

He looked up and the scowl of concentration on his face changed to a smile.

'Hallo, do you want to see the old man?'

'I want to see Dr. Harris, but the bell seems to be out of order.'

'It's been like that for months. The patients always go to the side door.'

'I'm sorry, but I don't know where that is.'

'Go back the way you came and turn right instead of left, that's the answer.'

'Oh, thank you. I am sorry I disturbed you.'

'That's all right. It's a pleasure. Don't tell me you are a patient—you look well enough.'

'No, I want to see Dr. Harris on business.'

'It sounds intriguing. Won't I do instead?'

'I am afraid not.'

Sylvia turned to go away.

'Why not? I am his son.'

'I thought you must be. Mrs. Bootle has made an appointment with your father for me to see him.'

'Mrs. Bootle?' The youth wrinkled his brow. 'Is she the fat old witch that has something to do with nursing?'

'That's right, but she isn't a witch; she is the kindest person in the world.'

Young Mr. Harris laughed. 'I'll take your word for it. She terrifies me. Now you are different. I shouldn't feel frightened of you.'

There was something flirtatious in his expression. Sylvia turned away.

'Thank you for your help. I will go round to the right door.'

'Now what have I said to make you run away like that?' he asked. 'Here, I'm sick of this puncture, I will come and show you the way myself.'

'There is no need, thank you.'

'There is every need. Pretty ladies shouldn't go wandering about this lonely garden by themselves.'

'Please, Mr. Harris. It is quite all right. As I said, I have come to see your father on business and there is no need for you to trouble.'

'Tell me what the business is.'

Sylvia felt it would be more dignified to tell the truth.

'I understand he is looking for someone to do a secretarial job for him.'

'And you are going to take it? Coo-er.' There came an expressive whistle. 'That's the best thing that has happened in this household for a long time. We need someone like you about the place.'

'I shall be busy working for Doctor Harris.'

'I say, is that meant to be a snub? You mustn't be unkind to me, you know.'

'I understood you were reading for Holy Orders?'

'That's true enough, but it doesn't say the reading will get me anywhere. I'm not clever enough to be a doctor and

I very much doubt if I am clever enough to be a parson. Besides, who wants to be a parson anyway?'

Sylvia looked at him in surprise. 'Well, why don't you choose some other profession?'

'What? And again which? It's got to require no private income; it's got to carry a salary with it; it's got to be such as befits a gentleman!'

He said the last words mockingly, but nevertheless Sylvia knew that he was stating facts.

'It does sound rather difficult.'

'It is, and if I have you to distract my attention I should think my Ordination will be at least half a dozen years farther off.'

'In which case perhaps I had better not see your father.'

'Now don't be stupid. I think there is really no reason to see him at all. Consider yourself engaged.'

Sylvia could not help smiling at his impertinence. At the same time she felt that things were progressing too rapidly and hurried her footsteps towards the side entrance.

'I say, you are in a hurry,' Dr. Harris's son protested. 'By the way, what's your name?'

'Wace,' Sylvia said briefly.

'What were you christened?'

'Is it necessary for you to know?'

'Now you are trying to snub me again. You are hard on a fellow.'

'I'm sorry,' Sylvia said, 'but think we had better confine ourselves to business.'

'What a hope you've got. Haven't you got a looking-glass in your house?'

Sylvia was blushing now and without more ado she hurried away from him and turned the corner of the house. Seeing with relief the side door at which she imagined she would receive attention, she knocked on it and it opened. An elderly man with a beard was standing inside.

'Miss Wace?'

'Yes, I am Miss Wace. And you are Doctor Harris?'

'That's right. Will you come in?'

There was a smell of antiseptic in the dark passage which led into an untidy, dusty consulting room. Sylvia, feeling nervous, followed the doctor into the room. He sat down at a big roll-top desk and indicated an armchair facing the light. Primly she sat down and awaited his first question; but try as she would she could not prevent the colour springing to her cheeks as past the window with his hands in his pockets sauntered the doctor's son whistling a popular tune of the moment, *'You are my honey, honeysuckle, I am the bee; I want to suck the honey up from those sweet lips you see . . .'*

Dr. Harris looked at her over the top of his spectacles.

'You are very young,' he said gruffly. 'Mrs. Bootle gave me to understand that you were older.'

It seemed to Sylvia that he spoke accusingly.

'I'm sorry,' she faltered.

18

Mrs. Bootle lowered herself slowly into the arm-chair in front of the fire and bent down to unlace her boots.

'Oh my, but I have had a day of it,' she said to her husband who, seated on the other side of the hearth, was smoking his pipe reflectively. 'First of all Mrs. Lockwood has twins this morning—the last thing we expected, or she wanted for that matter. But there they were and as bonny a pair of boys as ever you saw, though it meant a lot of extra work for me as you can well imagine. And then just as I thought I'd got her tidied up, along comes little Johnny Drew to say his grandfather was having one of his seizures. Well, I thought the old man was done for this time, but we got him round, and you mark my words, he'll be good for another ten . . .'

Mrs. Bottle got no further. The kitchen door was flung open abruptly and Sylvia came in. She was panting as if she had been running; there were two brilliant patches of colour in her cheeks and her hair seemed to have become loosened beneath her felt hat. She came forward into the light and Mrs. Bootle saw that she was trembling.

'Why, whatever's happened, dearie? You look real put about.'

'It is no use,' Sylvia said in a helpless tone of voice, 'I can't stand it any longer! I can't go back there, I can't!'

'Now just you sit down and take things easy,' Mrs. Bootle said. 'Here, Father, get her a chair.'

But Mr. Bootle had already risen and had drawn forward his own chair which Sylvia sank into gratefully. Then he walked across the kitchen and took his cap off the peg on the door.

'Going out?' Mrs. Bootle asked.

He nodded. 'I'll just pop up to the Cross Keys,' he said.

Mrs. Bootle knew that this was his way of being tactful. He was used to people coming in at all hours to ask his wife's help or confide in her, and as he put it himself—'He knew when he wasn't wanted.'

The door closed behind him and Mrs. Bootle bent towards Sylvia.

'Now, what's happened?' she asked.

Sylvia held out her hands to the fire. She looked white and shaken.

'It seems ridiculous,' she said, 'but I can't put up with that Harris boy any longer. I have done everything, really everything, Mrs. Bootle, to get him to leave me alone; but he won't, and I can't face going back there any more.'

'But, good heavens!' Mrs. Bootle said, 'why didn't you tell me about it before? I'll have a word with the doctor. I've heard tales about that young man, but I thought they were just a bit of gossip. I'd no idea he was pestering you.'

'Pestering is the right word,' Sylvia said bitterly. 'It started the very first day I went there and now it has become intolerable. He lies in wait for me.' Her voice quivered. 'Tonight he was hiding in the laurel bushes and he pounced out at me suddenly when I wasn't expecting it. It was almost dark in the drive and I was terrified, simply terrified. Oh, I know it sounds silly; and I am ashamed, utterly ashamed, Mrs. Bootle, of not being able to look after myself, that I can't put someone of that sort in his proper place.'

'There, there, don't fuss yourself. It isn't your fault.'

'But it must be. Other women have to earn their living. Why, the papers are full of women saying what they are going to do in the future. How have we got a chance of doing anything if the men won't leave us alone, if they take advantage of our being defenceless and weaker than they are?'

'I've always contended that a woman wants a man to look after her. It's going against nature that women should have to earn their living. Many's the time I've said that to

Father. Not that I haven't earned my own all my life. But then, there's the rub. It's the pretty women who find it hard, not the plain ones.'

Sylvia put her hands up to her eyes. 'Sometimes I hate my looks.'

Even as she spoke the words she knew they were not true. Could she ever forget that Sir Robert had once looked at her with admiration and she had known and been glad that he found her lovely?

'Well, don't trouble yourself about young Harris any more,' Mrs. Bootle said. 'We'll look round for something else.'

'And in the meantime I am nothing more than a drag on you. It is not right that you should work for me. You have worked hard and now you are keeping me who am young and active and ought to be earning enough money for myself.'

Mrs. Bootle laughed. 'Bless you, but you needn't be so dramatic about it. Why, you don't eat enough to keep a sparrow alive and we're glad to have you here. Now stop worrying, dearie; I'll go up and see Dr. Harris myself in the morning and tell him a thing or two about that son of his.'

'No, no, don't do that,' Sylvia said. 'He will only tell lies and say I encouraged him or something. He has accused me of that before now.'

'Why didn't you tell me?' Mrs. Bootle repeated. 'I'd have stopped that nonsense long ago.'

Sylvia did not reply. She could not explain that when Cyril Harris had forced his attentions on her she had felt ashamed of her imcompetence and awkwardness because of her own lack of experience. She had made every effort to be as cool and discouraging as she could, trying to keep her dignity and even shame him into leaving her alone. But he was persistent; it seemed impossible indeed to make him understand that any woman should not be flattered by his attentions. He was uncrushable and completely irresponsible and he managed to make Sylvia's life a hell for the ten days that she had worked for his father.

As soon as Dr. Harris had left the house to visit his patients, he would come creeping along to the room where Sylvia was working. Once she tried the experiment of locking the door; but he banged on it noisily, making such a fuss that eventually she let him in rather than risk his attracting the attention of the two maids whom Dr. Harris

200

employed. They would have known a good deal more if both had not been deaf and extremely old. Even so, Sylvia felt that they suspected her of encouraging Cyril. More than once one of them had come into the room to find her arguing with him or doing her best to keep him at arm's length.

Apart from the trouble he caused, she felt repelled by Cyril. He was an overgrown, spotty youth who did not take enough exercise and who, she guessed, indulged himself far too frequently the local public-houses. What she did not know was that he had a reputation for being a bit of a terror to the local girls and that his father had more than once been called upon to get him out of trouble and pay for him to retain his freedom. Anyone more unsuited to be a clergyman it was hard to imagine, but Cyril informed her that his chances were quite as good as most of the other undergraduates with him at Oxford and he expected to reform when finally he took Orders.

If he had been up at Oxford at this time, Sylvia felt she would have quite enjoyed working for Dr. Harris. He was a nice old man with a somewhat gruff and abrupt manner, and when she saw the muddle into which his personal affairs had got through neglect and overwork she felt sorry for him. Nevertheless with Cyril at home she could neither do her best for his father nor prevent herself from becoming terrorised by the continual physical attacks he made upon her.

'Come on, give us a kiss,' was his usual greeting. 'What do you think you've got lips for? Be a sport.'

When she refused he would try to compel her by more violent means. More than once Sylvia found herself forced to be undignified and struggle with him, and after a few days it became a real effort for her to force herself to go back to work the next morning. She lay awake at night thinking how she could drive Cyril away from her, but anger, rudeness or even pleading had no effect on him. He was attracted by her and he saw no reason why her feelings should be considered more than his own.

'Surely you must have some decency in you,' she said once.

'Not where you're concerned,' was the cheery answer. 'You're the prettiest girl I've ever seen; and knowing that, you can't expect me to miss my opportunities.'

'You are behaving like a cad.'

'What if I am?' he grinned at her. 'Besides, if you

201

dropped the grand manner for a bit you'd enjoy it. We could have a lot of fun together, you and I.'

'I don't want to have any fun with you. I loathe you and despise you. Now is that clear enough?'

'By Jove! you look pretty when you're angry.'

It was all the answer she got so she turned away in despair, perilously near to tears.

But tonight had been the last straw. She had understood from Dr. Harris that Cyril was out for the day, and she had really got ahead with her work, sorting out the more outstanding accounts and filing away letters which had remained unanswered long enough to answer themselves. She worked later than usual and only realised how the time had flown when it grew dark and one of the maids came in to light the gas. Sylvia stretched her cramped knees and put on her hat and coat.

'Here are two messages for the doctor when he comes in,' she told the maid.

'Very good, miss. I'll see that he gets them.'

'Thank you. Good night, Ellen.'

'Good night, miss.'

Sylvia let herself out at the side door. It was almost dark and she hurried round to the front of the house, the untidy, overgrown laurels casting deep shadows in the drive. She was hurrying along, wondering if Mrs. Bootle would be home and thinking that she would be glad to have her supper, when suddenly she felt someone spring at her. She screamed and in her fear it was a moment before she realised who it was. Then she heard Cyril's odious chuckle and felt his hot breath on her cheek.

'Caught you, my beauty!'

'Let me go!'

She tried to thrust him away from her, but he was stronger than she and now she felt his mouth seeking hers. Wild with rage, she hit him hard in the face. He swore.

'You little devil! I'll teach you to hurt me!'

For a moment under the pain of her attack, his grip on her was relaxed. She fought herself free, she heard the sleeve of her coat rip as he clutched her, and then she was away, running as hard as she could down the drive, through the gate and up the road. He followed her only for a few steps and she guessed that as there were several people about who might know him, he had given up the chase. But Sylvia never stopped running until she reached the cootage.

She felt dirty and besmirched that he should have touched her, and almost roughly she rubbed her cheeks. Then the helplessness of her position sapped away her anger. Was this the inevitable end of every attempt that she might make to earn her living? She looked across at Mrs. Bootle. Suddenly she envied her, her age and even her vast bulk, because both brought her respect and dignity rather than degradation and being pursued and mauled by men such as Cyril Harris. She sighed.

'What am I to do, Mrs. Bootle?' she asked. 'Does it mean that I ought to communicate with Uncle Octavius?'

'Not on your life it doesn't.' Mrs. Bootle's words were reassuringly vehement.

'Nevertheless perhaps that would be the best thing to do. I suppose if I appealed to him in the right way he would forgive me for having gone to Sheldon Hall. It might even give him a perverted kind of satisfaction to know that I had to leave there. He and Aunt Matilda would take me in. I might not be earning any money with them, but at least I would be working for my keep, they would see to that all right.'

'As long as I am alive,' Mrs. Bootle said, 'you shan't go to a man like that. I know his sort only too well. You should have heard the things he said when he arrived to find your poor mother dead and you gone. And the way he treated me! You'd think I'd been coining money out of your mother for years!'

Sylvia had to laugh. 'What did you say to him?'

'He got as good as he gave,' Mrs. Bootle remarked. 'But you aren't going to live with him, not if I can help it. A nasty sort of man, a type I never did care for, clergyman or no clergyman!'

'But what else am I to do?'

Mrs. Bootle sighed. 'Well, we'll have to find you something. We'll have to choose a place where there are no men about, only women.'

'Perhaps they won't want me either.'

'There will be some that won't,' Mrs. Bootle said dryly. 'But we'll find someone who will, don't you worry. Now what about a bit of supper?'

'Let me cook it for you,' Sylvia offered. 'You are tired, I can see that.'

'Well I'm not saying that my feet aren't a bit weary,' Mrs. Bootle admitted.

'Then I am going to do the cooking. Now you sit still

and if I do anything wrong you can tell me. But Mother used to say I was a very good cook.'

'And so you were,' Mrs. Bootle replied, 'and an economical one, too. And there's the test. If the food's there anyone can cook it, but if it isn't you've got to be a genius to make it tasty.'

Sylvia suddenly bent and kissed Mrs. Bootle's cheek.

'You are a wonderful person. If I lose confidence in one direction you always give it back to me in another. Perhaps I can go as cook to someone. Who knows?—somebody might be pleased to have me. They say there is a shortage of domestic servants.'

'I couldn't see you in service,' Mrs. Bootle said positively.

'Nonsense!' Sylvia replied. 'I think it is a good idea. I can't understand why we didn't think of it before. There are lots of houses where they don't have men servants and I shouldn't be likely to have trouble with the parlourmaid—not if I kept myself to myself.'

'You aren't serious,' Mrs. Bootle said. 'What would your poor mother say?'

'I don't suppose she would be any more shocked at my earning an honest penny in domestic service than she would be if she knew what I have had to put up with this last week,' Sylvia said.

'Well, that's true enough,' Mrs. Bootle said. 'And I'd just like to lay my hands on that young Cyril Harris.'

Sylvia hung up her hat and coat behind the door and put a big white apron over her dress. She smoothed her hair with her hands, but was too lazy to go upstairs and tidy it properly. The curls which had escaped lay on the nape of her neck and round her forehead, and now that her cheeks were flushed with the heat from the fire and the scared look had gone from her eyes she was amazingly pretty again. Mrs. Bootle watched her preparing the vegetables for their evening meal and she felt a sudden mistiness before her eyes. Sylvia's beauty was so delicate, so obviously something of the spirit as well as of the body that it was apparent to anyone perceptive that she could never stand on her own in a harsh, competitive world where women as well as men were seeking employment. As she bent over the table with her sleeves rolled up above the elbow she looked little more than a schoolgirl, and Mrs. Bootle had a momentary vision of her struggling against overwhelming odds. She saw her bearing insult after insult, being turned away from job after job, running away from them for the same reason always—because she would at tract the wrong type of man and was unlikely to meet the right sort. What will become of her? Mrs. Bootle wondered helplessly, and everything that was maternal in her big, generous body longed to protect this fragile, beautiful creature from the inevitable.

'There, if you don't enjoy this,' Sylvia said, 'I shall burst into tears. I heard Mr. Bootle say two days ago that he liked a pie and I thought then that I would like the opportunity of making him one.'

'I know who will enjoy it,' Mrs. Bootle said, 'and that's Bill. He's always hungry, that boy; but there, what growing child isn't? He ought to be back soon.'

'Oh, I'm not ready for him yet,' Sylvia smiled. 'I am going to make Bill something particularly delicious with the remains of this pastry.'

She picked up the rolling-pin. At that moment there came a loud knock on the door.

'Now I wonder who that is,' Mrs. Bootle said. 'I really can't go out again tonight. Someone will have to be very bad before they get me to move.'

The knock came again, impatient and peremptory.

'Oh, dear, can't people wait for a moment,' Sylvia cried.

She put down the rolling-pin and rubbed a little of the flour from her hands on to her apron as she turned towards the door. She flung it open and then stood transfixed as if suddenly turned to stone, for standing in the doorway, the light full on his face, was Robert Sheldon.

For a moment he did not speak, and Mrs. Bootle, twisting round in her chair, asked:

'Who is it?'

'May I come in?'

Sir Robert spoke to Sylvia, but she couldn't answer him. One hand went convulsively to the base of her white throat as if she could not get her breath.

Sir Robert took off his hat and bowing his head entered the cottage. In the small, low-ceilinged room he looked amazingly tall and so utterly out of keeping with the surroundings that even Mrs. Bootle was awed into silence. Seeing her sitting before the fire he moved across to her side.

'You must be Mrs. Bootle,' he said courteously and he held out his hand.

Mrs. Bootle got up out of the chair.

'That's right, sir.'

'Then I have you to thank, and I do indeed thank you very much for your letter. It was extremely kind and considerate of you to write to me.'

At last Sylvia could speak.

'A letter?'

Mrs. Bootle looked at her and appeared embarrassed.

'I felt it was my duty, dearie, to let him know where you were. It's not right for anyone to disappear as if the earth had swallowed them up.'

'Oh, Mrs. Bootle, how could you?'

Sylvia's eyes filled with tears. Even Mrs. Bootle had failed her—the one person of whom she was sure, of whose loyalty she was certain.

Sir Robert turned towards her.

'Mrs. Bootle has done me a great service; I have come to ask you to return.'

'No, never, never!'

Sylvia's reply was quick and seemed to come from the depths of her being.

'Won't you hear why I am asking you to come back?' Sir Robert asked. He spoke gently.

Sylvia had half turned her back on him. He could not see her face, only the little loose curls clustered against the whiteness of her neck.

'Please, will you listen to me?'

There was a note of authority in his voice.

Sylvia swung round. There were tears in her eyes; she held her head high and her hands were clenched at her sides.

'I don't want to hear anything you have got to say, Sir Robert. You have no right to come here. You know why I left your house. Will you please go.'

They faced each other across the small kitchen. Somehow it seemed as if they faced each other across eternity—man and woman drawn together, yet separated. Their eyes met and suddenly they were both spellbound as something magnetic, strong and vibrating passed between them. A moment passed. . . . Then as if she wrenched herself free, Sylvia repeated, 'Will you please go.'

'Not until I have told you why I have come here.'

Now there was a ring in Sir Robert's voice. His quiet gravity had gone. It seemed even as if he was no longer humble but commanding, taking control of the situation.

'Lucy is ill, very ill. She is asking for you. Won't you come to her?'

'Lucy.' Sylvia almost whispered the name. 'What is the matter?'

'She caught cold. When they told her that you had gone, she thought you were somewhere in the grounds and she went looking for you on her own. It was a raw day and she was insufficiently wrapped up. When we found her, she was wet through and weak with exhaustion.'

'Oh, Lucy, Lucy!' The cry came from Sylvia's heart.

'She is very ill with pneumonia and she keeps crying out for you. Won't you come back to her?'

A quiver passed over Sylvia's face. She made up her mind.

'I will come at once.'

She took off the apron which covered her dress, folded it and put it on the chair. Then without another word she went upstairs to her room.

For a moment neither Sir Robert nor Mrs. Bootle spoke. Then Mrs. Bootle asked:

'Is the young lady really bad, sir?'

'I am afraid so.'

'I'm sorry.'

There was a long pause.

'You'll be kind to her, won't you, sir?'

Sir Robert nodded his head; he knew that Mrs. Bootle was not speaking of Lucy. 'I promise you that I will.'

'She's been through a difficult time. She has no money and it's hard for a young woman to get employment.'

'No money?' Sir Robert looked at Mrs. Bootle and his brows contracted harshly. 'I never thought of that.'

'It's the truth.'

'Thank you for telling me.' He looked round him at the small, shabby kitchen. 'May I pay what she owes you?'

Mrs. Bootle drew herself up.

'As long as Miss Wace has no other home she's welcome here.'

Her words were simple, but there was a world of pride in them.

Sir Robert understood. He held out his hand without another word and Mrs. Bootle put hers into it.

'Thank you once again for your letter,' he said.

Sylvia was coming down the stairs and a moment later she appeared, her bag in her hand. She said nothing; but going across to where she had hung up her hat and coat, she put them on, pinning her hat firmly on her now neat head. She was very pale and her eyes seemed unnaturally wide and dark, but it was difficult to know what she was thinking. She appeared completely composed.

'I am ready, Sir Robert.' She spoke steadily.

'My carriage is at the end of the road. Good-bye, Mrs. Bootle.'

Sylvia came toward and kissed the old woman. Sir Robert had moved across the room and for the moment was out of earshot.

'Don't think too harshly of me for writing to him,' Mrs. Bootle whispered. 'Perhaps one day you'll thank me.'

Sylvia said nothing. She merely gave her a hug and then with a little strange sound which was neither a sigh nor an exclamation she turned towards the door which Robert Sheldon held open for her.

19

Sylvia glanced at Sir Robert from under her eyelashes. His face was set in stern lines and his expression gave her no clue as to what he was thinking. The rumble of the train had been like a musical accompaniment to the meal they had just eaten. It still seemed unreal to Sylvia—to be transported as if by magic from Mrs. Bootle's tiny, poverty-stricken cottage to Sir Robert's private railway coach which, attached to the northern express, was carrying them swiftly through the darkness.

Her thoughts were so chaotic and her emotions so twisted and tangled that she had found it difficult to breathe, let alone to think, as she and Sir Robert journeyed by road from Poolbrook to the railway junction ten miles away. They sat side by side in silence, the clop-clop of the horse's hoofs and the jangling of harness seeming sufficient without words to tell Sylvia that once again she was leaving her old life behind and going back—yes, back to Sheldon Hall.

It seemed to her, too, that Sir Robert was more than usually reserved and taciturn. She felt that he was unapproachable, had withdrawn into some proud inner silence which made him more inhuman than ever, a person whom she could in no way connect with the man who had held her in his arms, who had stared down at her with raw, untramelled passion in his eyes. When he spoke, his voice was courteous but cold; and when she glanced at him once or twice as they drove through the town and the light from the street lamps fell momentarily within the carriage, she saw his profile, stern, arrogant and aloof.

When they reached the station, they had been led by uniformed attendants to Sir Robert's coach waiting in a siding. They had entered it and instantly, it seemd to Sylvia that the atmosphere of Sheldon Hall re-enveloped her, for the pomp and luxury which was so much a part of the house was echoed in miniature within the railway coach.

One of the footmen whom Sylvia recognised hurried forward, but Sir Robert waved him aside.

'I will show Miss Wace where she is sleeping.'

Sylvia barely had time to wonder at his words before he led her through the drawing-room and there, standing outside the sleeping accommodation, was Ethel.

'Your maid will see that you are properly attended to,' Sir Robert said, and he looked at Sylvia as he spoke.

She understood what he was trying to convey without words, and in an agony of shyness felt the colour rising swiftly to her face. He was assuring her that he would not violate the trust she had put in him. Though they would be travelling north through the darkness of the night, Ethel would be there to attend to her and she would not have the humiliation of knowing that she, a woman, was alone with him in the privacy of his own coach.

Sylvia could not reply to him. Instead she smiled at Ethel, making a gallant effort to appear natural. A moment later when she looked round Sir Robert had gone.

'Oh, miss, I am glad to see you.'

The sincerity in Ethel's tone brought the tears perilously near to Sylvia's eyes. She went in through the door that Ethel held open for her. The neat brass bedstead, the washing basin and mirror seemed almost austere until she saw a great bunch of hothouse carnations arranged in a vase on the wall and the monogrammed sheets and pillowcases. Sylvia took only one brief glance at her surroundings, and then she asked the question which had been echoing over and over in her mind but which she could not force herself to speak during the long journey from Poolbrook.

'Is Miss Lucy dangerously ill?'

Ethel clasped her hands together.

'Oh, miss, I can't tell you how awful it's been.'

'What happened? Sir Robert has told me so little.'

Ethel took a deep breath.

'It started as soon as you had gone away. When Miss Lucy realised as you had really gone, she got in a terrible state. Nannie tried to soothe her down but she wouldn't listen. "I want my Wacey. I want my Wacey," she kept saying over and over again. And so at last to keep her quiet Nannie said, "I don't think Miss Wace has gone far, my dear; she'll be back before long, don't you worry?" Of course, Nannie never thought as how the child would take it for gospel, but Miss Lucy gets the idea in her head that you are hiding in the park. She says to me—you know, confiding like—"Let's go out, Ethel, and look for Wacey; she might be down by the rose gardens, or in the beech wood—she liked that walk."

'Well, I humoured her, thinking no harm. "I can't come now, Miss Lucy," I says; "but when I've done my work, perhaps we'll go and have a look—you and me."

'It was a nasty day—I think it was the second day after you'd gone—a damp drizzle and a mist over the moors. Nannie decided that she wasn't going out—you know how bad her rheumatics are at times and those damp mists always upset her—so she says to me, "Ethel, when you've finished your lunch you can take Miss Lucy for a turn in the garden, but she's not to go far and if it gets worse she must come in."

'Miss Lucy seemed pleased. "We can go as far as the beech walk, can't we, Nannie?" she asks.

' "No, you'd better stay in the garden," Nannie replies. "Keep walking briskly round the paths. I don't want you down with a cold."

'She didn't say any more, but that must have decided Miss Lucy, for I'd no sooner gone downstairs than she puts on her own things and is out of the house like a streak of lightning. Nannie doesn't realise that she's gone and when I go upstairs there's no sign of the child. I asks Nannie where she is and gets the answer that "maybe she's gone down to her grandmother."

'Well, I hung about for a bit and after a time I suggested to Nannie that she goes and asks Lady Clementina if she'd seen her. Nannie does so and her ladyship says she hasn't seen Miss Lucy since the morning.

' "I expect she's hiding somewhere in the house," Nannie says. "It's a nasty day, maybe she doesn't want to go for a walk after all."

'But I had my doubts because Miss Lucy was keen on that walk, I knew that. Well, we searched everywhere and at last I put on my things and went out into the garden to see if I could find her. I went down to the rose garden and on to the beech walk, but there was no sign of Miss Lucy. Of course, by that time she must have had two hours' start. I go back to the house thinking perhaps she will have come back, but there was no Miss Lucy.

'Then Nannie gets really worried and so do I. We go and tell Sir Robert. He was wild, I can tell you. He went for Nannie, and for me for that matter.

' "There's two of you," he said. "Surely you can look after one small child?"

'He gives orders for the footmen to start searching for Miss Lucy and he sends to the stable for a horse. Well, by that time it's come on to rain hard and it was cold, too—cold and nasty, and I can tell you, miss, my heart was in my boots thinking of that poor child. But what could we do? The men scoured the park, but there wasn't a sign of her.'

Ethel paused for breath.

'What had happened to her?' Sylvia exclaimed. 'Go on, Ethel.'

'Well, miss, she's found about seven o'clock just as it's getting dark. She had walked right up on to the moor.'

'As far as that?' Sylvia whispered.

'We had no idea how she managed it. she must have been so anxious to find you that she didn't even feel tired until she got there. But when she reached Blackstone she must have begun to think how far she was from home and all alone She was curled up at the foot of the stone itself and was fast asleep when Sir Robert found her.'

'So Sir Robert found her?'

Ethel nodded. 'Yes, he'd gone further than any of the others, seeing as how he was on horseback, and he caught a glimpse of her coat; it must have been a pale patch against the dark stone.'

Sylvia remembered the stone of which Ethel was speaking. It was a landmark for some miles around, situated on one of the lower rises of the moor which climbed skywards behind the house. It was a hard climb at the best of times, although she and Lucy had attempted it on various occasions. She imagined the child being driven by her impatience and her determination to discover the person she was seeking. Blackstone, like the beech woods, would seem to her a likely place of meeting; but when she got there and found nothing but emptiness and wind and rain, she must have experienced that sharp sense of disappointment and anti-climax which grown-up people know so well, but which they are apt too often to forget is just as acute and prevalent in children. Perhaps, Sylvia thought, Lucy had cried a little before, tired out and discouraged. She had lost the elation with which she had started on her search and had curled up at the foot of the stone and gone to sleep. She wondered what Sir Robert had said when he finally found his daughter, damp, dishevelled and perhaps, too, a little stupid with sleep and fatigue. But Ethel would not know.

'Sir Robert brought Miss Lucy back,' Ethel continued, 'and we gave her a hot bath and got her into bed. She looked all in, poor child, and then when I took up her supper I could see the colour coming back into her cheeks and I guessed, before Nannie took her temperature, that she was going to be ill.

' "Oh, don't fuss me, Nannie," she kept saying.

' "You've got to be fussed," Nannie answered. "You'll be in bed tomorrow, my lady."

' "But I didn't find Wacey. I must look for her again; I can't think where she has gone, can you, Nannie?" Miss Lucy cries.

'She says the same thing in almost the same words to Sir Robert when he comes up to see her in bed.'

'And what did Sir Robert say?' Sylvia asked, unable to restrain her curiosity although she felt that such a question was best left unasked.

'He didn't say anything for a moment,' Ethel replied. 'He stood looking down at Miss Lucy and we couldn't tell from his expression whether he loved the child or whether he was angry with her for what she'd done. Then at last he says, "Do you want Miss Wace as much as all that?" and when he asks that question Miss Lucy pushed away her supper and starts to cry. "I do want Wacey, I do, I do," she sobs. "I can't think where she is hiding. Oh, Daddy, do find her for me!" '

'And what did Sir Robert reply?' Sylvia asked breathlessly.

'Nothing. He never answered a word,' Ethel answered. 'But he pulls out his watch and we knew as he was wondering as to how long it would be before the doctor would arrive.'

'And when he came?'

'He was late, nearly eleven o'clock it was. He had been out on a case when the groom had called for him. Miss Lucy's temperature was high by the time he arrived, but she wouldn't rest, she lay there chattering away, calling for us if we left her alone for even a moment.

'The doctor gave her something as would make her sleep and said he would come again first thing in the morning. Long before he came we knew Miss Lucy was in for a bad illness. There was no leaving her—either Nannie or me had to be there all the time; and even when the nurses came it was always best for one of us to be about as she didn't like strangers. When she wasn't calling for you, miss, she was calling for us.'

'She kept on asking for me?' Sylvia asked in a low voice.

'That she did, and when she was delirious she cried something terrible, almost broke your heart to hear her. She got it into her head that you were unhappy or in trouble; she kept begging us to go and help you. It was awful to hear her at times. We had about four days of it and then Nannie said to Sir Robert, "I think Miss Wace ought to be sent for, sir." '

'When did she say that?' Fylvia asked.

'One morning when Sir Robert came up after breakfast to see what sort of night Miss Lucy had spent. The night nurse told him she'd been very restless and Nannie was trying to get her to take some milk, but she kept pushing it away, saying, "I don't want any milk, I want Wacey. When is she coming? Surely they have found her by now." It was then Nannie told Sir Robert what she thought.'

'What did Sir Robert say?'

' "Very well." That's all, just those two words and he walked out of the room. We felt he was going to find you himself that very moment. I quite expected to see you back in a few hours; but, of course, as the days went on we all guessed that he couldn't find you, that he didn't know where you had gone.'

'But . . . but what happened to my sister?' Sylvia heard the tremor in her own voice as she asked the questiion.

'Oh, she had left,' Ethel replied. 'I don't rightly know what happened, I never heard, but she went the day after you did.'

'So you knew that Sir Robert was making inquiries but couldn't find me?'

'We knew he was doing his best,' Ethel replied. 'The doctor said as how pneumonia had set in, and the child got weaker. All the same she kept asking for you; and when Sir Robert came up in the morning after the post had come, Nannie used to look at him hopefully. She didn't even have to ask the question. He knew what she wanted to know and he would shake his head.'

'And then what happened?'

'Miss Lucy kept getting worse,' Ethel answered. 'More nurses came and I was hardly allowed in the night nursery at all. Nannie went in, but they kept me out. I just spent all my time waiting on those nurses and running after them. I don't like them; stuck-up, starchy busy-bodies, that's what I think they are.'

'Yes, yes, go on.'

'Well, the day before yesterday I heard the doctor say, "Can't you do anything to find the woman, Sir Robert?" They were in the nursery. I was bringing in the coals. Of course, I listened, and Sir Robert answered, "I'm doing my damnedest. I've got the best detective agency trying to trail her, but it seems hopeless."

'This was early in the morning and when Sir Robert goes downstairs with the doctor the post had just arrived because I saw the postman going away. Well, I was clearing up and taking the nurse's orders as to what food Miss Lucy was to have, when Sir Robert flings open the door and comes striding into the room. He was smiling and there was a letter in his hand. He walks past the nurse and me as if he never saw us and goes into Miss Lucy's room leaving the door open and we both—without really thinking—follows. He goes up to Miss Lucy's bed. She's lying there with her eyes closed, looking so frail and thin, poor child—you'll hardly know her—and he says, "Lucy, Lucy, I have found ouut where your Wacey is and I'm going to fetch her. Do you understand?"

'And Miss Lucy says in a little, thin voice—you'd hardly know it was hers, "You're going to fetch her, Daddy? Now?"

' "Now," he says. "So be a good girl and try and get well by the time we come back." And with that he turns round and walks towards the door. Then he stops. "I want you, Ethel," he says. I was that surprised, miss, you could have knocked me down with a feather. "I want you to come south with me," he says. "Bring whatever clothes you think Miss Wace is likely to require."

'Well, I could hardly believe my ears, but I ran into your room and packed up some of your things. Of course, we had all known that Sir Robert's railway coach had been standing ready in Mickledon Station for days, but when we really started off it seemed too good to be true. And here you are! Poor Miss Lucy will be pleased to see you. I think it will save her life.'

Sylvia sank down on the bed and covered her face with her hands.

'Oh, Ethel,' she said, 'I had no idea the child would be so upset. I ought never to have left her.'

'Never you mind, miss,' Ethel said comfortingly. 'She'll get well now when she sees you. Why don't you change your dress and freshen yourself up before dinner?'

Sylvia did as Ethel suggested.. It was a joy to get out of the worn, faded dress she had worn all the time since she had left Sheldon Hall and slip on one of the dresses which Ethel had brought with her. When she looked at herself in the mirror she realised that in the time she had been away she had become shabby not only in appearance, but also in mind. She had let herself feel humble, she had let herself be humiliated; she had been afraid for her security; and all these things had taken from her something which seemed to come back to her now with the changing of her clothes.

She was just ready when she felt the jerk of the coach being coupled on to the train, and a few moments later they started off, the carriage swaying a little from side to side, the rumble of the wheels getting louder and louder as the engine which pulled them gathered speed.

'Dinner is served, miss.'

How strange the words seemed, hearing them again in such circumstances and after the dinners that she herself had cooked and served at Mrs. Bootle's.

Shyly, uncertain of herself and conscious that her fingers were icy cold from nervousness, she walked into the dining saloon. Sir Robert was waiting for her. There was food served on silver dishes by two footmen. Cooling against ice was wine to which Sylvia shook her head, but Sir Robert insisted.

'It will do you good,' he said. 'There is a long journey

ahead of us, and personally I always find it difficult to sleep in a train. Do you?'

'I have never been on a train journey at night,' Sylvia answered.

The conversation between them was stilted and formal, with long pauses when neither of them said anything, and although the food placed before them was delicious, Sylvia found it hard to eat it.

At last they finished and now as the dessert was brought in she glanced at Sir Robert and wondered what he was thinking.

'No fruit?' He raised his eyebrows as she refused the dish held out to her.

'No, thank you.'

'I don't want any either.' He turned to the footman, 'Bring the coffee into the drawing-room, and also the liqueurs.'

'Very good, Sir Robert.'

He rose to his feet and waited for Sylvia to precede him. She hesitated a moment unsteady owing to the swing and lurch of the train. Then she led the way and sat down on a soft, cushioned armchair. Sir Robert sat opposite to her, only a small table between them on which the coffee was placed.

Sylvia felt her heart begin to beat. She knew now that Sir Robert was going to talk to her. There was so much she wanted to know and yet she was afraid—afraid to hear it from his lips—afraid not only of that, but of him, too. She sipped her coffee, felt it stimulate her, and was glad of the sharp, bitter taste of it. Then at last the footmen withdrew—they were alone.

'I want to talk to you, Miss Wace.'

'Yes, Sir Robert.'

'I am grateful to you, very grateful that you are kind enough to return to Sheldon Hall with me. I was not exaggerating when I told you that Lucy is very ill. Your maid . . . er . . .' he hesitated for the name '. . . er . . . Ethel, will doubtless have confirmed what I said.'

'Yes, she has told me about Lucy . . . told me how she ran out searching . . . for me and that . . . you found her at Blackstone.'

'I still cannot understand how the child managed that climb alone.'

'Perhaps we can all attempt the impossible when we care enough.'

Sir Robert glanced at ther swiftly; then he looked away, picking up his coffee spoon and examining it carefully as if he saw one for the first time.

'Miss Wace, I owe you an apology. I want you to believe me when I tell you how desperately sorry I am for what occurred the night before you left my house.'

He had said it, and now the crimson blood rushed swiftly into Sylvia's cheeks. She felt herself quiver, her hands clenching and unclenching themselves in her lap.

'I am not going to try and excuse myself,' Sir Robert went on. 'That would be pointless. But I do want you to know that I was at the time labouring under a misapprehension. I had no idea then that your sister had come back into your life so very recently or that you had not seen each other for many years.'

'Who told you that?'

'Your sister.'

'And . . . and what has happened to Romola?'

Sir Robert smiled a trifle grimly. 'She left Sheldon Hall the day after you did.'

'But where has she gone?'

'Back to London.'

'But who . . . I mean . . . how . . .'

Sir Robert bent forward. 'Miss Wace, may I be very frank? Your sister told me the truth before she left. I insisted on it. Then . . . she went back to the life to which she belongs. She has promised that she will not attempt to see you or interfere in your life in any way unless you wish to see her. The first overture is to come from you.'

'She promised—Romola promised that? But why?'

Sir Robert's mouth tightened again. 'You will forgive my frankness—because I made it worth her while.'

'You paid Romola . . . money . . . to make you that promise?'

'Your sister was very hard up.'

Sylvia put her hands to her face. 'I'm sorry,' she whispered.

She felt as if every scrap of pride she had ever possessed was humbled to the dust. What could she say to the idea of Romola accepting money from Sir Robert, bargaining with him, making a contract which affected herself? It was done, it was arranged, and she had not been consulted—she could only burn with shame and horror.

'I hope you are not too distressed by this,' Sir Robert said. 'Your sister was quite satisfied.'

'You can hardly expect me to be . . . satisfied by such an arrangement.'

There was a flash of spirit in Sylvia's voice and eyes as she faced Sir Robert.

'No?' he questioned. Then suddenly his voice altered and softened. 'But, of course, you are both so very different.'

Sylvia dropped her eyes before his.

'I don't know what to say,' she muttered.

'Please allow things to remain as they are. Your sister will not starve.'

'But why should you do this? Why?'

Sylvia asked the question and then wished she had never spoken as she saw the answer in Sir Robert's eyes; saw it in one fleeting expression, so violent, so passionate that she must look away and feel the silence between them quiver and vibrate For a moment she felt something exquisite and tender draw and hold them both; then, harsh and abrupt, his voice broke the spell:

'There is no more to be said on that subject, Miss Wace. It is of other things that I wish to speak to you—of yourself and your return to Sheldon Hall. I make no excuses for the past, there are none that can be made. I can only promise you that nothing you have experienced will ever occur again. If you will look after my child and nurse her back to health I shall be deeply grateful and I shall show that gratitude by keeping out of your way, by inflicting my presence upon you as little as possible. Do you understand?'

'I understand.'

Almost before Sylvia realised what was happening, Sir Robert had risen to his feet. She knew that the interview was at an end, that he had finished what he had to say and was dismissing her. She stared up at him and in that moment it seemed to her that his face had altered, that it was no longer stern and arrogant but set with suffering. She would have spoken, but the words died on her lips. Obediently because it was expected of her, she rose to her feet.

'Good night. Sir Robert.' She did not put out her hand and he did not seem to expect it.

'Good night, Miss Wace. We shall arrive at Mickledon about eight o'clock tomorrow morning.'

'Thank you.'

He held open the door for her and she passed through it.

She felt the nearness of him—her shoulder even brushed his coat as she passed. And then she was alone in the corridor and the door had shut between them, separating them one from the other.

20

'Wacey, it's such a lovely day, do let us walk up to Blackstone.'

Sylvia looked up in surprise at Lucy's words, then she smiled.

'You really want to go there?'

'Yes, why not?'

There was surprise now in Lucy's voice and Sylvia turned away so that the child should not see either the smile on her lips or the astonishment in her expression. So Lucy had forgotten already! That should not really have been surprising, for a child's memory is short and yet it was hard to believe that the unhappiness and misery she had endured should have been so quickly erased from her mind. For Lucy had been unhappy with all the poignant, agonising pain which only children can suffer when, without explanation, things happen to them which change their whole little world and leave them quivering, helpless and alone.

How often had Sylvia reproached herself after her return to Sheldon Hall for not anticipating the pain her flight might cause Lucy! Until she saw what a pitiful echo of her former self Lucy had become through her illness, she had no idea that the child loved her so deeply and with such violence.

Lucy was thin and wasted and what was more her nerves were in a bad state. For the first week she would hardly let Sylvia leave her bedside; she would cry out for her, her voice rising piteously night and day to haunt Sylvia and reproach her.

At first it had seemed as if there was no chance of

Lucy's recovery. She was so ill, so listless that it was easy to believe that at any moment she might slip through their fingers and be gone. And then, as gradually Lucy became not only aware but assured of Sylvia's return, a change came.

'You are here, really here, aren't you, Wacey?' she would ask pathetically. 'You aren't going away again? Promise me you won't run away.'

'I won't leave you again, I promise you,' Sylvia would say soothingly; but a few minutes later the same questions would be repeated, and she knew that the worst thing she had done in her whole life was to create in Lucy a sense of insecurity, a fear of what might happen next.

Nevertheless by degrees—so slowly that it was hard to detect the change, Lucy began to get better. But by the time she was really on the road to recovery, Sylvia herself was almost a nervous wreck, tired out and exhausted with giving the child her own strength, with reassuring and comforting her, with trying to restore contentment to Lucy's small, shattered and perplexed mind.

It was only when at last there came a night through which Lucy slept without waking and she herself had therefore a proper rest that Sylvia became suddenly aware how near she was to the end of her tether. It was Nannie who, as usual, took things into her own capable hands and prevented what appeared to be an inevitable collapse.

'You are to stay in bed, Miss Wace,' she said as she brought Sylvia an early morning cup of tea; 'we shall have two patients instead of one if you don't.'

'I am tired,' Sylvia confessed, 'but why I should be after a good night . . .'

Nannie interrupted her with a laugh.

'A good night?' she ejaculated. 'Do you know how many nights you have been sitting up with Lucy or been brought from your bed because she was crying for you?'

'I have no idea,' Sylvia confessed. 'Time has ceased to count. How long is it since I came back?'

'Over six weeks,' Nannie told her.

Sylvia looked out of the window. 'I might have known if I had thought about it,' she said. 'It is nearly summer, isn't it?—and when I left it was still winter.'

She spoke softly and it seemed to her that beneath her own words there was some deeper meaning which she could not quite realise.

Nannie was brusque. 'You are to stay in bed, Miss Wace.'

'But Lucy . . .' Sylvia expostulated.

'You leave Lucy to me,' Nannie said. 'She is better, much better, and she has got to begin to think of someone else besides herself.'

'I can't possibly do it,' Sylvia said; but in spite of herself her eyes drooped and before she could rouse her determination to the point of getting up, she had fallen asleep. She slept the clock round and did not hear Nannie come softly in and out of the room. She did not even know that Lucy at one moment was brought, wrapped in blankets, to the doorway to see that she was really there. She slept and slept, drawing quickly from her dreamless slumber with the elasticity of youth new strength and fresh powers of endurance, even as a withered seed will spring to life again when it is fed by the warm darkness of the earth into which it has been planted. And when at last she woke, she was hungry.

Then with a quick jump of time—it had seemed only a few days later, although in reality several weeks—she and Lucy were walking in the garden, beautiful with the green tendrils and colourful blossoms of summer.

'Look, Wacey, roses. Which is your favourite colour? I like the pink ones.'

'I like the dark red ones best,' Sylvia replied and suddenly flushed as she remembered the traditional meaning of red roses.

Swiftly her thoughts flew to Sir Robert. She had almost forgotten him in these past anxious and exciting weeks; but now that anxiety was past and Lucy was well again, requiring only that little extra love and care which Sylvia was so ready to give her, it was inevitable that she should think and wonder about Sir Robert.

He had fulfilled his promise and had kept out of her way; but despite all reasoning which said she should be pleased, her heart cried out in protest. When he came to see Lucy, she withdrew. She would hear his 'Good morning, Miss Wace,' or 'Good afternoon, Miss Wace,' politely and coldly said, his eyes averted from her, his manner so aloof and distant that it was hard for her to believe that she had ever lain in his arms and known his lips against hers. At other times of the day they seldom encountered one another.

Only once when she was leaving Lady Clementina's bedroom had he stopped her.

'If there is anything you want, Miss Wace, either for yourself or Lucy, I hope that you will ask me.'

'Yes, Sir Robert.'

She had been tired; the night before had been a hard one, with Lucy desperate and hysterical, clinging to her and begging over and over again for a reiteration of her love. Sylvia, tired and weak and utterly lonely, had suddenly felt in need of comfort for herself. If only, she thought, there was someone in this cold, proud house to whom she could turn for consolation, just one hand she could clasp in friendship and in understanding, one shoulder on which she could lay her aching head.

She looked up at Sir Robert's face. It seemed to her that his expression was stern and indifferent. She was conscious of the weakness of her body and the trembling of her hands; she was over-wrought, of course, for despite every effort at self-control the tears suddenly welled into her eyes.

Then Sir Robert looked at her, looked deep into her eyes; and she saw in that moment through the veneer of indifference, sternness and pride, a man suffering all the torments of hell. For a long, long moment they stood there. For Sylvia the world vanished, leaving them alone on some planet of their own—man and woman. . . . Nothing else mattered, nothing else counted. . . .

The tension between them increased; the magnetism in him drew Sylvia and compelled her; she could not break away, could not turn her eyes from his. She made no movement, only her lips parted slightly. And then abruptly, harshly, Sir Robert turned and with a muttered sound, half a curse and half a cry of pain, he left her.

Sylvia leant against the wall, every nerve in her body quivering, the blood ebbing away from her head to leave her weak and faint.

It was a week before she saw him again. She was not even certain that he was in the house and was too proud to ask. Lucy had not noticed his absence; so long as Sylvia was there, she had no thought for anyone or anything else.

'I have never seen a child so devoted to anyone,' the doctor remarked to Sylvia one day.

'I suppose it is natural,' she answered. 'Her mother is dead and I am her only link with the past and the future.'

'All the same,' the doctor said, 'you must see that such a feeling doesn't get out of bounds, Miss Wace. After all, you may have to leave her for good one day.'

Sylvia raised her eyebrows. 'Why?' she asked.

The doctor smiled. 'Well, you are a young woman and not unattractive. I wouldn't be prepared to bet that you won't get married and have children of our own.'

He spoke jovially, but Sylvia felt the blood rush to her cheeks and she turned away quickly so that there was an embarrassed silence.

'I shall never marry,' she thought to herself, 'never, never.' And she repeated this vow when she was alone in her own room. It was impossible to think of marriage except with the one person, and to think of him was to bring up the old questions, the old speculations which inevitably taunted and teased her and for which she could find no answer.

What was the secret of Sheldon Hall? Why should Sir Robert hold himself aloof when he knew, as she did, that the whole fullness of life was theirs for the taking? He loved her. Sylvia was as sure of that as she was of her love for him.

Yes, he loved her; but there was some secret, mysterious barrier which kept them apart. It was not the difference in their rank which kept them apart. It was not the difference in their rank which Lady Clementina had so often pointed out. It was something deeper, something more important than the social standards or approval of a woman growing daily older, more difficult and more querulous. It was hard to please Lady Clementina in these days. Her voice rose shrilly from her bed, complaining and finding fault, scolding and admonishing. Purvis went around with permanently red eyes and the younger servants scuttled about the passages looking subdued and scared.

Once when Sylvia was going to Lady Clementina's room to report on Lucy's progress she heard the angry voices of mother and son through the closed door. She heard Lady Clementina say harshly, 'This house is more important than your petty feelings in the matter'; and Sir Robert's answer, 'That is for me to judge.'

She had turned and fled, ashamed of eavesdropping even for a moment. But all the same, she had pondered over what she had heard for the conversation confirmed something of which she had been certain for some time. Sir

Robert was obstinately opposing his mother's wishes regarding his marriage and driving Lady Clementina almost frantic by his refusal to fulfil her desires.

But all these things, even the promptings and agonies of her own heart, were unimportant beside the fact that Lucy was well again, almost her own self. She was still very thin and she had grown much taller since she had been in bed, while her head, shorn of its ringlets, was now graced by short, fluffy curls which framed her face like a vivid halo. She was prettier than she had been before, yet still so absurdly like her father that at times it gave Sylvia a heartache even to look at her. But she did not resemble him in character; she was impetuous, excitable and completely unreserved in a way he could never have been, not even as a child.

'Oh, come on, Wacey,' Lucy said now, dancing with impatience. 'If we are going to Blackstone we shall have to start; you know how long it takes.'

'Are you sure you can manage the walk?' Sylvia asked. 'It is a much longer one than you have attempted yet.'

'Well, if I get tired, we can turn back, can't we?' Lucy asserted with common sense.

'Of course we can. I will get my hat and warn Ethel that we may be late for tea. You change your shoes and then we will start. I won't be a moment.'

'Hurry up, Wacey, do hurry.'

Laughing at her impatience, Sylvia went to her own room and in a few minutes they were both ready. Hand in hand they went down the broad staircase to the hall. Usually they went out through the garden door, but today, without thinking, Sylvia let Lucy lead her down the main staircase and it was only when she saw Sir Robert standing in the hall that she wished she had been more thoughtful and insisted on their usual and less spectacular route. But it was too late now for regrets, for Lucy with a cry of joy had seen her father and running quickly down the stairs had already reached his side.

'Where are you going, Daddy?'

'Riding.'

'Wacey and I are going to Blackstone. Don't you wish you were coming with us?'

'I am not very fond of walking.'

'You know, Daddy, I think you are lazy,' Lucy said. 'Wacey thinks so, too. She said yesterday that everyone ought to walk, didn't you, Wacey?'

Sylvia, approaching Sir Robert more slowly, felt the colour rise in her cheeks.

'We had better be going, dear,' she said quietly, 'if we want to get to Blackstone before tea-time.'

'Oh, wait a moment,' Lucy said. 'I want to talk to Daddy. I haven't seen much of him lately, have I?' She looked up at her father.

'I have been busy,' he said.

Lucy frowned. 'I wonder what grown-up people do that keeps them so busy. You don't have lessons, and you don't have to do things for the good of your health like those awful exercises that Wacey makes me do. I can't think what you do all day.'

'You will know in time,' Sir Robert said.

He looked at Sylvia over Lucy's head and smiled easily and naturally. Sylvia smiled back at him. Today he seemed more approachable. She liked him in his riding breeches; he was really absurdly handsome, she thought. She wished the mere sight of him didn't make her heart beat so quickly.

'Will you come and see me tonight?' Lucy asked. 'I do want you to, Daddy.'

She was flirting with her father, and he liked it. Sir Robert bent down suddenly and taking her up in his arms kissed her.

'You had better come downstairs and have dinner with me,' he said.

Sylvia gave an exclamation. 'Oh, it is too late, Sir Robert. Lucy mustn't get over-tired.'

He raised his eyebrows. For a moment she thought he was going to insist on having his own way. Then he accepted her judgment.

'Very well, if you are not allowed to do that, Lucy, I will come and have dinner with you. What time do you have your meal?'

'Half-past six.'

'I will be there. And what shall I bring with me?'

Lucy clasped her hands together. 'Can I ask for anything I like?'

'Anything you like.'

'Ooh, then sugar plums, and the chocolates which Bateson puts out when you have parties and those funny brown sweets which look like chestnuts.'

'*Marrons glacés.* Yes, I will bring those, too. Six-thirty; I won't forget.'

225

'Oh, Daddy, that will be lovely!'

He kissed her once again. 'Enjoy your walk,' he said.

'We will,' Lucy answered. 'Come along, Wacey.'

They were moving towards the front door when they heard the sound of horses on the gravel outside. A moment later someone mounted the steps. Far away they heard a bell peal.

'Now who is this?' Sir Robert asked testily.

Bateson, who could not have been far away, crossed the hall and opened the door. Sir Robert stood irresolute as if he were debating whether to go or stay, but Lucy had turned back and stood at his side, slipping her hand into his as they waited. Now the door was open and they could see standing in the entrance a large man dressed in a blue uniform ornamented with silver insignia.

'Is Sir Robert Sheldon at home?'

Before Bateson could reply the man looked past him and saw Sir Robert standing there.

'Oh, there you are, Sir Robert. I wanted to see you.'

He stepped into the hall and then Sylvia recognised his uniform. He must be the Chief Constable. She remembered seeing the Chief Constable of Oxfordshire driving through Poolbrook to the Assizes.

'Good afternoon, Colonel Rochdell,' Sir Robert said, and his voice was cold. 'Is the matter an important one? I have arranged to go riding and do not like to keep my horse waiting.'

'You may consider it quite important,' Colonel Rochdell said slowly.

Sylvia had the impression there was an old antagonism between the men and that for some reason the Chief Constable disliked Sir Robert.

'In that case,' Sir Robert said, 'perhaps you would like to see me alone.'

'There is no need if you are in a hurry,' the colonel replied. 'There is no secret about what I have to tell you. I am here officially, Sir Robert, to inform you that as a result of information we have received, my men are at this moment exhuming the body of your elder brother, Sir Edward Sheldon.'

For a moment there was silence. Sir Robert stood very still, but Sylvia saw that his face had whitened and that his fingers had tightened over Lucy's hand.

'Under whose orders are you acting?' he asked at length.

'Under instructions from the Home Office,' the Chief

Constable replied, 'following a report I sent them some weeks ago.'

'May I have a copy of that report?'

'I see no reason why not,' the colonel replied. 'After we have removed the body, of course.'

There was something sinister and nasty in the way he said the last words, and like a flash it came to Sylvia. She saw it all so clearly; now at last she understood, knew what had always been in the back of her mind, hovering there, too terrible to be put into words.

Sir Robert had killed his brother and rid himself of the idiot who stood between him and the title. It must have been cleverly done to have aroused no suspicion at the time. And who could have raised the matter now? Even as she wondered she heard Sir Robert say:

'May I know the name of the person who caused . . . this action to be taken?'

'That also I daresay can be revealed to you later,' the Chief Constable answered. 'May I, without being indiscreet, suggest that "a woman scorned," Sir Robert, is often a very dangerous enemy?'

The man was enjoying this. He had the whip in his hand and he was cracking it. There was something almost nauseating in the gloating manner in which the words fell from his thick lips.

And then Sylvia knew; she knew with a horror that was physical in its intensity who had betrayed Robert, who had given information which resulted in this action on the part of the police. It was Romola, of course; Romola who had been scorned and who, despite Robert's generosity had taken her revenge. She remembered those long conversations with Purvis; she remembered Romola's suspicions; and she knew without having been there at the time how bitterly Romola would have resented being forced to tell the truth, being compelled by Robert to exonerate her younger sister and to confess that she herself was the perpetrator of all the lies and deception which had brought her to Sheldon Hall.

Yes, it was Romola who had done this. Sylvia felt as if the shame of it would cause her to sink through the floor. She raised her hands to her cheeks and thought that she must cry out; but instead she must in silence feel her heart beat slowly and heavily like a tolling bell and watch Robert's face sharpened and deathly pale. Yet he held himself as proudly and arrogantly as ever; his voice was smooth, unhurried and polite with an icy politeness which seemed to cut the air between himself and the Chief Constable.

'When you have finished your investigations, Colonel,' he said, 'I should be grateful if you would let me know the results.'

'When we have finished our investigations, Sir Robert, you *will* know the results,' the colonel answered, and Sylvia knew only too clearly what he suspected. 'There is one thing more,' he went on. 'You must not leave these grounds or stay away from this house till such time as I shall communicate with you. If you . . .'

Sir Robert interrupted him. 'I shall not run away.'

His words were decisive and somehow final, and for the first time some of the arrogance seemed to go from the Chief Constable.

'Well, I think that is all,' he said. 'I would like to say that I am sorry . . .'

'Good afternoon, Colonel Rochdell.'

The eyes of the two men met. The Chief Constable shrugged his shoulders.

'If you prefer it that way.'

'I do.'

Colonel Rochdell turned towards the door. As he reached it, Sylvia realised that Bateson was missing. He must have slipped away and she wondered if he were being tactful or he had any reason for leaving.

The front door was slightly ajar. Colonel Rochdell pulled it open and went out. Nobody moved; they stood there still and silent, listening to the horses' hoofs clopclopping into the distance. Lucy was still clinging to Sir Robert's hand.

Suddenly there was a sound from above them; it was a strange sound—a sound which suddenly turned to a scream. All three turned quickly and saw standing at the top of the stairs Lady Clementina. She was wearing a robe of red velvet over her nightgown. Her face was contorted, yellow and terrifying in startling, unnatural contrast to the flashing diamonds about her throat and the bracelets which glittered and shimmered on her wrists as she moved. Behind her appeared Bateson. 'My lady, please, my lady!' He spoke in a weak, helpless manner; his arms hung stiffly at his sides as if he wished to restrain her, yet dared not presume to touch his mistress. Lady Clementina ignored

228

him and his pleadings were lost in another scream which came from her lips.

'Where is that man? Stop him! Stop him, I tell you! He must know! Robert is innocent—yes, innocent! I did it; I killed Edward!'

Her voice, pitched high, rose in a shrill crescendo. It seemed strange that so small and frail a woman could produce such a volume of noise. Then her hands, claw-like with their yellow, bony fingers, clutched at her breasts as if compelled by a sudden agony of pain; her lips twisted and writhed; and another scream, this time of physical agony, rent the silence as she toppled forward. . . . She fell, and with a kind of sick horror, helpless and impotent, those watching her saw her fall. . . . She screamed once again, a scream of pain and fear. Then Sylvia flung herself on her knees beside Lucy, enfolding the child in her arms, blinding her eyes from the horror of what lay, broken, twisted and bleeding, on the marble floor of the hall.

21

How Sylvia managed to carry Lucy so quickly down the passage and out through the garden door on to the sunlit lawn she was never quite certain. She only knew that some urgency within herself drove her forward—an impulse to protect the child so strong that it gave her an impetus which swept away any uncertainty. Lucy was breathless when she set her down.

'What are you doing, Wacey?' she asked. 'Why did grandmother fall? Is she ill?'

'Hush,' Sylvia said severely, 'we haven't got time to talk. Come along, we are late.'

She took the child by the hand and started moving across the lawn at almost breakneck speed.

'But, Wacey . . . listen, Wacey . . .'

'Don't think about it. Let us talk about our walk,' Sylvia admonished. 'We decided to go to Blackstone. How long do you think it will take us? Shall we time ourselves by my watch?'

Soon she had the child talking spontaneously and naturally. The moment of darkness had lifted. The memory of that broken, bleeding, yet glittering thing which had lain at the bottom of the stairs was forgotten. Sylvia forced herself to talk, to be amusing, to laugh and to make Lucy laugh with her; and all the time the horror of it hovered at the back of her mind so that she dared not stop, dared not for a moment fall into silence lest all that had happened should overwhelm her with its intensity.

Only when at last they reached Blackstone to sink exhausted beneath it on the dry, budding heather did Sylvia turn her eyes to look back at Sheldon Hall. The great house sprawled out, necklaced by its terraces, and encircled by its gardens and park, seemed smaller and less awe-inspiring now that they could look down upon it. 'It is only a house,' Sylvia told herself, but she knew it stood for a symbol of so much else—for deep emotion, for hatred, for love and something stronger which had captured and held her prisoner both in mind and heart so that she could never escape from it . . . never.

'Sheldon Hall.' She repeated the name to herself softly. And then she allowed herself to think of Lady Clementina, of Robert and their secret which at last was revealed in all its crudity. So much which she had never understood was now clear: Robert's reticences, his reserve, the pain and suffering she had sometimes surprised in his eyes. How he must have suffered! Sylvia remembered his face when the Chief Constable had been speaking to him—pale, yet set sternly in lines of an iron self-control. Now she could understand that he had braced himself to take the blame for the crime his mother had committed. Suddenly Sylvia stiffened; a thought had come to her, and even while it presented itself in the form of a question, she knew the answer to it. Would Robert still be ready to take the blame? Yes; without doubt the answer was yes!

Who had heard Lady Clementina's despairing cry from the top of the stairs? Only herself and Bateson; both would be silent if Robert commanded it. But would she? If the police found that Edward Sheldon had been foully done to death as they suspected, was she prepared to stand by and see the man she loved die for another's crime? There she paused, a hand over her eyes. Was she imagining this? Was she torturing herself unnecessarily? How did she know that

Robert would take such a course? Lady Clementina was dead, her heart had failed her at last. A brave heart in some ways, even though misguided and led by false values, false standards and false gods. Surely a man strong and young and virile should not sacrifice himself for a woman who was already past punishment? Yet even while she battled with her own thoughts, Sylvia knew the truth.

Robert's pride would never allow him to besmirch his mother's memory. Somehow she felt that he might even welcome the chance of martyrdom; it would mean action after years of inaction; it would mean being definite, strong and courageous after years of repression, of subterfuge, of hiding his feelings and his thoughts. She remembered the frequent passages of arms between mother and son, the way Robert had seemed at times almost antagonistic to Lady Clementina. The thought of what she had done must have hurt him and humiliated him beyond words. But it would humiliate him even more should the knowledge of his mother's crime become public property. Better death for her sake than that her memory should suffer dishonour and disgrace!

'It is madness, it is madness, but he will do it!' Sylvia spoke the words out loud.

'What did you say, Wacey?'

Lucy was looking up at her with the trusting, loving eyes of deep affection. Sylvia put her arm round the small shoulders.

'Nothing, darling, I was talking to myself.'

'But I thought only mad people did that.'

'Perhaps we are all mad at times.'

Lucy looked at the house far away below her. 'Wacey,' she asked in a subdued voice, 'why did Grannie fall down the stairs?'

'I think it was her heart,' Sylvia answered gently. 'You see, your grandmother has had a bad heart for a long time, and that is why she stayed in bed; and suddenly, like a clock that has stopped ticking, it ceased to beat and so she . . . she has gone to God.'

Lucy accepted the explanation. She was silent for a moment, then she said:

'Whom did she kill?'

Sylvia paused and drew a deep breath. Turning she took both the child's hands in hers.

'Listen, darling,' she said, 'you love me, don't you?'

'You know I do, Wacey.'

231

'And you love your father?'

'Yes, of course.'

'Well, I want you to forget what you heard your grandmother say, for both our sakes. You are never to repeat it to anyone, do you understand?'

Lucy nodded. 'Not even to Nannie?'

'To no one. You are just to forget about it, and if anyone questions you, you don't know what was said. Will you remember that?'

'I will remember, Wacey. But did she kill anyone?'

Sylvia shook her head. 'I am sure she didn't. She just had a bad dream like you have sometimes, and she imagined things.'

'Poor Grannie. They are horrid things, bad dreams, aren't they?'

'Of course they are,' Sylvia answered. She released the child's hands and got up, shaking her skirts. 'And now we must go back.'

She felt her heart sink as she said the words. Yes, now they must go back, to find out what had happened, to watch Robert suffer, and to know that it was only a question of days, perhaps hours, before the storm would break and he would be taken away from them. . . .

From where they stood the trees hid the churchyard; only the spire of the little grey church was visible above the green spreading branches. Sylvia thought of men digging, the coffin being raised. She remembered Nannie standing with the tears in her eyes beside the plain gravestone, and the small, pitiful bunch of flowers she carried. Had she known then? Did she know how? She remembered the two swords that Lucy had found in the nursery, and once again she thought of the boy who grew older in body but not in mind, the young man who still played with toys; and almost in her heart she could find it possible to pity Lady Clementina. She, too, must have suffered, driven by her ambition, consumed with her love of the house and all it stood for, while the owner of the title, the head of the family, was concerned only with his playthings. It was hard, very hard, Sylvia thought to herself.

Her heart shrank from the thought of what happened afterwards. Was it possible that a woman, any woman, could kill her own son, could murder the child she had borne within her, simply because of an almost idolatrous worship for a thing made of bricks and mortar? It seemed to Sylvia at that moment that a dark shadow lay over Sheldon Hall. Now at last she understood the atmosphere which at times had frightened her. The house itself was a vampire, it demanded too much of those who lived within it. If it gave protection, it took in return something more precious—the integrity of those it sheltered.

'I am letting my imagination run away with me,' Sylvia thought, and taking Lucy by the hand she started to retrace their steps down the narrow sheep tracks which led them from the moors back to the shelter of the cultivated gardens. They went back far more slowly than they had come. Sylvia knew that her feet were flagging not because she was tired, but because she was afraid—afraid of what she would find on their return—afraid of seeing Robert's face, or knowing that he was suffering.

'What can I say to him?' she wondered; and knew in that moment that she loved him more deeply and more completely than ever before. At last she understood him; at last he appeared vulnerable and human; not a robot with whom she had little in common, but a man suffering agonizingly even as she herself had suffered.

She faced, too, the fact that even in that moment of shock and horror when she had first understood what the Chief Constable was saying, when she had believed that Robert was guilty of his brother's death, she had still loved him, loved him with every fibre of her being, with her heart, her mind, with her very soul. Were he a murderer, a felon, she would still love him; whatever he had done, however bad his crime, she knew her own love for him would remain unaffected. She might deprecate his action, might even be shocked by it, but still she would love him with an intensity of emotion which was beyond the point of criticism, almost beyond the point of judgment. That was true love, a love which could not be changed or altered, a love which remained when all else which life held dear had fallen and broken.

How could she ever—even for a few seconds—have believed him capable of such a crime? she asked herself. Robert would never stoop to an action that was dishonourable. He would never hurt, let alone kill, anyone for possessions, however great, however desirable from worldly standards. She might have known that greed was not part of his character, and she had no excuse with which to defend herself for those moments in the hall when she had believed him a murderer. But she had still loved him and now, if it were possible, she loved him even more. Always Robert had seemed so immensely above her, almost god-like in his omnipotence. But now at last he was a man—human, vulnerable. . . .

'Come on, Wacey, you are dawdling.'

It was Lucy who aroused her from her reverie, and at the child's insistence she hurried forward. The house lay just ahead of them; they entered the garden and Sylvia knew that in a few moments she must face Robert and her own future. She wondered wildly what would become of her. And what of Lucy? Then she thrust such questions away—it was Robert of whom she must think. Robert, only Robert!

Before Sylvia could stop her, Lucy had run round the corner of the house and was bounding up the wide stone steps which led to the front door. Sylvia had intended to creep in the back way; she shrank from entering the hall, remembering what had lain there crushed and broken an hour or so before on the marble floor. But Lucy had already forgotten, or at least the shadow of it had passed from her mind.

'I'm first, Wacey,' she called joyously from the front door, and went in.

Sylvia followed. The hall was deserted.

'Let us go up by the other stairway,' she said; but it was too late, Lucy was half-way up the main staircase and Sylvia was forced to follow her. There was nobody on the landing. Sylvia climbed the next flight and the next until she reached the third floor where Lucy was already chatting to Ethel in the nursery.

'We had a lovely walk, Ethel. We went right to Blackstone, and we did it terribly quickly, too. How long do you think it took us?'

Sylvia saw that Ethel's eyes were red with weeping. The girl gave her a glance over Lucy's head and instinctively Sylvia knew what she was going to say. Unperceived by Lucy she laid her fingers on her lips.

'Come along, Lucy,' she said, 'and get your things off. Your tea will be ready before you are.'

Lucy obediently ran from the room.

Ethel spoke quickly in a low voice. 'You have heard about her ladyship, miss.'

'Yes, I know,' Sylvia answered.

'It seems so hard to believe that she is dead,' Ethel gulped and the tears sprang to her eyes. 'She was a grand lady, nobody could deny her that.'

'Don't say anything in front of Miss Lucy,' Sylvia commanded.

'No, Miss, but we are all so upset you wouldn't believe. Why, Mr. Bateson, miss, he's been sobbing like a child.'

Sylvia slipped away before Ethel could say more. It did not appear from what she said that she knew how Lady Clementina had died; and Sylvia imagined that Sir Robert and Bateson must have carried her back to her room before summoning Purvis and sending for the doctor. Later some of the older servants might learn the truth, for secrets even in this house of secrets were hard to keep; but it would be sufficient for the younger ones to be told merely that her ladyship had died. And they, believing it to be the undramatic passing of old age, would none the less weep, finding, as so many people do, something tragic in the disappearance of an old milestone, of a face that was familiar even though unloved.

Having taken off her own things, Sylvia tidied Lucy's hair and took her back to the nursery. They were just finishing their tea when Bateson opened the door.

'Sir Robert would like to see you in the library, miss.'

Sylvia poured out another cup of milk for Lucy. 'Drink that, darling, and then play with your toys. I won't be long.'

She rose to her feet and saw that Bateson had waited for her. The man's face was blotched and for the first time since she had come to Sheldon Hall he looked human. Almost Sylvia could find it in her heart to be sorry for him, eavesdropper and informer though he was. She believed that with the death of Lady Clementina he had really lost a friend. Mistress and servant, they had yet schemed together and had found each in the other a basis of human relationship.

Bateson preceded Sylvia along the passages and down the stairs, but he did not speak. She remembered another occasion when he had led her in just such a manner to the library, the occasion when she had found Uncle Octavius waiting for her. He had been glad then, pleased that she should be humiliated and frightened. Now, though he said nothing, she knew by the set of his shoulders and the lowering of his head that it was Bateson himself who was humble. There was no note of triumph, no ring in his voice today as he opened the door and announced her.

'Miss Wace, Sir Robert.'

She went in slowly. Now that the moment was upon her she felt her heart beat quicker. She stood just inside the room, heard the door shut firmly, and then raised her eyes to Robert's.

He was standing in the window, his vivid head framed by the dark velvet curtains. He stood very still and for a moment she did not understand the expression in his eyes. She felt her hands trembling. Then she understood; he was waiting for her, waiting for her to make some gesture, to give him some word of comfort, this man whom she loved and who she knew loved her.

She went across the room and drew near to him slowly until, when they were only a few feet away from each other, she stood looking at him and saw the expression on his face. It seemed to her then that all words between them were unnecessary, she knew what he had been going to tell her. She knew the sacrifice he was going to make—a sacrifice for the pride of his house and to the memory of the woman who had been his mother. She knew all that, and because in that moment mentally they were as one, she dispensed with all formality.

'Must you do this?' she asked softly; and because he, too, understood that the barriers between them were down, he answered her simply:

'You would not have me do otherwise?'

She inclined her head.

'No,' she said, 'it is the honourable thing to do.'

And then as if he could restrain himself no longer he moved forward and knelt at her feet, and taking her hand in his laid his cheek against it.

'Oh, my darling . . .'

Her voice broke. She raised her other hand and touched his hair; it was firm yet silky beneath her fingers. 'Like Lucy's,' she thought, realising that he was in many ways nothing more or less than a little boy lost and bewildered in a world full of shadows, and sinister actions in which he had played no part.

Now his lips were on her hand—lips burning and possessive.

'I love you,' he said.

'You know that I love you, too.'

'How can you, while I can offer you nothing, not even my name?'

'I am content with loving you.'

236

'You are not ashamed?'

'Ashamed?'

There was so much joy and exultation in the words that he looked up at her and what he saw in her face brought him quickly to his feet.

'Oh, my dear, my beloved.'

He stood looking at her for one moment, and then he swept her into his arms. He held her very close, but when he kissed her it was the kiss of a man driven not by passion, but by something more sacred. For a long time their lips clung together and she knew at last that they truly belonged to each other—one indivisibly for all time and eternity.

After a time he released her. 'My darling, what is to become of you?' he asked.

She tried to smile at him with lips that were tremulous with the ecstasy she had experienced.

'Surely I should be asking that of you?'

'That is obvious and inevitable,' he sighed.

'Is it? Is there no hope?'

'I am afraid not.'

'You wouldn't care to tell me what happened?'

He glanced away from her and she thought he was going to refuse. Then he made a wide gesture with his hands.

'Why not? It would be almost a relief to speak, to be able to talk at last. All these years I have been silent, I have had to keep even my thoughts in check.'

'Poor Robert.'

Sylvia spoke softly.

'Oh, my darling, is this hurting you? If you had not come into my life I would not have cared, but from the moment I saw you I think I knew that you were the woman who was meant for me, the woman for whom I had searched all my life. But you came to me too late . . . much, much too late.'

'Is it too late?' Sylvia asked the question softly.

He stared at her as if he was seeking an inner meaning to her words.

'You mean . . . ?'

'I mean that I am yours, Robert, whatever happens to you; whatever the future holds for either of us I am still yours—now and for always.'

'Do you mean that?'

'Of course I mean it.'

'But what can I offer you?' he said. 'In a short while the police will return; they will take me away. They could do nothing else. Not all the brains and the skill in the world can save me now from what is coming to me. The only thing I can offer to the woman I love would be a name tainted and dishonoured, a name sneered at by all decent men.'

'And yet I should be proud, yes, proud, Robert, to bear that name; and whatever happens to you . . .' For a moment her voice faltered . . . 'I will look after Lucy.'

'You mean that?'

He reached out and took both her hands in his and raised them to his lips reverently, as a man might approach a shrine; then he looked deep down into her eyes and once again his mouth was near to hers.

'I love you, Sylvia. Will you tell me now, at this moment, that you love me.'

'I love you, Robert.'

It was as if they took their vows one to the other.

'You are sure that you know what you are doing?'

'I am sure.'

He thought for a moment.

'Our only chance then is to slip away, cross the Scottish border and be married at Gretna Green. If it is discovered that I have gone, they will suspect me of running away. As soon as we are married we can come back to face the music—that is, if you will face it with me?'

'There is no need of an answer to that question.' She raised her arms and clasped them around his neck.

The action, so instinctive and loving, fired him. He crushed her in his arms, and this time his kisses were burning and possessive.

'At last,' he said, 'at last you will be mine. I have wanted you, wanted you madly ever since that night I held you like this. Do you remember?'

She could not answer him because of the wonder and the glory that possessed her at that moment. She felt as if nothing mattered except this ecstasy and beauty which consumed them both like a flame, which held them united for one timeless moment while all the world slipped away and they were alone together.

'I love you.'

She heard his voice once again, felt his mouth on her lips, her eyes, her neck, and then she lay half swooning against his shoulder while his arms supported her, and his hand touched the shining gold of her hair.

'Mine! Mine!'

He had forgotten everything now in this moment of triumph.

22

The clock in the corner struck the hour. Five o'clock! Robert raised his head. When he spoke to the lips so close to his own, there was a tenderness in his voice which was all the more moving because it was in such utter contrast to the fierce, possessive passion with which he had held Sylvia a few moments earlier.

'We must leave shortly, my love—as soon as it is dark, so that no one will see us go.'

With an effort Sylvia roused herself to remember the urgency. Already she could imagine their flight through the night. It would be dawn when they reached the border, and then in the sunshine of another day they would become man and wife; they would belong to each other although, perhaps, it would be for only a few hours.

He saw the expression on her face as she thought of the future.

'Don't look like that, my darling,' he commanded, and releasing her from his arms he turned away to walk towards the window. 'Before you give yourself into my keeping,' he said, 'I want you to know the truth. You are the only person to whom I shall tell it and this is the last time I shall speak of it to anyone, but at least you shall know and understand what happened.'

He stood for a moment looking out blindly over the lawns and then he turned back to her.

'I loved my brother,' he said. 'I loved Edward as I have never loved anyone until I met you. I was the stronger and he the weaker, but we accepted it as the natural order of things and as children I don't think he minded my strength any more than I minded his frailty. We were happy; I suppose our close companionship sprang from the fact that my father and mother were busy social people with little time for us; we had to be complete in ourselves, and we were.

'As I grew older it was, of course, quite obvious that Edward was not normal. I went away to school, but he stayed here. When I came home in the holidays he could take no part in the games which I enjoyed; but still we were the same companions; and although when I look back I realise that I did the talking, I was content to have him as a listener and, perhaps, an admirer. That I loved him and he loved me was enough.

'As time went on, Edward remained a child, while I became a young man and it was then I began to put into words what I had always known in the back of my mind—that my mother had a kind of obsession for me while for Edward she had only disgust and distaste. Her attitude was too obvious to be misunderstood. I took it more or less for granted because though I had not realised it before, I had grown up in that atmosphere; but when my father died, her feelings were revealed very clearly.

'It was after the funeral and she had retired to her room, as I thought, to weep. I went up to comfort her, but I found her, dry-eyed, sitting at her writing table. She was still wearing her heavy widow's weeds, but her veil was thrown back from her face and I saw that in her hand she held the family tree. I was familiar with it, of course; it was a large genealogical table which had hung for many years in my father's study showing how our family had originally come over to England with the armies of William the Conqueror.

' "What are you doing, Mother?" I asked as I drew near to her, and then I saw that beneath my father's name she had added the date of his death in ink, and that after Edward's name she had put "Succeeded to the Baronetcy," and again the date.

'Stupidly I said the first thing that came into my head. "So Edward is now a Baronet? Sir Edward Sheldon! It sounds well."

'It was then that she surprised me. White-faced, and with lips that were taut with bitterness, she said passionately:

' "It should have been you! You! Not that puny invalid!"

'I stared at her in amazement, and quickly because I was

240

embarrassed I tried to laugh the moment off. But she reached out and grasped my hand.

' "This house shall be yours," she said. "This house, and all it stands for. I swear it! Yes, I swear it!"

'I was rather shocked and above all things embarrassed at such an outburst. But as time passed I began to see that she had spoken out loud only what was constantly in her mind. She hated Edward now. He was kept isolated in the nurseries with Nannie and she never went to see him if she could help it. The doctor came once a week and I suppose Nannie gave her reports on his general health. But all my mother's thoughts were for me and me only. She made me play my part in the management of the estate, she made me behave as if I was master of the house. She deferred to me and insisted that I should give orders.

'It sounds as if I was weak and stupid; but she was clever, very clever. It was partly to escape from her insistence and from her continual reiteration that I must marry and produce children that I started a love affair with a married women. There is no point in my mentioning her name. Sufficient to say that she got bored with me and gave me my *congé* when she found a more interesting and distinguished lover. Out of pique, and because her parents were clever enough to manoeuvre me into a position from which I could only have extricated myself dishonourably, I married Alice.

'We came back to Sheldon Hall for our honeymoon. I felt within me an urgency to get home immediately, caused, perhaps, by an unshakable conviction that I had made a mistake. I had written to my mother telling her I was being married and the time of our arrival, and she was waiting for us in the hall as we stepped out of the carriage. She was smiling, seemingly pleased to see us, and yet I had an uneasy feeling that something was amiss, that something had occurred which was more important even than my marriage. At times in my life I have had presentiments due, perhaps—or so I was told as a child—to my red hair. "Red-headed people are 'fey'." How often I have heard it said, but in my case it has proved true on more than one occasion. This was one of them. I had a definite sense that things were not right. I believe now, looking back, I had the feeling from the moment I put the ring on Alice's finger in a London church. I was sure of it when we were travelling northwards in the train, and it still persisted when I arrived back at my own house to find everything outwardly in order but, as far as I was concerned, with a sinister undercurrent for which I could not account.

'We had a celebration dinner that night. The chef excelled himself in his efforts to make the occasion festive. There was champagne, of course, and afterwards the staff presented Alice with a bouquet and Bateson said a few formal words of greeting and congratulation.

'But all the time I was watching my mother. There was something about her which worried me. What was it? I asked myself. Finally I noticed that amongst the group of servants in the hall Nannie was missing. I asked my mother where she was. "With Edward, I suppose," she said tersely.

'Something in the way she said it made me want to question her further, but there was no time. I had to make a speech on behalf of my wife and myself and when it was over my mother claimed my attention.

'There were various things she wanted to discuss with me—alterations to the estate, various problems which had cropped up since I had been away. It was all very boring for Alice and seeing her yawning I suggested that she might like to retire. Then she claimed my attention. I had no opportunity of either asking about Edward or going up to see how he was. Afterwards I was bitterly to regret being distracted from what had always been my practice of seeing Edward as soon as I returned home.

'In the morning when Bateson called me, he broke the news that Edward was dead. For a moment I couldn't believe it. I slipped on a dressing-gown and went along to my mother's room. She was sitting up in bed and I had the impression that she had been awake for a long time.

' "Bateson has told me . . ." I began.

' "Yes, he is dead," she answered, and there was something in the harsh tone of her voice and the look in her eyes which told me the truth. I had shut the door behind me as I entered and now I advanced slowly to the foot of her bed.

' "You killed him," I said quietly.

'She looked up at me fearlessly. Whatever her faults, my mother was never a coward.

' "Does it matter to you how he died?" she asked. "You are now the owner of Sheldon Hall."

'I stared at her with something like horror at her words. I prayed that it was not true, that she would contradict it, that she would refute with anger the charge I had made against her. I started to expostulate. I think that with my

242

white face and hesitating, shuddering sentences, she must have thought me a poor creature, she who was so calm, so convinced of her own infallibility.

' "It is the title of which we have to think," she said, "of the estate, and of the house."

'Her voice softened on the last word. She is mad, I told myself; mad in her love, her adoration, her worship of this place I call home.

'I said no more, but turned and left her and went upstairs to look at the cold, lifeless body of my brother. I had loved him and now he was gone, leaving me burdened with my mother's crime and with the thought that I had been instrumental to it.'

Robert's voice faltered for a moment and then as Sylvia did not speak he went on:

'You can guess what happened after that. I could not forget what had happened. How could I, knowing what I knew and haunted by the thought that my brother had been sacrificed to me, make anyone happy? My wife became bored with me; it was inevitable. I was a gloomy, taciturn husband, weighed down with my own unhappiness. I resented her gaiety, her desire to live, her longing for amusement. It was understandable that she should find such a life as ours intolerable and I was not in the least surprised when she ran away, although I had the idea that my mother had a good deal to do with it. She was impatient that we had no children, angry with Alice who could not be content to love this house even as she did herself.

'The rest you know. But what I never can tell you is how much it has meant to me to find you. I had grown to distrust all people. If I sought out women it was because I hoped that in their arms I would find, if only for a short time, forgetfulness of the horrors that surrounded me. I tried drink, I tried every form of amusement and vice; but never, never could I forget . . . not until I saw you—and then I fell in love. I could think of you with the trusting, young look in your eyes, your faint, uncertain smile, the brave way that you raise your chin when you are a little afraid, a little shy. And then, thinking of you, I could escape from myself—for a few moments at least, for I had only to look at you to remember that you could never, never be mine. How could I offer you in all your trusting innocence a life darkened by sin, a past stained with as horrible a crime as was ever committed in another's name?'

'It was not your fault.' The words burst from Sylvia's lips.

Robert looked at her and shook his head.

'I wish I could believe that,' he said. 'It would be the easiest way out, would it not? But I was the man—I should not have allowed my mother to become so domineering, to rule this house as she did, to make me her puppet as she made others. Had I been strong, more honest and a bigger man in every way, Edward might have been alive today.'

'You torture yourself.'

'Isn't it right that I should be tortured?'

His face was suddenly very sad. As he looked at her Sylvia knew that in his own mind he was aying good-bye to her, living that moment when he would be taken away, to die for a crime that another had committed. His eyes were searching her face, she knew that he was memorizing every line of it for the time when they would not be together. She wanted to cry out, to plead with him, to beg him to save himself, but the words would not come. He who so scorned dishonour should not be asked to commit it now for her sake.

Unconsciously she raised her chin and saw that he caught his breath as if at the beauty of her; then he bent forward and touched her lips very gently and tenderly with his own.

'Whatever happens, my dear, dear love,' he said, 'we shall have had our little hour together. Go and get ready. We must take someone into our confidence—I think it would be wise to tell Bateson and Nannie.'

Sylvia looked up at him trustingly, but for the moment she did not move; then with a deep sigh she turned to do his bidding. Even as she did so, there came a knock on the door. They both stiffened instinctively, afraid of the unknown.

'Come in.'

The door opened and they saw a familiar face. It was Nannie.

'Come in, Nannie. I am glad you have come, I was just going to send for you.'

Nannie entered and closed the door behind her.

'I wanted to speak to you, Sir Robert.'

'Come and sit down.'

He indicated a chair and then glanced at Sylvia who was standing irresolute.

'Will you wait one moment,' he said to her. 'I would like you to be here when I tell Nannie our plans.'

'Plans?' Nannie repeated the word and they looked from one to the other.

Robert took Sylvia's hand in his.

'Nannie, Miss Wace has promised to be my wife. We have only a very short time in which to get married. It has to be done secretly and hastily and we want your help.'

Nannie's eyes suddenly filled with tears and she smiled a little tremulously.

'Oh, I am glad, really glad,' she said. 'Now, Master Bobby, you'll be happy.'

She gave him the name she used when he was a child. It was a very long time since he had heard it from her lips and now it seemed to move him almost unbearably.

'Thank you, Nannie,' he said.

After a long moment during which it was impossible for her to speak, Nannie said:

'I have known for some time that you and Miss Wace were fond of one another; but I was afraid, sore afraid that you would never come together because of the dark things that lay between you.'

'You knew, of course, from the very first?'

'From the very first,' Nannie said. 'But you needn't be afraid, Master Bobby, nothing can hurt you now.'

Robert looked at her in surprise, and then wearily as if for a moment she had lit a little spark of hope which had as quickly flickered out, he said:

'I don't think you know what happened, Nannie, or what caused my mother's death.'

'Yes, I know,' Nannie answered. 'Mr. Bateson told me. I made him,' she added quickly as Robert frowned as if at the thought of disloyalty. 'I knew better than most there was only one reason which would have got her ladyship out of bed; and when I inquired who had called to see you and I was told it was the Chief Constable, I knew exactly what that meant.'

'Then you understand,' Robert said, 'why Miss Wace and I must be married at once, as soon as we can cross the border into Scotland. And you must help us, Nannie, because if it is discovered that I have left the house they will think I have run away.'

'There is no need for me to help you,' Nannie said. 'And there is no need for you to be in such a hurry, Master Bobby. You've got time and plenty of it, time to get married decently and without all the talk and scandal there would be about a runaway marriage; time to settle down quietly and happily; to have your children and bring them up to be proud of their heritage—though not to go worshipping it crazily as your mother did . . .'

'Listen, Nannie,' Robert interrupted her, 'you don't understand. Haven't they told you that they exhumed Edward's body? They have taken him from the churchyard. At this moment they are in all probability finding out what . . . what killed him.'

'And they will find nothing,' Nannie said.

She spoke positively.

Sylvia gave a startled exclamation, but Robert turned impatiently from her side, walked to his desk and sat down so that he was facing them both.

'You still don't understand, Nannie,' he said, and his eyes and voice were very tired. 'I can speak only before you because you are one of us. My mother told me that she had given Edward arsenic—that is what the police will find. Arsenic. And when they find it, they will arrest me for the murder of my brother.'

Nannie smiled pityingly.

'They won't find it,' she insisted. 'I know you have suffered these past years, but it wasn't possible for me to say anything. Besides, to be honest, I thought it would do you no harm to suffer, and if in suffering you opposed your mother's wishes and made things a little difficult for her—well, I felt she was getting her just deserts. Maybe it was wrong of me to hold my tongue. I am an old woman and a humble one, not in the position to pass judgments on anyone—least of all on you or her ladyship. Perhaps it was wrong of me, but now I will tell the truth.'

At last Robert was interested. He bent forward and there was no disguising the sudden light in his eyes, the eagerness with which he spoke.

'What do you mean, Nannie? Tell me what you mean?'

'I mean that when they dig up my poor baby's bones, when they examine him for the poison they are so certain is there, they will find nothing. Nothing at all. And they will have to inform you that he died a natural death—as natural as anyone could who had been abnormal from birth.'

'But I don't understand,' Robert said.

He looked across at Sylvia as he spoke, and then slowly

he put out his hand across the desk. She sank down into a chair on the other side of it and reaching out a hand, laid it on his. Their fingers were icy cold, but there was comfort in the mere touch of each other, for they were afraid—afraid of believing in the hope which was springing Phoenix-like from the ashes of their hearts.

Nannie wiped her eyes. 'I somehow never thought that the moment would come when I could speak of what I knew,' she said. 'I have locked it away all these years. My anger and resentment changed as time passed, so that now she is dead, I can't hate her ladyship as I did once.' She wiped her eyes again 'I loved my baby; I loved you both when you were little, but I'm not pretending to you that I didn't love Master Edward the best. He was mine, nobody else wanted him—his mother least of all. And he loved me. At times I almost forgot that he was not my own child, and I suppose—although I know it was wrong—I was glad of his weakness because he never grew too old to want me. He couldn't go to school, he couldn't turn away from me as you used to do, Master Bobby, and say, "I'm too old for a Nannie; I want a man to look after me." No, Master Edward always wanted me. He would look up with that little smile of his when I came into the room and he would show me his toys and ask me to admire something he was doing; and if I was out of the room for long I would hear his voice, "Nannie, Nannie, where are you?" and I would come hurrying back to him because he was mine and I was his. I was glad that sometimes weeks would go by and her ladyship would never come up to see him. She only upset him when she did He knew instinctively she didn't care for him, and she would speak to him in that sharp, cutting way which made him cringe and seem more stupid than he really was.

'The doctors told me that he would grow more infantile and more childish every year, but even so towards the end he had moments of sharpness and intelligence, although only I saw them It was at one of these times—after her ladyship had been to see him one day—that he said to me, "Don't let her come any more, Nannie; she will hurt me; she wants to hurt me, I know she does." I knew what he meant; I had seen the look in her ladyship's eyes, and though I could hardly believe it, I felt sure that she wanted to get rid of him.'

'That was after my father's death?' Robert interposed.

Nannie nodded. 'Yes. It was hard for her, of course, to

know it was Master Edward who held the title and all the broad lands that he could never see, and that this big house was his when he was content with just two rooms at the top of it and wanted nothing more. Anything he didn't like was "ugly." Then one day he told her ladyship to her face that she was ugly, and I knew from that moment that he was in danger. It happened the day before you came home with your bride.'

'The day before?' Robert interrupted.

'Yes,' Nannie answered. 'I can remember every moment of it very clearly. Her ladyship had come up to see Master Edward in the afternoon. She had stood looking at him for a long time. It was one of his bad days when he used to drone away to himself, sometimes whimpering a little. She made him worse, of course, and when she had gone he cried and I felt like crying, too; I had seen a look on her face which made me afraid. I wasn't feeling any too well myself and her ladyship had noticed it.

' "What is the matter, Nannie?" she asked.

' "I am afraid I've got a cold coming, my lady," I replied. "I've got a headache and a bit of a sore throat; but I shall be all right."

'She said nothing, but she looked at me in a rather a queer way. A few hours later, when I was thinking it would be a good idea to get off to bed early, Mr. Bateson knocks at my door. I was extremely surprised to see him; it wasn't often Mr. Bateson honoured the third floor with his presence.

' "Her ladyship's compliments," he said, "and she sends you up some hot milk with a touch of medicine in it which she is certain will cure your cold. She says you are to be sure and take it and get into bed right away."

' "That is very kind of her ladyship," I exclaimed. It wasn't often she was so considerate and I was genuinely surprised.

' "You won't forget to take it, Nannie, will you?" Mr. Bateson asked. "Her ladyship would be most annoyed if you didn't carry out her wishes."

' "I'll take it, Mr. Bateson," I answered. "I was just going to bed anyway."

' "I'll tell her ladyship," he said, and then he went.

'I set the milk down on the table and I began to think. It seemed to me very strange that after all the years I had been in her ladyship's service she should suddenly trouble about a cold of mine. I had had them one after another

248

when you were small children and was so hoarse at times I could hardly speak. It was a rare occasion if her ladyship remembered to ask how I was, let alone send me any remedy. The milk was very hot and I put the saucer on top of the glass and set it down by the fire. I might want it later, I told myself, to help me sleep; but if I could sleep without it, so much the better.

'I peeped in at Master Edward. He wasn't asleep, I didn't expect him to be; he slept a good deal during the day, and often he would be more wakeful at night than at any other time, but he was good and understood that he mustn't call me unless he wanted me very badly.

' "I'm going to bed now, darling," I said. "You can play with your toys, but don't make a noise because Nannie is very tired." He always had the light on, of course, and he had his tin soldiers spread over the bed, and a picture book.

' "Good night, Nannie," he said happily, so intent on what he was doing that he hardly troubled to look up.

' "Good night, darling," I said, and went off to my own room, leaving the door ajar as I always did.

'I got into bed; feeling drowsy and heavy with my cold, but I didn't really get off to sleep. It must have been nearly an hour later when I heard a movement in the next room. Someone was opening the door. My first instinct was to jump out of bed and see who it was, but instead I lay still. After a moment I heard somebody whispering, and then Master Edward's voice speaking normally, "Yes, Edward likes chocolate," he said. Somebody spoke again, still in a whisper, and after a moment Edward said, "Yes, Edward will drink it . . . yes . . . yes . . ." There was another whisper, but Edward didn't speak. Then I heard the door shut very, very quietly and straining my ears I thought that I heard footsteps going down the passage.

'I jumped out of bed and went into Master Edward's room. He was still sitting up in bed as I had left him; he had arranged the soldiers to march up the bedclothes and he was concentrating on making them slide down the other side. He smiled at the sight of me.

' "Who was that, darling?" I asked. "Who came in just now?"

'He looked at me steadily for the moment. He never was good at remembering names, and then I saw that beside his bed was a large cup of chocolate.

' "Who left that?" I asked.

'He shook his head as if he couldn't remember.

' "Was it your mother?" I inquired. I felt certain that the whisper had been that of a woman.

'He looked at me darkly. 'Ugly," he said, "Ugly."

'I looked at the chocolate. It gave off an appetising smell and yet I was afraid of it. Quite suddenly I knew why it was there. I knew, too, that the moment had come which I had been anticipating for so long.

'I stood and looked at my baby, at what had once been a little boy I had held in my arms and was now a grown man, but with an unlined, idiot's face, a wasted body and soft, white fingers playing with toys. I almost had it in my heart to pity her ladyship.

'Quite suddenly, as if another mind greater than mine was guiding me, I knew what I must do. There was no point in prolonging the agony. I went back into my room and fetched from the fireplace the milk Mr. Bateson had brought me. It was still warm and I took off the thick skin that now covered the top.

' "The chocolate will give you a tummy ache, darling," I said. "You drink this instead, to please Nannie."

' "Edward not thirsty," he said and tried to push it away, but I insisted. He was very obedient and would always do what I wanted, and to please me he drank it up quickly. I took away the glass, and I took the chocolate away, too, and emptied it down the sink. I put back the empty cup beside his bed; then I waited. About ten minutes afterwards Master Edward's eyes began to droop.

' "I'm tired, Nannie," he said, "so tired."

'He stretched himself out and some of the tin soldiers fell with a clatter to the floor; he gave what seemed to be a deep sigh and fell asleep.

'I went back into my own room. Half an hour passed and then I heard that same sound of someone coming into the next room. I knew who it was and why she had come. She moved very quietly; there was just a faint rustle of silken skirts and the very gentle clink of china and the closing of the door.

'The house was quiet. I went back to his room and stood by the bed. Edward was snoring gently. He looked relaxed and at peace; the sleeping draught must have been a strong one.

'Once again I saw him as he was, rather than as my love pictured him—helpless, growing worse year by year and yet—as the doctor had told me—perhaps living even after he had lost all touch with reality. He might not even know me, he might even become utterly senile—a living corpse. Perhaps it was better this way; I tried to make myself believe it.

'I drew the spare pillow from behind his head very gently and put it over his face. I held it there—held it over him until my own arms became numb; till the prayers which moved my lips became only a hopeless jumble of words. And then—then—when I moved, I knew that my baby was dead.'

Nannie covered her face with her hands. There was silence in the room, utter silence. Only Robert's fingers tightened over Sylvia's—tightened with a strength which left them white and bloodless.

After a moment Nannie recovered her control.

'I knelt all night beside his bed,' she went on. 'I locked the doors; I wanted to be alone, undisturbed, with the person I loved best in the world.

'When the morning came, I washed in cold water, dressed myself and was ready when the girl brought me my morning tea.

'You are early this morning, Nannie,' she said.

'Master Edward's had a bad night,' I replied. 'I don't want anybody to disturb him. Bring his food into this room and when he wakes I will take it in to him.'

'All that day I was the only person who went into him. I sent no message, although I was quite sure that her ladyship was waiting to hear from me; I remained silent. I hated her. There was bitterness and anger in my heart, but I was not certain yet how I could make her suffer, how I could hurt her for what she would have done to her own son.

'At luncheon-time I was told that you were married and on your way home with your bride. The news which excited the rest of the household considerably, left me cold for the moment. I could think of nothing except my baby lying still and white in the next room. I had laid him out myself—I had learnt to do that many years ago from my mother. He lay there with a face utterly at peace, the poor, thin, wasted hands crossed on his narrow chest, and I placed some flowers between his fingers.

'Mr. Bateson himself came up to tell me that all the staff were to assemble in the hall after dinner to bid you and your wife welcome. I told him I couldn't leave Master Edward.

' "Isn't he well?" Mr. Bateson asked casually—too casually, and his eyes wouldn't meet mine as he spoke.

' "I'm afraid he has caught my cold."

' "I hoped that was better after her ladyship's cure," he said. "You took it, of course?"

'For a moment I thought I would frighten him by telling him that I hadn't, and then suddenly I felt utterly weary with the whole thing. "Yes, I took it," I said, and I saw the relief in his face.

'I spent another night alone with my boy and in the morning I went down to tell Lady Clementina that her son was dead. I saw the triumph in her face and heard it in her voice, but I betrayed none of my own feelings or gave her the slightest inkling that I thought anything else than that he had passed in his sleep. The doctor pronounced it heart failure. It was only me who could have told them that it was his breath that failed—failed because I with my own hands had murdered him.'

'You mustn't say that, Nannie,' Robert said hastily. 'You were not the murderer; you only gave him the kinder death, without pain or suffering. He might have suffered the other way.'

'That we shall never know,' Nannie replied wearily. 'But at any rate, I believed that I was doing the best for him, and, as it turned out, it was the best for you, too, Master Bobby.'

There was a sudden tenderness in her voice and in the expression of her face which brought the tears springing to Sylvia's eyes. She knew then that Nannie still loved the boy in Robert—the little boy, lost and bewildered in a strange, frightening world, whom she, too, had found and loved.

Robert got to his feet. He left his desk and stood beside Nannie, and though he was a tall man and she was a very small woman he did not seem to dwarf her.

'I can't say thank you, Nannie,' he said, and his voice was unsteady. 'You gave both Edward and me a love for which no words of thanks could ever be adequate. I can only ask your forgiveness and that in the bigness of your heart you will stay on with us in the future to try to make this house a happier and better place.'

Nannie gave a little laugh and she wiped away the last of her tears.

'Why, Master Bobby,' she said, 'why do you think I should be leaving you now? And where should I go if I did? This is—my home.'

Sylvia had risen from her chair; she moved to Robert's side, found the shelter of his encircling arm and laid her head in utter trust against his shoulder.

'That is what we have got to make it, Robert,' she said in a low voice. 'A home.'

Nannie looked at them and put her hand over theirs.

'God bless you both,' she said; 'and I believe He will.'

She went from the room, a little woman with great dignity; a woman who had never failed the great love within her own heart.

There was a long silence as the door closed behind her, and then Sylvia sighed.

'I can't believe it is true,' she said. 'We need not be afraid.'

Robert repeated her words softly, 'No, we need not be afraid.'

She looked up at him to see the almost unbearable happiness in his eyes. And then he went down on his knees before her and hid his face between her breasts.

9